NASHVILLE

Also by Pat Booth:

TEMPTATION
MARRY ME
SPARKLERS
BIG APPLE
MASTER PHOTOGRAPHERS
PALM BEACH
THE SISTERS
BEVERLY HILLS
MALIBU
MIAMI
ALL FOR LOVE

NASHVILLE

Pat Booth

LITTLE, BROWN AND COMPANY

A *Little, Brown* Book

First published in Great Britain in 2001
by Little, Brown and Company

Copyright © 2001 by Orcam Corporation
All song lyrics © 2001 Pat Booth

The moral right of the author has been asserted.

A CIP catalogue record for this book
is available from the British Library.

HARDBACK ISBN 0 316 64875 2
C FORMAT ISBN 0 316 64876 0

Typeset in Sabon by M Rules
Printed and bound in Great Britain by
Clays Ltd, St Ives plc

Little, Brown and Company (UK)
Brettenham House
Lancaster Place
London WC2E 7EN

To FAITH HILL from Star, Mississippi.

Your magical country music inspired this book.

PROLOGUE

LeAnne Carson was about to marry the man she loved, but she was not in love with him. This unsettling truth was in the forefront of her mind as she walked down the aisle of St Edward's Episcopal Church in Nashville, Tennessee. Purcell's *Trumpet Voluntary* sounded grandly on the organ, and LeAnne shook gently as she walked to join her husband-to-be. You were allowed to be nervous on your wedding day, but the enormity of the commitment she was about to make had LeAnne's guts in turmoil beneath the fine French ivory-silk dress that hugged her thin waist. In the Appalachian Mountains where she came from, 'divorce' was a dirty word of the kind you spelled out in front of the children, like in the Tammy Wynette song.

The mist of the veil hid the colour high on her cheeks, and the wide-open roundness of her beautiful blue eyes. Where there should be joy, there was doubt. Anxiety hovered around the edges of her certainty, plucking at it, eroding it like a wild sea demolishing a sandy island in a storm at night. She could see Henry smiling at her, encouraging her, and the pastor, relaxed at his side. Sunlight danced through the stained-glass windows, making crazy patterns on her wedding dress. Behind her, LeAnne sensed the presence of her retinue . . . the eight bridesmaids, the maid of honour, and the two adorable little children, one of each gender . . . all essential ingredients of this so ancient ceremony. To have and to hold. From this day forth. Evermore. She would have to ignore the voice that told her to turn back. In sickness, and in health . . . as long as they both should live. LeAnne took a deep breath. The music was near to its climax. She was near to Henry. In minutes, her new life would begin. But all she could think of was that her dreams were ending.

Henry Stone shared none of his wife-to-be's uncertainties, but he, too, was worried. When a man from the top of the pile marries a woman from the bottom, the class divide that separates them is never more apparent than at their wedding. He was chiefly worried that there might be embarrassment of some unspecified kind. The important things were achieved. The girl he adored was about to be his for ever. She was close to him now, and he reached out his hand in welcome. She would be nervous. Every woman was. She walked steadily, the long train rasping over the iron gratings of the aisle, but she would be trembling. Beneath the veil, the glory of her face would be haunted by the ghost of worry. His heart beat firm and fast in his chest. In seconds she would be his. He would protect her. At a stroke, she would have all the security that the Stone millions could provide. LeAnne Carson from the Smokies above Gatlinburg would become a Stone of Belle Meade. She was marrying into the Social Register, into one of Tennessee's oldest and most aristocratic families, and the poverty that had stalked her life like a spectre was about to be banished for ever before the wedding feast. Henry loved LeAnne without reservation, totally. Never for one second had he had doubts about the wisdom of this wedding. But . . . as his hand reached out for hers . . . he felt the fear. His? Hers? It was there somewhere, like a fine mist on a mountain morning. It permeated the air, hovering over the happiness like the wind that had blown away the substance of the Old South, leaving behind only its aristocratic formality.

Mary Stone watched calmly from the front pew. Behind and around her clustered her mighty family and its powerful friends. The Governor was there, and both senators, led like puppets on a string by the campaign contributions that the Stones had paid since long before the war that everyone in this church referred to reverentially as The Lost Cause. But the Stone money was more than mere money. It was old money. And they were ancient friends, going back for generations, from the days of King Cotton through the cheers of Chancellorsville and Fredericksburg to the bitter tears of Gettysburg and Sherman's bloody march through Atlanta to the sea. Many of these people, the husband's 'side' of the church, wondered about Mary Stone's feelings at this moment. They saw her smart floral dress, her extravagant hat, her perfect pearls, and they speculated on what the matriarch of the Stone dynasty might be feeling as she watched her son and heir, Dr Henry Stone, marry a hillbilly cracker girl from the misty mountains, a girl hardly used to wearing shoes. She picked a guitar, apparently. At the wedding breakfast, would she pick her teeth? The men shifted uncomfortably in their morning coats, starched collars and pinstriped pants, and the women arched their necks in their scented, white-gloved Southern finery. Mostly they looked across the aisle . . . at the opposition.

The Carsons and their ridge-runner mountain friends stared proudly back. They were the outsiders, the rebels here. Like their ancestors of the Confederate rank and file, who had gone to their deaths in glory – a ragged army against the blue-uniformed might of the North – they were not ashamed. There was not a cutaway in sight, not a dinner jacket, and few enough suits . . . and those that were on display shiny, unpressed, ill-fitting. The women wore clothes from racks in stores that sold food and tools as well as frocks, and their gnarled, gloveless, hard-working hands gripped the polished mahogany of the pews, and would leave marks upon them.

Mary Stone's wise old eyes saw it all, through the surface to the depths. It was time the Stones's genes had a transfusion of energy. The blood was beginning to run sluggish in the family veins. Henry Stone, her fine-looking son at the altar, had brains to spare, and the best education that money could buy, but, the truth be told, Mary found him a little dull, a tad conventional, lacking in the spirit that she personally liked in a man. Of course, she loved her son, but her wise love was not blind. Andover, Vanderbilt, a glittering career in medicine and a trust fund that would keep wolves from the door until Judgement Day, had a way of draining the spunk from a man. Behind her were similar men and women. On the other side of the church, however – on the bride's side – the folk had been pressed into sterner stuff by hardship. They looked like they could still walk through the cannon fire while giving a rebel yell, and LeAnne Carson, her soon-to-be daughter-in-law, was one of them, and a beauty to boot. Her children would not be short of the backbone required for the deadly serious business that was called life.

From Mary's point of view, the whole church was full of family. The Carsons and the Stones shared a common heritage. All had come over on boats from England. Only then had their paths separated. The Stones had found riches and position; the Carsons poverty and privation. But there was no basic difference in the blood that fed the daisies and the grass in the fields over Shiloh and Antietam. The upper classes and the mountain folk possessed the pride of those who knew who they were. It was the upwardly mobile carpetbaggers in the middle who suffered the soul-sapping silliness of insecurity. So what if there would be 'inappropriate' 'Praise the Lord's and 'Amen's from the bride's side of the church. Who cared that Mary's guests resembled penguins and sweet-smelling flowers from a carefully cultivated herbaceous border, while LeAnne's outwardly more motley crew looked like scarecrows and flora from the vegetable patch. It was blowing in the wind that, outside the upper-class church, the battered pick-up trucks made uneasy bedfellows with the Rolls-Royces and the German cars that the rich preferred. At the end of the day, LeAnne Carson would produce Stone heirs with balls and backbones, whatever happened to the marriage along the way. It was the long view that Mary Stone had been brought up to consider. After all, people were merely potential crosses in a graveyard. Today's 'ideals worth dying for' would be the footnotes in tomorrow's history books. A true daughter of the Confederacy knew that. Mary smiled as her son took LeAnne's hand, and held her head high as she always had and always would. It was going to be all right. It always was.

'Can you just smell the goddamned money . . . ?' Eileen Early leaned towards her husband in the front pew of the hill-hawk side of the church.

He half turned towards her and smiled wryly. 'Don't think any of it's gonna come our way,' he whispered none too quietly. His dark blue suit smelled of sweat and mothballs, and he flicked a big finger into his too-tight collar and eased the soup-stained necktie looser.

'It went Luke's,' she said and nodded to emphasise her point. LeAnne had just passed her, staring straight ahead, shaking like a leaf. Seemed like she was going to an execution, not a wedding. Eileen's stomach lurched in sympathy with her sister's. She knew that LeAnne loved Henry Stone, but Eileen knew, too, that she was not 'in love' with him. Did that matter? It certainly hadn't mattered much in her own perfectly satisfactory marriage. But on your *wedding* day, all dressed up like that, in a ten-*thousand*-dollar dress, weren't you allowed to hope for a little magic? She banished the thought. Thoughts did not provide fat bacon for the table. And it was feelings that brought out the best tunes on a fiddle. Action and emotions were what counted in the cradle-to-grave struggle that was life. Thoughts just made you miserable.

She was looking forward to the food, and the drink. It would be good. Money knew how to eat, and the difference between brand whiskey and popskull moonshine. So when the Good Lord had blessed this union she was going to enjoy herself, and maybe give some good ol' boy with a prostate and a plantation a flirtin' he had long forgotten about.

Eileen felt her stomach surreptitiously. She wasn't showing yet, but she was three months gone. She smiled happily. LeAnne would be close behind. Would their kids be friends? Would they sing duets, sweet and low on the porch on the cold mountainside? Girl and boy? Again an alien thought formed in the clear sky of her mind. Would the money difference keep their children apart? Would it interfere with the close relationship that she had with her sister? It would certainly be the end of LeAnne's dreams of being a country singer. The 'other side' of Nashville didn't 'do' country. They had people to work farms for them, and wrote off 'cowboys' as being from out West, which hadn't counted in the heyday of old Dixie. Why sing about trains, drunks, lost love and all the bullshit that went with it, when you could be listening to Wolfgang Amadeus Mozart or somebody else with an impossible name to pronounce?

Eileen bit her lip. What happened when you gave up your dreams for security? What happened when you sacrificed your ambitions for duty and love of family? She swallowed nervously. The truth was that LeAnne was marrying Henry Stone in large part because of their little brother, Luke. Right now, he was in Vanderbilt Medical Center, and about to be transferred to Sloan-Kettering in New York. He was dying of leukaemia and the Carsons had diddly squat in the way of insurance. Luke's cure was being financed entirely by Stone money. The medical campaign to save him was being directed under the brilliant command of Henry Stone himself . . . and all because he loved and would marry Luke's sister. It wasn't the whole story, of course. LeAnne loved him in a fashion. On paper, in the flesh, he seemed all but impossible not to love, so handsome and well spoken, so clever, dependable and so very, very rich! But the passion wasn't there. Maybe it would come, thought Eileen, smoothing her worn frock over her still mercifully flat stomach. And maybe one fine day Tennessee would be allowed to secede from the Union and all the damned Yankees would go home, and leave folk to run things the way they liked 'em. Mmm. It was better to think about the sippin' whiskey that would be coming at the breakfast or whatever they called it, and the country club plutocrat who was about to get the flirtin' of a lifetime. It didn't bear worryin' about. At the end of the day, the little sister who had frolicked barefooted and in rags through the bittersweet childhood they had shared was hitching herself to millions of dollars. That wasn't so bad and, hell, it was only a marriage. It wasn't like it was a life-and-death affair.

The pastor, smooth of tongue and oily of appearance, was pretending to think otherwise. 'Welcome to St Edward's,' he boomed in mega baritone, 'old friends,' and he bowed to Mary Stone and her clan, 'and new.' His smile deepened to show his fake sincerity as he turned towards the white-trash side of the unbalanced equation that was the congregation.

His words reverberated around the magnificent building, echoing back into the silence created by the end of Purcell's predictable piece. He knew nobody was listening. The mountain crowd had his measure, and so did the plutocrats. Words were cheap to both groups, neither of which really required a middle man in their dealings with God. Dixie and religion have an easy relationship. Father McClellan, drafted down from a snobbish parish in New England, where worship was merely another part of social activity like hunting, riding and playing golf, had never quite understood that.

'We meet on this solemn and wonderful day to witness the joining together in matrimony of Henry and LeAnne . . .'

Henry let go the hand he had taken, and stood back as LeAnne unveiled herself. He saw only the brilliance of her smile, not the nervousness at the edges of it. He smiled back at her.

'I love you, darling,' he said, surprised and thrilled that his wonderful woman had taught him to say things like this. She had opened up the Pandora's box of emotions, long closed to him by the family tradition of the line of phlegmatic Stone ancestors. This was her day. Women loved weddings; every man knew that. And he, Henry Stone the fifth – although he would rather have died than use the vulgar Roman numeral – had spared no effort in making sure that the day would be special. From the sculpted simplicity of the dress to the careful extravagance of the ten-carat D flawless diamond ring, a family heirloom from ante-bellum days, everything had been thought of. Back at home, the tent on the velvet lawns of Harbour Court would already be full of Taittinger and bustle, the bunches of gardenias mountainous in size and heady in scent, the orchestra tuning up on Dixie. It would not be just for today. From now on, LeAnne was free from worry. He would look after her. Her adored brother would be pulled back from the brink of the grave. LeAnne would be showered with her husband's wealth, and her whole life would become a wonderful voyage of discovery around the glittering Stone world of European holidays, culture, and all things worthwhile and honourable. He smiled at her, and she whispered, 'I love you, too,' and Henry Stone, who had never really been happy before, marvelled at the experience.

LeAnne took a deep breath as the pastor droned on. 'Many of you have experienced the magic of this moment. But many of you also know that marriage is not something we can take for granted. It must be worked on, tended like some much-loved tree, like some . . .' Soon the deed would be done and, like Macbeth, she thought that it were well it were done quickly. Henry stood like a stone wall beside her. He was a good man. Not the best and the finest of men, but solid and good-intentioned, and when he said that he loved her, he meant it. She had nothing to worry about now, except for Luke, and somehow that anxiety had diminished. Whatever happened it would be in God's hands. Everything that was humanly and medically possible would now be done for him. Dr Henry Stone was in control of the situation and LeAnne marvelled at the way the other doctors jumped when he spoke to them; how they were suddenly more willing to explore exotic treatments; how they simply tried harder. That was what she was marrying into. She was acquiring the power of the old-money world, still the greatest power of all. But she knew that there was a price, and that price, at the tender age of twenty, would be her freedom. Never now would she play the honky-tonks and beer joints of the Broadway. Never, through the smoke and the smell of stale beer, would she hear the applause of the hardest crowds. She would not walk Music Row, land a contract and sing out her heart and her songs to an America that needed them. She would trade hard-won fame and the thrill of self-achievement for the prestige of marrying into the heart of the Southern aristocracy. And she would pay for the wedding dream that was so many women's in the hardest currency of all, the dreams that were her own. So again she took a deep breath and tried to keep the smile in place, and the tears to the fine mist that filmed over her eyes. Tears of emotion, Henry would think. And in a way they were.

The pastor's clichés were droning to a close. He stepped forward. 'We are here today to join in holy matrimony . . .'

'That's right! Marry 'em, preacher!'

The slurred cry came from the middle of the bride's section, to nervous laughter from the congregation. LeAnne was glad of the release of tension. It sounded like Uncle Isaiah, sounded like he had been at the flask of corn whiskey he carried everywhere. LeAnne wasn't embarrassed. She didn't 'do' embarrassment because she was proud of her creek-and-holler family, each and every one of them. She had never been taught to be anything else. The Carsons had always been poor, but they had never doubted themselves. You got what they gave you, straight in the face, never behind the back, in plain and simple words and sometimes in a fist. McClellan didn't like to think of himself as a preacher man, but to men who called a spade a spade that was what he was. Henry smiled indulgently; McClellan, superciliously; LeAnne, naturally. Suddenly she felt all right. The clouds had lifted, except for one small one that was heavily lined with burnished silver. Sooner or later, she was going to have to get around to telling Henry she was pregnant.

CHAPTER

ONE

Savanna walked towards her father. He turned and she could see from his expression that the worst was about to happen. He was leaning over the nurse's station talking to one of the attending physicians who sat at a chair before a sheaf of notes. The clock on the wall said 3 p.m. precisely.

Henry Stone stood up straight as he saw his daughter approach. 'Excuse me,' he said to the doctor, and walked quickly towards Savanna, taking her arm and steering her towards a quiet part of the corridor. His furrowed brow said it all. He spoke quickly, in clipped sentences. Was it the doctor in him, or just his personality . . . laconic, taciturn, precise even in his dreadful sorrow?

'Probably the end of today, or tonight. Best, I think. We aren't holding back on the painkillers. I'm sure that's the right thing to do.'

You mean you're killing her, thought Savanna. She wasn't cross, just numb. Her father was a good, good man who worshipped the ground that her mother walked on. To be instrumental in hastening the end of the person you loved, to save her pain, was the finest kind of courage. She just wished her father could be a little more direct. And then, of course, she didn't want that. Tears welled up in her eyes.

'Is she conscious?'

'In and out. Go and sit with her. I've been there all morning, and I'll take over later.'

He's saying, 'I don't want her to die alone,' translated Savanna.

'Oh, Daddy, isn't there anything else . . . ?'

'No. No, darling, trust me. It's God's business now. Do you think we haven't tried everything? This is me, Savanna. Your daddy.'

He shook his head from side to side to emphasise his point. She nodded. Words had to be said, questions asked, for formality's sake. It wasn't about answers. Specialists had been flown in from across America, but it was a straightforward case. Breast cancer. Lung and liver secondaries. Chemo was history. Radiation a hideous memory. Surgery simply contra-indicated.

Savanna, her tear-stained face the image of her mother's simple, straightforward beauty, was destined for pre-med. Her nineteen years in a doctor's household had taught her how to sum up odds; how you didn't strive officiously to keep alive; how, at the end, death was natural and a doctor's job was to ease that passing.

'She was asking for you earlier. I think she knows.'

Knows it's near.

Savanna took a deep breath. She looked down the corridor at the door to her mother's room. This might be the last time she saw her alive. Her father was trying to prepare her for that. And she didn't know how she could be prepared for such a terrible tragedy. Oh, yes, her brain knew. Intellectually, she understood. But her heart screamed 'no'. It was so unfair. Her mother was not yet forty, she had led a blameless, selfless life and brought joy to everyone who had met her. Why? Why? What the hell was God's game?

Her father took her hand. 'Just tell her you love her. That's all she wants to hear,' he said.

'As if she doesn't know.'

He squeezed her hand, and then, feeling its coldness, he drew his daughter in towards him and hugged her.

'Oh, Daddy. Oh, Daddy!'

'I know, darling, I know.' He held her tight, binding his sorrow to hers, and they clung there together for support, for strength to face the loneliness that would follow. It would be just the two of them then . . . and they had needed LeAnne so desperately to bridge the gulf that separated an authoritarian traditional father from a head-strong, spirited daughter whose mind belonged to nobody but herself.

'I'd better go. She's alone,' said Savanna, pulling back from him.

'Yes,' he said.

So she turned and walked along the corridor and opened the door of her dying mother's room.

She lay whiter than pale against the sheets, gripped by the cancerous anaemia of her terminal illness. Her eyes were open, but she had to moisten her lips with her tongue before she could speak. 'Hello, my darling.' LeAnne tried to hold up her hand, but it fell back again, as Savanna hurried towards her.

Savanna felt the tears come as she crossed the few feet that separated her from the mother she adored. She sat down on the bed, scooping up the hand that had tried to greet her. She bent over and nuzzled into her mother's neck, feeling the thinness of her new-grown hair, and smelling the so-well-known scent of her.

'Don't die, Mommy,' she whispered. 'Please don't die.'

'Darling, darling. Don't cry. You mustn't be sad, well, just a little bit, I guess.' LeAnne smiled at her. 'We're all leaving the station sometime, darling. Just, I guess I'm catching an earlier train, and you and Dad are gonna wait for the midnight special.'

'Midnight train to Georgia,' said Savanna, trying to smile through the tears and knowing she ought to be brave. Carsons and Stones were, and would be, that.

'I'm hoping for something a little better than Georgia, and with acoustic guitars. Hold the harps.'

'You're going to be all right,' said Savanna definitely. There was something to be said for denial.

'Course I am, little darlin'. And you are, too. But you have to look after Daddy . . . and not fight with him. Promise.'

'Me and Daddy, fight?' Again Savanna tried to smile through the grief.

'That's what worries me. I was the oil that kept you from grinding each other up. I'd die happy if I could know that you and he would love each other for ever.'

'We won't fight, I promise you,' said Savanna. 'I swear it, Mommy.'

'But don't you let him run your life, either. You hear me, darling. He's headstrong, but you're spirited, more than I was. You have to walk that line between loving him and not being ruled by him.'

Savanna looked down at her once-beautiful mother, now thin and racked by disease. How frail she looked, like a spent leaf hanging by a thread to the tree, waiting only for the evening wind to fall for ever. Her mom was trying to tell her something. Beneath the generalities there were specifics.

'I loved singing with you the most,' she said. 'No one on this earth has a voice like yours.'

Savanna turned her face to one side. 'The best voice in pre-med?' she asked.

'Best voice somewhere,' said LeAnne, managing an enigmatic smile.

'What are you saying, Mom?' But Savanna knew.

'Follow your dreams, my darling. Whatever they are, make sure they are yours and no one else's.'

'What were your dreams, Mom? They weren't being Mrs Henry Stone, the professor's wife, the aristocrat's woman, the Southern belle with the balls, were they?'

'No, they weren't, but I regret nothing. Especially you, my darling. You made it all wonderful. You were the string of fairy lights around my heart. Whenever I felt sad, one look at you could make me happy again. That's all it took.'

A big tear rolled down Savanna's cheek, and she wiped it away. It seemed as if her mother's voice was fainter, as if she was fading out of focus, becoming blurred.

'So much happiness you gave me, my darling, thank you, thank you.' She squeezed her daughter's hand and Savanna could barely feel the increased pressure.

Savanna felt the presence in the room of a coldness, an otherness.

'Mom! Are you OK? Shall I get Dad?'

'No. Not Dad. I think he would feel the need to say something that somehow didn't sound quite right.'

'Sounds like Dad.'

'I loved him, you know. Very much. He is a good man. So good.'

'I know, I know, but don't talk in the past, Mom.'

'That song we wrote . . . The shape of a curl, the touch of a hand . . .' She sang in a still surprisingly strong voice, and Savanna joined her in harmony . . . 'Precious memories and yet . . . there's a reason to remember to forget.'

LeAnne lay back smiling, exhausted by the effort. 'Could have been a big hit. Could yet be. Could yet be.'

'That was your dream, Mom, wasn't it?'

'Oh, yes. Seems silly now, but it was. Dreams. So insubstantial, and yet they are all we have. We have to live as if it all mattered. Can't afford to think it doesn't. Except perhaps now. You are young, my darling. Will and dare. Then, when you get old, know and be silent. Trouble was I never got old. Never got to know or to be silent. Got a feeling that even if I'd gotten old, I'd have always felt young.' She paused as if to draw a deep breath and once again Savanna felt the closeness of infinity, the oneness that would soon be all there was.

'I'm not frightened, you know,' said LeAnne suddenly.

'But I am, Mommy. I am,' said Savanna and the tears came with a rush now, a sobbing stream of sadness that was past words.

'I'll be with you for ever, and waiting for you, my angel. I'll see you always from now on, not just sometimes, when you are not busy with your life. I'll be there on all the dark nights and on all the joyful mornings. And you will have such a good life, my sweet, because you are such a good and strong spirit and so brave. Stronger than all the Carson boys, and the Stone ones, too. My little girl.'

And she began to sing, softly, gently, the words that she had sung to Savanna so many times in the nursery at home.

> You'll be all right with me,
> Whatever may go wrong,
> Through heartaches and disasters,
> I'll always ride along.

Savanna sang, too, her voice unsteady through tears that would not stop.

> As the world deals threes and aces,
> A pair we'll always be,
> Look around. I'll be there.
> You'll be all right with me.

And then Savanna realised that it was a duet no longer. She was carrying the tune alone, because at last her mother had left her. She had gone on the wings of angels to the better place than Georgia, and she had been singing as she'd left. Her mother's hand was still in hers, and an expression of eternal peace was upon her face. Her race was over, her suffering finished. She had gone as she would have liked to have lived, perhaps *had* lived, with a country song for ever in her heart.

Now grieving was for the grievers, and mourning for the mourners, and the wave of blinding sorrow crashed over Savanna as the gap opened wide between the living and the dead. The business was starting . . . the almost impossible business of trying to remember to forget.

CHAPTER

TWO

The Carson family used the barn for just about everything, storing corn, animals, and the rusty decaying machinery they called West Virginia lawn furniture in these parts. But today they were using it for a dance of sorts . . . the barn dance wake that LeAnne Carson Stone had insisted on in her will, to the horror of her husband and the surprise, but not astonishment, of everyone else. The conditions had been specific. No sadness, only joy fuelled by whiskey and the music that LeAnne had loved so much. And it was to be a Carson business from start to finish, in the mountains, and not a stuffed shirt in sight with the exception of her husband . . . who was already beginning to see it as some kind of cunning revenge.

Children washed round Henry Stone's feet like eels in a barrel, dirty, noisy and dressed in their very best finery, which looked to his patrician eyes like dishrags before laundry day. He resisted the urge to kick out at them as they surged like surf around the immaculate ice sculpture that he resembled. They screamed and shouted near the pain level in a dialect that he could barely understand and he shifted a bit in his perfect Savile Row suit, and black silk tie, and in the lace-up black walking shoes with their Southern shine that rendered looking-glasses superfluous in his presence. On the floor was sawdust at best and dirt at worst, and there were places where the free-flowing keg beer had rendered it treacherous. People milled around drinking from paper cups as if it were a picnic, or straight from bottles as if it were a ball game.

But it was neither. It was the post-funeral gathering for his beloved and respected wife and the honoured mother of his only child and heiress. It should have been held in the decorum of a tented annexe to the vast conservatory at Harbour Court, with hushed voices, mournful faces, and the full panoply of restrained upper-class grief. But his wife's will had put paid to that. He had not dared to override it, after he had broached the subject with Savanna and watched her furious reaction.

'Nice to be around people who know how to have fun,' said his mother's voice. She had approached from behind, and now, as she spoke to him, she raised an antique silver flask to her lips, the one with his great-grandfather's initials and crest engraved upon it.

'Mother!' he said in horror.

'Oh, what?' she said, sipping anyway. 'For God's sake, Henry, don't spoil this party like you do every other one.'

She was dressed quite unlike himself, in twill trousers, and a shirt that might have been vaguely Hawaiian, with brown riding boots which were perfect for the treacherous barn floor. She must have changed in the limo on the way from the graveyard. God, his mother was impossible. He prayed that once, before he died, just once he would get the better of her . . . but he wasn't banking on it. She knew his Achilles heels, and there were far more than two of them.

'I don't spoil parties,' he said, reduced at a stroke from Professor of Surgery at the Columbia College of Physicians and Surgeons to the level of whining child. 'Anyway, this is not a party.'

'Looks like a party, smells like a party, sounds like a party,' said his mother. 'That makes it a party, young man, and you spoil 'em.' She said the last part with the authority of a matriarch that could not be confronted.

Parties from his youth loomed up. The time he had twisted his ankle during the eightsome reel; when he had been sick from overdoing the chili, all over Maybelline Beauregard's frock; the time he had told the dancing instructor that his foxtrot footwork had been 'sloppy'. He reddened up at the memories. His mother did not need to cite chapter and verse.

He sniffed in general disapproval. As he drew the air into his nostrils . . . mountain evening fresh mixed with sweat, beer, whiskey . . . he had to admit that it smelled like a party, although not the delicate kind that he was used to at Belle Meade, the ones he was so good at spoiling. He could have a heart attack at this one and nobody would notice, or care.

'You all right, Daddy?' said Savanna. She took his hand.

He didn't look all right, he knew that. His daughter wore faded blue jeans and a simple white T-shirt, the youthful equivalent of her grandmother's garb. She looked stunningly beautiful, although he could see from her reddened eyes that she had been crying. He remembered her, tight beside him, at the cemetery as they had lowered her mother into the cold flat Tennessee ground in the Stone burial plot. She had shaken with grief then, but somehow now she seemed to have risen to LeAnne's posthumous 'occasion', as his own mother had clearly done . . . and everyone else for that matter. Not for the first time in his life, Henry Stone found himself the odd man out.

'I'm as all right as I can be in the situation,' he said stiffly.

'You need a drink,' said Savanna.

'I don't drink at funerals.'

'Chinese do,' said his mother abruptly. 'And they've been around a hell of a lot longer than the Stones and their grand "old" family. Welsh, too, for that matter. Party pooper!'

'Oh, Mother, will you *stop* it,' said Henry. He felt like stamping his foot. Half the time he loved his mother, half the time he felt like performing open-heart surgery on her.

'Mrs Stone, will you do me the honour of a dance if I promise not to step on them dainty feet of yours?' Uncle Matt Carson's blood alcohol level was rising fast from the redness of his face and the bits of beer foam clustered in his whiskers. He took off a none-too-clean hat and bowed down from a thick waist, in a gesture of *Gone with the Wind* elegance. It was not a manoeuvre he was used to performing, and it was with difficulty that he reattained the upright position. He half smiled, half leered as his world spun round.

'Why, sir, how gallant. I would surely like to join you in a two-step, if you will forgive my arthritis and lack of practice, sir.'

'You'll have to forgive a heck of a lot more than that, ma'am,' said Matt with deadly accuracy and a confident smile as he bore Mary Stone away to the circle in the hay which was the dance floor.

'See you later,' said Mary Stone, with a twinkle in her eye as she looked the mountain man up and down and liked the brawn she saw.

'Mother is *impossible*,' said Henry. 'That man is drunk.'

'That man is my Uncle Matt,' said Savanna simply. 'And he plays the meanest fiddle you ever *heard*. Anyway, I think Grandma can handle herself OK. Remember the time she shot the burglar in the butt.'

Henry did not like to be reminded of things like that. Somehow he had his mother up on a pedestal, separated from the world by white gloves, servants, and millions and millions in the funds. That she was almost brutally human was a vast factor of her personality he chose as a son to ignore.

'Dad, come outside. You've got to see this.'

He followed her gratefully. She had her mother's figure, the same tight bottom and full breasts in the same tight jeans and plain white T-shirt that LeAnne used to wear. LeAnne's personality was in her daughter, too, but Savanna had inherited his obstinacy, his cussedness, his certainty that he was right and that others were wrong. In vain could he see any other genes of his in his daughter, and for some reason he was glad of that. It was a bit like having LeAnne live on. God, he was going to need that . . . but not *everything* about LeAnne. This crazy party for instance was a bad, bad idea, and in the poorest possible taste. All this noisy, simple music played by noisy, simple people who drank too much and thought too little. They said the first thing that came into their heads. Came straight out with it. They had no filtering mechanisms at all. Not an idea of what was done and what not done. Thank God Savanna would soon be back at Columbia, her teeth sunk deep into the core curriculum. Greeks and Romans, that was what she needed right now. And afterwards, the grind of med school. That would knock off some of the rough corners she had inherited from her mother.

Outside the barn it was a different world. The night was cold on the mountainside, but the stars were burning bright in the heavens. It seemed they were laughing down at them, their twinkling gaiety in tune with the cheerful music that wafted out from the barn. He looked up, and breathed in deeply. He did not get to the Smoky Mountains that often, but each time he did they left their mark upon him. What must it be like to be born amongst them? How wonderful it must be to grow up on the hillside with the smell of the ragwort in your nostrils, the blanket of blossoms in spring, the flame azaleas, the yellow-fringed orchids of summer. How fine to be surrounded by the snow-capped peaks in the brutal winters, huddled around smoking fires against the mountain mist that wrapped the cabins on the dark nights and the damp, wet, early mornings. He felt the spirit of the mountains and it was LeAnne's spirit, and Henry sensed her closeness.

'You can feel her looking down, can't you?' said Savanna. 'She said she would.'

Henry said nothing. He *did* feel that, but it was the kind of super-stition his scientific mind was unhappy with, although, like every other genuine Southerner, he trusted in God.

'Sometimes, I think I didn't understand her . . . fully,' he said. Suddenly, he felt guilty. He had given her everything, including his love, but had he ever really bothered to *understand* her? He had simply assumed that she wanted what all women wanted, children and security and things, and so he had provided them. But she had also wanted this wake. She had wanted it enough to put it in her will. And he didn't understand it. Yes, she loved her family and respected her roots. She was a Southerner, for God's sake. But this! He couldn't escape the idea that his wife was trying to tell him something from beyond the grave. Was she gently reproaching him, or passing on some different, and more inaccessible, message?

'You know, my grandparents are both buried down there by the clump of trees. Side by side,' said Savanna suddenly. She pointed in the moonlight to a copse a few hundred yards down the mountain.

'Really? Oh, yes, I remember Mom showing me once.'

Once again he felt the guilt. He hadn't thought to wonder if his wife would have liked to be buried beside them. It simply had not occurred to him. The tradition was that Stone women went to ground in the Stone burial plot, to be joined by their menfolk later, or the other way around. But now he wasn't certain.

The music wafted out from the barn on the brisk breeze.

'"Some assembly is required for this heart after all". One of Mom's songs she wrote,' said Savanna. 'Remember?'

'Yes, of course,' said Henry. It was vaguely familiar, the words childishly simple, romantic nonsense really. But it was a pretty tune, if of no consequence. LeAnne had been proud of her songs, and he had pretended to be proud of her when she'd sung them. He'd encouraged her . . . hadn't he? It had been an eccentric hobby, and he'd have preferred that LeAnne had learned to play bridge properly, but she never remembered where the cards lay – or cared for that matter.

'Hi, y'all. Takin' some air? I was fit to burn in there.'

They peered into the darkness.

'Oh, hi, Steph. You remember my dad, Dr Stone, don't you? Dad – Cousin Steph. All grown up like me.'

'Well, hello there, Stephanie.'

He leaned forward and shook the hand of his wife's niece. She performed a funny little half curtsey as she took it, which embarrassed him. 'Eileen's girl,' he said, with some relief that he had got it right. 'And Tom's,' he boasted. Doctors were good with names.

'Your grandma is dancin' up a storm there with Matt. They cleared the floor,' said Steph with a laugh. She was tall and thin, rangy like a colt with nothing anywhere to spare, not in muscle or conversation. She had a long face which was just the wrong side of pretty, but you could tell she was closely related to Savanna whose rounder face sat firmly beyond the borders of beautiful.

'Oh, God,' said Henry.

'You gonna come sing, Savvy?'

Henry winced at the nickname.

'I don't know that I feel strong enough.'

'We could sing a sad song . . . Aunt LeAnne loved sad songs.'

Henry wanted to contradict her. What did she know about 'Aunt'

LeAnne? LeAnne's songs were either fast or slow. He had never analysed their 'sorrow' content. Anyway, weren't all country songs mournful in some way or another? He was glad Savanna didn't seem to want to sing. How could one sing with one's mother barely cold in the ground? It was downright morbid, if it wasn't disrespectful. What *could* LeAnne have been thinking about when she had arranged this whole business? How on earth had Carmichael at the law firm been conned into going along with it? He just might move the family business, except that his mother would overrule him. Hell and damnation! Why was the world ganging up on him when everyone should be feeling sorry for him? But Savanna had not given up on the idea of singing.

'Like "You Dreamed Dreams"?' said Savanna, enthusiasm creeping into her voice.

'That'd do it.'

'Do you really think, Savanna . . . ?'

'Let's go back inside,' said Savanna, taking her father's hand. He was bewildered, but he was also hurting. He had lost his wife, and now he was a fish out of water fighting for survival in the middle of her over-the-top family. Despite his impressive intellect, he was powerless, an emotional illiterate in a gathering of emotional grown-ups.

The party seemed to have gathered strength in their absence . . . perhaps because of it. The band, composed of an ever-changing stream of Carson relations, used as its platform the back of an old truck that had lost its engine and its wheels. It was easing out a version of the 'Tennessee Waltz' that was awash with melancholy, and on the floor the two-steppers glided smoothly like oil on troubled waters. Savanna picked out Grandma and Matt. She had him well trained already. He wore a frown of concentration as Mary Stone matched his turns and his rhythms, and put him through a whole range of her own. She was laughing regally, her head thrown back. And Matt, smiling uncertainly, never having been as near to a real lady before, was clearly ambivalent about the feeling.

'What is Mother doing dancing with that drunken . . . man!' said Henry Stone.

'Can't dance when he's sober. Can't play the fiddle either when he's dry, some say. Me, I've never seen him sober,' said Steph without any trace of humour. It was just a polite social comment. The sort of remark Henry Stone might make about someone's golf handicap or whether or not they had been a marine.

'Next, they'll be line dancing,' said Henry, unable to keep the contempt from his voice. Both Steph and Savanna laughed at this.

'You try line dancin' in the mountains, you get lynched,' laughed Steph. 'That's for Yankee trash tryin' to be South.'

'Oh,' said Henry. Perhaps he just wasn't the expert on this. He always deferred to his colleagues on complex biochemical matters. A man should know his limits. He stared around him in confusion. What *was* all this? What was going on? And then, of course, he knew. LeAnne *was* trying to show him something from beyond the grave . . . her other world, the one he had never acknowledged, never known about. His mother was already climbing her learning curve with spectacular success. She would, wouldn't she? She didn't know what it was like to be a fish out of water. She was the sort of fish who would have colonised the land, as the evolutionary forebears had. You could put her down anywhere and she grew like a weed, yet always managed to look like an orchid. No wonder he loved and loathed her all at the same time.

He tried to put on his sociological hat. The Carsons who weren't two-stepping were clogging. This type of dancing seemed reserved mainly for the children, with adults forming an enthusiastic ring around them. The waltz had moved on to a speedier bluegrass tune with much fiddling which seemed ideally suited for the flying steel-tipped boots of the family youth. Their upper bodies hardly moved and their hands were folded across their chests, while their faces wore looks of tight concentration. They were blond and blue-eyed, or red-haired and freckled, and Henry remembered that these mountain people were direct descendants of Britain's Celtic rejects. This was Irish folk dancing, these were Irish jigs, devised by the Riverdancers of hundreds of years ago. There was Scotland in the music, too, and all the time the plaintive wail of those to whom the deep emotions, grief, rage, love and hatred, came far more easily than to most.

There were trestle tables around the floor on which bedsheets had been stretched, and on which sat pitchers of beer and bottles of whiskey with no labels. The liquor was dark, vicious-looking stuff, home-distilled, that would send you away tonight and bring you back tomorrow with a vengeance. His daughter and her cousin steered him to the corner of one such table and sat him down. For once Henry was content to be told what to do. His ancestors had ordered these people's ancestors into the blue-belly musketry, and they had gone with a cheer. Had they ever understood each other, the leaders and the led? These people's forebears had never owned a slave, far less a cotton plantation. Yet they had died cheerfully for no greater reason than that they were not prepared to be bossed about by strangers. They had walked into cannon-balls simply because they didn't want to be told that they had to stay in the Union Club when they had decided they wanted to leave it. Henry's family had had a whole lot to lose in the war between the States. These people's ancestors had had only their pride at stake, and in dying for it, they had never lost it. And they had passed it on in their genes to people like his wife and their daughter.

'Hello, darlings.' Grandma was back, looking coolly flushed from her dance-floor exertions. 'Well, my my, that gentleman can surely dance a two-step, and now he promises to play a mean fiddle. Quite a character, your uncle, Savanna. Your brother-in-law, darling.'

Henry, shell-shocked, could think of nothing to say.

Aunt Eileen – Steph's mom and LeAnne's sister – could. She approached the table, none too steady, and put a sweaty hand on the immaculate serge of Henry Stone's besuited shoulder.

'You wanna dance, Dr Stone?' she said.

Grandma opened her mouth. Instinctively, Henry knew it contained the story about his telling the dance instructor that his foxtrot was 'sloppy'. He jumped to his feet. He could deal with anything but that. 'I would love to,' he said, noticing his mother's and his daughter's mouths drop open. Steph's expression mixed disbelief with horror.

24

He took a deep breath, as Aunt Eileen, sweating profusely and red as a beet, led him towards the floor like an aristocrat to the Paris guillotine.

'A two-step, I think,' he said as if diagnosing a particularly tricky cardiac arrhythmia.

'Surely is,' she said over her shoulder with a laugh. She took him in a firm grip, and Henry was relieved that he was allowed to keep the male position. The clogging sound had been replaced with something more danceable. Then, he noted with alarm, it slowed some more, as if taking its cue from his arrival on the dance floor.

'More like a waltz now,' said Eileen cheerfully, drawing him in closer to her warm and well-covered body.

Could LeAnne really be related to this person? A sister? A much-loved one? It seemed all but impossible.

'This is not easy for you,' said Eileen into his ear.

For some ghastly seconds he wondered if she was referring to the proximity of their bodies.

'I guess it is not the way you do things over in Belle Meade.'

Oh, God, I'm going to have to talk, thought Henry. 'A little beyond my experience . . . sheltered life,' he tried.

'Different way of grievin',' said Eileen. 'Same grief.'

'Of course.'

'Mountain folk don't like cryin' unless they're singin' a sad song. Better to cover it up. Get drunk. Pretend it ain't happened.'

Henry took a deep breath. This was probably not the time for a discussion of the psychoanalytic mechanism of denial. Freud tended not to fly well in the Smoky Mountains, south of the Potomac generally.

'We have our own ways of covering up emotions, too,' he said truthfully. The dignified Stone gathering of softly spoken friends would have been a deeply emotionally constipated event, as unsatisfactory to Eileen as this was to him.

'Well, I know LeAnne wanted you to come here and see this. I know 'cos she told me. Wanted you to see where half your daughter came from.'

Henry almost stopped dancing. Was that it? Was this about Savanna, not him? And if so, what did that mean – 'Don't try and force her to be something she's half not? Let her marry a cracker? Don't give her too much cash? Pull her out of Columbia and stick her in Georgia Tech?'

'Half my daughter came from my wife, and I knew my wife exceedingly well, believe it or not,' said Henry coldly.

'LeAnne was special. She was a real lady like your family. But deep down she was a Carson like us.'

The expression 'warts and all' hung unspoken in the air.

Henry fought against the impulse to be impolite. But, genetically speaking, Eileen was right. Environment could do only so much, and probably not very much, to change biological inheritance. Mercifully, amidst much groaning of fiddles and strumming of acoustic guitars, the music ground to a stop. This time, Henry was the leader back to the relative safety of the table.

'You dance well, dear,' said his mother.

But another Stone was speaking. Savanna had taken over the mike, and Steph stood beside her on the stage.

'As you all know,' she said, her voice firm. 'As you . . .' The silence descended gradually, almost grudgingly. Badness was going to have to be confronted. 'Mom asked for this . . . this . . . evening, wake, I guess. We're all family here, and I don't have to explain to you what I've lost and Dad's lost, because we all of us lost the same thing, the same wonderful person, Mom.'

She paused, smiling through the beginning of tears.

'I hear her sayin' get the hell on with the party,' shouted a cousin from somewhere.

'I hear that, too,' said Savanna. 'Is that Cousin Willy? An' you go right ahead drinkin' while I'm talkin', 'cos that's one of the things we know you do best.'

They laughed at the good-natured response, glad of the chance to do so.

'The last time I saw my mom, she said she would be looking down on us and I know she is tonight, wishing only that she could be here to sing. You remember how she liked to show us Carsons who had the best voice in this family, even if Matt played the best fiddle. Now,

I don't really feel like singing, but I'm going to anyways, because I think Mom wants me to for some reason. She even told me the song . . . or I feel she did. I love you, Mom. We all do. And I know you are still here with us and always will be. You give me somebody to live up to and oh, my God, I miss you . . .' Her voice caught on the barbed wire of feelings . . . 'I miss you an' the saddest thing is I'll not hear you sing again . . .'

There was the grave's silence as Savanna fought not to lose it. 'So here's . . . here's "You Dreamed Dreams".'

Matt had joined the band, and his plaintive fiddle took up the challenge of the song for LeAnne Carson Stone. Steph joined him, with long, deep chords on acoustic. Then drums, more guitar, and the back-of-the-neck voice that sent ghostly fingers down the spines of all who heard it – Savanna's solo.

> The day you died, I lost my faith in the pain of the partin',
> But in the morning, I found God again,
> In the sunlight, in the shining heavens he created,
> You were home, but life will never be the same . . .
>
> You dreamed dreams, your fantasies kept you alive when
>   you were living,
> In a world where people die before their death,
> How I'll miss you and the love that you were always giving,
> I'll dream too,
> Make dreams come true,
> I promise you, with my last breath.

As she sang, she caught her father's eye, and she sang to him and to his wife's family through a mist of tears that were in his eyes, too.

And then Henry Stone knew what this was all about. In the starkness of his sorrow, he realised the truth. He and his beloved wife had a fight on their hands. From beyond the grave, they were battling over what would become of their daughter.

CHAPTER

THREE

'There's one of those in Nashville,' said Stephanie. She peered up through the steamed-up window across the vast quadrangle that was the centre of Columbia University. Her hair was messed up and her eyes full of sleep. She moved a finger towards the glass and made a little hole to peer through.

'One of those whats?' said Savanna. Her accent was cut off from her cousin's by the Mason-Dixon line. It seemed something of an accident that Tennessee and New York were part of the same country. If Pickett's charge had broken the Union centre at Gettysburg, they might not have been.

'The big building with the columns,' said Stephanie. 'It's like the Parthenon. They copied it in Nashville. That's why they call it the Athens of the South.'

'Oh, shit,' said Diane. 'Spare us the guide-book stuff. Look, you couldn't do something useful like make coffee, could you?' Diane turned petulantly in her bed. She had been too drunk the night before to take off her make-up, and she looked like a clown gone wrong, a bad-tempered, beautiful one.

'I surely will,' said Steph obligingly. 'If y'all will tell me where it is.'

'Don't let her boss you about,' said Savanna sharply. 'She hasn't gotten used to the shortage of Filipino maids around here. That's why we have to wade through dirty knickers from dawn till dusk.'

'Oh, don't,' said Diane theatrically, pulling the bedclothes over her head. 'I'm too hung-over for a fight. Forget the coffee. I don't think I could keep it down anyway.' Diane let out a sigh of resigned pain. Why did everything have a price? Why couldn't they make alcohol that made you feel terrific the next day? What was the point of having people like Bill Gates on this earth if they couldn't dream up the necessities? Then she wouldn't begrudge him his billions.

'You sure?' said Steph. She climbed back into bed with Savanna with whom she was head-to-toeing it in the other single bed. Diane didn't intimidate her. Few people whose head you'd held over the lavatory bowl the night before did. 'How you feelin', Savanna?'

'There have been better mornings,' said Savanna, leaning her head against the *Good Will Hunting* poster just below Matt Damon's waist. Her remark could have done for most mornings these last six months, with or without the headache and dry mouth. There was a mournful, wistful feeling in her words, and Stephanie heard it, and understood it. She could still feel the cold mist in her nostrils, hear the meaningless drone of the pastor's words in the sorrow of the grave-yard. Stephanie had hardly known her aunt, but Savanna had worshipped her mother. There was a part of her that would never heal.

'You got class this morning,' said Stephanie.

'Homer. The *Iliad*,' said Savanna absent-mindedly.

'I thought you were doing pre-med. What's all that Greek stuff about?'

'Homer was a Roman,' said Diane. She spoke from beneath the sheets but the sarcasm wasn't hidden.

'Writing about Greeks,' said Savanna sticking up for her cousin again. She had the measure of Diane. She was a bully who needed to be stood up to. 'We have this thing called the core curriculum. Columbia is the only Ivy League university which has it. Everyone does a general course for the first two years. Then you get to specialise. It's the broad-education thing.'

'Sort of dragging things out. Expensive,' said Stephanie, who was practical.

'Finishing-school for the rich,' said Diane, coming up for air, and braving the surly light of campus dawn. 'And if you're on a scholarship you don't pay anyway.'

'I guess you learn how to drink.'

'Or how not to,' laughed Savanna. 'Hey, shit, Diane. You barfed on the Bed, Bath and Beyond rug.' She wrinkled her pretty face in disgust.

'Only a tiny bit,' pleaded Diane. 'I'll get it dry-cleaned. It's no big deal. You should have seen what Orlando did to Melissa Richardson's. That was way past cleaning. Dry or otherwise.'

'You're all a load of winos,' said Stephanie with a laugh.

Diane sat up in bed, her eye make-up dangerously askew, a mascara'd eyelash leaning like a detached retina. 'Winos? Winos?' she repeated in rhetorical horror. 'We are *not* winos. Claret-os. Great burgundy-os. Dry Martini-os but decidedly not winos. Winos drink inexpensive booze.' She wrinkled her nose at the thought.

'It all looks the same the next morning on the rug,' said Savanna definitely. 'That is your job for the day, Diane. I live with your underwear and your eye-pads knee-deep in the bathroom, or should I say barfroom, and yesterday I slipped on an open lipstick and nearly broke my neck. And remember what Hemingway said to Fitzgerald when he said the rich are different from us . . .'

'They have more money,' parroted Diane, shaking her head and pulling a face, frustrated that her game of baiting Savanna's poor relation from Nashville was doomed from the start. 'What happened with Mitchell last night?' She changed the subject to the always more promising one of boys.

'As in who did he end up with?' said Savanna. She looked at Stephanie quickly.

'Me,' said Stephanie. 'Like I took him back to his room and got him . . . like *put* him into his bed.'

'You put Mitchell to bed? You can't do that!'

Neither Savanna nor Stephanie felt the need to ask why. Somehow the onus was on Diane to explain why such a thing was impossible.

She looked around her desperately, clutched her aching head and said, 'You're not at Columbia.' Somehow aware that this was an insufficient reason, she added a very lame 'You're from Nashville.' Her straight 'A' mind was in alcohol-induced 'F' mode. Stephanie and Savanna laughed out loud. So, after a short pause, did Diane.

'Oh, all right. OK. So I blew last night, and I'm sorry for the mess, and thanks for looking after me . . . and, oh shit, did Mitchell see me . . .'

'Mitchell had problems of his own,' said Savanna. 'And right now he's on the East River and has been for the last hour,' she said looking at her watch. 'So his problems are not over. He is thinking only about his coach. He is not thinking about you, Diane, I swear it.'

'How can people *be* athletes?' moaned Diane. 'It's so much easier to be bright.'

'Apparently not this morning, it isn't,' said Savanna darkly.

'Oh, God, I've got calculus in half an hour, and I couldn't play *Trivial Pursuit*.'

'Calculus *is* a trivial pursuit,' said Savanna in a jaundiced voice. She slipped out of bed, and stepped carefully on to the clean part of the rug. She ran her fingers through her short blonde hair, and on cue it fell to frame her face. She might have walked straight from a salon. Her long T-shirt was a spotless white, barely covering her butt and the tops of her bare legs. Diane, in stark contrast, was still partially dressed in a Prada sheath which looked as if it had sustained mortal wounds.

'Well, look at you, Miss Spick-and-Span. Where were you when it hit the fan?' mocked Diane in a wheedling tone of voice.

'Taking your clothes and make-up off before going to bed is hardly Miss Spick-and-Span,' said Savanna smiling. 'And when it hit the fan, or rather the pan, I was holding your head to make sure you didn't follow it in. So was Steph.'

'Yeah,' agreed Stephanie. 'Down South we always have a big breakfast . . . eggs, ham . . .'

'Stop her, Savanna,' said Diane, burping and wiping the clamminess from her brow with the back of her hand. 'Or that rug . . .'

'Hold the regional cooking commentary,' said Savanna quickly. 'She's done action replays before.'

It was cold but mercifully quiet in the bathroom. Savanna splashed water on her face and sighed. She looked at herself in the mirror. She was young enough to get away with late nights and lots to drink. She was nineteen now, and she was well the right side of beautiful. She had her mother's features, prairie-wide-open, guileless, Donald Duck eyes and a pert, pretty nose. Sometimes she envied Diane her olive-skinned angular sultriness, the more sophisticated end of the great-looking spectrum. She, in contrast, was the all-American ideal, rounded like Debbie Harry of Blondie, but with a tummy flat enough to be a Shania-like bellybutton act at the Opry. She could have done with being a bit taller . . . she wouldn't be accepted as a catwalk model, although she might be able to do catalogues . . . and she could have been, well, perhaps odder-looking, more *unique*. Men carried on conversations with her chest, and everyone turned to watch when, bejeaned, she walked away from a table. Certainly she had plenty, perhaps too much, 'attack'. So overall it was a pretty good deal. But. But. Inside she felt like shit. And she wondered if it would ever stop. The pain hadn't lessened. There was just this great gaping void that ached inside her. So she sighed again, and massaged the cold water into her cheeks, punishing herself for feeling so bad, as if it were a shameful indulgence. She eyed the john speculatively. Luckily the cleaning up had been done last night, mainly by Steph with amused, sleeves-rolled-up tolerance.

Savanna sat down on it to pee. She pulled her T-shirt round her. It was a bright cold Manhattan September morning and the New York weather hadn't decided between winter and Indian summer. The Columbia dorm heating system was therefore in schizophrenic mode. This morning Stacey Hall had been looking for sixty and gotten forty. But it didn't matter. Savanna wondered if anything would really matter again. It was good to have Steph here. Good to have found Steph again after all these years. It was funny how families could drift apart without rows or bad feelings, just a separation based on different lives, different locations. Steph's mom, Eileen, had stayed around Pigeon Forge and married a session musician who didn't get hired a whole lot. In stark contrast, LeAnne, Savanna's mom, had married into the grandeur of the Stone family, of Nashville's super-smart Belle Meade area, and now of Fifth Avenue and Connecticut. That simple fact of wealth, and her father's prestigious position in the medical profession, had proved a great divide that only Christmas and birthday cards had bridged. Then, at the funeral, in the desperate grief she had found the gangly cousin with whom she had once had a fist fight as a young child, and recognised a soul mate beneath the surface differences of rich and poor. So she had asked her to come up to Columbia and stay, and Stephanie, who was passing on college, had surprisingly agreed.

Savanna finished peeing, and Stephanie peeked her head round the door. 'Dying to go.'

'Sure.' Savanna smiled at her cousin. 'Sorry about Princess Diana.'

'Oh, she's just fine. I think she's funny,' said Stephanie. 'Didn't seem to mind about me putting her boyfriend to bed. Do you all drink like that every night?'

'Not *every* night.' Savanna didn't sound too certain. Was it every other night? Every three nights?

'Funny,' said Stephanie. 'Back home it's the losers who drink. Not the winners, like here.'

Savanna looked at her. It wasn't said to be rude. It was a bemused social comment. Savanna thought about her words. She was right. The audience would be wasted in the beer joints of the South, but the act was usually sober, making the money, the one with the future. He or she might sing about drowning sorrows in whiskey, but Garth Brooks didn't drink at all. Neither did Steph.

She thought of Diane, and herself, and Mitchell and the others . . . the trust-fund kids. Were they winners? Did their gold and platinum credit cards make them that? Did their Ivy League university? Or were they simply winners at choosing the right parents? And was that winning? 'I made my money the old-fashioned way . . . I inherited it.' Ha! Ha! But on whom was the joke? Weren't they just versions of the six-pack sixty-a-day guys in the 'HARDY ELECTRIC' T-shirts and their women shouting the odds on some Southern Saturday night on a long ride to nowhere with drink as an anaesthetic for the pain?

Steph had been the real heroine of the night before. She had headed off the fights at the pass, got everyone home, put everyone to bed, made sure nobody died of inhaled vomit or hypothermia on a cold bathroom floor, and cleaned up the mess afterwards. And all she'd gotten for her pains were discouraging words from a hung-over Diane who had tried to minimise her for failing to be a right royal pain in the ass like everyone else had been.

'You still play Aunt LeAnne's guitar?' said Steph. She accentuated the first syllable of guitar just as Savanna's mom had done.

'Sure. All the time. Specially lately.'

'She was surely one helluva singer, your mom. You too, when you were young. I remember Christmas once. We were all pretty jealous, us being the hillbillies and y'all from Belle Meade and outsinging us.'

Savanna watched her. Steph was taller than she, plainer, thinner, hungrier by far, and truer to her type. Being a young songwriter in Nashville and waiting tables to pay for the habit was country's equivalent to the bus stop on Hollywood and Vine. But Steph believed, and while there was belief there was hope, although right this second Savanna was thinking that while there was sleep there was hope. Nobody had told her that college nights were busier than college days.

'Hey, your T-shirt is a little short on me. I look like I'm in some soft-porn movie.' Steph laughed unselfconsciously. She was very sure of herself. So was Savanna but somehow it was more of a surprise that Steph was. After all, she was a fish out of water here amongst the college crowd . . . not being academic; not being able to talk the small talk and not wanting to; drinking diet Coke and suggesting subways while everyone else was calling cabs.

'I think dorm life is more slasher/horror genre than soft porn,' said Savanna smiling. 'All the girls are on synchronised periods, and at night it's "Scream 2000".'

'But you enjoy it,' said Steph. Somehow it was a question. 'It seems like party time USA.'

'But not Music City, USA.'

'No, not Nashville.'

'I envy you Nashville.'

'Why? It's your town too. You have that big old house. I remember going to tea there once, and being scared stiff, but your grandma sat me on her lap and made me laugh. She was a darlin'.'

'Yeah, she still is. Sometimes I don't think she's Dad's mom. She's so funny and he's so damned serious, and self-centred, and buttoned up . . .' Savanna shook her head to express her deep misunderstanding of human nature. 'But what I mean, well, I don't mean Nashville . . . I mean dreams, and having them, and doing something about them, working at them, for them, all the time. OK, so you're here, on a holiday, but you're not really here, Steph. I can see it in your eyes. You're thinking about songs, and where you've placed them, and wondering how good they are, and who's going to buy one. Your eyes get all somewhere else, even when some brainy millionaire's son is trying to pull you before he gets too drunk to. That's what I envy. Because you can do it. You might do it and then one day the Dixie Chicks are singing your song, and then everyone is, and it's Grammys and Sony sending jets and shit like that. And I'm still flogging through Aeschylus or calculus or some hot new piece of science that will be tomorrow's flat-earth theory.'

'And until the Chicks bite, I go right on serving blue plate specials to construction workers who think a tip is a pinch on the butt. And you spend your time wondering whether to see *Rent* for the tenth time at a hundred bucks a ticket, or to take that plastic card out to LuLu's with the guy who's planning his first cyberspace venture-capital deal. I wonder who most people would want to be.'

'"Most people" aren't us. Come to think of it, "most people" aren't most people. Put it this way. Would you trade? Right now, would you be me?'

'I'd like to sing like you. I'd like to own that '29 Gibson and look like you, cute as a button, sweet as honey, and get up on a stage and sing my own songs and *kill* them out there.'

'You would?' said Savanna. Steph's vehemence was tangible and touching. She meant every word of it. 'But no Columbia and the irresponsibility of youth?'

'My life is real serious,' said Steph simply. 'There are things I have to do, and time is running out.'

'At nineteen?'

'Sure at nineteen. I don't have to find out what I want to do. I *know* what I want to do. Always have.'

'So do I,' said Savanna, a trifle too fast. 'I want to be a doctor.'

'There you are. You know what I'm sayin'.' But Steph put her head to one side when she spoke. 'What kind of doctor?' she added.

'Oh, a doctor doctor,' said Savanna with an impatient wave of her hand. She was acutely aware that it wasn't an impressive answer. Had Steph been asked what kind of a songwriter she was or wanted to be, she would hardly have answered, 'Oh, one who writes song songs.'

'I haven't got as far as thinking "speciality". Too busy with the Greeks.' She tried to laugh it off, and Steph laughed to help her through the moment. That was Steph. Diane would have nailed her indecision and vacillation to the wall for all to see and sneer at. 'My grandma says she's still trying to decide what she wants to be when she grows up,' said Savanna. More laughter. Still no humour.

'I guess medicine is in the genes.'

'And country.'

'Oh, yes.'

'I wonder if I'm any good,' said Savanna, the germ of an idea forming. 'Mom used to say I was, but Mom was Mom.'

'You could sing as well as her, couldn't you?'

'Maybe a bit better, I think.'

'Then you are good,' said Steph. 'You got that Gibson here?'

'Under the bed.'

'Let's find out?'

'Now? Hung over?'

'Excuses!'

'OK, you're on. Let's do it.'

They exploded into the bedroom.

'Shit, I thought you two had pissed off. I'm trying to crash here.'

'Fuck off, Diane,' said Savanna. 'Clean up, caff up and ship out. Calculus calls.'

She started to scramble around under her bed on her hands and knees.

'Can't you put on some underwear, Savanna? I'm not feeling that strong.'

Savanna hauled out the guitar case. Steph sat down on the bed, her eyes shining. It was years since she'd seen the legendary Gibson that had been her aunt's prize possession.

'You're not going to make a noise, are you? Oh, please don't. Please don't,' wheedled Diane, her head poking up from the covers like a bedraggled ostrich.

'I don't say that when you're plumbing that cock diesel on the football team,' said Savanna, 'and that is noise noise. Jesus! This is going to be a lullaby. What shall I play, Steph? I know – one of Mom's. "It was a Lucky Day when you Broke my Heart."'

Savanna ripped into a neat, economical introduction, milking the strings of rich melody, the old wood humming happily. It went fast, and with great accuracy, no fumbling, nothing missed, nothing fluffed. And then Savanna began to sing.

> It was a lucky day when you broke my heart,
> Though it felt like hell, and I fell apart,
> But where the bone is broke is the strongest part,
> Thanks to you, what was weak is now a real tough heart.

> A real tough heart, but tough, not hard,
> Ready to play with the cowboy crowd,
> When there's hearts to be broke in the name of love,
> It'll be the man, not me, who's the turtle dove.

The room was full of a certain magic. Savanna didn't sound like anyone. She was not a little bit unique, or even unique in a different way, she was Savanna. Steph, who knew country music like a priest knew prayers, tried first to pinpoint it, out of habit. Patsy Cline meets Nanci Griffith, the hint of Loretta, Faith Hill singing to her husband . . . but then she gave up.

This was the new old, or the old made new. It didn't cross over from mainstream country to pop, because it was already in both places at once. Savanna's voice was synthesis. The thesis and the antithesis had merged. Steph knew she had never heard anything quite like it.

'Oh, God,' she said simply, and her hand was at her mouth.

But the real impact was elsewhere. Diane, sitting up in bed, looking quite dazed, said in a bemused voice, 'Jeez, that is actually quite good.'

CHAPTER

FOUR

The box sat on the Barcelona table. It was big, cardboard, and square, and the Giacometti and Brancusi bronzes that flanked it seemed put out by its presence. On it, in black marker, were clearly printed the words 'FOR SAVANNA'. Beneath that command, in her mother's cursive writing, was an order in brackets, something of an afterthought . . . ('Only for Savanna'.)

'I suppose that means I'm not to open it. I supposed that was what it meant when I found it.'

Savanna nodded. Her father walked over to the vast picture window of the vast *pied-à-terre* that was his New York apartment and stared moodily at Central Park. He held the glass of Bourbon in his hand as if it were a talisman with limited powers to ward off evil spirits. His body language was clear. He was irritated that the packet was for Savanna alone. It smacked of secrets. He was being excluded by his dead wife. He had felt to some extent excluded by LeAnne when she was alive, but then he had done more than his fair share of excluding. In fact, he had specialised in it. Was this some form of revenge?

'Do you want me to open it now?' said Savanna.

'Do what you like,' said Dr Stone. 'Yes' was what he meant.

Savanna tried to pick the box up. 'It's heavy,' she said.

'I'm sorry to drag you all the way over here for this,' said her father. He managed to imply that his wife's cardboard legacy was a small, rather irritating distraction from the more important business of the living.

Savanna frowned. That was so like him. Once again, her perennial anger at her father bubbled up. Why was he so goddamned insensitive? He missed her mother in his fashion, but it was a miserable fashion. Couldn't he cry, break down, like a real man? There was a difference between maintaining a stiff upper lip and a Teflon one.

'I think I'll take it back to the dorm and open it later,' said Savanna to punish him. 'It'll be easier to carry all wrapped up.'

'Probably just newspaper clippings,' he said dismissively.

'I'll find out later,' said Savanna. And you won't. You'll have to ask. *Oh, by the way, what was in the cardboard box – clippings, was it?* He would hate having to ask that question.

Henry sipped petulantly at his drink.

'I suppose I'll have to call up for a porter to help you carry the thing downstairs,' he said. 'After dinner, that is. You are staying for dinner, aren't you?'

'That was the plan,' said Savanna, as if she had signed a contract it would be dishonourable, but attractive, to break.

'Good. We'll go downstairs. It's so easy, and they've got a new chef. Quite decent in patches, sort of curate's egg as they say in England.' He laughed without humour.

Savanna slumped down on a black Eames chair, the latter-day equivalent of relaxing on a bed of nails. Her father was a bit like a road traffic accident, horrifying but fascinating at the same time. He was very good-looking in a distinguished, highly polished way, and effortlessly grand. It was a heady combination, brains and class, old money and new, and that cold self-confidence that only the truly emotionally constipated could carry off. No wonder her mother had fallen for him. When she had been younger, Savanna had quite fancied him herself. As a young teenager she had always gotten a laugh by saying that she couldn't see why incest was such a dirty word. But Oscar Wilde had been right when he said 'Children begin by loving their parents. After a time they judge them. Rarely, if ever, do they forgive them.' Right about her father, wrong about her mother, that is. Somehow the battered cardboard box, marked 'Only for Savanna' in her mother's wide-open hand, was more impressive and interesting than her father in his immaculate suit with its sloping, perfectly cut shoulders, razor-creased pants, and glistening black lace-up brogues. The box would have a warm inside; Dr Henry Stone looked as cold as a tailor's dummy.

'Any excitements in the OR today?' said Savanna watching him.

The desire to wind him up was strong. He didn't do excitement.

'Couple of CABCs and a valve replacement. They went well.' The 'as always' hung unspoken in the air.

'How old were the by-pass grafts?'

'Oh, I don't know, eighty-one and seventy-eight.' He turned around and the swallow that he took of the Bourbon was more a swig than a sip. He was on to her.

'Striving officiously to keep alive,' said Savanna with a laugh. 'Wasn't that what Grandpa used to say?'

'They both have loving families. They are fit. They have as much right to treatment as anyone else. The world doesn't belong to the young, you know.' But it reached him. The medical world was divided on the advisability of replacing compromised coronary arteries in the old who were much more likely to have problems with major operations. Greedy surgeons often took risks to get the big fees in situations where there was no consensus on which course of action was 'right'.

'You'll be making those decisions one day,' he said confidently. 'Don't think they're easy.'

'I don't think anything about being a doctor would be easy.' Savanna twiddled her hair with her finger, and stared out of the window as the lights of Manhattan began to glint in the rapidly gathering dusk.

'You're not having second thoughts, are you?' said her father sharply. It was precisely the reaction she had been going for.

'No. No,' she said distantly. Her trumpet sounded the faintest possible note, riddled with indecision.

'Because that is what all this college is about. It's not inexpensive, you know. We Stones have a tradition of giving back.'

'Tell that to the slaves your ancestors died trying to hang on to.'

'For God's sake, Savanna. What's got into you tonight? Am I imposing on your time here? Are you deliberately trying to irritate me? I know this is an upsetting time for both of us, but we should pull together.'

'Oh, sorry, Daddy,' said Savanna. Her eyes suddenly filled with tears, and her stomach churned with the familiar sense of loss. 'An upsetting time. It's just that . . . just that sometimes it seems you don't miss Mom at all. I know you do, but it seems you don't, and I do . . . all the time . . . so badly. *So* badly.' Her shoulders sagged and a tear crept out on to her cheek.

Her father simply hovered. He took a step towards her, one back. His hand described an ineffectual circle, as if he wanted to reach out and touch her shoulder, but recoiled from the gesture at the last moment. He coughed awkwardly. He lived with death. People died around him all day long, and all night long. Sometimes they died under his knife. *Because* of his knife. You won most, but you lost some, and in the end death was always the winner. Losing LeAnne of breast cancer had been a terrible, terrible thing. But you couldn't indulge in feelings. You had to go on, keeping up appearances.

'We all grieve in our different ways,' he said, trying to keep the stiffness out of his voice. Then he made a far too early attempt to lift the mood. 'How's life in the dorm? That girl you're rooming with still untidy?' He smiled as if he had made a joke – a wan, rather hopeful smile.

'Yeah,' said Savanna looking at him in astonishment through bleary eyes. His lack of sensitivity was on a truly astounding scale. Had she inherited it? *Any* of it? If so, it must be cut out like a cancer. 'Stephanie has been staying. Cousin Stephanie.'

Her father's blank look was replaced by one of total disinterest as the word 'cousin' located Stephanie in his memory bank.

'Oh,' he said.

'She's a songwriter in Nashville.'

'*Is* she?'

Savanna wiped her eyes with the back of her hand. Her father wondered about offering her the immaculate linen handkerchief in his breast pocket, and then thought better of it. Tears unremarked upon cleared up faster than those made a fuss of.

'We played some songs together. She thought I was pretty good.'

'*Did* you? *Did* she?' Her father sat down on the sofa beneath the Kandinsky of a violin. He shot his cuffs, and crossed his immaculately trousered legs. His shoes shone in the subtle, subdued lighting. He smiled neutrally. Whether or not Stephanie existed, and what she did, even Savanna's talent for singing – all these subjects were about as interesting to him as the activities on an unknown and unknowable planet. Seemingly aware of his shortcomings in this area, he tried unsuccessfully to hide his lack of interest. 'Your mother always played well,' he said. 'I liked it when you two sang together.'

'Mother didn't just play well, she played brilliantly. And she sang better than she played. She could have been a star. Bigger than anyone.'

Savanna's tone had turned bitter. Anger was replacing sadness. Anger was often the end product of Savanna's emotions.

'She *was* a star. Our star. But I don't think she'd have wanted to be on TV or anything like that.' He laughed at the silliness of the thought.

'Are you sure?'

'I was married to her.'

'She was my mother.'

'You are not seriously saying that Mom wanted to be a country music performer?'

'Of *course* she did. How could you have that talent and not want to use it? She just didn't talk about it, because you always put her down about it, and about her family being hillbillies, and all that wrong-side-of-Nashville stuff.' Savanna was sitting forward now. 'But she had her dreams. *I* know about them. I think it is so *sad* that you didn't.'

'Savanna, you are upset . . . you . . .' He took this tack with patients sometimes. Patients were often upset. The prospect of death was often unsettling.

'I am upset. You are goddamned right, I'm upset. I'm upset that Mom could spend her whole life with a man who never bothered to find out what she wanted, what was going on inside her head, what her dreams were. I'm upset, incredibly upset, that my father could be so insensitive, so tone deaf, so devoid of any emotion not to *know* that Mom had this wonderful, almost unbelievable talent. It's like living with an angel and not noticing; a saint and not recognising it. I mean, you couldn't *hear* her, you didn't *see* her, you never even bothered to get to *know* her. And you want me to be a doctor like you. Why? What have you got? What talent do you have that hundreds, thousands of others don't have? You're a plumber, Daddy. At the end of the day, all you do is fit pipes. And because you fit them on humans everybody thinks you're God, but you're just unblocking drains, really. It isn't such a big deal. But when Mom sang, God was listening. I guarantee you. And he's for sure not watching when you are sewing away under the arc lights, giving some geriatric a few more wheezy painful months in your expensive hospital. You've got art on your walls, Dad, but you've got none in your soul. Mom had a heart full of it. Now, if you'll excuse me, I'm going to pass on your dinner invitation and go back to the dorm with Mom's box. Because with the cardboard and her writing, and her newspaper clippings, or whatever, I'll be close to something warm and loving and caring . . . something that's actually alive . . .'

They both jumped up, both equally angry, both feeling equally wronged. He didn't try to stop her as Savanna heaved the big box off the shining table, and lugged it towards the door. She had the weird feeling that she was taking her mother's ashes away from him, although she had been buried in the cold, hard Tennessee ground. The box's contents were heavier than cuttings; books perhaps, something important, she couldn't help feeling. She wanted to know where her father had found the box, but she was too proud to ask. The Parthian shot she had designed especially to wound him lay hanging in the shocked and shaken air of the apartment. Her mother had never really been at home here amidst the state-of-the-trend modern art, the grey marble, and the desirable fifties' black leather furniture. But it had suited her father with its hard angles and the sacrifice of comfort on the austere altar of good Manhattan taste.

He did not help her to open the door, watching her with irritation as she struggled with it. He needed her more than she him. He had plans for her, and she could frustrate them, maybe would frustrate them.

'Goodbye, Dad,' she said.

'Goodbye,' he said stiffly.

They would be in touch. In this life you did not have many fathers and mothers. They might be impossible, but they were never replaceable. But the slamming door slammed on the part of Savanna that had been the obedient daughter. And if she was going to be a rebel, she had better find herself a cause.

CHAPTER

FIVE

Savanna sat on her bed and opened the box. There was a note written on bubblegum-pink writing paper.

My Darling,

When will you read these words, and where? I'll be gone,
my darling, but I believe that I will be able to look down on
you, and I will be doing so now, right this minute, my precious
daughter. All my life is in this box, and I give it to you . . .
because you and Daddy were all my life, yet you were the
one who understood me most. I kept a journal. No one knew
about it, and I revealed nearly all my secrets in it . . . and now
you will know them, Savanna. I hope that you won't find this
morbid, but I don't think you will. You have such a sense of
life and fun, and I hope that you will laugh as much as I
laughed sometimes in these pages, and cry fewer times than I
cried. You will also find all the songs I ever wrote. Some you
will remember, because we used to sing them together, but
others you won't have heard. There are tapes, and pictures,
and I have tried to be honest and make a photograph of my
life as I saw it . . . very differently, I suspect, from the way you
thought I saw it. Maybe it is a selfish thing that I do now. I
have worried about that. But then I think that all knowledge is
good and all mystery is waste, and if you never know your

own mother, who then will you ever know? I don't want to influence your life, my darling Savanna. It is yours and yours alone to live, although Daddy might not share that sentiment! But I want you to know the places where I went wrong, or where I wonder if I did, because one can never be sure about what might have been. Some say they have no regrets in this life. Lucky them. My regrets are to do with my dreams. I never reached for them. I watched them from the back seat in the movies of my thoughts, because reality seemed so much safer than illusion and because the toughest thing is to take, or make, the chances and opportunities. There is so much fear in this world, and now I am beyond it all how silly that fear seems and how little power or point it has. You are braver than I was, Savanna, and I hope this box and its contents make you braver still. Be strong, my darling. Be of good courage. Don't blame Daddy for anything. He is a good man, and always has been. In fact, don't blame anyone. Just live life to the full and fear nothing. You have brains, beauty and talent, my Savanna, and a fierce morality (and temper, my sweetheart). Use it all well. And I will be watching you always, from the front row of the stalls of your life, loving you and cheering you on. Think of me, my angel, because I am not dead. I live in you, and in your children, and in theirs, and in the wind that blows in the evening, in the chill of the morning, and in every note you will sing. This is not 'goodbye', my darling. As you read these words, I am saying 'hello'.

'Hello, Mommy,' whispered Savanna, and her eyes filled with tears, as she began to dig deeper into the box, laying the note on her pillow. The first book, bound in dark brown leather, was inscribed simply 'Diary'.

CHAPTER

SIX

The afterburn of the Phoenix sunset fired the sky. A warm wind blew
in from the desert. Aron Wallis could sense the anticipation in the
hot, dry air . . . and another emotion that was very like fear. It was as
if all who watched knew this would not happen again. Not exactly
this. Not ever. Aron noted the faces, frozen in suspended ecstasy. The
girls were young, some barely teenagers, but there were mothers,
too, blue-jeaned, cowboy-booted, many in cowboy hats. He saw the
perspiration on far-from-stiff upper lips, and he brushed by T-shirts
that were warm with hot women, and tank-tops that showed jail-bait
bellybuttons, many pierced with rings bearing the DD initials. And
there were men as well, macho, and unashamed. Dwight Deacon
could do it for all of them. He had transcended gender with his
music. His appeal was universal. Everybody wanted him.

Which was why Aron was there. Because Deacon *was* Polymark
Records, sixty per cent of their North American sales, and this was
the first extraordinary concert of his three-year World Tour. Aron's
boss had been quite clear at the breakfast: 'Dwight told me personally
he'd appreciate your support, all of you, whether you work with him
or not. This is a big moment for our company, boys.'

The secretaries had jammed the switchboard getting first-class
seats to Phoenix. Actually, Aron had been looking forward to it. He
had artists on the road, and about to tour, and Deacon, possibly the
world's greatest showman, and its bestselling recording star, was the

man who showed how a concert should be staged. He had helped with the production of one of the great man's early hit albums and had a signed photograph of 'DD' on his piano to prove it.

Steam spun like cotton candy from the edges of the giant stage. It came from the F-100 performance smoke generators, primed with water and mineral oil to make the artificial fog. Aron was caught up in the group fantasy, aware of the power of the raw emotion around him. Some of the beautiful young eyes that were able to force themselves away from the stage took in his stick-on, the backstage pass that these Deacon fans would die for. Aron's was a top-of-the-line 'ALL ACCESS' with its own passport-sized photograph of him, and a hologram of the Deacon trademark 'DD'. The eyes stopped at the pass. They missed Aron, the man, completely; although, young and darkly good-looking as he was, and on the fast track to success as one of Nashville's hottest record producers, he would have fulfilled the dreams of most of the young but totally preoccupied girls in the vast stadium. He didn't mind. This was show business. His business. And you didn't mix business with sex unless you were a performer, or a performer's hanger-on, and needed some help getting down from the adrenaline high of the act.

The smoke was building fast now, as if the Devil himself were blowing an infernal wind in a doomed attempt to delay what must happen. And then the lights were blazing – some 500 pairs of fixed, and 150 'varis' capable of travelling everywhere to make sure that the star shone wherever he went. A young girl, pressed right up against Aron's shoulder, was weeping silently, oblivious to him, both her hands pressed to a delectable mouth. Any guy on the football team would have died for her, but tonight, this moment, she belonged to a man physically capable of being her father. Suddenly her single shout pierced the quiet; her voice, thick with the accent of the Delta, hovered on the edge where ecstasy met sorrow, where sadness collided with joy.

'Come *to* us, Dwight.' She paused poignantly and then the single word, 'Please!' Aron stared at her. Her 'Dwight' was all strung out, her 'please' had the upturned inflection of deep Mississippi. He could actually feel her body quivering against his.

Her prayer was answered. As if cued by that lonely voice in the hugeness of the auditorium, everything on the stage began to move at once. A curtain backdrop, glittering like the Field of the Cloth of Gold, fell away. At the same time a mighty chord struck: A minor, known in Nashville as the 'people's key'. It was the sign. The roar from the crowd drowned the music, but the chord, amplified a thousand times, fought back. Two walls of sound collided. The irresistible force crashed into the immoveable object and then the screams of 80,000 were quieted by the on-stage spectacle that unfolded. A giant guitar case, 1,000 feet high, was revealed, suspended from hidden scaffolding. It was bathed in a bright yellow light that illuminated the blood-red 'D' which was the single initial it bore. The music now had taken form. A super reality invaded the borders of the illusion that had gripped the crowd. They had cried to this song, made love to it, quieted the kids with it on their automobile rides to nowhere.

> There's a little bit of Memphis in my soul,
> Can't forget the Delta, the blues, the rock 'n' roll,
> In Smoky Mountain mists hillbilly made me whole,
> But it was here in Nashville that I found my way,
> Yes, it's country from Nashville that I play today.

They were swaying and singing along to the Deacon signature tune. They tapped their urban cowboy boots and clapped their hands above their heads in time to the inescapable rhythm. Aron, showing solidarity with the beautiful girl beside him, joined in and was rewarded with a brilliant co-conspirator's smile. Latinos, African Americans, rednecks, everyone was in this together, Aron couldn't help noticing. The new country music, Dwight Deacon's music, had brought them together in a way that they hadn't known before; other music had for so many years kept them apart. Country was now a symbol of the growing national unity for which America had searched so painfully for so long. And soon the 100-million-selling solo artist would be among them, one of them, appearing just for them.

The doors of the guitar case swung open as the music intensified. Who would see him first? Where would he come from? Where would he be? The secret had been carefully kept, although the press had been full of rumours of the extraordinary expense of this country music extravaganza, a show that it was rumoured would dwarf the extravagant rock productions of the Stones, U2, and Metallica. Inside the guitar case was a huge acoustic guitar, completely lifelike, its six strings made from rope-like steel hawsers. Strobe lights played across the yellow-brown of the old wood, dipped tantalisingly into the cavernous central hole on which all eyes were now focused. A rumbling explosion shook the stadium, and a bright flash of light, and then, back-lit in an orange glow, a platform began to slide out of the very centre of the guitar. A figure, dressed in a long white robe, head down, drew 160,000 eyes. A muted roar came from the crowd, but they were ready for tricks. With Dwight Deacon, showman supreme, nothing was ever as it seemed. The music quieted and a voice spoke.

'May the spirit of his music, and the love in his heart warm you all tonight with the help of God.'

And then it happened. A giant holographic halo of light appeared from nowhere in the sky above the stage before the vast guitar. It descended, hovering down like a spaceship from a distant planet. As it did so, a platform rose from the stage. On it was a man in black skin-tight Wrangler jeans, his head held low, his face shielded from the eager eyes by the rim of a John B. Stetson beaver hat, size seven and five-eighths. He held out both hands to one side. His wrists dangled limply. One foot was placed behind the other. The imagery was unmistakeable. There was no cross, but Dwight Deacon had been crucified. He was dead and soon . . . he would ascend into Heaven. Which is what he did. He looked up. A hundred and fifty spotlights caught him. But the brim of his hat still shaded the hypnotic eyes that his audience had come to see. From stage right, a girl with long blonde hair ran across to him, bearing a black acoustic guitar, and at last he spoke.

'God bless you, Phoenix. Thank y'all for comin', and if the good Lord will forgive me, we're sure as hell gonna bust butt tonight.'

He leaped forward as the roar of the blissful audience provided the wind for his vocal wings. Now they could see his eyes, round with wonder, unblinking in the lights, scanning the crowd in awe, sucking energy from them, and sending it back to them multiplied a thousandfold. Memphis. The Delta. Bluegrass from Kentucky. The rock of Elvis, the blues of Muddy Waters, the soul of the Motor City. It was all inside him, the eyes promised. It was all there. It was his synthesis. The Dwight Deacon sound was now America's sound, and the crowd adored him for the ability to share that he had given them. But it was more than the music. It was his need. They sensed his desire for them. They had given him the fame that he needed as much as the air that he breathed. It was nothing to do with the billion dollars he was rumoured to have made; the hire-and-fire power he had in the music industry; the cosy chats with the President in the Oval Office. It was all about fame, that universal, unconditional love of strangers. To a man from Mars, it might have seemed there were 80,000 fans in the stadium that night. But really there was only one: Dwight Deacon himself. He had entered what he liked to call 'The Place', where everything was heightened, every experience more real, where time slowed down, where happiness was total. He only reached 'The Place' at moments like this, and he lived for it and would die for it. The music was the message, and the message was love: love for the audience, which was converted into the end product that he craved. What Dwight Deacon needed with the desperation of the damned was unconditional love for the strange, inexplicable, alienated creature he had become.

Aron watched in awe. He ran his hand through his thick, black hair, and his brown eyes narrowed. He didn't very much like men . . . women were the superior gender in every aspect of his book . . . and he liked Dwight Deacon a good deal less than most men he knew. But this was magnificent. It was a triumph of showmanship, entertainment lifted to some transcendent level where human emotion was so deeply engaged that it could be milked for cash like a full cow in a secure stall. None of his artists came close to Deacon in their ability to do anything like this, and he wished like hell that they did. That it was based on bullshit was a billion miles from the point. In truth, there was no Memphis in Dwight Deacon's soul, if indeed he had one. He couldn't remember the Delta blues, and he was on record in the office as having said he didn't like rock 'n' roll. His endless battle with his weight problem was solved by wearing tight Wrangler jeans like a corset. So in fact he was more roly-poly than hillbilly, and on the few times he had been to the Appalachian Mountains he had told Aron personally that he had found them unpleasantly cold and wet.

But none of that mattered. All that mattered was the package . . . the big round innocent eyes, the sensual mouth, the image of the man and the muscle of his music. All that counted was that he be number one for ever, that his Soundscan ratings should prove it and his 'hard-ticket' sales should agree. His *Billboard* ratings and R & R chart positions must sing in perfect harmony the truth that must never be denied . . . that Dwight Deacon was an American legend, now and for ever, amen. For the time being the superstar would settle for that. Was it really too much for a man to ask to be God on this earth?

'Do you know him?' drawled the girl next to him. She nodded down at Aron's all-purpose pass as if it were an open sesame to the Pearly Gates.

'Oh, yeah, a bit,' said Aron. She smiled hard, and moistened her lips. Her white tank-top was wet with sweat. No bra. No need. Aron was better-looking than Deacon, he knew that. And at twenty-five he was seven years younger. OK, so he was perhaps a little olive and aquiline for Miss Mississippi with her piano-key teeth, shimmering hair, and her Bambi-big eyes. But, purely from the looks point of view, he was a better bet than the billion-dollar man. That, however, was without factoring in fame, and fame was life's ultimate distorting mirror.

'What's he like?' she drooled. There was a contract on offer. She had signed it in the blood of her teenage longing. 'Show me Deacon and I'll show you me.'

Aron took a deep breath. He had been asked a question. What was Dwight Deacon like? Actually, it was an interesting question. The short answer was that he, the rest of the world, and possibly even the star himself, hadn't a clue. This was not, however, the answer required by the teenager in the jeans so tight he could actually see her panties outlined beneath the soft blue denim.

'Like nothing at all on this planet,' he said with an encouraging smile. It was the nearest he could get to the truth.

Kirstie Stevens was in love. It wasn't just love, really, it was bigger than love. More like religion and love of God, but it was sexual, too, and she felt the adrenaline rush as she watched her idol. She went to every Dwight concert that she could afford, and many that she could not, and it was always the same. They gave her a high so high she could hardly remember it afterwards. No longer was she plain, ordinary Kirstie who worked at Peaches in Nashville selling records. In the presence of Dwight Deacon she became transformed. It was like he had the Midas touch or something, because he turned her into a goddess. She felt so powerful when she could see and hear him, and it was only a matter of time before she touched him, because she was a fan club member now. Soon it would be Fan Fair in Nashville, and Dwight would sign her CDs, her T-shirts, her arm, and the Polaroid picture in which he would pose with her. She wondered a lot about that day. Would it show visibly upon her? Would she have marks from his touch, like mystical country music stigmata – his guitar strings imprinted across her hand, or his finger-marks across her breast above her heart? She felt faint at the thought . . . deliciously, deliriously faint . . . and the waiting made it better. She had to be worthy, and worship correctly. She had to be the best and most diligent member of his audience, this and every other night. When he told them to sing, she would. When he asked if they were having a good time, her scream of 'Yes, Dwight' would be the loudest. She only wished with all her heart that hers had been the voice that had pierced the sudden silence just moments before, pleading with him to come. But maybe it was wrong to ask Dwight for things. Too presumptuous. Sacrilege, perhaps. Kirstie was not quite sure.

Then she saw him, or rather it. He was a man attached to an 'ALL ACCESS' pass that had DD's picture on it, like on a credit card. She scarcely saw his face, but she stared at the pass and it scrambled her already curdled thoughts. This guy was one of them, one of the chosen people. Like an angel or something. He must actually know Dwight Deacon in the way you knew ordinary people, or he probably did. Her eyes were wide, and the 'ALL ACCESS' man saw her expression and cocked his head to one side as he squeezed past her, as if puzzled by it.

Kirstie looked hard at his face, and wished she was prettier. She had good hair and good teeth, and, she liked to think, a good heart. But she was wide of hip, and small of breast, and her skin with its weak suntan looked sallow and greasy. She was plain really, and ordinary, except that Dwight made her very, very special.

Dwight was her secret. At the store they would joke that she had a crush on him, but all the girls had crushes on someone. Mostly they were Goth girls heavily into the hard rockers like Slipknot, Placebo, Feeder, and Korn. But they didn't know the half of it. They didn't know about the shrine that was her studio apartment to which nobody was ever invited. They had no clue about the files she was building up on DD from the Internet, a dossier that thickened every evening as she plundered the electronic world for everything she could find about the god she so deeply adored.

The guy with the 'ALL ACCESS' pass was almost past her. There was a slim chance. A window of opportunity. Kirstie must seize it.

'Hey, guy,' she said. She reached out and touched him on his disappearing shoulder. 'Hey, guy,' she said again.

Aron stopped and turned.

'You got a pass!' she blurted out.

'Yup,' he said with a kindly smile. 'Guess you wanna know what he's like.'

'No,' she said quickly. 'No, I know that. I just want to buy the pass.'

He laughed quickly, and shook his head.

'A thousand dollars,' said Kirstie. She had 2,000 in the bank.

'Honey, a *hundred* thousand, and I'm tempted. If Deacon heard I'd sold my pass to a fan, he'd crucify me.' He made to move on. The girl had a strange expression on her face. They came in all sorts and shapes and sizes in the crowd, and that was just the bodies. It made Aron nervous to speculate on what was going on in the heads.

'Dwight wouldn't crucify anyone,' said Kirstie with a puzzled, indulgent smile. Clearly the guy didn't know him at all. Maybe he was just some guy from the arena. Obviously he had nothing to do with Dwight.

'No, maybe he wouldn't,' said Aron, smiling again. 'Of course he wouldn't. Not Dwight.' Hell, this was business. Fans were built on dreams. Music was. It allowed you to dream; drugged you and dragged you into dreams. Aron himself was an arch illusionist in the field in which Deacon was the grand master. Crucifixion would be the mildest penalty imposed by the superstar on someone who sold a backstage pass to a fan. But nobody wanted the public to know about his temper, and the public didn't want to know. Bliss was preferable to the folly of wisdom, wasn't it? So he hurried on, learning more about the game he was playing that went by the name of work. But he would have learned something else if, like Superman, he had had X-ray vision.

He would have learned that Kirstie carried a Dan Wesson .357 Magnum revolver in her little leather purse. Serious fans took their business seriously. If anyone ever threatened the superstar, Kirstie would be there to save him. After all, who knew what happened to a heroine when she saved the life of her hero?

CHAPTER

SEVEN

Steph and Savanna walked into the Manhattan honky-tonk, and threaded their way through the tables to the bar. Savanna carried her guitar case. The barman noticed it immediately. Starstruck hopefuls were always trying a shot at the microphone.

'I think they already gotta band, lady,' said the barman.

'We're on our way to a gig,' said Steph quickly.

Savanna put down her black canvas guitar case by the side of the bar stool.

'Oh, where you playin'?' The barman looked vaguely interested. A lot of kids tried to get on the stage of the Silver Bullet. Some tried to talk their way on; some just jumped up. But this girl sounded South, sounded right. He had her from the mountains where about six states met: the Carolinas, the Virginias, Bluegrass Kentucky. Hell, she might even be from Tennessee. The barman had been in Manhattan too long now, too long to go back, but the 'algia' part of nostalgia meant pain. Folk forgot how homesick you could get.

'We're playin' for some kids over at NYU. Fraternity thing,' said Savanna. She sounded like her mom sounded when she was around her Southern family. She'd gotten that down.

'You girls are a long way from home,' said the barman with a wistful smile. 'I'm hearin' Smoky Mountains. Appalachians, at least.'

'Pigeon Forge,' said Steph with a smile.

'*There* you go. What can I get for you two ladies?'

'Couple of Buds.'

He didn't ask if they wanted glasses. Pigeon Forge didn't do glasses. 'You got it.'

'Fooled him,' said Savanna, smiling broadly.

'Heck. He didn't need no foolin'. We *are* from Pigeon Forge,' said Steph. 'You gotta start thinkin' right about this thing, Savanna. You are the real thing. You are classic Coke, cousin. Don't go forgettin' what it is you got. I'd choke rattlesnakes to sound like you and that Gibson. These Travoltas gonna die and go to Heaven if we get you near that mike.'

Savanna eased herself on to a stool and steadied the Gibson. She twisted round and cased the room. The mike was there all right. Centre stage and flanked by others, and a drum kit. The band were off, and the floor was half full of gliding two-steppers doing a reasonable job to a kick-along Merle Haggard. Big-city cowboys danced smoother than country folk, and the tourists usually outdanced the locals in Nashville. There wasn't enough smoke or testosterone to make this a card-carrying beer joint, and there was a fifty:fifty women-to-men ratio, unheard of in a genuine honky-tonk. It was TNN country. They'd probably do line-dancing lessons during happy hour.

The Buds came up sweating cold.

'Who's playin'?' said Steph. She'd had this planned. The only way you got a shot at the mike was if the band said so.

'Some kids out of Austin.' The barman nodded his head down towards the end of the bar where four guys were drinking. 'Call themselves the Lonesome Doves. Say they've got a deal coming up with Mercury, but they all say that. They've got a couple of fast ones that kick ass. I've heard worse.' He laughed as he moved off to serve someone else.

'Larry McMurtry,' said Savanna.

'Yeah, Mercury will have to change their name,' said Steph. 'They shoot doves.'

'And eat them,' laughed Savanna wickedly. She looked down the bar at their targets. They seemed a quiet enough group. They would be fish out of water in the big city, and maybe feeling it. Bands were divided into two. There were those who played places like Manhattan where they got paid; there were others who stuck to Nashville tighter than ticks on a hound dog, working for tips, but always close to the folk who could make the big time happen. The Lonesome Doves might not want it badly enough, and be prepared to surrender a mike for five minutes. Steph knew Nashville acts who would rather perish in eternal flames than do that.

'OK, let's do it,' said Savanna.

They stood, and sauntered down the bar to the band, who looked up in friendly fashion as they approached. Savanna left the guitar back where it was.

'Hi there, Lonesome Doves,' said Savanna. 'Hear you guys are from Austin.' She didn't smile too much. The doves were a hat act, and they touched them respectfully as the girls approached. They were in between sets, and drinking Cokes. In other words, they were sober and Southern and therefore polite.

'Has our mighty reputation preceded us, or have you been talking to the bartender?' said a good-looking, thin guy in a check shirt, conch belt and blue jeans.

'Bartender,' said Steph with a smile. 'I'm a songwriter in Nashville. Heard you had something going with Mercury. Hot label right now.'

They exchanged glances. The Mercury deal was hardly baked in the cake. And it would be a development deal if it was anything, not an out-and-out contract, i.e. no serious money. 'A songwriter from Nashville' could mean anything from a good networking opportunity to a girl looking for a free beer.

'Songwriter? You sold any we might have heard?' It was said pleasantly by a short guy with long sideburns. He wore a string tie with a turquoise stone that fixed him from Texas or thereabouts.

'One on a Kathy Mattea CD. *Love Travels*. Jo de Messina used one. Nothing top twenty. Yet.'

'What was the Kathy Mattea?' said a long, lean guy crouched against the bar in a doomed effort to make himself look smaller.

'"Patiently Waiting".'

'Hey, I know that one. With the guitar lick intro . . . and the piano. That's a good song, lady. You know that one, dude. You remember that one.'

He clapped his friend on the back, genuinely pleased at the memory. These boys had done their time. They probably had a 300-song repertoire they'd trailed a 100-mile radius round Austin.

'Yeah . . . something about some hick a girl was dating and how when she got paid she was outta there. Tell the guy I've had it with the waiting bit . . . that's a neat song. Pretty tune.'

Steph blushed and smiled. There was no pleasure more intense than folk knowing your song.

'I'm flattered and I'm Steph,' she said. 'This is my cousin, Savanna.'

They tipped their hats again, and the girls put their beers on the bar with the band's Cokes. Jim and Jackson, Mike and Red. They were already friends . . . Confederates and musicians in a Yankee town.

'That your guitar down the bar, Steph?' said the tall one trying to be shorter, who was Mike.

'No, it's Savanna's. She's the voice. And the face. And the body,' said Steph generously. She didn't know what jealousy meant. Nor had she forgotten the plan.

'What do you play, Savanna?' said Mike.

'Own songs. And my mother's.'

'She a performer, your mom?' said Jim, the short guy, gently.

'Dreamed of being. Could have been. Didn't do it,' said Savanna.

'Ain't easy,' said someone. 'Doin' it,' he added. They were all a long way from home, and they weren't paying many bills. It was all in the name of hope.

'Hey, man, why doesn't she play one of her mom's songs in the set. Nobody'd mind.' Jim addressed his remark to Jackson, the best-looking of the Lonesome Doves, as also apparently the band's leader. He looked quickly at Stephanie who had written a good song for Kathy Mattea. She had given the testimonial. If Savanna could sing an eighth as good as she looked, she'd put a shine on the whole outfit.

'OK, you want to try it?' he said. 'You been up there before?'

'Oh, yeah,' said Savanna. It was a half truth. She'd done cook-outs, barn dances, porch sessions but not strictly a stage like this with the backing of some Mercury hopefuls from Texas.

'Better go get your guitar before someone steals it. You want to do fast or slow?'

'Slow. Sad song. Called "Remembering to Forget".'

'Sad song. That's good. We are all so goddamned cheerful, we're short of those,' he said in a purposefully mournful voice.

Savanna felt the thrill. When she had walked in, the bar had looked half empty. Now it looked half full.

The Lonesome Doves were eyeing her speculatively. They were taking a chance. It was a kindness. But there was an aura of confidence about her, and the sorrow she had so suddenly and so genuinely conjured up when she spoke of her mother had touched them all. Her sad song would not lack emotion.

'Thanks, guys. I appreciate it,' she said, hurrying back to retrieve the Gibson.

'Savanna from Tennessee. You want a second name?' Jackson called after her.

'Stone,' she called back over her shoulder. She paused. 'No, Carson. As in Kit. Hold the Stone.'

'Savanna Carson from Tennessee singing her mom's song "Remembering to Forget".' Jackson practised half out loud for himself. As he did so, he thought that Savanna Carson Stone might take quite a bit of remembering to forget.

Across the room the manager was giving the band a sign. It was time. They ambled up on to the stage and took up their positions. They didn't feel they had to clear Savanna with him. It was a spontaneity thing, and they had been there three weeks now, and the smiles round the place said that takings were up. Every now and then, one of the Doves would check out Savanna and Steph as they sat on bar stools turned towards the stage to catch the action. The band wanted to impress, but to hide the fact that they did, and to that extent the whole evening was turning into a communal first date.

'Sweet guys,' said Steph. 'Can't believe they knew my song.'

'Can't believe I'm going to get to sing, before people who have actually paid,' said Savanna.

'It really starts when they pay *you*,' said Steph with a laugh. She looked at Savanna. She was flushed, but cool. No sign at all of stage fright. 'I hope they don't drown you out. They didn't look or sound like shit-kickers, but you never know with Texans. How you feelin'?'

How was she feeling? Like something was beginning. She felt peaceful, easy. It had all gone so smoothly, as if it had been rehearsed in advance on some ghostly stage with everybody word-perfect, and standing on their chalk marks. Then she remembered what Steph had said. Singing for nothing was not a career move, but neither was it blowing in the wind.

'That Jackson guy. Briefs or jockeys?' she said.

'Ah, so he's the one you like,' said Steph. 'Briefs. One size too small. Hanes from WalMart in Austin. Read somewhere that jockeys make you sterile. Took it pretty seriously.'

'Nah,' said Savanna. 'Briefs. Two sizes too small so that he can still paint those blue jeans over them. Fruit of the Loom. Changes them twice a day. Has a thing about cleanliness.' She pushed her hair back out of her eyes. Jackson looked at her quickly as he adjusted the height of the mike until it was precisely in the position it had started out.

'Cleanliness? A country singer? In your dreams.'

'Dwight Deacon is *very* clean. Apparently.'

'Deacon is not a "country" singer,' said Steph definitely.

'Snob!'

'Haven't got much to be snobbish about besides music.'

The Lonesome Doves cut her off. One, two, three and they were racing away into a novelty song about a guy who pissed his wife off by saving all his 'lovin'' for his Nascar. They listened critically. They played well together, and the song was original. Jackson gave it a jolt of personality to go with a neat, twangy Texan delivery. But the X-factor was missing to the ear that could hear. You could tell immediately, in the first few bars. Right here, on this stage, was probably the top of the line for the Doves.

Savanna tapped her toe to what turned out to be 'a little song we wrote called the "Nascar Blues".' As she listened, she thought, different dreams, that was what life was all about. Without dreams there was nothing. You had to live 'as if' it all mattered desperately. 'As if' happiness depended on something happening. 'As if' it was vitally important that your dreams came true. Her mother's diaries were full of regrets. Being a mother, a housewife, the partner of a successful surgeon might have been a valuable life for those who dreamed domesticated dreams. But her mom had been blessed, or cursed, with vast talent and immortal longings and had lived as if she had never possessed either. The Doves were squeezing the small dry apple of their talent until the poor pips squeaked. Her mom had left prize-winning grapes to wither on the vine. Savanna's chin pushed out in determination as they delivered a respectable cover of Garth's 'If Tomorrow Never Comes'. The trouble was they managed to leave the very faintest impression that it would not be much of a disaster if it didn't.

'Is Garth country?' whispered Savanna.

'Sometimes.'

'It doesn't matter that he has a degree in marketing? Never lived on a farm?'

'But he *believes* he did. It's all about what you believe and what you sound like. There's a moment when you can get to fake sincerity so well it turns into the real thing. People who can do that are rarer than the genuine article.'

'Nietzsche,' said Savanna half to herself. 'It's all a question of the will.' Somehow it seemed wrong that it should be. Shouldn't beauty just 'be'? Effortless. There. Not dragged screaming into existence by some cold, calculating will, an act of pain and suffering like our own birth. She was aware that this was a Columbia thought process. It was somehow alien in this Manhattan surrogate beer joint with its pretty waitresses and preppy trend-surfers who'd caught on to the magazine articles that country was 'cool'. Maybe thinking like this was another thing Savanna would have to remember to forget.

Cutting into her thoughts and lopping them down to size, which was Steph's art, her cousin said, 'Writing is work. Singing should always be a joy.'

Savanna simply nodded.

'Is the Gibson tuned?'

'Yup,' said Savanna.

'They'll probably do a few quick ones to warm everyone up, and then call you up there to slow 'em down,' said Steph, looking around the room and sizing it up. It was filling up nicely. There were tables with chequered cloths, and the previously empty bar now had a coating of people. The crowd were dressed in everything from Wall Street suits to somebody's idea of what might have been worn on a covered wagon.

'Are you two ladies with the band?' said a baby-faced teenager with a friend.

'Would we be imposing on you, were we to join you?' said the other kid with a pleased smile, wedging himself in against the bar next to Savanna.

'English major? NYU?' said Savanna in pure Park Avenue.

'Oh,' he said simply. Then, recovering, 'How did you know?'

'Conditional subjunctive. The more formal "imposing", rather than the vernacular "boring".'

Steph giggled.

'Oh,' again. These girls were probably not 'with the band'. Possibly, the guitar nestling between the bewitching legs was an up-market Spanish number and the girl was at Juilliard. Possibly, more had been bitten off than could reasonably be chewed.

The baby-faced kid, fortified by more beer than his friend had drunk, pressed on. 'Why not Columbia? Why NYU?'

'Because at Columbia it is not considered cool to talk in a stylised way as if the last war was the Revolutionary one.'

The tables of attempted patronisation had been neatly turned. Ivy League Columbia effortlessly outranked vast NYU, and the implication was that Savanna was at it. The two kids out of their depth did what kids do in that situation. Nothing. They hung on in there with blank, confused faces, sipping at their Millers as if their lives depended on it.

Jackson, head Dove, came to the rescue. An in-your-face song about a husband's infidelity, 'You're not just leaving home, you're leaving love tonight,' had been up-tempo, foot-tapping, despite references to crying children, and a bewildered dog . . . 'you shout and shake your finger, but he just wags his tail.' After the song, he spoke confidentially into the microphone.

'And now, ladies and gentleman, we have a surprise for you. A very beautiful and talented lady from Pigeon Forge in the great state of Tennessee is going to sing a song for us tonight. It's called "Remembering to Forget" and her name is Savanna Carson . . . you remember that name, folks . . . come on up here, Savanna.'

The ragged applause strengthened as Savanna crossed the floor into the spotlight, undoing the Gibson as she climbed up on to the stage.

'Now that is a guitar, ma'am,' said Jackson half to the mike and half to Savanna.

'It was my mom's – '29 Gibson.'

'That is *sweet*,' he said enviously.

Savanna arranged herself on a stool, one leg crossed beneath her, guitar across her lap. 'Thank you,' she said into the microphone. So far they were clapping her beauty. She turned to the band. 'G, OK?' They nodded back to her. The room quieted.

'Thank you all. This is a song my mother wrote, and I wish she was here to play it for you tonight. But sadly she passed away six months ago, and so it's dedicated to her. I feel she's listening. It's called "Remembering to Forget".'

She began an intricate introduction, her fingers way down home on the neck of the guitar, and as swift and sure with the plectrum at its belly. If there had been any doubts in the minds of the Doves, they were already long gone. The girl could play, and you could hear from her speaking voice that she could sing. Which left the tune. Once through the intro and they had it . . . an uncomplicated chord structure and rhythm that would rely heavily on voice and lyrics for its effect.

G
The face of a child,

G7
The shape of a curl,

　　C　　　G
Precious memories and yet . . .

　　　　　D7　　　G
There's a reason to remember to forget.

　　　　G
The smell of his skin,

　　　G7
The sound of his laugh,

　　C　　　G
But my eyes are gettin' wet . . .

　　　　　D7　　　　G
Once again, it's time to remember to forget.

G　　　　　　　　G7
Without forgetting, I can't go on,

　　C　　　　　G
In this lonely world without you,

　　　　　　　　　　D7
You were my son, you were my joy, you were my love,

　　　G　　　　D7
And in God's twilight, amidst the shadows,

　　C　　　　G
Round the old house I go walking

　　　D7　　G
As I dream of you in Heaven up above.

Savanna dug down deep, mining memories. Her mother's brother, Luke, had died as a child, and Grandma Carson had never really recovered from the tragedy. His illness had made a huge impression on LeAnne Carson, and had in fact been responsible for the chain of events that had led to her unlikely marriage to the aristocratic Henry Stone. Here was where country music came into its own. It was about simplicity and honesty; it was devoid of cynicism. There was no fake rock rebellion; rappers getting rich by milking the misery of the streets. This was not about beautiful boys and girls playing to pre-teenage little-girl fantasies, it was about the raw emotions. When it was happy it was happy; when it was sad it was sad. People joked about it – freight trains, whiskey, crying, loving, leaving, dying – but in the end those feelings were real.

The film of moisture came easily to Savanna's eyes, and the throaty catch to her voice. She closed her eyes and threw back her head as she sang, exposing her long white neck. And all around the room sound quieted, movement slowed, until there was nothing but Savanna and the Gibson and the memories that must be forgotten if life was to go on. One by one, the Lonesome Doves withdrew from the accompaniment, realising instinctively that they were subtracting, not adding, to this performance. They looked at each other, frank wonder on their faces, because they had not heard this good before. There had been no advance warning, no preparation, to soften their shock.

At the bar, Steph, too, was caught up in the general sense of surprised awe. Savanna's voice had real force. There was simply no ignoring it. And it wasn't anybody else's, it was hers. Steph knew country like the recipe for toast, but now she didn't even try to look for sources. The raw emotion was focused, aimed by a narrow corridor of notes from the Gibson, and shot from Savanna's throat with the power that Chairman Mao said could only come from the barrel of a gun. Even the two college kids whose idea of the Deep South was formed on barely remembered spring breaks to Daytona and Lauderdale, were open-mouthed by Steph's side. And then it was over.

> And if I forget to remember, I'll be betrayin' you so that
> My darlin' I'll continue to remember to forget . . .

There was a stunned silence. Nobody clapped. They just stared. The quiet continued. Everyone seemed frozen in space/time.

Waitresses stood motionless in suspended animation, their trays of food and drink hovering like low-flying birds in a smoky sky. Savanna looked around her, blinking in the spotlight, as if awakened from a trance. Jackson, the lead Dove, was the first to break the spell. He began to clap, and Steph did too, then a table with hats near the stage. Section by section the others joined in until the whole room – band included – was rocked with applause. Even the wait-resses joined in. There were shouts for more, and general cries of encouragement and gratitude. Savanna smiled and raised the Gibson to acknowledge the clapping which seemed to roll on and on, with some people standing to applaud.

'Oh boy, thank you. Thank you,' said Savanna.

Steph watched it happen. She watched the addiction start in her cousin's wide-open eyes. This was what only entertainers knew about. How often in this life did you give such pleasure, and were thanked so effusively, so publicly and so immediately for it? Here was the antidote to the lives of quiet desperation that many led. Here was being appreciated, getting attention. For this magic moment Savanna was the only person in a room chock-full of people. Here in fact was the microcosm of fame. It was where it all started. It was the place the once-famous would try to return to even when the applause had long since gone. Steph smiled. She had been hoping for this, and it had happened. What would Savanna do now?

'Play another one. Quick. You've got 'em in the palm of your hand,' Jackson whispered generously.

But no. Instinct said no. 'Thank you all so much for hearin' me out,' said Savanna. 'That's all for tonight.'

And she climbed down from the stage as they bayed for more, and made her way over to the bar.

'Wow!' she said. She was sweating through her T-shirt, beneath the black leather jacket.

'Yeah, wow!' said Steph, hugging her. All around people inched nearer to her. 'Great song, lady.' 'Boy, you sure can sing.' 'What you doin' in New York City, lady? You oughta be in Nashville!'

'That last one was right,' said Steph. 'There's a contract down there with your name on it. Trust me. That was far, far better than good. I remember that song when your mom used to sing it. Got to me then. But not like just now. Where did you get that finger-work, cousin? And where you bin hidin' that *voice*? I always thought you talked like a friggin' Kennedy, or one of those kinda guys.'

'It just comes out like that,' laughed Savanna. She looked around her. They were still checking her out, people twisted round at tables, women getting irritated with men whose eyes lingered just a tad too long, or whose praise was a mite too effusive. She had created a buzz. She had made a stir. And now the poor Lonesome Doves were trying to catch up to the place she had taken this audience, and failing dismally so to do.

'You liked it, didn't you?' said Steph.

'I *loved* it.'

'Yeah, I know,' said Steph, watching her closely. 'Not like doing it for friends, family, neighbourhood. Real strangers. That's what gets to you. People you've never even seen before liking you, loving you, thinking you are just great. Anonymous love. And all you have to do is sing for it.'

Savanna was quiet. Steph was right. This had been an epiphany. She had something. There had been no build-up, no hype. She had come from left field and nobody had expected anything of her. But it had felt like a triumph. She felt totally unreal. It was as if she had ceased to be Savanna, and been magically transformed into someone else, the girl on the stage, the singer of the song, the one they had all loved; no longer a rich man's daughter tucked into the core curriculum at an Ivy League school. The feelings she had experienced on stage were super-reality. The rest was a dusty humdrum black-and-white world that she no longer wanted a part of.

'You OK, hon?' said Steph putting her hand on her arm. 'I think you got it bad.'

Savanna nodded and smiled. She knew what it meant, of course – Nashville.

EIGHT

'Aw, shit.' Savanna yanked the card from the slot in the wall, and pulled up her collar to try and stop the rain trickling down her neck. 'He's cut me off. The bastard's cut me off already. How does he *do* that? Banks simply are not that efficient.' She stamped her foot in irritation.

Steph wound down the window of the Bronco. 'No cash?'

'Zip.' She ran back to the car, and jumped into the driver's seat. She was soaked. And penniless. The latter, she had never, ever been before.

'You don't have a savings account?' said Steph.

Savanna looked at her as if she were mad. 'Savings account, what the hell is that? No, I don't have one. Money is for spending, not saving. You simply put your card in the wall and out it comes.'

Steph shook her head. This one had a long way to go. It was one thing being bitten by the singing bug; it was another to turn your whole life upside down to run with it. Poor people had an easier shot at fame. They wanted and needed a whole lot more, and they didn't have anything to give up. Right now, Savanna was experiencing plutocratic parental displeasure with a capital D.

'You don't balance your cheque-book.'

'The bank balances the cheque-book,' said Savanna, puzzled.

'You mean you don't have an allowance, like spending limits?' Steph couldn't get the hang of it.

'Yes,' said Savanna, absent-mindedly. 'I have spending limits.'

'How much?'

'What I spend,' she said, as if it was obvious.

Steph laughed out loud. 'Savanna, are you ready for the real world?'

'I live in the real world,' said Savanna, a little defensively. 'At least I did, until he cut off my card. How can he *do* that?'

'He wants you to give up this whole Nashville idea.'

Savanna shook her head. The confrontation with her father had been a nightmare as she had known it would be. But it had been stimulating, too. Standing up to him. Trading insults toe to toe, wondering if he would hit her, daring him to. There had been some old scores settled in that argument, and she had landed some verbal punches where they had hurt. But Henry Stone was not without power. The Lord giveth, the Lord taketh away. Cash, credit cards, money in all its multifarious shapes and forms was the gift of the father.

Now, the spigot was going to be turned off. Savanna had never earned a cent, red or otherwise. She was a brilliant college student who could read Caesar in Latin and solve calculus problems on the back of napkins. On the other hand, she didn't know how to sell a bag of chestnuts to a rich, hungry tourist on a cold street at Christmas. It was at moments like these that Henry Stone was really grateful that his daughter was basically useless at one thing nobody had ever thought to teach her: how to make money. She had needs all right, but the means were his. All she had to do was toe his line, and the money would pour out of the wall again, and once more the plastic would be an open sesame to more or less anything she bothered to want. It was so simple. So satisfying. He who paid the piper called the tune, and the tune was Columbia and med school and, much later, the Stone money when the grim reaper turned up to take him away. Nashville! Ha! God, what was it with the women in his family? Where had he failed them? What the hell was the matter with Mozart? He might even come to terms with Marilyn Manson. But country music? Dear God! They had spent the last three generations keeping the guitar-pickers out of Belle Meade only to have them blossom on the inside. It would have been a bad joke, if it weren't apparently so serious. He blamed the cousin . . . whatever she was called. And LeAnne, who had filled her head with silly dreams. If Savanna wanted to go to Nashville for a holiday, then she should go down and stay with Grandma.

'Have *you* got any money, Steph?'

'Not your kind, sweetheart. You can stay with us, but there isn't much to go around until McGraw starts buying my songs, and Shania and Reba.'

'Wait a minute. I've got this car.' Savanna banged the steering wheel to emphasise her point.

'Isn't this how we were going to get to Nashville?'

'Yeah, but with no money for gas, and motels and stuff? And this would be like *capital*. I mean, it must be worth something. Do you think $15,000?'

'Shit, I don't know. Is it leased? Is there a loan on it?'

'Don't be crazy,' said Savanna. 'It's mine. I think,' she added.

Suddenly, she had doubts. Had her father put it in his name to get some insurance deal or something? She'd never really checked. It had been a sixteenth birthday present, the keys in a box, the car outside wrapped in ribbon in traditional upper-class American style. A nice new blue Ford Bronco with double airbags to keep the birthday girl safe for her family future. There had been a *lot* of talk about safety.

'Well, don't you have paperwork, like in the glove compartment?'

'Of course,' said Savanna, opening it up. 'There, you see. Owner. Savanna Stone. That's me, I can sell it. Then we can take the Greyhound to Nashville,' she said hesitantly. 'Hey, that will be fun. I've never been on a Greyhound before. OK. Where do we sell it? Where Dad bought it, I guess.'

'You sure you want to do this?'

'Sure, I'm sure. What's not to be sure? But, hell, maybe we should fly to Nashville. If we get fifteen for the Bronco, you could trade in your Greyhound return.'

'It was a round trip,' laughed Steph.

'But we don't want to arrive tired at Sony, or MCA or whichever record company we try first.'

'Oh, God, Savanna. That is not how it works. You've got to get some *experience*. Clubs. Gigs. Maybe join a band. Cut a demo. Make contacts. They're not even going to *see* you on Music Row until you have an agent. And you can't get an agent until you've done time. It's the way things work down there. Believe me. I know. It's like being a doctor. You have to go to school. You have to take the exam.'

'Bullshit,' said Savanna. 'If you want it badly enough, you can cut through all that stuff. You said I was good enough. Everyone liked me at the Silver Bullet. You remember that agent who said to Garth, "You haven't a chance, man." Who has the last laugh now?'

'As long as you're not some rich kid out there on a whim and a dream,' said Steph.

'I'm not rich any more,' said Savanna, suddenly thoughtful. She wasn't. Her father would not relent. He was proud. Arrogant, even. He didn't merely like his own way, he worshipped it.

'If I had $15,000 in the bank, I'd be rich,' said Steph.

'Yeah, well, it isn't even a year at Columbia. Not even close with extras.'

'Jeez.'

The rain was coming down harder. Savanna flipped the heater on. She looked at her CD player, the sound system with its woofers and tweeters and extra bits that had tumbled out of Christmas stockings. Was she an hour away from losing this car she had loved so much? She felt the edges of a downer she didn't need if she was to go through with this. Doubt suddenly picked at her. She was blowing a vast inheritance for a chance in the lottery of success where the odds against you had zeroes that rolled on to the horizon. Or was she? This wasn't about money. This was about being your own person, living a dream. The pay-off would be self-respect, with or without the achievement. In this life you could live your own, or somebody else's. It was as simple as that. The latter was often safer; the former was where the pay-dirt was, the genuine kind, the kind that made looking in the mirror a good experience rather than a bad one. And there was something else, too. There was her mom to prove it all to, and there was the applause at the Silver Bullet. Oh, yes, there was that. That was the kind of reality that turned dreams into truth. She wanted to hear that sound again. Badly. Soon. So she fired up the Bronco, and drove through the sleepy village to the junction with the interstate where Oliver's Ford dealership was.

CHAPTER

NINE

The car salesman, finding himself in the unaccustomed, but seriously powerful role of a 'cash buyer', sniffed the air like a hungry, randy rat.

'You want to sell it? For cash? Now? You want another? You don't want to *trade*?'

He smiled at the horrific beauty of it all. The girl who owned the car was a fox, and he hadn't had an Altoid for half an hour. Shit. That always happened. Sooner or later, he was going to have to bite the buck and see the dentist.

'Yup. It must have a value. I guess you guys have a book, or something.'

Or something. Oh, yes, they did! The 'cash-value-for-used-car-book', no part exchange, was a mimeographed bundle that was also known as the joke book. The joke was always on the seller of the car.

The polyester suit might have been Dacron, or some newer, nastier fibre. It vibrated unpleasantly against the tie, and ground gears with big fake-gold cufflinks.

'Can you prove this is your car, lady?'

'Ms Stone,' Savanna corrected him. 'Yes.'

'Sorry, I'm Gary.' He put out a limp hand and his eyes narrowed. He looked like a weasel now, one that would climb up a woman's skirt, and burrow into her underwear.

'OK,' said Savanna, tossing her head in exasperation. 'Savanna and Steph.' Had there been a Ford-sponsored seminar on how to *buy* cars for cash as well as sell them? It seemed a certainty. She showed him the certificate of ownership, and her passport as ID.

'Going away?' he said cunningly.

'No,' said Savanna. 'Some of us have passports just in case we want to go away, you know, as a spur-of-the moment thing.'

The weasel didn't know. He was not one of the ten per cent of his countrymen who possessed passports. A cash sale by a young girl with a passport sounded like a movie about rich-kid crime. Maybe a slasher one. He moistened his lips. The documents were in order. So was the driver's licence. She flashed the defunct gold card. The girl was definitely classy, although she was dressed in jeans like everyone else.

'I bought it from you. At least my dad did. Dr Henry Stone. Professor Stone?'

'Ah.'

That changed things. The Stones were from around here; he'd heard the name. There would be a record of the sale. He smiled horribly. He was going to clean up from this baby. He shot a sidelong look at the car. It looked clean, very clean. It would have extras, a great long list of them for daddy doctor's girl. It was maybe two and a half years old and would have cost nineteen. No loan. He could move it this afternoon at sixteen. Could he get it for ten, and be the toast of the showroom for deal of the day?

'I need to go and make a couple of computer checks. Just formality. I'll be right back.'

'Why?' said Savanna when he'd gone. 'Why do they have to be like that? What law of human nature says so? I mean, you wouldn't find somebody who looks so crooked in San Quentin. I mean, I just know this guy is going to steal from me.'

'We could try someplace else.'

'This is a cross-country thing. A world thing. You walk into any place they sell or buy cars and this guy is there, this same guy. He is generic. The motor companies clone them, or something. They have them on a production line, and the last things to go on are the cufflinks and the tie. It's like "Hello," he lied.'

'Wait a minute,' said Steph. 'I'll be back.'

Savanna stalked around the brightly lit showroom trying not to catch the eyes of the swarming sharks, with their smirky, smarmy smiles. They sat in cubicles, some in shirtsleeves, and they leered at her over the shoulders of the client sheep they were shearing.

A few minutes later, he was waddling back towards her. He came too close, invading her space.

Steph arrived simultaneously behind her. 'Savanna, can I have a quick word. They've got a '97 Bronco in the lot, not such a good sound system as yours, but very similar. They want $17,000,' whispered Steph, as Savanna backed away to listen to her.

Next came the charade of inspecting the car. He ran his fingers lovingly over the two tiny surface scratches; peered doubtfully at the immaculate engine; clucked worriedly as he listened to the purring motor when Savanna turned it on. He avoided looking at the top-of-the-line music system, and appeared not to hear as Savanna listed the extras.

'The trouble is,' he said at last, flashing a cunning look at Steph whom he had seen comparison-shopping in the lot, 'we have one of these on the lot right now. Been there for months, very little interest. And, well, I shouldn't tell you this, but it belonged to Matt Damon which makes it attractive to some . . .' He laughed at the ridiculousness of that being a factor in the buying of a car. 'And my boss just told me, we've taken a couple more similar ones in part exchange. So we simply wouldn't be in a position to offer you a competitive price. Frankly, you'd be better off someplace else. Someplace they're not loaded up with '97 Broncos.'

Savanna wondered if killing them was legal. It ought to be. Certainly it should be a mitigating circumstance, like the wind in the Mediterranean . . . the Puniente or the Levante . . . which was well known to drive people mad.

Yes, she could go somewhere else, and receive a different-coloured dollop of bullshit: a knock in the engine; the wrong colour this year. 'Had a lot of problems with the late '97's, to be absolutely frank.'

'Why don't you do your sums, or whatever, and give me your very best cash offer. Like a here-and-now deal.'

'You won't like it,' he smiled.

'I know I won't like it,' said Savanna shortly. She would not like anything that crept through the Altoid haze in this man's mouth.

'$12,000,' he said, and sighed.

'Done,' said Savanna, as Steph looked on, horrified.

His eyes widened, but he was not fazed.

'Let's sign that up now,' said Savanna.

'All righty,' he said. And then, 'All righty.' Quite suddenly, he looked hunted: a fox perhaps, or a coyote. Certainly nothing as benign as a rabbit. 'Step into my office.'

They crammed into the cubicle. A long-suffering family stared morosely from a photograph frame on his desk. He fished out a contract and scribbled away furiously. 'There,' he said. 'You sign there.'

Savanna took the contract and signed it. 'Where do you sign?' she said.

'Oh, I get my boss to sign. He's the man with the money!' He laughed an oily laugh. The man with the money. What a very good joke! 'Be back in a flash.'

He was. His mouse-like face had achieved a saddish expression. He placed the contract down in front of Savanna. Across it someone had scrawled in big capital letters: 'SORRY SAVANNA. NO CAN DO AT THIS PRICE. 10 IS OUR BEST OFFER.'

Savanna stared in disbelief at the offending piece of paper. 'Are you an agent of this company?' she snapped, picking a card from a dispenser on the salesman's desk. 'This card says so.'

'Yes.'

'Steph, did you witness a verbal contract to buy this car for $12,000?'

'Yes.'

'Good. OK. Here is what is going to happen. I am going to ring the family attorneys, Stone, Leggat and White, of which my uncle is senior partner. We are going to sue Oliver's Ford for non-performance of contract, inconvenience and consequent damage flowing from breach, and punitive damages for lack of good faith, bearing in mind . . .'

Ten minutes later, with a cashier's cheque for $12,000 in Savanna's pocket, she and Steph were in a taxi on their way to the station. Savanna was acutely aware that for the last time she had used her family connections, her education and the legal savvy that went with it. From now on she was on her own. She had just her voice, the Gibson and her mom's good wishes between her and whatever country music and Nashville could dream up to torture or to pleasure her.

CHAPTER

TEN

The 'spare' room at Savanna's aunt and uncle's house was the sofa bed in her uncle's den, a room that doubled as a storage unit, a makeshift studio, and a space to flow into when the small house became too full to make movement easy. It was, however, clean, warm and well lit, and if it wasn't exactly 'Rooms-to-Go' colour coordinated, it provided everything that Savanna needed and it was free. She liked the guitars stacked against the wall, the loudspeakers and amplifiers, and the paraphernalia of Nashville. There was even a photograph of Reba inscribed 'To Tom, with love.' He had worked as a session musician on one of her earlier albums.

Savanna curled up on the sofa bed. On her knees sat her mother's diary. She rationed the amount she read, and she didn't read it in chronological order. Somehow her mom was even more alive that way, sometimes young looking forward, sometimes older looking back. But overall there was the warm sensation of changing seasons, of the dance to time's music that ebbed and flowed through life. Children became parents and then their children, too. Leaves fell from the trees in winter, but in the spring they would shoot again. It all went on as it always had and always would. Death was a door and immortality was memories. These memories now were alive. It was as if Savanna were having a conversation with her mother . . . one of the real close ones you always wish you'd had more of.

It seemed so silly to pack up a bag and the old guitar and take
a Greyhound to Nashville like all the others when I could have
flown first class, but that was the way I dreamed of doing it. I
never wanted it to be easy. I wanted to work for it, sweat for
it, force it to happen through an effort of the will. So often in
life, the journey is more fun than arriving. You'll find that,
Savanna, if not when you read these words then sometime . . .
I bet. When Daddy fell in love with me, and I was so in awe of
him, and then when we married, he said, 'You don't have to
worry about money any more, LeAnne. You don't have to
worry about anything, ever. You never have to work, and you
never have to speak to anyone you don't want to . . .' I don't
think he was thinking of the country club committee when he
said that, or Alice Cabot, or Majorie Polk, or . . . well, you
know the list! It sounded so wonderful at the time, like a great
burden dropping away. It was wonderful in a way but there
was a little thing called freedom missing, and being in control
of my life. I'm not moaning, my darling. I chose it, and so
much of it was so magnificent; you most of all. There wouldn't
have been you if I'd spent my life on a bar stool in Nashville
scraping by on tips and hanging out with would-be singers
with egos as big as their hats and no sense at all! I used to
discuss it in Pigeon Forge, with Momma when she was still
talking, and Dad and Grandpa, and they all gave me what
I ended up calling the Nashville lament. 'Your chances of
making money as a singer are next to nil, hon. Streets of that
sad town littered with broken dreams and kids who'd swap
every song they'd sung for a thick steak.' Everybody thought
they were doing me a favour. Perhaps they were. I guess it sort
of worked, marrying a millionaire instead and not eating
steaks on account of the low-fat diet! But I kept turning on
TNN and seeing all these folk who weren't starving, but
instead they were singing their hearts out and making good
music, and driving great big cars and I just wondered how
they'd reacted when they'd heard the old lament. Only one

way for certain the lament's going to come true, and that's if you never give it a shot in the first place. So I saw myself in real seedy joints, maybe for years, before something happened. That way it was going to be years before I got downhearted.

'Supper's on the table,' Steph called up the stairs, and Savanna closed the book with a little sigh, and stowed it away in the locked case beneath her bed. Well, she wasn't starving. Meatloaf and cabbage were coming up the stairs in scented form, and there would be cornbread and gravy, and ice-creams, too. Just what a girl needed to win the prize pig show. But in this family, food was something you didn't waste and she respected that.

Her aunt looked at her with the love, concern and slight anxiety you might reserve for a pet Martian. Eileen had always loved her sister LeAnne, but their worlds had been so far apart it had been difficult to bridge them. In the end they had kept in touch mainly by telephone, apart from a couple of nervy visits up North by Eileen that had not been a great success. The titanic presence of Henry Stone had seen to that. While far too well-bred to be openly patronising, he had kept slipping subconsciously into that mode without realising it – 'I've never really seen the point of the Chardonnay grape. The French didn't either until thirty years ago. What wine do you drink, Eileen, at home? Gallo? Oh! Interesting!' Eileen was a fattened version of her elder sister, of whom she had always been a little in awe, coarser of feature and without LeAnne's fine skin and perfectly proportioned face. She was formidably 'sweet', but a fine mist of fear pervaded her, and she always watched her husband, a bearded, kindly man with a gut and broad shoulders, as if she half expected him to hit her; something he had never, ever done.

'Goodness, girl,' she said. 'We gotta build you up. Don't they feed you at that college of yours?'

'Oh, yeah, the eating thing,' said Savanna with a laugh. At Columbia, food was the stuff that came up with the drink.

'Don't go stuffin' her, Eileen. She's gonna be a belly-button act. You don't see Shania stuffin', and that girl got a butt like a billion dollars.'

Steph ran her eyes up to the ceiling in mock embarrassment.

'Bill Gates has got a hundred billion dollars, and I wouldn't thank you for his butt,' said Savanna.

Eileen looked worried. She was never very good at standing up to her husband. He'd put good food on the table, even if they were economising on the heating right now.

'So how are we gonna get Savanna started, Dad?' said Steph. 'What's the plan?'

Her dad earned a precarious living playing sessions and she had loved and admired him enough to have caught his musical bug.

'Sounds like she's short of practice, experience, from what you say. How many songs you sing, Savanna?'

'Maybe a dozen I could perform. Originals. I guess twenty or thirty covers.'

'Well that lot ain't gonna get you through an evenin' on stage. The way you want it is that two out of three requests you can have a stab at 'em. Otherwise the drunks get nasty, and that's just the girls in the crowd. And they're jealous anyways.'

'Couldn't I fund a demo with the money from the Bronco and take it round Music Row?'

Tom laughed. 'No, girl, you gonna need that money. You don't want to go off half cock. Get good and ready first. Sometimes you get a first chance in Nashville. I heard of a few who got a second, never of one who got a third. Pass the gravy, Eileen, hon.'

'Dad's right,' said Steph. 'It's no good us usin' up the limited contacts we got. They just gonna ask where you've been playin', how long, you know, have you paid your dues, starved a bit, struggled a bit, got the fire in your belly that'll stop you freezin' in the ice-cold of the music business. Not that it's you, 'cos you can sing like a bird, but any hint of that rich-kid-on-a-country-music-whim crap plays *real* bad round here. Like, Belle Meade is a *big* secret. The guys in the business would have passed on a Patsy Cline out of pure revenge if they thought she'd come from there.'

'Could I try a talent night at the Bluebird?'

'Even the talent night is deep-end at the Bluebird. Get easy round a stage first. Get the feel of handling an audience. You have to listen to 'em as much as they listen to you.'

'That's it,' said Tom, his mouth full of meatloaf. 'It's a two-way thing. That's why Deacon is Deacon. He could raise havoc with an audience of deaf mutes, pardon me bein' politically incorrect. You stop hollerin' for a second, and those big eyes of his find you like a searchlight, turn you right on again, like a toaster. At the Bluebird you're basically singing to Amy, but she's an audience, too. You learn how to touch a room full of hollow-legged drunks. Then maybe you gotta chance of connectin' with her.'

But Savanna was not downhearted.

'Well, you guys just point me in the direction of anywhere you think might take me. And I'll go from there.'

'Ray Willis over at the Guitar Bar on Lower Broad might be a good start. It's not much of a place . . .'

'The Guitar Bar?' said Steph. She didn't sound sure.

'Yeah, afternoon slot, for a couple of hours, maybe. Get Savanna plugged into what it's all about.' He gave a somewhat ominous half smile with his eyes as he chewed his corn on the cob like a harmonica, dripping butter down his chin.

'It would be like a stepping-stone,' said Steph. Again there was a doubtful tone in her voice.

'One small step for a girl . . .' said Savanna cheerfully.

'Don't you worry, hon,' Eileen said. 'We'll look after you. You got a place for as long as you like, an' if it don't work out, then nothin's lost. LeAnne's baby sure gonna be safe with us.'

'Yeah,' said Tom, slopping on the gravy and warming to his theme. 'And when you done a few months at the bar, then maybe we can scoot you in the door at the Gibson for a bit of refinement, polish you up a bit, kinda . . .'

'And I can help with the writing when you're not playin' or workin'. Show you the places you can go wrong when you're not real used to it,' added Steph.

Savanna heard the subterranean message loud and clear. She remembered the words of her mother's diary: it was the journey not the destination that counted. She was being offered another type of security blanket. OK, it was a very different kind from Columbia and the Stone millions, but a safety net nonetheless. She would sit there, and her ma's family would pour maple syrup down her throat, keep her warm, and manage her attempt to take off in Nashville. She would be given a hand-up here, and a leg-up there. Then, if it all went right, Tom, Eileen and Steph would take the credit. And if it all went wrong, they would shake their heads sadly at the predictability of life, and say that, anyways, they'd done their best for the girl, and given her some sort of a shot at the illusion of Nashville fame.

Savanna knew what she had to do. She had to start all over again. She had to throw away the life jacket, and jump into the deep end. It was the way to learn how to swim. It would be the only way of getting credit for the success that she believed with every ounce of her being would one day be hers. It was easier for a poor man than a rich man to pass through the eye of the needle, the Bible had said. Today, people were beginning to understand that at last. Affluenza, they called it . . . the crippling, debilitating disease of not having to try. To fight when you didn't have to; work when you didn't need money; land a job when people were queuing up to land it for you . . . that was genuine hardship of a peculiar sort, because only the tiny minority experienced it. It was the poor-little-rich-girl syndrome. How could you ask anyone to be sorry for a millionaire? But if you stood the question on its head, it made sense. How could you ever respect yourself if you never had to earn your self-respect?

'I'd like to say something,' said Savanna.

They didn't usually say things like that around this dinner table. Everyone started listening.

'I do appreciate what you all have done for me, and what you would do for me if I let you. But I've been giving this a lot of thought. I've decided that if I'm going to do this, I'm going to do it on my own. *All* on my own. I could stay here, and I really appreciate the offer. And I could stay with Grandma, but Dad has already told her not to take me, and I don't want to be "taken" either. So, instead, I've decided to find a place of my own. I've decided to do whatever all the other hopefuls do who arrive on the Greyhound every day, whatever that is. I'll make all kinds of mistakes, but at least they'll be *my* mistakes. And if it happens for me, it'll be me that did it, all on my own. I don't want to sound ungrateful, and I love you all very, very much, but I know you will understand . . .'

''Course,' said Tom, chewing his lumpy potatoes, and looking at her like she was mad.

'I don't know,' said Eileen.

'Well,' said Tom. 'Ain't that the American way?' His voice was full of doubt that it was. He also doubted, even if it *was* the American way, whether or not it ought to be. There were crazy schemes and dreams on this earth, and there was making it as a singer in Nashville without any inside help and no track record. Still, they'd be there when she failed. They could always take her in when the gas meter needed too many coins in winter, and the food money ran out. 'But you get into trouble with sleaze-bag guys, an' debt collectors an' the rest, you know where we are. There's a couch here even when we got company, and Mother is always cookin' somethin' or other in that kitchen . . .'

Eileen had tears in her eyes, but she recognised the determined glint in her niece's expression.

'May the good Lord protect you,' she said.

But Savanna knew otherwise. Her mom would.

CHAPTER

E LEVEN

'Oh, my God, shit, Savanna, that roach is as big as a *cat*!'

Steph wasn't the kind to pull a hissy fit on something as common-place as a palmetto bug, but it was symbolic of the general decrepitude of Savanna's bedsit. For every bug you saw, there were a hundred unseen. From the size of this one the whole room must be constructed from insects.

Savanna gave a half-hearted swipe at it with a rolled-up copy of the *Tennessean*. She missed, and it waddled, rather than scurried, away. Steph had the strong impression that had she not been there, the roaches would have been left to do their own thing.

'Wow,' said Steph.

'A bit primitive,' said Savanna. She gave a dismissive laugh that didn't dismiss a thing. She was aware that she'd let things go a bit. Including herself. There didn't seem to be much alternative. She couldn't afford a cleaner, and all her life there had been an army of those. Vacuuming, polishing, dusting, dealing with the ring around the bath were all relatively new to her life, and she dealt with them by simply avoiding them.

'It's just the fridge is so small, and there isn't anywhere to put food away,' she said by way of explanation. 'Can't afford an exter-minator,' she added. It was becoming apparent that the roach and its size had made quite an impression on her cousin.

'You can get stuff from the hardware store, and spray it yourself,' said Steph. She was worried about her cousin. The dirt was one thing, but the black rings under Savanna's eyes, her lank, less than clean hair, the unpressed blue jeans! Savanna was bottom fishing in Nashville, working shifts at a fast-food joint by day, writing, singing the odd set, hanging out with writers most of the night. It was the trial by ordeal that everyone went through, but her cousin seemed ill-equipped for the life.

'How's it all goin'?' said Steph. She saw Savanna from time to time but there was a distance between them, and it came from Savanna. Somehow, the unspoken agreement was that they would be close again when Savanna had some kind of success . . . but not until. That looked like not until hell froze over, at the rate she was going.

'I never thought flipping burgers would be part of the training. But better than cutting up corpses. Maybe.' Savanna laughed to show she still could. 'The writing is great. And when I sing I hit the right notes, just like Caruso. Only thing missing is anybody thinking my stuff is good.'

'*We* know it is,' said Steph with feeling. It was.

'*We* don't count,' said Savanna and her laugh went a little bitter. She was getting the measure of the game. Natural selection was its name, and evolution was a gradual process. For the fittest to survive, they had to struggle. It was the weeding-out process. Maybe it was like hazing in a fraternity. You had to show you could take the shit before you were worth anything, and then when 'overnight' success hit after years of pain you were good and ready for it. You'd done your four years and post-grad in the University of Music City Life, and the diploma was the hit single; the degree was the record contract.

'You want some coffee, Steph?'

Steph looked doubtful. The sink was full of unwashed cups and plates. The kettle looked as if it had an inch of gunk inside. Even the Taster's looked like it had been around for a while and would need to be chipped off the block it had become.

'Sure. Any news from your dad?'

Savanna picked a cup from the basin and held it beneath a spluttering tap in a process akin to washing it.

'When he doesn't know what to say or how to say it, he writes letters,' said Savanna. 'He sent me a beautiful one the other day. Pure Dad. He said that he would have nothing more to do with me, and there would be no more money . . . zip, zilch. He wants me home, and he wants his own way.'

It took Savanna a minute or two to light the gas with a match. It didn't seem to be flowing too freely.

'And he told Grandma to do the same. Not that she'd listen to him if he told her to leave a burning house. But then there's my pride. I don't want to do it with Grandma's help, or his help, or anybody's help. I just want to do it on my own. You understand that, don't you, Steph?'

Steph didn't. It made no sense to her at all. Fighting to make it in Nashville did not include looking gift horses in the mouth. You took a steak where you got it, a ride when it was offered, a leg-up whoever was handing it out. Her expression said what was on her mind, but then she had never been a poor little rich girl. Maybe it was different for them. Maybe they had *more* to prove.

Savanna saw Steph *not* getting it. She made the coffee, and sat down at the table, sweeping off a whole load of half-finished songs, magazines and the dead wrappers of two or three Snickers bars.

'Steph,' she said. 'Here it is. I am going to do what I set out to do in this town. I don't care if I die here. I don't care if I get carried out of here in a box, and still haven't made it. At least I'll have tried. I won't have chickened out. I'll have made my own mess my way, like fucking Frank Sinatra.'

There was vehemence in her words, and Steph felt her worry collide with pride in her cousin. Her admiration for the seemingly doomed martyr was mixed with concern for Savanna's mental state.

'But you look so tired, Savanna. And this place . . .' She held out her hands to encapsulate the termite-infested old wood building that Savanna was trying to live in. 'Couldn't you just move back in with us?'

Savanna spoke to her kindly, her voice quiet, her words coming slowly for emphasis. 'I know I look a mess, Steph. I would, wouldn't I? There isn't any hot water here. The shithouse is outside, which is a drag when it rains. The couple upstairs make love all night like they're working on some over-the-top porn movie with a director on speed. The guy next door is almost certainly a serial killer, and the landlord only gets out of bed to collect the rent and go through the underwear drawers of the single white females he prefers to rent to. This is not the Ritz-Carlton. But it is where I am determined . . . *determined* . . . to prove to the world and to myself, and to my father . . . and to my mother . . . that I can survive on my own, doing the things I want to do in life, and not the things other people want me to do. If I have to give up a few million bucks to get to be mistress of my own game, then I don't care. I smell of burger fat. I don't sleep. I am rejected by music people every which ways . . . but this is not Bosnia. This is not Dachau, Steph. This is just the American nightmare before it turns into the American dream. It's like Robert Redford saying about girls, "Where were you when I needed you?" When I look back, this will be my finest hour. I'll be *proud* of it. It's not like "My daddy bought me a record company for Christmas." If I want enough, need enough, I can make it. It's just a matter of time. Nothing can stop me, but myself.'

'I sure hope so, Savanna,' said Steph, her trumpet sounding the note of uncertainty. She had had a little speech prepared about how sometimes in life it was better to face up to realities, and let go of dreams that refused to fly. But that was out of the question now. Savanna had spoken. There was no discussion. It was just a question of what the nerve-racking cup of coffee was going to do to Steph's stomach.

'One day, you'll be a believer, too,' said Savanna gently.

CHAPTER

TWELVE

Savanna was discovering all sorts of things about being poor. It was difficult to look good if you were. The time and money for creams and facials and haircuts were all in short supply. And it cost hard cash just to keep cool or warm. When you were poor, your temperature was never quite right. That made you either irritated or vulnerable, often both. Then there was food. She had never yet been hungry, but never before had she eaten things she didn't particularly enjoy, like carbohydrates, simply because they were inexpensive. That made it easier to be fat if you were poor, and later on, presumably, in a downward cycle, it made it easier to be thin. Cable TV had gone for the odd reason that the bill had not been paid. That had been quite a shock, but the telephone being cut off had been a bigger one. She bought clothes because they were warm, or durable or in the sale . . . so in winter she looked like a shapeless bundle, and in summer, like now, she looked kinda cheap. The fact that everyone else did helped a bit. Fan Fair at the State Fair grounds in June was some sort of polyester and Bermuda shorts ugly parade. So Savanna tried to concentrate on the music that blared from every direction, rather than on the nerve-racking appearance of the middle-American fifty-year-olds who loved it.

Savanna's first year in Nashville was almost over, and it seemed fitting that this was her first Fan Fair. She was still an outsider. She was there, but she wasn't really *there*, and now, for the first time, she was beginning to wonder whether she ever would be. Doubt had arrived, and it had been certainty that had been keeping her going. She looked around her. Here was country music natural selection in the raw. The fittest were the star survivors with the biggest crowds around their tents. In Nashville, fans equalled success. The sun was burning and there was no breeze. The wet-rag heat of the humid summer lay over the fairgrounds. To wait in endless line for a Polaroid of oneself with the object of one's affections was a measure of determination and 'loyalty'. That would eventually be translated into airplay time, record and ticket sales, and ultimately the hard cash of serious fame.

It was interesting to notice the sub-plots. Some 'big' stars had splurged on tents to match the size of their names, and yet the people around them were sparse in number. Others, with not much more than an autograph table, chair and a canopy against the sun, were swamped with high-energy fans. Eric Heatherly, the new Mercury signing – a guitar-playing, singing Elvis lookalike from Memphis – was besieged and loving it. Jo de Messina was in strong comeback mode, as was Lee Anne Womack. In contrast, the Marty Stuart and Travis Tritt displays seemed in decline . . . maybe as a backlash against their mildly anarchic attitude to the Nashville world, their 'no hats' tour, the fact that they were 'cowboys' who could think; Music City philosophers in a place where 'philosophy' was a rude word. The real high-flyers like Tim and Faith, Shania and Garth, had been no-shows this year, their superstardom transcending the need to keep the grassroots support well watered. Girls, Savanna couldn't help noticing, seemed to be doing much better than boys.

Fame came and went. A tide taken at its ebb led on to fortune. It was difficult to define the fickle fingers of fashion but they were plucking unseen at the strings that controlled the careers of these singers. All was destiny. Every hair had its number, every grain of sand its place in the plan of the mysterious master of the game.

Savanna was suddenly sorry she had come. It was supposed to be a fan fest, but there was something strangely depressing about it. The ordinary people seemed weirdly passive as they stood still in the hot, wet discomfort to touch some mere mortal with egotistical dreams. They confused the 'star' with the music he played, the art with the artiste. If the music got their emotions going, they believed he or she would. But in fact the star would likely be a shy, or brash, showman who saw nothing but applause in the hands he shook, and dollar bills in the CDs he signed. Yet, Savanna aspired to this. This was *her* dream. Was it a tawdry one, less grand by far than the medicine she could one day have dispensed, less satisfactory by miles than the lives she could have saved?

And she wasn't even hacking it. She had bummed this ticket from one of the Music Row secretaries, who had taken pity on her endless attempts to see people who might make a difference to her non-existent 'career'. Now, she searched through the tight pockets of her jeans for change to buy a greasy chili-burger that she wouldn't have dreamed of eating a year ago.

She knew that, mentally, she was saving the best for last. The talk of this Fan Fair, and there was always a central 'story' to each, was Dwight Deacon. The big DD had, as always, gone in the opposite direction from the crowd. While the high and mighty usually regarded it as a sign of their power that they could afford to stay away, Deacon had taken the biggest tent at the fair. The point – and it was a point that was not lost on anybody that mattered – was that he had the crowds to go with the big splash he had made. They snaked round and round, literally thousands of them, laden down with Deacon merchandise for the great man's bleeding hand to sign. It would be long hours in the relentless steam-bath before they reached that Nirvana, and gazed on the fattening Buddha, but they were resigned to all kinds of earthly torment for their moment of celestial bliss. Wow! It was impressive, if sickly so.

Savanna handed over her change carefully and reluctantly. The chili-dog was a clip at two bucks. Once again, she felt the doubt. She remembered the days when money had been no problem, yet here she was thinking about the price of junk food. That made her like everyone else, or most people. That was supposed to be good, wasn't it? Wasn't life supposed to be hard work, and struggle. Struggle, God! It certainly was that. The only protein in her one-room 'apartment' was the roaches. She could have fed the Deacon fans with a stew of them. She bit gratefully into the greasy frank, and wondered if Amy, the proprietress at the Bluebird, would be satisfied now. It was about time for another shot at the Bluebird talent night. Twice she had tried, and twice she had failed to make the cut. The strange message from the all-powerful Amy had been the same on both occasions: 'Honey, you sing real good, and you write real well, but, sweetheart, it all comes too easy to you. You look like you have never *suffered*. Know what I mean? Come back again and see us when you have.'

Savanna smiled at the memory. At the time, Amy Kurland's attitude had simply astounded and infuriated her. She had not understood what the guru of Nashville singer-songwriters had meant. Now she was beginning to. It wasn't just about the songs and the music and the voice. It was something more. It was about depth. Meaning. Suffering, perhaps. The emotions had to be true, and to be true they had to be felt. You couldn't sing about the hardship of riding a freight if the Platinum Amex could get you there first class by American. OK, stars like Dwight and Garth were rich now, but that was only because the 'then' had filtered into their voices through the osmosis of pain. Amy's turn-down had hurt the most, because the Bluebird was *the* place in Nashville, and Amy's judgement counted for a lot. But it wasn't infallible. The only person to whom she had ever given a straight 'A' was David Wilcox, whoever he was, and today he was probably serving blue plate specials at a meat-and-three. To Garth Brooks, she had given an 'A minus'. And to Savanna, as yet, nothing at all.

She wandered over to the front of the Deacon line, where the bouncers clustered, eyeing her suspiciously as if she were about to try and jump the queue. It apparently took all sorts to make a DD fan. They ranged from grandmothers to teeny-boppers, and there were as many men as women, as many straight as gay. Right up at the front they were asking people to open up their purses for inspection. Nobody wanted some nutter to stick a knife into Deacon before he was right and ready to become a legend, and to ascend into Heaven as a final celestial boost to his already stratospheric record sales. Just then Savanna felt a tap at her shoulder. The voice was urgent.

'Hey, guy. Can you help me? I'm really in a hurry. Can you just look after my purse, while I take my turn? They're holdin' my place in the line, but I don't think they can hold it for long. I bin waitin' four hours.' She thrust her purse at Savanna hopefully. 'Got some personal things in there. You know, like women's things.'

Savanna saw the small flustered girl, plain as mashed potatoes, yet as excited as a Queen before her coronation. Here was a prototype fan. Deacon would be the prom date she never had, the cherry on her pie, the star of her steamy dreams.

'Sure,' said Savanna, taking the purse which was surprisingly heavy. 'Thanks for trusting me.'

'Oh, thanks, thank you, lady.' The girl made as if to dart off.

'Give him my love,' said Savanna with a laugh.

The girl stopped in her tracks. She turned and blurted out, 'You *know* him?' over her shoulder.

'No, no,' said Savanna, amazed at the response her joke had had. She waved a hand to show she was kidding. 'It was a joke.'

'Oh . . . a joke,' said the girl and the crestfallen look in her eyes was more eloquent than the Gettysburg Address. How could anybody make a joke about Dwight Deacon! About knowing him! But she recovered. By the time she was back at the front of the line Savanna could see that the flushed expression of excitement was back in place.

'What's your name?' shouted out Savanna. 'In case we get separated.'

'Kirstie,' the girl called back, as she disappeared into the inner sanctum.

Kirstie took a deep breath as if in a strangely superb church. It was quiet in here, and cool. Large fans distributed the air. The walls were festooned with posters of Deacon, and a song of his played soft and low, like the organ did just before the service. It was dark, and the line of people was subdued. They were shepherded into a snake which turned in on itself like a coiled rope. Finally, they were fed past two outsize cut-outs of Deacon lit by hidden spots into a tent within a tent, in which the saviour sat. The woman in front turned and whispered to nobody in particular, 'He hasn't been to the bathroom in ten hours. Security guy told me.' Kirstie simply nodded. Nobody smiled. Somebody said, 'Really?' with great interest and without a hint of mockery. Everybody in line came with souvenirs for the star to sign. Security guards roamed the queue, issuing numerous instructions about how the fans were to behave in the presence of the man himself. 'Only two signatures per person. No body parts unless Mr Deacon personally requests it. One Polaroid per person. This does not count as one of your two signatures. Mr Deacon only has a minute per fan. Please remember this. If you feel faint or unwell, please say so immediately.'

'Why would anyone feel unwell?' said Kirstie, feeling oddly sick. Nobody replied. Everyone looked mildly discomposed and flustered. Not a few appeared to have been competing in Dwight Deacon's bladder-defying competition, shifting from foot to foot uncomfortably. The tension was mounting. Kirstie had been thinking about this moment for a year. She had a little speech prepared. In fact, she had written it down, but it was in the purse that she had given to the girl outside. That, and the gun. Thank God, she had seen them searching the fans up ahead. Nobody would understand that the only thing she cared about was protecting Dwight, not harming him. She smiled at the ridiculousness of the thought. How could you hurt the thing you loved most in all the world? She meant 'person' not 'thing'. No, actually she really did mean 'thing', because Deacon was nothing so ordinary as a mere person. She knew that, yet she had never met him.

'About five minutes, now,' whispered a guard, patrolling the line and watching the fans carefully. 'You all all right?' he asked. And then a strange sea change came over the crowd. They seemed to recapture the devil-may-care gaiety that had characterised them during the early hours of the line. Sporadic laughter appeared, a few jokes were cracked. The tension seemed to ease. It was as if, faced with the ultimate experience, the fans had rediscovered reservoirs of strength and fortitude, even scattered patches of irreverence.

'I just might throw up over his cowboy boots,' said one leathery grandma, to patches of daring laughter from the crowd. Kirstie managed a weak smile at such levity.

Kirstie was nearly there. Two guards flanked the opening to the tent within a tent. A curtain hid the idol from his idolaters.

'Step inside, miss.'

Kirstie went in, and there he was. He sat at a raised table, and he looked as if he had been up all night. His eyes were red and bleary. A fixed, rictus smile was plastered in place as he turned towards Kirstie.

'I have waited . . . I have waited . . .' she tried.

'Hello, darlin',' boomed Deacon. 'What's your name?'

He didn't have the time for her stuttered rubbish. This one was a worshipper. He could tell 'em a mile off. In and out, and on to the next. She wouldn't remember a thing about this minute of her life, and neither would he. It would be gone as if it had never been. The Polaroid would be the only evidence that flesh had touched flesh. She was pale, but she was not a fainter. Adrenaline would carry her through, and the hollerin' would start later while he was trading good-natured insults with the feisty-looking grandma who followed her.

'Kirstie,' mumbled Kirstie, all speech gone. Dwight took the two CDs from her trembling hands. He did so gently as if removing the knife from the hands of a usually harmless person who had, for inexplicable reasons, just killed somebody. 'To Kirstie,' he wrote in a big round hand. 'Pretty as a picture. My love, Dwight Deacon.'

'That *is* Kirstie with a K and an E?' he queried. 'I just had a Chastiti.'

Kirstie didn't know what he meant. He knew she didn't. The Polaroid man jumped forwards. Kirstie began to tremble. The world whooshed around her. 'My love, Dwight Deacon.' Love. Dwight Deacon. Kirstie with a K. He wasn't real. He was super-real. He jumped up and held her tight. 'Heeey?' he said in a loud, cheery voice, and the camera whirred and spewed out its square of celluloid. 'Enjoy,' said Deacon, with a nasal twang, or was it a booming base.

'This way, miss,' said a minder.

It was over.

Kirstie blinked as she was shot like a cannon-ball into the sunlight. She began to cry on cue, shaking with surrogate emotion. She felt sucked dry by the power of the man, by his fame, by his beauty. She had two CDs in her hand, and a square of a Polaroid that was still developing. Through her tears, she tried to look at it. Love. Dwight Deacon. He came into being before her misty eyes. There was the hat, the big conch belt, the smile, the teeth, those arms around her. Around Kirstie. She was holy. She had been touched by greatness.

'Ooooooh,' she said.

'Kirstie?' said Savanna. 'Are you all right?'

Kirstie looked at her, not recognising her, startled. Then she saw her purse, and remembered.

'Oh, hi, yes, thanks, I'm fine. Oh, God, better than fine. Wonderful. Wonderful.'

'How was he?' said Savanna, transfixed by the effect that the brush with stardom had had on this young girl. Was this normal? She guessed it was.

'He was great. Great!' said Kirstie. She thrust the Polaroid at Savanna as proof of Deacon's greatness, but she wouldn't let Savanna hold it.

Savanna stared deeply into her eyes. She had to understand this thing. It was quite a business. Industrial-strength adoration built on bullshit.

'You like his music?' she said.

'His music?' said Kirstie, as if she didn't understand. It was beyond music. Above music. Did you love God because of His music? You loved God because He was God, and you couldn't not love Him.

Savanna tried to see inside the looking-glass world of the obsessed fan.

'What did he say?'

'I don't know. I can't remember.'

'Was he nice?'

'Nice?'

'I mean friendly.'

'Can I have my purse back?'

Kirstie looked at Savanna strangely, as if the girl were asking crazy questions and she wanted nothing more to do with her. Savanna handed it to her.

'Thanks for looking after it,' said Kirstie.

'No problem.'

'I'm sorry,' said Kirstie suddenly.

'Why sorry?'

'I'm kinda not myself. You see, Dwight and me . . . we have this kinda . . . well, it's sort of special. I can't say it . . .'

She splayed open her hands to show that mere words wouldn't cut it, and she gave a tangled smile. 'I mean, it's not just music . . .' she said. She backed off, then turned away, and hurried from the scene of her confused epiphany. Her large round butt waddled as she went, and her pin shoulders were hunched beneath mousy square-cut hair. Her T-shirt was a Deacon one, surprise, surprise.

'Weird,' thought Savanna. She walked on, strangely depressed. Was this the end result of the fame game? To attract life's misfits. Again, medicine seemed a nobler calling, and a more dignified one. She hadn't talked to her father in a year, but suddenly he seemed a far more attractive figure. His only crime had been wanting to protect her from the tawdriness of poverty and failure, and she had not allowed him to. Instead, she had trawled Music Row, and had all the traditional Music Row experiences. The secretaries had been mostly little Hitlerettes, but on the occasions she had been allowed to filter higher it had not been much better. A man old enough to be her grandfather had told her she had 'promise' that they had to discuss over dinner. A guy young enough to be her brother had asked to see her belly button. A man who reminded her a bit of her father had said her demo was good and to come back in a year so that he could see if she was still there. Apparently, not many young singer/songwriters made it a whole year through Nashville's school of hard knocks and dream assault courses. Well, she was still here, but barely . . . and she was getting desperate.

Over to her left was one of the stages, maybe Sony's. One of their lesser signings was belting out a song that had scratched the edges of the top forty for ten minutes. She sang as if she were at the Oscars or the Super Bowl. Her need was palpable. Not many were listening. Fan Fair was primarily about meeting stars, not seeing them perform. You could do that at the county fair in the early days, and on TNN later. Savanna took a seat at the back in the full glare of the sun. This singer was way ahead of her in the game, but it didn't seem to have done a whole lot for her. Her smile showed as much desperation as was in Savanna's heart. So much for the lower rungs of the ladder of success.

'Hey, Savanna!'

The lean kid sitting next to her wore a hat, dark Levis, conch belt . . . the uniform.

'Walt. Walt Thomas. Remember? We was standin' next to each other at the Bluebird at the open audition . . . one of 'em . . .' he added.

'Oh, sure, Walt. I remember. How's it going?'

'Pretty bad,' he said with a shrug and a grin. 'Maybe a Yankee from Buffalo didn't have no business down here in Tennessee.'

'Yeah, Amy said I hadn't suffered enough, whatever she meant by that.'

'Amy told me to get the hell out of town on the next bus,' said Walt with a sad little laugh. 'Should have listened to her. Best advice I ever had in Nashville.'

'Didn't work out?'

'Hell, no. Nearest I got was as a waiter caterin' an event at Martina McBride's place. Slipped her a tape, and my boss fired me for it!'

'Yeah, I haven't got round to slipping tapes yet. I hear people are pretty sensitive about it.'

'Specially if the stuff on it is shit,' said Walt. The bitterness was out in the open at last. When you ceased to believe in yourself, then the days of getting others to believe in you were over for good. 'How about you, Savanna? You can really sing. I remember your set. You can write, too. That was one of your own songs you played.'

'Thanks for remembering. No, I'm pretty much up against it. Got a job at the C on Lower Broad for a few weeks. Afternoons. Like dead time. No one else wanted me. Forget Music Row. What you going to do?'

'Head back North. My uncle has a lumber business. Says I can start there in the winter. Glad I tried it, though. Gave it a shot. No regrets. 'Cept every time I turn on TV, or the radio, I'll be thinking . . . could have been me.'

'If this . . . if that . . . luck, chance, right time, right place . . .'

'Yeah, all that stuff. You've been there, I guess. Guess we all have.'

'And I dropped out of an Ivy League, and gave up a career in medicine, and my dad won't speak to me, and I'm blowing Nashville . . .'

'Bummer,' he said, but it was all the same. Dreams were dreams. You gave up your life for them. 'Crazy C turned me down a couple of times,' said Walt, throwing her a crumb. There was a camaraderie about Nashville failures. You couldn't tell anyone else what it was like; you had to have been there. 'Well, I'm going to walk around some more. I don't think this Dixie chick is going to give us any secrets.' Walt nodded at the Sony signing, still belting it out on stage.

Savanna stood up. She hadn't failed yet. Walt had. He was going back. She was still there. That opened up a gulf between them.

He tipped his hat to her. 'Good luck, Savanna.'

'Mind your picking fingers around those chain-saws,' she said with a smile and a laugh. 'Good luck, Walt.'

She walked on. The crowd around Deacon's tent was getting bigger. It coiled around the superstar's marquee like a mile-long boa constrictor, squeezing the juice from his fame. And then the crowds began to thin out, until there were hardly any people at all. This was also-ran territory, and the unlikely-but-just-possible newcomer patch. The tents were very small. The fans were thin and mean here, darting about like barracudas, swallowing an autograph there, a CD here from fawning, ingratiating performers who lived at the lowest end of the Music City food chain. How like life it was. The fans were the bosses here; loud and demanding, dropping the names of bigger and better performers, and using up lots of conversation time. Gone were the minders, the heavies, the trappings of fame and power. There was just the music and the wits of whoever it was who had just taken their first small step for Nashville man and woman . . . a booth of their own at Fan Fair. Savanna watched a small determined blonde 'star' fending off the attentions of a big tall 'fan', who looked like he might get nasty after a few beers. Then she heard her name called for the second time that afternoon.

'Savanna!'

She turned, and there he was. A Lonesome Dove. The short one; the one called Jim. She remembered him instantly. Now here he was and wearing his hat. Were they still a hat act?

'Jim Lonesome Dove,' said Savanna.

Her eyes worked faster than her mind. They had a booth. There was a table, four chairs, no fans, a box of CDs and a couple of posters. The single – it didn't look like an album – played on constant loop on a hidden tape deck. It sounded vaguely familiar to Savanna.

They all slipped into instantaneous recognition mode. Why did they remember her so easily? They cascaded off their chairs and clustered around her. 'Hey, Savanna, hey, Savanna, you were our good-luck charm.'

The story tumbled out. The day after Savanna had sung at the Silver Bullet, the Mercury guys had called to say the development deal was off. They had had all their hopes pinned to it like a star on a sheriff. It was the end, the *coup de grâce* to a musical future they had all known in their hearts was dead. They had begun planning their separate and ignominious retreats to Austin. Then, their world had turned yet again.

Mike, still trying to be shorter than his six foot four, took up the story. 'And I'd done this thing, ya know, like I was real ashamed, I hadn't told the guys. Sent me our demo down to Vince Gill's agent in Nashville, weeks back, way back. Shit, that very same night the agent dude walks right into the Silver Bullet and asks for the Lonesome Doves, like you and your cousin did. Said who he was. Said he was always in New York. Said he'd seen our set. Said did we want to go down to Nashville and try out for Capitol. His tab. And, baby, that was it. That was it. An' here we are with a top forty, made twenty-seven, and a pay-or-play deal for an album. They said to come and try Fan Fair. Get the feel of the town, boys, they said. An' here we are. Half an hour ago we had a fan. Dude with prostate problems who couldn't wait in the Dwight Deacon line. Bought a CD. Seemed put out there weren't no T-shirt.'

'Yeah,' said Red, 'we gotta fix that T-shirt problem. Had 'em back in Austin.'

Jackson, the leader and the looker, said, 'It was the night after you came down and sang. We all figured out you were like the snow white dove . . .'

'On the wings of a snow white dove,' sang Savanna.

'That's the one,' said Jackson with a laid-back Texan smile.

'And the Doves weren't Lonesome no more,' said Red with a cackling laugh.

'Not even Doves, no more. They changed us to "Texas Sky", on account the sky was the limit, they said.'

'I heard that "Texas Sky" song. That was a great song,' said Savanna, slapping her hands together. 'This one,' she added, waving her hand to indicate the backing music.

'Wrote it on the plane to Nashville,' said Jackson. Again there was the slowed-down smile.

'They either take ten minutes, or ten years. My mother used to say that.'

'Ain't that right, ma'am,' said Jackson. 'How about you? What's your life bin like?'

'Oh, brick walls and bullshit. You know the scene. Like you after Mercury backed out and before Capitol hit. But there wasn't a Mercury. No bites at all. I'm pretty much washed up. Thinking about my own Austin.'

She laughed to show she didn't care. The gloomy silence that greeted her speech showed how much they all realised she did.

'Gotta gig down on Lower Broad. Beer joint called the C. Drop in one . . . afternoon.'

The silence deepened. Afternoons on Lower Broad! The good news was there wasn't much further to fall.

'We could introduce you to our agent. He'll hear your tape,' said Jim. The others nodded vigorously, but without enthusiasm.

Nashville had worked out its own variation of the sword in the stone. Only when the secret and unknowable conditions had been mysteriously met could the sword be withdrawn from the stone and used to cut a swathe through to success and fame. The sending a tape to Vince Gill method had probably failed for thousands, just as losing lottery tickets would end up merely as scraps of torn-up dreams in the trash.

But there and then, as she sat surrounded by the Lonesome Doves who were now reaching for the Texas sky, she knew what she would do that very night. She would get her demo to Dwight Deacon. If you were going to fly a hopeless kite you might just as well fly it amongst the biggest stars.

THIRTEEN

Aron Wallis's father was somewhat in awe of his son. This, in part, was because he had turned out so differently from the Aron after whom he had been named. Aron Wallis Senior, aristocratic, cultivated, gentlemanly, had taught classics at William and Mary, and it was always assumed that Aron Junior would follow in his academic footsteps. Certainly he had the brains for it, and in the early days the inclination. Classics was a little out of date for the latter part of the twentieth century, but young Aron had discovered an interest in philosophy, which was a thoroughly acceptable alternative. Professor Wallis had had connections at Cambridge University in England, and it was with no difficulty that his son obtained a place at Trinity, the college of Russell, Wittgenstein and G. E. Moore who were, arguably, the greatest mathematical, linguistic and ethical philosophers of the age.

So, when Aron returned home to Charleston from Trinity, Cambridge with a double first in Moral Sciences and a failed marriage to a fellow student who had turned out to be a serial cheat, it looked as if he was destined for the groves of Academe. Yale, Princeton or Harvard should probably have first shot at his son, Professor Wallis thought.

It had therefore come as a wild shock to the family when Aron had decided to become a record producer in Nashville. The Wallis family, however, specialised in shocks. They had endured a few during colonisation, the Revolutionary War, the Civil War and the Reconstruction, plus an unpleasant financial blip in 1929. So there was a certain amount of sang-froid about Aron's departure for Tennessee soon after his return from Cambridge. 'Isn't country music about philosophy?' had been his mother's comment, and Professor Wallis, who valued his Italian wife's intuition and commonsense, was inclined to agree that it was. What's more, he had a Southerner's respect for a man who made up his own life, and didn't allow others to make it up for him. The Ancient Greeks and Romans, whom Professor Wallis so much admired, specialised in thinking and acting for themselves.

So, today, the philosopher *manqué* was testing the acoustics of the still reasonably new Nashville stadium and was trying to persuade Newt Fulsome, one of his stars at Polymark Records, that his voice sounded good there.

'I don't think I'm reachin' into the back.'

Aron wrapped his navy blue overcoat tight round him against the cold, and walked to the back of the stadium. Fulsome and he had not read the same books, because Fulsome could hardly read at all. However, Fulsome *could* sing and write good wholesome philosophy of the kind that Aron had not run into much at Trinity, Cambridge. His big hit of the moment was about a dying man comforting his ever-loving wife with comments about the universality of death and the shortness of life: 'Some of us jump the evenin' freight, others hang on for the midnight special, but we're all leaving Tucson 'fore the early mornin' light.' Aron thought it deep. It was the sort of sentiment that appealed to him.

'I can hear it perfectly from here. All the nuance. You're not losing anything, Newt.'

A hundred yards away on the stage, Newt Fulsome nodded. He trusted Aron. Aron was good, not maybe the best yet, but getting there. Fulsome, however, in his honest moments realised he was headed in the other direction. His fading career had been kick-started by 'Leaving Tucson', not least because of Aron Wallis's superb production of the CD of the same name. Fulsome thought Aron was a funny guy in those funny English clothes, and with the accent that sounded like an ad for an English airline mixed with George Plimpton. But what mattered in Nashville, anywhere really, was delivery of the goods. Apparently, Wallis had had this thing for country music since he was a kid, couldn't sing a lick, and so had gone into producing. Heck, who cared? Fulsome would have sold his soul to the Devil for a hit, and as far as he could see, Aron Wallis was a long way from the Devil, although a long way from a country boy, too.

Aron walked back to the stage. 'How does it feel?'

'Good, I guess. You sure it was reachin' the back?'

'Newt, we are number seven with a bullet, man. Would I bullshit you? I'm ridin' your coat-tails right now. I am the flea on your butt, and the beer in your belly, man.'

Aron could talk like that, too. He could do anything. He only had one difficulty in life. Wanting things enough. Motivation. That was more precious to him than the air that he breathed. The trouble with philosophy was you questioned things. Thought was action's enemy, and it was action that delivered the bacon in the year 2000. The real problem was to persuade yourself that bacon was worth the effort.

'OK, then I guess we are through. I just wanted you to check things over. You're the man, Aron. You put those fiddles in. An' I didn't want 'em. Everyone says they make the song.'

'You made the song, Newt. Wrote it. Sung it. Who cares about a couple of fiddles?'

'Yeah, you and me both, we know it ain't that easy. A hit comes from all over the place, Aron. Mixin'. Sellin'. Plain old luck. This is yours, too.'

Aron smiled. It was nice to hear, and rare in the music business where ego was the fuel that drove ambition. But then Newt had been down as well as up. He'd seen the other side of the industry's coin, and watched people turn from close 'friends' to distant strangers. A guy like Deacon passed out praise with the same enthusiasm as pints of his blood. You could write a hit for Dwight, arrange it, produce it, stick it at number one with the bleeding stumps of your fingers, and he wouldn't cross the street to piss on you if you were on fire. Not that Aron held it against him personally. It was just another way of treating a world it took all sorts to make. You could be Nietzsche, or you could be Plato. Both had had something to say, and you didn't get good words without discouraging ones . . . except home on the mythical range.

'I'll split then, if you're cool,' said Aron.

'You wanna ride?'

'No, I'll walk down Broadway to my place. Hang out in the District. Make like a tourist!'

'I remember when they had singers down there,' said Newt. 'Used to do Tootsies myself. Upstairs room. You was in diapers, man.'

'Never needed diapers, man, I was saving my stuff for the music industry.'

He waved goodbye to his singer. He had several others like Newt, but he had a soft spot for the recently redeemed has-been. Finding new talent in Nashville was a popular activity. Recycling old talent and making it new again was akin to raising the dead. That made you a miracle worker.

The cold wind hit him hard as he walked out on to the street. He wound his blue cashmere scarf tight around his neck. The weather was coming from the flatlands to the West, straight out of Memphis. Gracelands weather. He turned right on Broadway, past Tootsies where Newt had done the upstairs room. The Ryman, which had been a church, hovered over this end of the street like a blessing. God, it was cold. He walked fast to make some body heat. It reminded him of Cambridge in winter when the howling wind came in across the marshes they called the Fens, straight from the North Sea, just as it had done a thousand years ago, blowing the island's ancestors with it. Aron smiled as far as he could with his face half frozen. Life was so weird. It was an act of will, and it was acts of chance. He had sat in his room one afternoon by the fire, and the decision had been whether to resign from life or join it. To become a philosopher would basically have been resignation. But what was the alternative? It had to be something difficult, and yet romantic, something that caught his dreams . . . but what were his dreams . . . surely he wasn't supposed to have any? So he had gone back to his early life when youth dealt only in dreams. Country music had been his 'thing' then. God only knew why. But it had been. When he heard it on the radio and TV he felt the thrill. He had sung along, badly, but he had remembered the words of all the songs, and the names of the singers. Country was so simple and his mind was so complicated. It was like an antidote. And it was hopeful music, balm to the ears of a young cynic. Aron had started cynicism a bit before he had been able to spell it, aged around five.

He let his mind go a bit. 'Leaving Tucson.' Ten billion years. That's how long life had been going. If you wanted to take that time to cross America you'd be allowed only one step every 2,000 years. Recorded history would be the last few steps before you hit the beach. Each life was a mere moment in the mist of eternity. The midnight special against the evening freight? It didn't make a blind bit of difference when you died, only that you did. Aron quickened his pace. There was just as much bullshit in Cambridge as there was in the music industry. Perhaps more. Probably it was just everywhere.

He breathed in the cold air deeply. He was getting to love this town, but towns weren't all there was to love. There were women, too. And women were not easy. He'd got it wrong the first time, but that was a fifth of his life in the past. If at first you don't succeed . . . sooner or later, he would have to try, try again.

CHAPTER

FOURTEEN

Savanna took a deep breath, air that was equal parts second-hand Marlboro, stale beer, and whatever sawdust smelled like. She peered through the darkened room. To call it a honky-tonk would be to give it too much credit. It was just a bar with a stage, and she was on it.

She tried to sound upbeat, although including the barman her total audience numbered four.

'Well, hi, y'all. I'm Savanna, and I'm real pleased to be playing here at the Crazy C. Later I'd like to do a few of my own songs for you, but right now let's start real slow with one that did real good for Shania. This one's called "From This Moment On".'

The two guys at the bar didn't turn round. Luckily their baseball hats were back to front so she didn't feel quite so excluded. A guy at a table had five empty bottles of Bud lined up, and a face that glowed in the gloom. He was ape-shit and proud of it, which was why he hadn't allowed the barman to take away the empties. He leered at Savanna through mindless eyes. The barman, wiping down the counter, bothered to look up as she introduced herself. She had 'auditioned' a week earlier singing a Tammy Wynette number – 'D.I.V.O.R.C.E.' – which usually struck a chord with the fifty-plus age group. 'You can try the two-to-four for three weeks, hon,' he had drawled. 'It'll be pretty quiet. Tips only. No beer.' He hadn't bothered to say that he'd liked her voice, her delivery, or anything like that, although he had. Just allowing her to play, here in Music City, for tips and no beer, was compliment enough.

Savanna took the Shania Twain nice and easy, milking it for melancholy. It went well with the mournful ambience of the Crazy C, a place whose craziness took the form of a seemingly deep depression. Probably at midnight, it would jump. Here in the afternoon, it was death. She lost herself as she played. She could do that, and it felt so good. New York was light years away. She was back home again. Savanna smiled as she sang the sad song. Country allowed for that. In this music there was precious little difference between the good times and the bad times. She sat straight on the chair, and pushed out her bejeaned leg, starched and creased Nashville style. The lizard boots were no longer new, but they were too expensive for the dirty jar at the front of the stage on which someone had written 'TIPS' in black indelible marker. Still, the jar went with the territory. Anyone singing in a bar like this would be living off what got put into it. Savanna, when she had started out doing gigs, had never expected to be one of them. The first use she had put them to was to get her telephone back on.

She finished Shania. The drunk clapped, making a business of it, as if he were spending energy that he couldn't really afford. Nobody else did. One of the baseball guys at the bar half turned, not giving Savanna the full benefit of his standard bar-fly ugliness. 'You do any Garth Brooks?' he growled.

'I'm twenty, and female, and you want me to sound like Garth Brooks?' she said with a laugh. Damn it, she still had to learn this. The audience, any audience, had to be massaged. This was all about friendliness, making people love you, creating fans out of thin air. Fans alone had the power to make the dreams come true. Her laugh saved her from giving offence. Just. The barman had a glint in his eye. His bottom line was to sell beer to the couple of losers at his bar. He didn't want them insulted by his singer. Singers were far cheaper than two a penny in Nashville, Tennessee.

So she closed her eyes and launched into 'Friends in Low Places'. Her reward came fast. The two guys at the bar ordered up a couple of Buds and the drunk staggered across the floor and, with the reverence of a church-goer placing money on the plate, dropped a filthy dollar bill into her 'tip' jar. She smiled her thanks as she growled out the music. One more buck and she had a burger.

As with most of the bars on and off Broadway, the amplification of the song was blown out into the street to attract cruising drinkers to the free music. As an added incentive, the stage was in the picture window. That was one of the reasons so many of the singers in the afternoons were girls, the drinkers at this time being almost exclusively male. Savanna's blonde hair, much longer after a year in Nashville, her crisp white shirt and tight butt were a potent 'come-on-in'.

Aron, walking past, took in the visuals and tied them up to the music. He paused. Garth Brooks, from a blue-jeaned blonde with a strong voice. His body language showed his indecision. To stop or not to stop was the question.

He shook his head, and smiled, and then walked on quickly, looking at his watch as he did so. 'I don't have time for this,' he thought. Then he stopped again, and turned back, drawn to the strange combination of sight and sound that he had just witnessed. He hovered at the window, trying to catch sight of the girl in profile. But her back was squarely towards him. That left the music. She sang hard and true, hitting all the right notes, in a voice that was distinctively different. The song, of course, was all wrong for her, which made it doubly admirable that she was doing so well with it. Aron exhaled. Face to face she was bound to be a disappointment; life was full of them. But the voice was good, very good. Curiosity alone carried him inside.

Aron took one look at Savanna and at once was mesmerised. She was beautiful, an unevenness giving to her face a surprising asymmetry that was at once alluring and slightly unsettling. Her mouth was large, and her lower lip seemed to protrude slightly, making its upper partner seem severe by comparison. Her eyes, too, were uneven, the right larger and rounder than the left which was more oval than oblong. But these seeming deficiencies in uniformity were drawn together by remarkably strong pure blonde eyelashes. These were startlingly wide apart. Her small neat nose, fuller at the bottom than the top, drew her extraordinary eyes and mouth into a secret harmony that was decidedly attractive. Her hair, Pantene-perfect, was long and lush. There was no real style to it – fancy haircuts were expensive – but her fringe framed a face that had not quite decided whether to be long or round. Aron Wallis could not take his eyes off her as he walked into the Crazy C, and he did not. The result was that he bumped into a table, and nearly knocked it over. The menu, stained with tomato and barbecue sauce, and sitting on a blue plastic base, clattered loudly as it hit the floor.

'Friends in Low Places' ended at Aron's noisy arrival. He was acutely aware that he was blushing as Savanna said, smiling widely at his evident confusion, 'Welcome to the Crazy C. Hope you haven't injured yourself.'

He lifted up a hand, and half smiled to acknowledge her welcome. He tried to calm down. Sometimes people called him 'Mr Cool'. It was an image he liked to cultivate. Something had gone seriously wrong with his persona this afternoon. He looked at the bar speculatively, and then at the ten or so empty tables.

'What's your name?' said Savanna. She had the microphone. Aron turned again, mild panic plucking at him. This was normal Nashville stuff, especially in a dive like this. Talk to the audience. Ask them where they are 'from' – 'Gee, I always wanted to visit Nebraska.' However, Aron Wallis of Polymark Records was not in the habit of hanging out in beer joints in the middle of the afternoon exchanging pleasantries with the no-hope singers. Music Row was where his office was and Garth, Reba and the offices of the big Nashville labels were his natural neighbours.

The drunk turned around to look at him. So did the couple at the bar. It seemed they all wanted to know his name and it would be downright unfriendly of him not to provide it. Here in the Southland only Yankees prided themselves on being too busy for manners.

'Aron,' said Aron.

'Hi, Aron,' said Savanna, 'I'm Savanna.'

Aron sat down hard. The bartender approached him grudgingly, because of the way he was dressed. From beneath the overcoat the sharply pressed pants of an expensive dark suit broke over Cole-Haan loafers. The usual clientele in their jeans and Dexters picked up their own drinks at the bar and carried them to their own tables.

'What'll you be havin', Aron?' he said.

'A Perrier water, please,' said Aron. He was regretting this already. And yet he wasn't. Ambivalence, an emotion he rather enjoyed, surrounded him like the stale air.

'Club soda do?' said the barman.

'Could you put a slice of lemon in it?'

'Guess I could do that.' He stumbled away.

Savanna watched him. What the hell was he doing in here? He was a fish out of water. But was he? The city was rigid with talent scouts. That was why people came from all over to work here for nothing when they could be earning decent money in New York, Florida, or even Czechoslovakia. People didn't come to Nashville to get rich. They came here to get famous. There was all the difference in the world between the two, although the two often walked hand in hand. Could he have heard her sing outside, and slipped in to check her out? Was this her break? Was this guy slumming it from Music Row, trolling the strip, next stop Robert's 'Western World', after giving Tootsie's 'Orchid Lounge' a roll?

Whatever. She aimed her next few songs at him, and he applauded politely. He looked like a Northerner, who had lived for some time in the South. His skin was olive, his face aquiline, maybe some Italian in there, or a Jewish heritage. He had a suntan which he wore well, and from the cut of his coat which he didn't take off, and the shine of his shoes which were Southern-bright, he was well-heeled. Aron. That was a name that said a lot. Elvis Aron Presley. His mother would have been a fan. Did that mean that, as in the words of the Deacon mega-hit, he had a little bit of Memphis in his soul, a bit of the Delta, some blues and rock 'n' roll? He had nice eyes, small and brown, but soft and somehow gentle. He was in his mid twenties, maybe older, with plenty of thick black hair, swept back from a high brow in a uniform direction with no parting. It was long at the back, turning up a bit at the edge of his coat collar where the baby-blue cashmere merged with the dark blue of the serge overcoat. He clapped politely as she finished her set. Savanna made the decision fast as she stood up. She walked up to his table, and stood over him. He looked up at her, smiling, slightly self-conscious.

'Looks like I've been singing just for you,' she said.

'Singing very well,' he said.

'Well, thank you, sir.' Savanna mock-curtsied. This man was no beer-bellied busted cowboy. He seemed shy, and she liked shy guys. They allowed her to give her natural extroversion an outing.

'Look, would you think me rude if I asked you to join me?' He half stood as he issued the invitation. 'And can I offer you somethin' to drink?'

'I was fixin' to have an iced tea,' said Savanna, sitting down as he sat. His voice had the hint of a down South accent if not a Deep South one. He spoke slowly, unhurriedly, and he had almost lost the 'g' of something. The word 'drink' had turned up slightly, giving a life to the last word of his sentence that was unusual above the Mason-Dixon line. If he hadn't been born here, he had spent a long time in the southland. He would know not to use the term 'civil war', but he would drive a Jeep not a pick-up and would scarcely know the difference between a Remington 12-gauge and a .243 Custom rifle. He wasn't gay. That meant he was married, but he wore no ring.

He organised the tea efficiently, lubricating the potentially surly barman's attitude with a fat tip.

'I really like your songs,' said Aron. 'Oh, forgive me. My second name is Wallis.' They shook hands. His grip was firm. He looked her straight in the eye as he spoke.

'Which ones did you like best?' She was testing him.

'Oh, the one about the spring, summer and winter of love. Those were good lyrics. "I saw the future and us together for ever in the heartland." That was pure country . . . Patsy Cline voice to go with it. But then I could detect a Nanci Griffith influence, too. I also liked "Remembering to Forget". Great lyrics. Great song. That one could cross over big time. It'd be nice to hear some drums and fiddle in the background to go with the collector's Gibson you've got there. You fixin' to get a band together?'

'Wow,' said Savanna, impressed. 'I guess that means you're in the music business. Aron Wallis . . . should I know you?'

He laughed, throwing back his head. 'I'm just a faceless backroom boy,' he lied.

'With a label?' Savanna tried to sound cool, but she didn't feel cool. This was what it was all about. It could be a break. The little thing called luck that made the difference. Out there, across America, was a vast audience crying out to be entertained. And here, in Nashville, and in a thousand towns across the South there were legions of singers who wanted to give the public what it wanted. Only a handful would be chosen. Talent was not enough to pass through the eye of the needle. You had to find someone with power who was a believer in your potential.

'Polymark,' he said simply.

'Dwight Deacon,' said Savanna in something between a whisper and a croak.

'I haven't worked with Deacon for a while but, yes, he's with the label. Sometimes I think he *is* the label.'

'What's he like?'

Aron smiled. Why did pretty women keep asking him that? He ran his fingers through his hair and took a deep breath. 'You're not a stringer for the *Globe* by any chance, are you?'

'Not with the *Globe*,' laughed Savanna.

'Well, there's that saying about a puzzle wrapped inside an enigma covered in a mystery? Something like that. He's sort of weird. Deep. Obsessed, I guess. With being a hero, an icon, something bigger than a legend. His music is almost incidental to that. It's good, it's great even, but if he could make more people follow him by turning him-self into the Pied Piper he'd go there in a flash. Image, marketing, packaging, he cares about all that more than any other artist I've ever worked with. And he has to control it all. Doesn't trust anybody. Wants to be the Duke, Elvis, Abraham Lincoln all rolled into one.

You know, I bet he dreams in a hundred years they'll tear down that old Statue of Liberty and stick him up there instead.'

'Jeez, and to think I sent him a song.'

'You sent Deacon a song? Which one?' Aron was impressed. 'Did he acknowledge it? Did he get it?' Aron had to ask but he knew the answer would be no. No artist even opened unsolicited material, especially not Deacon. Nobody wanted plagiarism suits.

'I don't know. I mean, I just sent it to his office. It was a thing called "Roots and Wings" . . . about how if you have roots then you're in a better position to be able to fly. It's about good parenting, I suppose. Making a kid confident enough to feel they can do any-thing, by giving them values and encouragement, and a code to live by.' Savanna blushed, because she wasn't quite telling the truth. He didn't seem to notice.

'I'd like to hear it.' There was a strange look in Aron Wallis's eyes. Savanna could see it and she knew what it was. He liked her. He was attracted to her. She was confident enough in herself to realise that one helluva lot of men did, and that confidence increased her ability to draw them to her.

'I'd be happy to send you a copy of the demo I sent Deacon. Should I just mail it to Polymark?'

In answer, he dipped into the pocket of his coat, drew out a wallet, and extracted a card. 'Sure, I'd like that. I'd be real interested.'

Savanna looked at it. It was simple. Engraved, with no splashes of vulgar colour. It simply said Aron Wallis, Polymark Records, pro-ducer. There was a telephone number, a fax number, and an e-mail address. She tucked it into the back pocket of her jeans.

'So how come you ended up here in the Crazy C? You don't look like a small-town girl. Don't sound like one. Don't feel like one.'

'You want my bio?' Savanna smiled, teasing him. 'The real one, or the tweaked one?'

'Hold the spin. We add spin later.' He laughed, too.

They were both enjoying this. Savanna was aware that she ought to be singing again soon. But the drunk had staggered out, and the couple at the bar were drinking as fast as they could anyway. Right here with Aron Wallis, Polymark producer, was quite definitely the place to be. And she had the definite feeling that it would be the place to be if his card had read Aron Wallis, Pet detective, too.

'OK. How about this? My father's family have lived in Belle Meade for about a hundred years. He's a famous surgeon in New York at the Columbia College of Physicians and Surgeons. My mom was hillbilly stock from the Appalachians and my dad met her when he was on the staff at Vanderbilt. I guess the music comes from Pigeon Forge, not Belle Meade!'

Aron Wallis's eyes opened wider. That was quite a reach for a girl singing in a place like this. His quick mind put it together fast. Belle Meade was the area of Nashville where they looked down their noses at the entire country music business. They had been there first when Nashville had been a banking and insurance centre, way before the Grand Ole Opry and before Jimmie Rodgers, the first country super-star, had decked himself out in cowboy garb even though he was a sickly railway worker from Mississippi. To this day none of the town's musical heavy hitters had dared to live in toney Belle Meade amongst the socialites. They didn't want to go where they weren't welcome.

'So what do your fancy relations feel about you singing down here? Or is it just a little something you do on the side for fun?'

Aron hoped that wasn't true. He sensed strongly that it wasn't. The girl could sing. Some of those Appalachian genes had gotten into her vocal chords. And she could write. The package was picture-perfect, and even the image might not be the disaster it sounded on paper. Nashville these days was all about conflict. Genuine country versus 'crossover'. The perennial 'authenticity' issue. Did you have to look like a cowboy and sound like Hank Williams and Loretta Lynn to call yourself 'country'? Or could you pillage the mainstream, and top both the country and the pop charts as Deacon had done, and at the same time stay true to 'country' tradition, whichever that was. Here was a girl whose whole family represented conflict. Old money and class merging with mountain roots, moonshine and guitars to pro-duce a new synthesis. Hell, this girl was Nashville before Nashville was Nashville. From the look of her body she could be both a belly button act like Shania but with brains, education and class. After all, Vince Gill's father was an attorney; Trish Yearwood's the vice president of a bank; and Garth Brooks had a degree in marketing. So why should it matter that this girl's dad was a surgeon? Aron could see the press kit – 'Country Doctor's Daughter'! Class, sex, and talent were a potent brew.

'No, it's not for fun. It's for real,' said Savanna. 'It's deadly real. And my dad doesn't like it. He won't even accept that it's happening. I was at Columbia and I dropped out. I'm staying here until it happens. However long that takes. My dad wants me to be a doctor like him. But it's not what I want. I want this.'

She spoke vehemently, not to impress, but because that was the way the words bubbled out of her. She wanted. She needed. And she wondered why.

'Does it come from your mom?' Aron was looking at her intensely. In his mind he was already moving on to stage two. He needed desperately to hear this. This was the most important part of all. To succeed against all the odds you had to want with the desperation of the damned. It was the thing that made fame so tragic, but it was the vital ingredient. First you wanted it. Then, when you had it, you fought to keep it because you were driven by the fear of losing it. And then, last of all, you lost it. Because one day people tired of you, and another group, wanting like you had wanted, pushed you into the oblivion you dreaded. At every stage of the fame game there was heartache and tragedy but, inexplicably, it remained the most potent drug of all.

'Yes, I guess it's from Mom,' said Savanna. 'Her family were dirt-poor, and they played music all the time. Singing didn't cost anything. She taught me how to play and sing. And in a way, I think all her life she would have wanted to take a chance at this. But it didn't work out like that. She met my dad, and he was rich and suave, and good-looking, and it was like, "Hey, here's security, and a family and never having to worry about anybody being cold, or hungry, or sick, or anything." So she let herself fall in love. Only thing she had to give up for all that was her dream. She died of breast cancer.'

'God, I'm sorry, how awful,' said Aron quickly.

Savanna waved it away. 'I'm not going to make my mom's mistake,' she said.

'No, I don't believe you are,' said Aron Wallis leaning forward slightly in his chair. To Savanna, it was not quite clear if this was a prediction or a promise.

'So what does your boyfriend think of the move to Nashville?'

'Did he come with you?' was the real question.

'No boyfriend,' said Savanna, smiling and then looking down. 'Does your wife enjoy being married to a record producer?' she said quickly.

'No wife,' said Aron. 'Divorced four years ago.' And it was his turn to smile.

CHAPTER

FIFTEEN

Aron walked into a low-slung building that looked like a shingle shack on a suburban street. Just off Music Row, it stood close to similar, but more souped-up, houses where the record labels of Nashville lived. The door banged behind him, and the receptionist looked up.

'Hi, Aron,' she said. 'He's right upstairs, and expectin' ya.'

Aron waved his hello at the almost pretty girl. In her spare time, she cut demos for aspiring songwriters who couldn't do justice to their own compositions. But she hadn't got what Aron liked to call 'the factor'. On all levels she was close. Looks. Voice. Personality. But on all she fell short, and a miss was as good as a mile in Music City. Of course, she didn't know it. Nobody could tell anybody for sure that they weren't going to make it in this town. Partly it was because nobody really knew. So they just recounted the *odds* against success like a mantra, and hoped it would scare away the dreamers who weren't sufficiently hooked on their dreams. There were tour bus drivers in this town who'd had top twenty hits. One wasn't enough. Come to think of it, nothing was enough. The fame game never ended. The success sport never ceased. It was the one sad subject nobody in country music ever dared to sing about.

Aron hurried towards the stairs. The receptionist was prone to trying out her new songs on him, hoping that one might stick. She did so now.

'God made bad boys to tempt good girls . . .' she tried. 'God made . . .'

'Sounds like Lorrie Morgan,' said Aron as he took the stairs two at a time. He smiled over his shoulder at the trilling would-be songstress. His money was on 'pearls' as the rhyme.

She shook her head, and looked away still singing, as if pretending she hadn't really meant to engage his attention. As Aron opened the door at the head of the stairs, he heard the word 'pearls'. Sometimes, he just knew it all. But then that was what he was paid all the money for.

The guy behind the desk stood up as Aron closed the door behind him. He wore a brown boot-polish suntan, below luxuriant grey hair. Horn-rimmed glasses clung to a beaky nose. His cream silk shirt was open at the neck, no jacket, and his initials PC were stitched in blue to the place where a pocket might have been.

'Goddamn it, Aron, take a look at this.' He thrust a photograph at Aron. It was of a boat, rigged for fishing.

'Yours?' said Aron, taking the photograph and feigning interest. When you'd seen one boat, you'd seen them all.

'Will be this weekend. Forty foot of dreams come true, and Saturday I'm in the Gulf Stream catching sail-fish. How does that grab you?'

'Somebody has to do it. Glad it isn't me,' said Aron with a laugh. 'Makes me feel sick to my stomach just looking at the thing. You're a better man than I am, Pete Cook.'

Pete laughed. Richer anyway. The boat, if it could speak, would be saying half a million bucks. Aron was on his way, but he hadn't got that kind of spare change yet or the $75,000 a year it would take to run the money-eater.

'Sit down, boy,' said Pete. 'Wanna Coke or something?'

Aron put up his hands. 'I'm fine. All caffeined out. Your girl downstairs sings a neat tune.' The word was she was a little more than the receptionist.

'Yeah,' said Pete, looking away at a wall covered with records and trophies. 'She doesn't give up.' He wanted out of the subject.

'OK, so what have you got for me? You found some girl down there in the District. I didn't know they still found 'em down there. What were you doing? Taking some kids to the Hard Rock or the Nascar?'

It was *touché* for the receptionist reference. Broadway these days was mostly for tourists. It wasn't very obvious what a hot producer like Aron would be doing hanging out down there.

Aron by-passed the question, much as Pete had dropped the receptionist.

'Heard her outside on the speakers. Took a look inside. Stayed for the set. And she's very good. Very, very good,' he added.

'How does she sing?'

They both laughed.

'No, Pete, I'm serious here. Like you about your boat.'

More laughter.

'I feel about my boat like a redneck feels about Shania's belly button. You picked the wrong analogy there, boy.'

But already it was time to get serious. Nashville wasn't New York. You were allowed pleasantries first, in fact it was insisted upon. But you couldn't keep a sacred subject light for long. Undiscovered talent was rare as gold in the Gold Rush, but when it was found it was lottery time. They still laughed at poor old Meadows who'd turned down his shot at Garth. Nobody wanted to be Tennessee's longest running joke. Aron was a bit too much of a Southern gentleman to be entirely to Pete's liking, but he had made platinums with Tritt and Gill . . . and they didn't specialise in failures. If he said a girl was good, she probably was. On the 'very good' the jury would always be out until the record was up there on the *Billboard* charts in black and white for all to see.

'So where is she? Where's the demo? Or are you going to sing the thing yourself?'

They were the right questions. The honky-tonk angel should be there right now, sweating bullets with a rictus smile. At the very least there should be a scratchy demo. A picture was worth a thousand words, but a thousand words didn't add up to a single note.

'I want to go slowly with this one,' said Aron. He was aware that what he was saying sounded odd. If she was genuinely hot, the thing to do was to go for her like a bat out of hell before some other slick scout found her. But he wanted to go slowly with her. With Savanna. Savanna Carson Stone. Her lips had curled so cutely as she'd sung and she had that sound, that distinctive meld of mountain music mixed with something quite different. What was it? A Fifth Avenue sidewalk next to a country lane? Traffic that wasn't tractors? Class meets country? The two had only met once before but it had been quite an act. Minnie Pearl, God rest her soul, had become famous for the $1.98 label on her hat, but she'd been at the Belmont Academy for Ladies not 500 yards from this house. Years ago she had looked down on it, in every sense of the word, when it had been a lodging-house where the servants had lived. Famous doctor's daughter goes country. The girl who didn't just cross over, but crossed the great divide, between the country of the cowboys and the country of the cattle barons. 'Roots and Wings'. She had sung him the song unaccompanied, smiling and singing low in the beer-sodden bar.

He had been captivated by it, by her, by everything, the totality that was Savanna Carson Stone. He had liked her thin wrists and small back, and her surprisingly large breasts. He had liked her small, economical butt atop the long blue-jeaned legs. But mostly he had liked her smile and its warmth and the way she had leaned across the table as she had sung without any hint of embarrassment or self-consciousness. It was one thing to be up on a stage, doing your thing, in control of the mike, and therefore to some extent the room. It was another to pitch a song in music, unaccompanied, to a guy who knew what he was doing, and had very publicly done it.

'OK, we're going slowly. What exactly does that mean, son?'

Aron smiled. 'OK, Pete. I know this isn't really the right way to do things, but I wanted you to have first shot at this. Polymark are for the big boys and girls, and their newcomer stable is pretty darned full right now. This girl needs your touch here at Vantage. She needs a smaller stable. A slower, steadier start. That's my feeling anyway. Vantage is Polymark, so I have no conflict.

'Vantage is ninety per cent Polymark,' Pete corrected him. Everyone knew he had ten per cent, including Aron. But it was always important to nip these slips of the tongue in the bud before people got used to saying them.

'Yeah, sure, I know, but you know what I mean.'

Pete nodded. He moved the picture of his boat from one side of his desk to the other. He could all but hear the snap of the big fish taking the line off the outriggers.

'What's her name . . . if that's not too fast?' he said.

'Oh, Savanna Stone. Of the Belle Meade Stones.'

'Well, praise the Lord, Aron, you found us a real live lady in low places.'

'Her daddy married a mountain girl. Dirt-poor. A pickin' family.'

'Tell me they sing together like the Judds.'

'Nope. Her mom died a while ago. She's bright as a button.'

'Not so bright if she's playing Broadway and dreaming of music videos when she should be nailing down an Ivy League education and marrying some East Coast sissy boy with a trust fund and a page in the Social Register. Her poor father must be having a cow, as my daughter would say.'

'She isn't doing so badly,' said Aron, pulling Pete up to order. 'She's got me pitching her. Though I say it myself, that puts her a few points ahead of the game.'

'Yeah,' said Pete. 'I guess it does. So what do you want from me?'

'I want you to stake me for a low-budget demo. "B"-list musicians. An afternoon at the longest. One song. This one called "Roots and Wings". I'll produce for nothing. You get first crack at a contract if you like what you hear. If not, I get to keep the demo, at least Savanna does.'

'Seven session guys and an engineer. The back room at the Squash House studio. Sounds like around five grand without the producer . . .'

'About,' said Aron.

'For a shot at a nobody.'

'A "somebody", says Aron Wallis.'

'And if I don't like her, and turn her down, and then some other studio picks her up on the back of my demo, and she's the next number one then . . .'

'You've not only passed on a star, you've paid five big ones to do it. But you won't pass, Pete. Believe me, you will not pass.'

Pete sat well back in his chair and laughed. It was a neat trick. He'd never heard of it before. Aron was standing on his reputation which was a pretty tall chair, and asking Pete to stake the demo. That way, when the demo came in he'd already be invested. He'd actually *want* to say 'yes' rather than the 'no' that was Hollywood's and Nashville's favourite word, because it cost nothing.

'So you haven't tried it on the boys next door?' Pete wanted to be sure Aron wasn't shopping this one around. Not that he was likely to risk his reputation in an industry so small and so talkative.

'No way. Polymark are so geared to Dwight, they hardly do unknowns any more. He gets crazy as a bedbug when he sees Polymark PR bucks goin' out on anyone else. Spends all this time looking over his shoulder to see who's going to be stealing his air-space. Good Lord, I sometimes wonder if that one is really on this planet. He's a single walking advertisement for the downside of success.'

Pete nodded, hardly daring to agree. It must have been like that round Stalin or Hitler, he thought. A loose remark that might get back to a paranoid superstar, and suddenly you were on his enemies list. Unlike Nixon's, that was a list you didn't boast about being on in this town.

'OK, Aron. Make the cut. I'll stake you for first pick. But if it's down the drain, my friend, you owe me one. I'll tell you one thing. You got me interested. Nothing like having to put your hand in your back pocket to do that!'

They both laughed, but Aron took a deep breath afterwards. It was immediately followed by the surge of adrenaline. He wanted to cut Savanna's demo, but more than that he wanted to hear her voice, and see her face when he told her what he had done for her.

CHAPTER

SIXTEEN

The receptionist was still trilling away in the foyer of Vantage Records as Aron bounded down the stairs. An all-purpose hum transformed itself into distinct lyrics and music as the producer appeared. In Nashville, you never knew . . .

'Can I use the telephone, Mary-Lou? Hey, that's a useful little song you've got goin' there.'

She smiled, blushed, and Oh, yes, he could use the phone.

Her 'Be my guest' sounded a bit to Aron like 'Be my lover'. He wondered idly if she'd be being sick in the Gulf Stream this weekend on Pete Cook's boat or whether the wife would have that doubtful honour.

He fished the card out of the pocket of his jeans. He had written Savanna's number on the back of it. As it was early in the morning, and she had the afternoon set at the C, the chances were good she'd be in.

He waited. The receptionist smiled at him encouragingly, showing him her best profile. She didn't look a quarter as good as Lorrie Morgan, but she was taller and younger. Years and inches were on her side.

'Hello?' She seemed surprised that anyone was ringing her.

'Savanna? This is Aron Wallis. Remember me?'

'No, I don't think so. No recollection. Remind me.'

She was very cool, and playful like a wise kitten. He had not expected gushing oil, but he was relieved anyway. Unknown

singer/writers and name label producers could have horribly syco-
phantic relationships.

'That little impression?' he laughed.

'Wait a minute. You were the guy without the baseball hat. The
one who was sober with the good sense of humour . . . pretending to
be a record producer at Polymark. Now, I have you. You gave me
your card. You got a brain surgeon's one, too?'

Again, he laughed. 'I have some news for you.'

'News?'

'Oh yes, but it's not "over-the-telephone" news.'

He saw the knowing look flash across the secretary's face, and he
felt the pang of shame. She would have heard similar lines. This was
hardly the Kremlin/White House hotline. The information he had
for Savanna fell way short of nuclear. He just wanted to see her
again. Soon. More than he had wanted to see any woman so soon for
a very long time. He felt the thrill of wanting.

'Oh,' said Savanna, on to him like a cat on a mouse. 'So we have
to meet to hear this "news".' She mixed laughter in with the words,
telling him she was enjoying this game, that she wanted to play, too.

'Vitally necessary.'

'Like when?'

'Like now.'

'Like where?'

'Well, I have a meeting at noon, and I'm up on the Row. We could
meet . . .'

'Polymark?'

'No. No, that would be a little difficult. I'll explain when I see
you.'

'My, are you not the mystery man, Aron Wallis? There I was thinking this is a nice Southern gentleman, and all the time you are James
Bond.'

He couldn't meet her at Polymark. He'd just pitched her to
Vantage, which was different by Pete Cook's ten per cent.

'I know,' said Savanna. 'Country Music Hall of Fame. You know
where that is!'

Aron laughed out loud. 'I haven't been there in years.'

'Nor me, but it's near. And as I'm going to be in it one day, perhaps I ought to check it out. They'll think we're tourists. You can throw me the microfilm over Elvis's gold Cadillac.'

'OK, meet you in the entrance. Tickets are my treat. How long?'

'Give me twenty. Oh, hey, and Aron . . . listen . . . even if your news is a fizzle, I'm glad you called, and it will be nice to see you again.'

She put the telephone down. So did he, more slowly. He knew he was blushing. The singing secretary was smiling at him. Oh, shit! He had totally blown his cool. Where had that detachment gone that turned the women on like radiators? Where was the icy profession-alism? Where the 'who cares' ennui of the man with the key to the doors that mattered? The Music Hall of Fame! Savanna was right. He was coming across like Pierce Brosnan on a bad day. Already, the director would be sending for the scriptwriter for a bit of polishing. But then, another thought came, a better one. In twenty minutes, he would be telling Savanna about the demo. There was an old tradition involving the rewarding of messengers with good news, especially when the messenger had manufactured the message. He was about to please a girl. And not just any girl.

CHAPTER

SEVENTEEN

Savanna threaded her way through the tour buses, and the strag-
gling tourists, and pushed through the glass doors of the Hall of
Fame. It had never been much of a place. Small and unobtrusive, it
made no architectural statement at all. Country was not interested in
buildings. Most of the stars lived in houses that could be suburbia
anywhere. But it was a suburbia without hedges, or many trees, so
that one house ran on into the next; when Martina McBride hung out
the washing the star six houses away could see the colour of her
underwear, giving no privacy at all.

Savanna saw Aron immediately, and the excitement that had
gripped her on the drive was peaking now. It was two things at once.
The news, and him. They could be separated. But the news was the
mystery. Savanna had a list of possibilities. He had found her an
agent. He was going to introduce her to a better class of beer joint.
He was going to represent her himself. Least attractive of all was the
possibility that it was just a scam. 'No news. I just wanted to see you
again.' That would be a pain, and make him a pain, but it was low on
the list. Savanna considered herself good on characters. She had liked
him. He had seemed laid-back and honest, maybe with a moody side,
plus a bit of existential *angst* that would be fun to unravel.

She saw him first, staring at an Alan Jackson poster as if he couldn't
understand what it was doing there. Aron looked black as midnight
in the same coat, but somehow more Armaniesque. He seemed more

fashionable than traditional, with some sharp shoes that were not as safe as yesterday's Cole-Haans. He stood out starkly from the fat, polyester-clad tourists who drifted around in Day-Glo colours and trainers. Nor did he look like an insider. In fact he looked like himself, and nobody else. That was a good start in the looks department. Savanna was close enough to touch him by the time he saw her.

'Why so deep in thought?' she said.

He started, and then smiled in the confusion.

'Savanna. Hi! Great!' Then he seemed to register he had been asked a question. 'I was wondering what it must be like to *be* famous, sort of officially famous, to the extent you are in a museum dedicated to fame in the abstract. I mean, did somebody ask Alan Jackson for a pair of his boots to go in a glass case in there? Imagine picking through your closet and choosing the ones that will be immortalised. Would you choose the comfortable ones, the ones you really liked? Or maybe the bastards that pinched; or the expensive ones to show you were rich; or the battered ones to show you were cool. Or would you just have some roadie go up and make the choice for you? I mean, would it be a big deal, or a joke, or a bore, or none of the above . . . but some more sinister, perhaps fetishistic, thing . . . ?'

She laughed. She had known he was a thinker, but a thinker who could 'do'. Or was he a 'doer' who could think?

'Smelly ones,' she said definitely.

'Smelly cowboy boots?'

'Yeah, and then see if they came back, all embarrassed, and said, "We can't take these, these are smelly." Or whether they would just stick them in a specially air-sealed case, and then put out rumours you had smelly feet. Then, one day, long after you had forgotten, you'd get a call from Dr Scholl's PR guys and make a million bucks on TV selling fragrant soles . . .'

He laughed, and looked her up and down. She didn't say anything he didn't like. She didn't look like anything he didn't dream about. She was standing there, young and untouched by the hand of fame. It was ridiculously early, but Aron believed in love at first sight. He tried to remember the first time he had seen her. One milli-second, he had been expecting the horse's ass, and the next he had seen her in profile. Had that been the magic moment, Savanna growling the Garth song, as he had stumbled over the table and made a mini fool of himself in a dirty bar? He could still see the ketchup-stained menu spiralling to the floor, but his heart had been telling him things then. Yes, that had been it. First sight. Oh, Aron Wallis! Was love neurosis, as Freud would have it? Or was it just lust by another name? Whatever. It seemed to be floating around, waiting to strike at people when they had banged into tables and expected horse's behinds. That made it an odd little business, but a significant one.

'What the hell are we doing here in the Country Music Hall of Fame?' said Savanna, smiling as she watched the effect she was having on him. It was lucky she only liked people who liked her. That was a far from common quality in a woman.

In answer, he held up two tickets.

'OK,' she said, happy to play along with the game. 'In we go.'

In they went.

'When do I get the news?' whispered Savanna.

'Now if you like,' whispered Aron.

'Why are we whispering?'

'It's a bit like church, isn't it?'

It was. The light was dim, and side rooms that might have been side chapels contained small knots of quiet people gazing reverentially at the artifacts. These consisted mainly of clothes, guitars and photographs . . . from Dolly Parton's dresses to the guitar Garth Brooks had smashed on stage. It was strangely subdued, a million miles from the excitement of a stage performance, or even the playing of the music that had enabled these people to become famous in the first place. It was as if an Art Hall of Fame had contained Picasso's toothbrush, Monet's spectacles, Fragonard's dagger.

'You are cutting a demo for a major label, and they are picking up the tab. Nothing guaranteed, but I think we have a very good chance.'

'What?' Savanna yelled, at the top of her voice. Everybody turned to look at her. This was hardly a place where you raised your voice. 'How did you *do* that?'

She looked as if she was about to launch herself at him. A bear-hug was a definite possibility. Aron wondered how best to make sure it happened.

'You deserve the chance. It's self-interest. It's what I do.'

She came at him then, throwing her arms around his shoulders and launching herself upwards so that he had to bend to take her weight. He was aware of her hair against his face as she hugged him, the sweet smell of it, of her, the touch of her breasts, flattened against his chest.

'Whoa!' he said as the breath was deliciously squeezed from him. He set her down, and he did so gently, hanging on around her waist to ensure that she was still up close, way inside his personal space. Her face was flushed with excitement and exertion, and he was right up near to it. He could smell her breath . . . strawberries . . . and feel the warmth of her. Her eyes were wide open and so was her mouth in a magnificent smile. Her teeth glistened. She was ridiculously, impossibly, kissable. But Aron was not an opportunist, and he hated himself as the magic moment faded. Who dared, won. All around were the memorabilia of those who had seized moments by the scruff of their necks and turned them into fame and fortune. Instead he smiled at her enthusiasm.

'You are a genius, Aron Wallis. I am so *excited*. Which company? Where? When? What do I have to do? Tell me! Tell me!'

They wandered past Elvis's gold Cadillac as if it was a Toyota Camry in a car-wash.

'Vantage Records, wholly owned subsidiary of Polymark's. They specialise in new talent. Polymark is pretty much running on Deacon and a few other big ones right now. It won't be a top-of-the-line session, but the "B" list in Nashville is better than the "A" list most places else.'

She threaded her hand into his as if she had known him all her life. 'God, I can't wait to tell Dad. He'll freak!' Then she went quiet. She felt like a Roman general at a triumph. There should be a slave behind her saying, 'Remember thou art but a woman.'

'It's a beginning,' said Aron gently. His whole being was concentrated in the hand she held. He felt light-headed, light on his feet, light, period. They had entered the movie section . . . films about Nashville . . . the posters from the few films with country music themes, mostly failures, were festooned around them.

'It's my chance,' said Savanna. 'You've "discovered" me. I feel like they are making the airtight box for my boots right out there in the back somewhere. What do you get for "discovering" someone? Well, I guess in polite Nashville society . . . a peck on the cheek?'

But he didn't get that.

She took the half step towards him, pushed both her arms around him, and kissed him full on the lips. Nor was it the kiss of a niece, or a sister, or a friend. Her mouth was a little bit open, and he could taste the delicious wetness of her, just briefly, tantalisingly so. Then she pulled away from him, still smiling, but in a different way now. He had discovered her all right.

CHAPTER

EIGHTEEN

Savanna parked the well-used Honda she'd borrowed for the day in the small lot beside the nondescript cedar-lined, one-storey building. A small sign had said 'Squash House Studios' outside. The lot was full of even more decrepit-looking vehicles; red pick-ups, and cars of uncertain vintage, all American. There wasn't a Japanese auto anywhere. The only foreign car was the neat little sport BMW, and Savanna knew instinctively that this was Aron Wallis's ride. She looked at her watch. It was twelve noon. She wasn't late, everyone else was early. It seemed impossible that anyone could be more eager than she. Apparently they were. She had gone for strict punctuality, which had necessitated parking for a quarter of an hour tucked out of view down the street behind the Country Music Hall of Fame. The others had decided to be fashionably early.

Inside the building, it was dark and dingy, smelling vaguely of a school hall where someone had just smoked a questionable cigarette. There was no reception. To the right a sign over the door said 'Studio', so in she went.

The room was full of men. None of them looked as if they belonged there. Savanna's idea of what a Nashville studio looked like and the reality did not gel. She reminded herself of Aron's words: 'Squash is not a state-of-the-art facility, but we can do the job there.' The same looked as if it could be said for the musicians. They were either too fat or too thin, too short or too tall. Most appeared semi-blind, blinking under the lights in glasses that didn't go with the cowboy hats that several of them wore. They held instruments, smoked cigarettes, and their faded jeans were tightly in tune with their jaded dreams. They looked dirty, poor and short of sleep. In fact they looked as far from the image of the 'new country' that was sweeping America from coast to coast as the Devil himself from Grace. Savanna knew that these musician guys were strictly for sessions like this. They didn't travel, they weren't part of a star's group. They were the guys you didn't put out there on show because they were charismatically or aesthetically challenged. This was the rule in Nashville. It worked well, because for every musician with personality and a presentable appearance, there was one without. Usually the one without was the better musician. The ugly tried harder. They had to in life.

Nobody had shown the slightest interest in her as she had walked through the door, and so Savanna just stood there. She said 'Hi' to nobody in particular. Nobody said 'Hi' back.

The finger on her shoulder made her jump. She was nervous enough anyway. The forbidding appearance of the assorted pickers and pluckers who milled about wasn't helping.

'Savanna, great. There you are.'

'Here I am,' said Savanna, with a nervous but wide-open smile.

The butterflies were loose, but she was still able to separate off the excitement that was caused by seeing Aron . . . Aron the man . . . from the free-floating *angst* of the imminent recording session.

'Guys, say hello to Savanna Carson Stone. Savanna's family come from Nashville, and she sings like a bird.'

The *déjà vu* eyes fixed on her, some breaking into reluctant smiles. She didn't *look* like Nashville but, if she was, that made her folk, and folk got the benefit of the doubt even if they were crazy enough to embark on the abortive moon shot that was the run at stardom. A big beer-bellied guy said 'Hi y'all', although Savanna was in the singular. As if to emphasise his pleasantry, he pulled off a quick riff on an old guitar that was way better than good. The others tipped hats, raised hands, nodded, or showed tobacco-stained teeth. The songstress sure did look *clean*. That probably meant she couldn't sing a lick. Still, as

'B'-group session guys pulling a four-hour stint, they were each picking up $300. That was baked in the pecan pie even if the girl's voice
was ugly as a mud fence.

A woman came through a door at the back, followed closely by
another. They looked better than the men, but not a whole lot. They
wore the standard once-white T-shirts and once-pressed jeans over
sneakers. Their eyes came with beer baggage, as did their guts. Both
women had taken the Nashville precaution of buying Wranglers a
couple of sizes too small to act as corsets. Savanna knew these were
the back-up singers. They were introduced as Charlene and Cherry-
Anne. Pretty soon it was whispered round the room that they'd done
vocals behind Johnny Cash on his San Quentin album, which put
them both firmly the wrong side of fifty-five.

'Let's go up, Savanna,' said Aron. She walked behind him, carrying
her guitar case to the upper part of the split-level room.

A swivel chair in biscuit-brown sat like a starship commander's
seat before a console of complex machinery. At the back of the room
was a sofa covered with a similar pseudo-suede material in matching
colour. In the room below, a set of drums dominated. Two or three of
the musicians had followed Aron and Savanna up the stairs and now
stood around telling each other quiet jokes that Savanna wasn't
intended to hear.

'OK,' said Aron, calling the odd meeting to some sort of order.
'Let's make some music.' He clapped his hands as if to drum up
enthusiasm, and the lack of any obvious response made Savanna feel
worse. How could anything good come out of this unpromising situation? Both the location and the people seemed a million miles from
a hit country song, from any sort of song, come to that. Aron turned
to Savanna, his voice definite, as if by mere leadership and force of
character he could make things happen. 'Savanna, if you just run
through the song once, these guys will have it.'

Savanna looked uncertain. There were no notes. No music. There
wasn't even a sheet with the words on it.

Aron picked up on her doubt. 'Trust me. This is how it gets done.
One run through and Dylan on the acoustic here will have the chords

down in the Nashville Number System. Then he copies them on the Canon, and the other guys each get a page. They can take it from there.'

Two or three of the players nodded. Their eyes said, 'Boy, this one is green!' The lounge cowboy with the acoustic guitar had a notepad laid out on the wood of his instrument, and a chewed Bic biro in his mouth. 'Roots and Wings' was about to be written down musically for the very first time.

Savanna took her guitar from the case. This was very hard. There was no feedback from an audience. The room was all but devoid of interest. She wasn't performing and she wasn't on a stage. She was simply 'running through' the number so that some hard-bitten musician could commit it to memory. It was downright mechanical, but of course it had to be done. Sometimes your dreams got you into the sort of places you hadn't dreamed about at all.

She stood, her feet apart, picked out Aron's face, and focused on it tightly. She began to sing. The acoustics of the room made her song sound tight, and arresting. The cloth wallpaper and white tiled floor sent the sound scurrying back to her, and the angled walls diffused it, bouncing it back in different directions and at different times. The result made it sound new and interesting. Savanna picked up strength from the sound she herself was making. It was her first time in a studio. She got better and better as she went along. The words conjured up memories of her childhood, and emotions began to arrive in the room. The acoustic guitar player still jotted down the chords, but Savanna noticed the change of his expression. Boredom was disappearing. The others, too, began to still. From trying not to look too uninterested, they started attempting not to show enthusiasm. It was all there to see in the body language, and it transferred itself back to Savanna, and the music she was making. Aron most of all summed up the essence of the reaction. He swayed his head to the music in the Nashville way that meant he liked it.

She smiled at him as she told him her story, of the roots that had so miraculously turned into wings and allowed her to fly away to another world.

The song came to an end, and there was a long silence. Savanna didn't know what to expect. Where she came from it would have been polite for someone to have said something nice.

'Can you believe she sent that song to Deacon?' said Aron. He knew what the people who knew were thinking. He was inside the minds of these folk. They pretended they'd seen it all, but their eyes were wide open now. Savanna had opened them.

The man who had been doodling the chords down on his pad of paper said, 'That's a real pretty tune, lady.'

A couple of the others nodded. Aron smiled.

'Surprised Deacon don't use that one, 'cos he ain't got no roots nor wings,' said someone. He paused. 'Between ourselves,' he added to a couple of isolated laughs. They had the phrase 'You'll never work in this town again' in Nashville, too.

'OK, boys, let's get to work.' It was instantaneous. They ambled downstairs, and while they did so the drummer, who had taken up his position at his set while Savanna sang, let go a riff that caught the tempo of 'Roots and Wings' to perfection. It was a little faster than she had sung it, but right on beat. They took up their positions below the RPG diffusers, small blocks of wood suspended from the ceiling to disperse the sound. An assistant handed round the photocopies of the song's chords, each containing a bare series of numbers which the musicians knew represented A minor, a C or a G. Aron sat down at the console above them. In front of him were forty-eight columns of green lights, each reaching in a pencil-thin line six inches tall towards the band of red lights above it. Savanna stood close behind his shoulder. She was aware of his aftershave. It smelled good. So did the quiet power he exuded. The scent of confidence. He pressed a red button which allowed his voice to penetrate to the musicians below. 'Boys, give me a preliminary run through, will you. Do you have it, or would you like Savanna to sing along to orchestrate things?'

The acoustic guitar player leaned towards his mike. 'No, we got it, Aron. Let's lay down a track.'

'Go for it,' said Aron.

'One, two, three, and . . .'

Down in the windowless studio, the engineer, crouched over the quarter-million-dollar cockpit panel, started to twitch and roll around like a break-dancer as the music burst into life. He banged buttons and flicked switches. His ears craned towards each separate component of the music in turn, winding up the right bits, toning down the wrong ones. The acoustic instruments, guitar and piano, were separated from the harder ones by isolation booths around the perimeter of the studio.

'Can I talk?' said Savanna in a hushed whisper.

'Sure,' said Aron laughing. 'You can even sing along if you like.'

'How can they pick up the song so fast? Just on one run through.'

He half turned and smiled. 'These guys are pros. The second best is pretty good in this town.'

Savanna smiled her excitement. Down below they were all working for her, for her career, for her song. Fiddle, drums, acoustic guitar, electric guitar, piano and pedal steel guitar were all making intricate music of the tune she had written with her mother. The song that had never been written down was now being played in a way that it had never been played before. It was difficult to believe.

'Let me have more drums in my ear,' yelled the acoustic guitar player into his mike, as the engineer turned up the volume on the twelve mikes that surrounded the drum set.

'Put a bit more of a wang on it. Open it up,' yelled Aron excitedly, punching down on the red button so that he could be heard on the floor below.

He swung his head from side to side. This first track was laying down well, and the first one was the vital one. It set the tone for the session. The guys liked the song. They were letting their own creative juices flow on to it, and the Sony 3348 Digital Multi Track Recorder was laying it all down on DAT. Later, they could do anything with it.

Forty-eight different sounds sat on top of the audio tape as if they were in separate compartments. Forty-eight individual noises could be added, subtracted, divided, multiplied at will. Then the whole could be joined together again so that nobody could know what the wizard had done. Once the base track was down the fiddling and sleight of hand would begin. Only then would the finished product, as perfect as smoke and mirrors could make it, be ready for the addition of Savanna's vocals. Reality would be improved on. Every phrase, every note would be scrutinised and manipulated until the sound, totally manufactured, seemed genuinely authentic. Sometimes, Aron wondered if all this science was cheating. But he never wondered for long. The real sound of Nashville was the sound of money spilling out of a slot-machine when some smart-assed producer like him hit the jackpot with a number one crossover hit. Aron didn't lose sight of the objective. They were still a long way from a single, although not as far as they had been. When 'Roots and Wings' came together like the dream he intended, the demo would set Pete's pants on fire. In no time, Savanna's ink would be dry on a contract. The next of these sessions would be with the 'A' team, in a class studio like the Soundship, with songwriters like Harlan Howard and Ronnie Dunn sitting regally on the ice-blue sofa.

'That's it,' said Aron at last. He pressed the button once again. 'That's it, boys,' he repeated. 'Now the fun starts.' He turned to Savanna. 'We've got the base track laid. Now we get to play around with it.'

'What about me?' said Savanna with a laugh. 'When do I sing?'

'Last but not least, Savanna.' Aron looked at his watch. He couldn't afford too much perfection in the time available. He would have to control the obsessional part of his personality. The musicians had wandered up and now they were hanging about chewing gum, munching moon pies and watching seamless loops of Headline News that played on a monitor hanging from the ceiling. Aron had them, one by one, replay parts of their tracks, concentrating on the steel player who had made the most mistakes. Then, at last, it was Savanna's turn.

'OK, Savanna, you're up.'

Savanna fought the anxiety. Thought and feeling were the enemy. Action the friend. She just had to stand up and do it. But every time she allowed herself to dwell on the importance to her life of this moment, fear swamped her. She swallowed hard, picked up her guitar, took a deep breath and walked down the stairs to the body of the studio.

'Good luck, Savanna,' said Aron, half to himself.

She took up her position in front of the mike. Aron, behind the glass in the control room, had his hand in the air. The engineer wandered over and placed a small rug beneath Savanna's feet to prevent reverberation. Then he placed a pop filter – a round, saucer-shaped piece of nylon mesh – in front of the microphone to prevent sharp 'P's and 'T's from disrupting the balance of the sound.

'You'll hear the back track in your earphones, OK.' It was Aron's voice. 'Guitar opening, then I lower my hand, and off you go. Give it everything first time, but remember we get to do this over and over.'

Savanna picked up the earphones, and put them on. There was a crackle of quiet static. She put both her legs apart, leaned in towards the mike and waited, looking up at Aron. Then the guitar kicked in, playing a fast riff of chords, and his hand dropped down. Savanna Carson Stone's roots had wings.

Immediately, she was lost in the music. She had been playing this song all her life, but never to a professional, almost unbelievably creative, backing like this. The background singers, behind and to the side of her, gave a deep richness to the lyrics and they lived again, like a painting restored to vivid brightness after years of benign neglect.

She watched Aron's face as she sang, and she could see her words hit home. She too was going back, to that simpler place in time, to her own back pages.

The wispy evening mist was beginning to cloak the mountains. Savanna shivered as the low wind blew. She nestled backwards into her mother's warm skirt, feeling her legs through the thick cloth, and the comfort of the closeness. They were all gathered on the porch of the old cabin, sitting in chairs, Grandpa standing off to one side, looking out over the mountains and smoking; with them, yet somehow distant as always. He watched the far horizons as if for danger. It was as if he were always on guard against something from somewhere that might harm the family he had raised. Or so it seemed to

Savanna from the perspective of that distant country that was child-hood, where adults were both simple and complicated all at the same time.

Her father had not come for this visit. He seldom did, and Savanna was glad of that. Here she had her mother to herself, and she could revel in all the things that weren't allowed at home. She could paddle in the running river at dawn, the bass jumping in the shallows; she was allowed to scamper free in the driving rain as the cool, humid air from the Gulf was forced up the high sides of the mountains until it could hold its moisture no more, and rain poured down on the high firs and the low cottonwoods, making the hills live, and creep, and crawl, and burst into flower as a celebration of God's goodwill to mankind.

'I'd better play the "Waltz", I reckon,' said Uncle Joe.

'I reckon you had, Joe,' said LeAnne. 'Never let it be forgot that you lost your first love to your best friend.' She laughed, joshing her brother, and Savanna smiled.

'Did you, Uncle Joe? Did you?'

'This song was written with me in mind, little Savanna. Me in mind. An' I saw them two, a couple of weeks ago in Pigeon Forge, and I didn't know which one to pity most. Sure was a lucky day when I got my heart broke, an' that's God's honest truth.'

'How can it be lucky to break a heart?' said Savanna. It didn't sound like a happy thing to have happened. She was aware of the dif-ference in the way that Joe spoke, and the way that she spoke, and her mommy spoke. He sounded like Grandpa. It was called hillbilly, apparently, and it went up and down like music even when they weren't singing which was not very often.

'Well, now,' said Joe. 'The thing about hearts is they mend. Takes a bit of time maybe, but like a bone that's broke, they's stronger for it after. Not many a heart's been broke twice by love. Sorrow, maybe, but not love.'

'Did you ever break any hearts, Mommy?' Savanna twisted around. Her mother was so very beautiful it seemed all but impossi-ble that she hadn't. But then she had gotten married to Dad almost before she was old enough to fall in love.

'Never did,' said LeAnne with a laugh.

'Well now, sister, that may be true an' it may not be true. But if I remember anything at all, I remember one young kid, that had a pretty deep track in his heart. Don't know if you'd diagnose it as *broke* exactly . . .'

Grandpa turned to them then.

'Are you going to sing that song or are you going to talk us all to sleep?'

Savanna wanted to hear the story, but Mommy was blushing deeply, her cheeks red with embarrassment. Grandpa had turned to look at them now, and his words hung in the air, taking on some of the characteristics of a command.

Joe tossed his head with an enigmatic smile, and plucked on the banjo that lay across his knee. 'You going to join me in the harmony, sis?'

'I will,' said LeAnne. Part of her confusion still remained in her voice. The blush was not fading, but at least it was ceasing to deepen.

Together they sang the so-well-known words of the 'Tennessee Waltz', LeAnne singing high and clear, and the sound they made, sad and slow to the plaintive twang of her uncle's banjo, sent shivers down Savanna's back, but warm ones now. Grandpa joined in, his voice cracked but brimful of melody, singing a bass that took care of the low end of the tune. The sound seemed to tumble out from the porch, past the moths that danced by the kerosene light, falling away down the hills, a gentle avalanche of music. Savanna didn't know the words, but she had already picked up the sound, and so now she hummed along, stealing the parts of the rest of her family in turn, experimenting. She felt her mother's hands on her shoulders as the family sang, encouraging her, until they were all swaying to the tune of the waltz that all those years ago had told a tale of treachery, betrayed friendship, and broken promises.

But all the way through the song, despite being lost in it, Savanna was wondering about that boy whose heart might not have been broken but might have been cracked; the memory that had painted a sunset red on her mother's cheeks.

The song ended, and Savanna was all set to return to the subject that Grandpa had so effectively changed.

LeAnne seemed to sense her daughter's intent. 'I'll do "Roots and Wings",' she said, and Savanna noticed the haste with which she hurried to perform the song.

Savanna had finished. There was silence in her earphones. She took them off. It was as if she had returned from long ago, and her mother's voice still resonated in the air where her own had been. For an instant she had that feeling of waking in a strange place, and not knowing where you were or why you were there. But it was gone in a flash, to be replaced by the immediacy of the studio. Suddenly, they were all clapping. The back-up singers to her right were smiling as they applauded. Aron's voice came over the speaker system.

'Wow, Savanna, that was great!'

In the background, she could hear the hard-bitten veterans applauding too, although they were out of sight. She was full of the thrill of it. This was what it was all about. To be lost; to be merged in the peak flow. The true goal of life was what she had just experienced. Happiness was absence. Joy was the passage of time so fast that when it ended you didn't know where it had gone to. Was that what Nirvana meant? She had had the experience a few times before, usually on stage. You didn't think at those moments. All was movement. Everything was on automatic pilot as some ghost of creativity moved you. It was what artists lived for, struggled for, dreamed about. The time that time forgot, when effort ceased, and the will was not needed. Then spirits could be summoned from that vast ocean of art. They came when they were called, and they performed for free.

In the control booth, Aron Wallis could hardly contain his excitement. Down below him, Savanna, looking for all the world like the ultimate living doll, the package that could sell itself without singing at all, had just unleashed a tune and a voice that had the entire studio twisting on its own guts. The reaction was visceral. He could feel it. The song was a hit. He didn't even have to fiddle with it. He would, but he didn't have to, although perfection could always be improved upon. That was article one of the state-of-the-art producer's faith.

The acoustic guitar player, the most experienced musician in the group, said it all. 'A man could fiddle around with that one, and end up behind, not ahead.'

'Yeah,' said Aron, almost to himself. Again he pressed the red button. 'Savanna, why don't you come on up here, and we can discuss this thing,' he said.

And then Savanna was bounding up the stairs towards him, and Aron Wallis was full to the brim with conflicting emotions. Part of him was thinking *Billboard* charts; but that part was receding. What he wanted to do was to take the girl in his arms and kiss her. That first time would never be enough.

CHAPTER

NINETEEN

The saloon of the trailer was fuller than was comfortable. The atmosphere was downright unpleasant. Dwight Deacon sat in the armchair and exuded menace. His black jeans and black boots were up on the coffee table, and on his muscular knee was a copy of the *National Examiner* tabloid.

The headline was quite certain.

'Cassie Stewart suicide. "Dwight Deacon killed me," says note.'

'I'll sue their asses. That's the end of them. They're dead. Dead!' He stabbed his finger into the air to emphasise his point. The lawyer looked at him. Thin and bespectacled, he didn't relish delivering this bad news. Suing a newspaper successfully in America was like walking on water. Carol Burnett and Jesus wee about the only two who had done one or the other.

'You see, they're not saying you killed her. They're saying the note says you killed her. It's the opinion of Stewart that you . . .'

'Aw, shit!' exploded Deacon. 'Does it cost me money to hear you say that? This is malicious. They mean to hurt my career. That's what this article is. It's an assault on my image. Cowboys don't kill women. They don't make people commit suicide. It's not what they do, ladies and gentlemen. Take it from me. Does anybody here think that is what cowboys do?'

He stared around the room aggressively. They were all one way or another employed by him: the publicist, the business manager, the attorney, the Polymark liaison guy, two or three hangers-on in the 'general crony' category. Now, they actually had to respond to the furious question. They nodded their heads from side to side in grave denial. Nobody saw the humour in the situation. Mortgages were deeply 'not funny'.

Deacon's eyes were wide as the Mississippi; wide and a little bit mad. They'd all seen him get like this once or twice before, and all had wondered at those moments just how sane Dwight Deacon actually was. Now, there was a strange light behind his eyeballs, the flickering flames of some private internalised hell.

'How did they get this?' he said, his voice quieter and somehow even more deadly.

The question was addressed generally. Everyone looked hopefully at everyone else. Then they all zeroed in on the publicist.

'Word is she wrote them a letter before she topped herself.'

Deacon tapped his knee with the palm of his hand, and glowered at them. Cassie Stewart was a drunken has-been of a singer whose band he had muscled his way in on way back at the beginning. It was true that he had ended up displacing her, before jacking in the band and moving on himself . . . but that was show business. He would, wouldn't he? God had given him talent, and in the end audiences decided who they wanted to hear. Breaking up the Stewart band and ruining her career was not murder, nor was it driving someone to suicide. He personally had had all sorts of problems from time to time, and he had turned them into other people's problems. That was what you did with grief. You passed it on like a hot potato. God, he hated losers. God, he hated drunks. How could anyone on this earth kill themselves when there was so much to prove, so many goals to achieve, so many battles to be fought and won?

He picked up the newspaper between thumb and forefinger. 'Dwight schemed to get me out of my own band. My career never recovered. It's my belief he used his power and success in the country music business to make sure I never worked again,' he read, his voice dripping with sarcasm. He sat forward in his chair in an attitude that was strangely threatening. He was powerfully built, like a baseball player with the hint of a weight problem, but lots of muscle, too. His face was storm-dark, belying its round, baby-faced appearance. His unblinking eyes roamed the room like dangerous tank turrets searching for any expression that might fall short of 'horror at the lie'.

'It's just so deeply unfair,' said the Polymark guy. 'She was drunk from dawn till dusk and dusk till dawn, and she could never sing a lick anyways. Not for the last twenty years.'

'Not ever,' barked Deacon, correcting the minion.

There was a chorus of 'yeahs'.

He sighed and looked towards Heaven, as if the ways of the Good Lord were mysterious indeed. He took a deep breath. This was not the first time. This was a weekly business. But it always hurt like hell. America was fascinated by health and celebrity. Exactly half its interests were his interests. The downside was the constant trial by tabloid, and the impossibility of stopping the lava flow of half truths, half lies and terminological inexactitudes that were spawned by America's lenient libel laws. You did not merely have to prove that what was written about you was untrue and damaging, you also had to prove malicious intent on the part of the publication. The attorney was right. To prove something as intangible as an intention in the secret mind of another was no easy thing to do. There had to be evidence, like a letter saying, 'I hate Dwight Deacon and am making up this lie specifically to damage him.' That was not the sort of letter that tabloid journalists were in the habit of writing.

'So, it's the usual pathetic response,' he said wearily. 'We call the friends, get Hazel Smith on board, sweet-talk the usual suspects. But I'll be answering questions on this one for the next fifteen years. More. Much more.'

A roomful of hearts missed a beat, and stomachs rolled. Was that how long they were all going to have to put up with the ego man? Still, it would mean the money was still rolling in if he was around for all those years . . . job security of sorts, promotion possibly, wives and mistresses partially pacified.

'We have denials with all the cred reporters . . . Dwight feels real sorry about poor Cassie whom he always admired . . . the sadness of alcoholism . . . dreadful disease . . . tried to help, but help always refused . . .' said the PR, hurrying his words.

'Shut the hell up and listen,' said Dwight, raising his hand for silence. 'Here's what we are going to do. Someone cassette this. Put out a Dwight Deacon release about Cassie. Loved her dearly. Admired her more than anyone. The soul of country. A sad depression. *Hint* at a drink problem. I did my best for her. Tried to take her along with me. Did for a while. You can't stop someone who is determined to self-destruct. Nobody can face the responsibility of the failure of their career. They need scapegoats. I was around, and I am happy to be hit on. I'm big enough, *man* enough, to take it. And she gave Dwight Deacon his start. Dwight Deacon will always be grateful for that. Dwight Deacon will never forget her, and he prays that the grace of God will go with her, and that she will find her happiness in Paradise.'

The notes of the press release had turned imperceptibly into a prayer, which had merged unnoticeably into a blessing. Dwight Deacon, star in the Heavens, had seemingly parted company with the earthly Dwight. He was talking about himself in the third person, and everyone in the room had the strange sensation he was talking about two different people.

Now, Dwight Deacon closed his eyes and breathed in deeply. Fame. All his life he had fought for it, and there was a sense in which he had achieved it. But, like the mirage in the desert, it moved away from you, as elusive as a rainbow, as unreal and intangible as a dream. Fame was the ghost in the machine. It was the soul to the body; the essence that could neither be touched nor captured. He had battled all his life to get to it, and there was nobody in the whole wide world except Dwight Deacon who didn't reckon he had achieved it. But fame was what other people had. It was never yours. It couldn't be owned. It was deeply and meaningfully relative. He had sold one hundred million albums, but there were seven billion people in the world. He had hardly started on owning the earth, and already they were plotting to take away what little he had. Paranoia coursed through him. The *National Examiner*. The people in this room.

Cassie Stewart, cold in the morgue. The competition out there taking up radio time that should be his, selling concert tickets that would deplete the fans' finances so there would be less for them to spend on his shows. Now this. The *National Examiner* had delivered a powerful dent to the image he had created.

Then Dwight Deacon called a stop to the whole unproductive business of thought. That was enough. Stop! He had to move on. Deal with it . . . that was his motto, and he had dealt with it. When next he spoke there was a sea change in him. It was as if yet another spirit had walked into his body and taken it over effortlessly. The aggression was gone, as if it had never been. The new Dwight Deacon was in homespun philosopher mode.

'Funny thing, suicide,' he said. His tone was conversational. The regulars knew a reminiscence was coming up. He often started a story like that: 'Funny place, Texas'; 'Funny emotion, guilt'. He lay back in his chair, suddenly relaxed by the subject of suicide. There was even a half smile around his mouth, hovering seemingly between melancholy and humour.

'I remember back in the old Tucson days playing a bar that had this waitress . . . best-looking girl you ever seen. She had a chest on her . . . like . . . well, ya know, amazing grace. Body like an angel, I swear. Saturday nights they had this wet T-shirt contest, and anyone could join in. Thirty-seven-buck prize. Every week the hard-assed rednecks would try and get this babe to enter the competition, and she was havin' none of it. She was a real strong girl, with a real neat personality to go with that body. She sure was bright. Never could understand why she was waitin' tables.' He looked around. They were hanging on his every word.

'Anyways, this one night . . . whether they got some Tequila into her or not . . . I dunno . . . she said she'd go for it. And it came down to her and this other girl I'd never seen before, who looked pretty darn good, too. And they stripped down to nothin' at all. The two of them just weren't fixin' to lose. I've never seen anythin' like that competition. Never anything, before or since. Both those girls wanted to win so bad. There were those two girls and these shit-faced hayseeds full of fightin' liquor just hollering for them to go the whole hog. An' it came to the prize, and the guy who owned this bar, the darkest, dank-est crap-hole you ever did see . . . he decided to split the prize fifty:fifty. That waitress, she went *berserk*, screamin' and yellin' and carryin' on like she'd been bitten by a rattlesnake. "Y'all seen my body for $18.50. Y'all seen my body for $18.50," she kept on yelling. I can hear her now . . .'

He tailed off. His face was faraway in some smoky hell of neon beer signs, amidst a sweating, swearing crowd of drinkers, and a naked lady who deserved better was shouting over the din.

'And two days later, she strung herself up in the rest room. Hanged herself. Dead. Suicide. Used a guitar string. An F, I think it was. Weren't no G.'

Quite suddenly there were tears in his eyes. He swallowed hard once, then twice. Nobody knew what to say because nobody knew what to think.

'You know,' said Dwight Deacon, and there was a catch in his voice, 'you know, in a way I felt responsible. I was the band. I was there. That girl was too good to strip off in that shithouse of a bar.'

He stood up suddenly, and there seemed to be a weight on his broad shoulders. Guilt. Shame. Something that Deacon didn't do.

'I'll catch you guys later,' he said in a quiet, contemplative voice, and he walked out of the room.

Nobody spoke. Everyone had seen yet another side of the extra-ordinary enigma that was Dwight Deacon. Was it a gentle side? Had he loved the girl? Or was it another exercise of his supreme ego . . . that anything that happened near or around him was his personal responsibility because of the power of his personality? 'Funny thing, suicide,' the story had started.

But everyone in the now seemingly empty room was thinking, 'Funny guy, Dwight Deacon.'

CHAPTER

TWENTY

Dwight closed the door behind him, and wiped a tear from his eye. Jeez. He hadn't thought about that girl in years. What had been going on in her head? He shook his. There were no answers to questions like that. Nobody knew what was going on in the minds of others. You just had to control the controllable things, keeping track of the bucks, and all the other stuff. He flopped down on the sofa and scooped up his black acoustic guitar. You never knew when a song would come and he needed to chill out from the scene next door. He struck a few chords at random, and listened for a tune. And the same thing happened again. The chords sequenced themselves round a melody he was finding increasingly difficult to get out of his mind.

> The time will come when our folks must die.
> But mine gave me something to remember them by,
> Now I'm soaring through the sky,
> They gave me roots to grow, and the wings to fly,
> Roots to grow, and wings to fly.

Darn, it was good! It was getting better. For some kids out there in fan land it could even be true. It certainly hadn't been for him, but it probably had for the kid who'd written it. He wondered who she was. He wished he'd not erased the name and telephone number that had been written on the tape in black marker. It had been a girl, that he knew. Some spunky kid had trespassed on his property, opened the door of his Range Rover, and stuck the tape into his cassette player. He hadn't come across that one before, and now he smiled. All singers in Nashville were slipped tapes at every hour of the day and night: in the john, on the street, some even got thrown up on to the stage with the roses and the underwear. You couldn't listen to them. Most were so bad they would pollute your mind with their mediocrity, and plagiarism suits were the curse of the industry. But this one he had heard by mistake, expecting Bob Seger and getting Ms X. 'Roots and Wings' . . . that had been the name of her song and it was maybe five weeks now, maybe more, and it wouldn't go away.

Dwight Deacon continued to play around the melody, experimenting with diversions, but none of them was as good as the original. There was something inescapable about the song. It had to be the way it was. Try as he might he couldn't improve on it. Dwight put down the guitar and placed both hands behind his neck. Once again he closed his eyes, so that he could think more clearly. He was going back to Nashville in the middle of his endless tour to record a CD. Some of the material was already laid down; fast up-tempo stuff that he was pleased with, and had a few singles in it . . . maybe two. But he needed a big weepy ballad. That was what he was short of. 'Roots and Wings' could be it. But did he own the copyright? No, the unknown girl did. But she had trespassed on his property, and she had broken into his car – at least she would have if he had locked it. Then she had left the tape. Was it therefore a gift? Almost certainly. Would she have taken the precaution of registering a packet with the tape inside, sending it to herself and keeping it sealed? That way the postmark would be proof that the song was created before that date. No way. This kid was an amateur with 'Roots and Wings' and the courage to take chances. That was in the song. It was about her, if she had written it. That made her interesting. Yet she didn't exist. She was out there somewhere in the shadows of the Nashville wishscape, dreaming out loud, with poetry in her soul.

Deacon shifted, suddenly uncomfortable on the wickedly comfortable leather sofa. Because he knew what he was going to do. The company had been begging him for more Dwight Deacon songs, ones he had written all by himself, words and lyrics, the Full Monty. The fans liked that, and what the fans liked they must get. Sacrifices must periodically be made to the god of fame. He made the decision, then and there. *He* had written 'Roots and Wings'. He had dreamed it up in the middle of the night. He had warbled it sleepily into the cassette recorder that all songwriters kept by their beds to catch the elusive songs that would be long lost to memory by the jingle-jangle morning. The faceless girl would never complain. If she did, who would believe her against the word of Mr Nashville himself, the one who made music that the town really loved . . . the magical sound of cash registering, the swish of banknotes being counted, the luscious clatter of slot-machines playing the big prizes?

Yeah. That was it. He'd play it for them as soon as they got back, and they would like his song, and love his creativity. It would be one more sign from Heaven that Dwight Deacon was not dead and would provide for Polymark for years to come.

CHAPTER

TWENTY-ONE

Aron Wallis's loft in the old part of Nashville looked out over the Cumberland river where First Street met Broadway. Through the big picture window which had once been a loading bay, he could look down into Fort Nashbrough, the 1930s replica of the eighteenth-century frontier fort. He could also see the suspension bridge that brought the Greyhound hopefuls to town. More to the point, across the river, he could make out the low rows of houses where his past and his future lay. Tomorrow he would be in one of them, Savanna by his side, the red-hot demo in his hand, and a brand new future would open for both of them. He breathed in deeply and let his breath shudder out of him in excitement and anticipation. 'Roots and Wings' was going to be a hit. Nobody who had heard it in the studio doubted that, and nor did he. It was a question of handling it. It was a question of how best to wind Pete up until he put maximum bucks on the table for a year's contract plus options. It wasn't just the money. The more they invested, the more they would have to run after their investment. That was how the music industry worked. If you bought, for peanuts, a so-called 'new kid' contract, you could afford to leave the song out there on the inhospitable slopes of radioland, and let it take its chances. If you were in deep, you unleashed the full force of your PR department on the hardened programmers and promoted with a capital 'P'. That way they knew you were a believer, and believing tended to be contagious. Tomorrow he hoped for a deal memorandum for at least one album, of which 'Roots' would be, he felt certain, the lead single. He would be going for an advance that was at the high end for a beginner. Also he wanted Savanna to avoid a 'pay-or-play' deal in which, for any reason at all, the record company can decide against making your record and pay you instead the miserable 'scale' rate per song of $271.73. Aron was aware of his conflict of interest. He was employed by Polymark. He should be trying to get Savanna as cheaply as possible. His heart was making him do the opposite. That was about as far as he had got. That . . . and inviting Savanna to dinner.

He looked at his watch. She wasn't late, but she wasn't early either. He walked over to the state-of-the-art music system and pushed the tape into the dual deck. When she walked through the door he wanted her song to be playing. Was it too soon to call it their song? He shook his head to still the thoughts that were rattling about inside. It was going to be difficult to separate business from pleasure in this situation. Aron didn't see himself as a Svengali. He had never created a star from nothing. He was instead the consummate professional. He was the man the big names wanted when they needed to try something a little different, kick-start a fading career, or leapfrog into a new direction. So this was fresh ground for him, and he couldn't help questioning his motivation. He was, after all, single and childless, after a marriage that had ended like a peculiarly banal country song, the sort of thing that Pete's receptionist might well have written. His wife, a fellow undergraduate at Cambridge whom he had worshipped, had been a sex addict, and he had been the last to find out what everybody else, following the rules, had failed to tell him. It was amazing how much he had learned about her since the divorce. Their life together hadn't been so much a lie as a fantasy dream sequence. Nothing had been as it seemed. No story had been anything but a lie. What would they have called it on amateur night at the 'No Hope Café'? 'Ain't Nobody as Blind as a Married Man.' He shook his head, and smiled as he thought about it. It was over now. Four years had just about rubbed out the emotions attached to the memories, but the experience had left him scarred as these things do. Women as a species were to him guilty until proven innocent, and even then they remained under suspicion. Was Savanna different? Well, she was young. There was quite an age difference. But she had about her that innocence that even his sorely tried emotions could recognise. She had worked hard enough to get into Columbia. That meant she had worked very hard indeed in this world, where the young worried now in the way the middle-aged had worried a few decades ago.

He walked over to the piano on which he kept the signed portraits of the stars he had worked with. Their heartfelt messages went way beyond the all-purpose good wishes that the fans got at Fan Fair. 'To Aron. I owe it all to you. You're a genius. Your friend Dwight Deacon.' That just about said it all. Anybody who had seen the message was gob-smacked by it. 'I owe it all to you.' From Dwight Deacon! Deacon calling someone other than himself a genius, without an exclamation mark and a couple of question marks, was so far out of character as to amount to a psychosis. People would pick it up and laugh, and say, 'Man, what was he on when he wrote that stuff, 'cos I'd for sure as hell like to try it?'

What made the difference? Why was Deacon so much bigger and more important than all the others put together? He sang well. He chose good songs. He had a great road show. The best. But that was only half the story, hardly the story at all. He had the magic. Somehow, his whole was far bigger than the sum of his parts. He wasn't really good-looking. Pleasant, yes. But not handsome. And he was really too heavy for the cowboy image, too cuddly, and way too clean. It was impossible to analyse, but even in the photograph the X-factor came through. The eyes had it. They seemed to follow you everywhere. Aron moved to one side, and yes, they were on to him. Then to the other, and they seemed to swivel after him. What were they saying? 'I need you to love me.' 'Please adore me, and together we can do anything, become anything.' But people hated to be needed. In Aron's experience women seemed to recoil from it, especially young pretty ones who liked a tough old time from their rangy, macho males. Yet women were the basis of Deacon's career. Aron tried again, as he had so many times, to analyse the man's appeal. It was what after all he did for a living – trying to calculate in advance what would work; trying to predict what people would like; seeking endlessly to find the mysterious ingredients of the musical recipe that would be universally accepted.

The doorbell cut into his speculations. How like Dwight Deacon to be able to take a red-blooded male's attention momentarily way from a girl like Savanna.

He hurried to the door.

She stood there looking much as he had seen her for the first time on the stage. Her clothes were more or less Nashville uniform, but the overall impression was what counted. That was summed up in one word. Energy. From the tip of her blonde hair to the points of her expensive brown lizard boots, Savanna Stone was peculiarly alive. It was as if she had been freshly charged at the mains. If she were one of those batteries that you could test with your fingers, the white line she generated would have run way off the scale.

'Hi, Savanna. Come on in.'

'Wow, so this is your pad. What a great view. This is like SoHo down South.'

'Yep, missy. I guess this building is even older than your Grandma's place at Belle Meade.'

'You must come out and see my grandma sometime.' She swivelled around, half smiling, aware that he had taken a mini-shot at her, testing her to see what her sense of humour was like. That was what this was all about. Getting to know you. It was the best part of any relationship, that time right at the beginning when everything was new and exciting. Things could go right, or wrong. Every smile, every gesture, nuance, tone of voice was a revelation about the other's character.

'Oh, they wouldn't have a record guy like me out at Belle Meade. I'd have to live out at Brentwood, Goodlettsville or Hendersonville, with the music people.'

He made it light. Somehow he gave the impression he transcended the social divide that still separated classy sheep from musical goats in Nashville, Tennessee.

'Nonsense. We have a country singer every other year now at the Swan Ball.'

She laughed at the ridiculousness of it all. But it was true. Johnny Cash had made the breakthrough a decade before, but the Belle Meade crowd her father's family came from still winced when people referred to Nashville as Music City, USA.

'Every *other* year?' said Aron with a laugh.

'Well, we don't want to go overboard, do we?' said Savanna, affecting a snobby Deep South accent, and striking a Scarlett O'Hara pose with her hand on her hip and a toss of her head.

'Tell you what,' said Aron. 'If we do a record contract tomorrow, you get to take me to the Swan Ball. How about that?'

'Top hat, white tie and tails?'

'I have nothing else in my closet.'

'Then it's a deal,' said Savanna.

Aron walked over to his stereo system and flicked a switch. Soon 'Roots and Wings' filled the huge room, bouncing off the polished teak floors, and the old red brick walls, and flowing round the comfortable but well designed modern furniture. Savanna swayed delightedly to the song. She could hardly believe she and her mother had written it, or that the voice, so throaty and full of country soul, was actually hers. It seemed like a con trick. This was somebody else singing. She tried to explain that to Aron, but he laughed away her doubts.

'They all say that when they hear the first tape,' he said, shouting above the music. 'This is the beginning of the new you, Savanna. The Savanna of myth, not reality. From now on there are two yous, and sometimes you'll be confused as hell just who you are. Fame is schizophrenia. Maybe one day you'll end up like Dwight Deacon. He calls his famous version DD, and talks about him in the third person. DD needs to talk to the President about that idea for a "Peace on Earth Day" and then he takes off his hat and says, "Jeez, I need to take a leak."'

Savanna walked over to the piano and picked up the 'DD' photograph. 'Mmm. Genius. I owe it all to you. Pretty impressive. Thank God he never used my song.'

'I'm sorry to disillusion you, but those guys never play those tapes. If they did, they wouldn't have time for anything else. They just bin 'em, and that's that. In fact, if he had decided to record it, that would have been worth a lot of money to you. If he used it on an album that went triple platinum, you'd pick up $180,000-plus. If he went single with it, you could retire right now.'

'But I don't want to retire,' said Savanna. 'I don't want the money. I mean, I don't want to sound like some brat, but I just have always somehow had money, you know. It's no big deal. What I want to be is right. Is listened to. Is to create and to make people happy. I just want that feedback. You know, that feeling of having an audience like you. I've done so little of that, but it feels so *good*.'

Her eyes danced as she talked, and she waved her hands in animated comment on her words. Her mouth was so expressive, her teeth so incredibly white and perfectly formed. Boy, she had it. She had *it*. And even though she didn't know, she was saying all the right things. To be a star only one thing mattered. Wanting it. Needing it. Settling for nothing else. The rest was smoke, mirrors, talent and a whole lot of luck. She'd articulated the most important part. The thrill of anonymous affection. That was the key ingredient. So many people wanted to impress their families, friends and loved ones. That was what drove the masses on. But a few wanted something subtly different. They wanted the unconditional love of strangers in a darkened auditorium, the very essence of that weird and wonderful thing called fame.

'You know, I bet he did hear my song,' Savanna said suddenly. 'Because you know what I did? I went out to his ranch one night, and his car was parked in the driveway, that souped-up Range Rover he drives. I stuck it in his tape deck.'

'You didn't!' Aron was genuinely amazed. 'Hell, you might have got shot, or eaten by the dogs he keeps out there at his ranch.'

'I sure did.'

'God almighty, Savanna. Thank God I found you. Looks like you were heading for the county jail.'

'Nah, I'd have talked my way out of it.'

Of course, that was true, and her confidence was so attractive, and so necessary if she was going to live up to his expectations of her.

'You know,' said Savanna, 'what I think it is that Deacon has?'

'The world wants to know, especially me,' said Aron.

'I think he's crazy,' said Savanna. 'You look at him and you sort of feel he's got this crazy passion just for you, like a total mad obsession. And it's not scary, because of course you don't know him, and he doesn't know you. But there's a spine-chilling quality to it, and a bisexuality, too. A sort of androgynous all-purpose all-consuming love for his fans. That's what those crazy eyes are saying. I'm going to get you. Have you. Own you, and there's not a thing that you can do about it. Maybe Shania does it a bit with that leather dominatrix look, and all those "I'm going to be tough on you" lyrics and "I couldn't care less" themes. Giving up freedom to someone stronger than yourself. You know, in the land of freedom, nobody really believes in freedom any more. It's like too much responsibility.'

'Did you take sociology, psychology, anthropology?' said Aron with a laugh. He was getting in deeper every moment, and he didn't know if that was cool or not. Business and pleasure had been mixed before in Nashville. Sometimes it was the most potent brew of all. Faith Hill and Tim McGraw's marriage had done each other's careers no harm at all. Neither had that of Shania and her star English record producer husband Mutte Lange. The music industry was riddled with examples: the Estefans; Sony's Mottola and Mariah Carey; Celine Dion and her genius promoter husband.

'Well, you know him, genius. What's he like?'

'Terrifying.'

'Why?'

'Because if he wanted me fired, I'd be fired.'

'No way.'

'Way.'

'The business is *that* cynical?'

'*All* businesses are that cynical.'

'So you sort of have to "handle" him.'

'Kid gloves.'

'One day maybe you'll have to "handle" me.' It sounded the very opposite of a threat.

Savanna liked Aron, more and more each moment. He was shy, and she had never been accused of that. He was quiet, talented, clever, and good-looking in a cool, understated way. He was also fun . . . fun to wind up a bit. She knew that he liked her, and Savanna was one of those high-self-respect girls who thought that showed good taste. It was those who were unsure of themselves who felt like they deserved a bad time from a fella, like those battered wives wandering from one wife-beater to another.

'If I ever get to handle you, maybe I won't bother putting on the kid gloves.' That was raising the ante plenty, and Savanna felt the beginnings of a blush. But she had started this and she wasn't sorry that she had.

'You mean bare hands?'

He just laughed. So did she. She had both her thumbs stuck in the pockets of her blue jeans, and she sort of leaned forward into the joke that was hardly a joke. Her breasts were firm against the pressed white cotton of her shirt. Her butt curved away, tight and turned up like it had been in the window of the Crazy C when he had first set eyes and ears on her.

He took a step towards her. She did not move back. This was very close. They both felt it. She was ready for him. She would kiss him. She wanted to. He knew it. And it wouldn't be the first time. The laughter sparkling in her eyes was changing to another emotion, and Aron knew that his own eyes mirrored it. But he also knew it was too soon. This must be savoured. So, instead, he reached forward and took her hand which she gladly gave him. It was cool, and soft, and he squeezed it and pulled her in towards him, in a gesture that was inside intimacy. She went with his flow, close within his space, but not touching his body. They hovered there for a moment, neither quite knowing what would happen, each ready for anything.

'You going to bare handle me?' she said. Her voice was husky, throaty like on the tape, like when she was singing. It was halfway between a question and an invitation.

He could smell the scent of her now, soap and some low-key perfume, understated, sophisticated. Better still, he could smell her breath as she spoke to him, fresh and smelling somehow of strawberries. He breathed in, trying not to show that he wanted the air that had been in her chest to be in his. His heart was hammering. His whole body was at maximum alert, sensitised, ready. Where he touched her hand it seemed they had merged. The cool had warmed. Their senses intertwined at the interface. Essences had joined. Souls communicated. Bodies seemed strangely irrelevant in this moment of promise.

He knew somehow not to go on. But it would happen. If not now, then at some other even more perfect moment. She, too, shared his certainty. She uncoiled from him, and he let her go only because he knew he could get her back. It had started in the museum, but now it had momentum.

It was called falling in love.

CHAPTER

TWENTY-TWO

Savanna tried to lie still in the dark, but the adrenaline was pumping like a creek after the rains. It seemed like the sweetest coincidence that her chance had arrived at the hands of Aron. She had learned so much about him the other night. He, too, was a fish out of water like she was . . . but a fish supremely capable of adapting to the new environment. His family was old, and he talked of them lovingly, and the fierce brilliance of his mind was always bobbing up, just when you thought he was a man who cared about little but country music. To some extent he was damaged goods. The wife had left her mark, but that was nice, too . . . that he could trust, that he had dared to commit, even if he might be shy of it a second time.

'Steph, are you awake?'

She had stayed at Steph's that night. She had somehow wanted to be near her roots. It was pitch-dark in the bedroom, but Savanna couldn't sleep.

'Sort of,' said Steph in a sleepy voice.

'I can't sleep.'

'It's called excitement, hon. I think I got some of it, too, on your account.'

'I mean, what if this guy says "no" tomorrow? He could. They do. It's the way it goes, isn't it?'

There was silence in the darkness. What Savanna said could not decently be denied, certainly not by Steph who had heard the 'N' word in every tone variation in the book . . . and a few that were not in the book.

Savanna shifted about in the small bed, waiting for some encouraging words.

'But look, this Aron guy is a player,' said Steph. I've looked him up. He's hot. He's *recently* hot. He's pulled old Newt Fulsome out of the grave, and turned him around. Fulsome's telling anybody who will listen that Aron Wallis saved his career. "Leaving Tucson" was bulleted at three in yesterday's *Billboard*, up from seven. It's got a shot at a one. That means Wallis is flavour of the week round here. And Vantage have paid out cash already, nothing signed. That's a first. They do newcomers. Cook's an old hand. The song is great. Just great. The demo is magic. I mean, how can they say "no"?'

'With the greatest of ease,' said Savanna. But Savanna wasn't really thinking of the demo just now, all she could think of was Aron. She had never felt like this in her life. She loved his dark looks, so opposite to hers, and his soft brown eyes that combined a wily innocence with a warmth that touched her in the heart. She tried to ask herself if she would have felt the same if he had been a banker, a poet, a butcher, a candlestick maker . . . and the answer was a reserved 'yes'. Because you couldn't wonder what people would be like if they were different. It was hard enough working out who they were when they were being themselves.

'Would you like him as much if he hadn't "discovered" you in the C?' said Steph, who it seemed to Savanna specialised in telepathy, or commonsense . . . the two being basically the same thing.

'Oh yeah, sure,' said Savanna. 'Well, probably. I guess it helped.' She laughed. Outside, the riverboat horn moaned in the misty blackness.

'But he has been a "gentleman" so far,' said Steph.

'He isn't gay,' said Savanna, cutting to the chase.

'No, I didn't mean that,' lied Steph. 'I mean he seems a gentleman, must be eye-openin' for him swimmin' with those sharks at Polymark.'

'I think he can give as good a nip as he gets,' said Savanna speculatively. There was something deep-down strong about Aron, that was belied by his well-dressed, non-macho appearance.

'Well, I sure look forward to hearin' all about that first nip.'

'I nipped him in the Hall of Fame.'

'Tongue nip?'

'Sort of wet . . . damp anyway . . . moist. I don't think I could swear to tongue. You have to get things right. It's half the fun.'

'Half?'

'Well, a hundredth anyway.'

'It's all working out so well, isn't it,' said Steph.

'It had better be,' said Savanna with feeling. 'That bastard tomorrow had better say "yes".'

'Be nice if the Polymark guy said "yes", too.'

'Oh, very funny.'

'Remember your guy works for Polymark, too.' Steph thought she might just put that one in. Getting started was the big thing, and nobody paid much for starters . . . but there were deals and deals. If Savanna was going to make it . . . if . . . then she mustn't sign anything that would tie her up to chickenfeed for the rest of her career. Although Savanna was hot for this guy, Steph's beady eyes hadn't run over him yet. Steph had been bitten on a couple of songwriting deals, and it was no fun.

Savanna was quiet for a minute. To be careful in this life was almost as much of a risk as to be a gambler, she thought. There weren't very many guys who made their first million on their sixtieth birthdays. She was so young now. If she screwed up, she could just turn around and do it all again. Not to dare was to lose. Not to chance was to fail. Not to trust was to be closed to opportunity. In matters of the heart, and in business, it was the same. You could go through life, roaring like a lion, at full tilt, head held high. Or you could creep through it like a mouse, sniffing for danger, twisting and turning to watch your back.

'Well, the fella likes your song, your voice, you . . . he can't be all bad,' said Steph. She had delivered her warning. There were knives in

Nashville as well as rhinestones and good ol' Southern fried everything.

'Thanks, Steph. I guess Dwight Deacon played for tips once.'

'Nope. Every "tip" was negotiated in triplicate, witnessed, signed
for . . . trussed up like a legal chicken.'

'Boy, is that guy a legend in his own lunchtime. But he passed on
my hit. That makes him fallible. I guess he did me a favour by not
picking it up.'

'You'd have made a fortune.'

'I'm going to do that anyway. What I want is a career.'

But it rankled, in the darkness, somehow. Deacon was no fool. He
was perhaps the shrewdest man in the entire world's music business.
He must have heard her song, yet he had passed on it. Why? Because
he didn't like it enough? There was no other explanation. Dwight
Deacon didn't think 'Roots and Wings' was hit material. It had to
dent a kid's confidence. How many things musical was Deacon
wrong about? Maybe he thought it was a girl's song. Maybe it was.
But guys had childhoods, too. Didn't they need 'Roots and Wings' as
badly as their sisters?

CHAPTER

TWENTY-THREE

The receptionist in Pete's office tried a fast one as Aron and Savanna hurried in for their appointment. 'I'm just an Okie, Singing Karaoke,' she trilled. 'Neat, huh?' Aron raced past her, half dragging Savanna by the hand in his wake lest her natural politeness should tempt her to linger.

'Baby, you get closer every day,' said Aron gravely as he swept past.

'He's up there, waiting on you. Thanks, hon,' said the girl. She meant 'thanks' for the encouragement.

Outside the office, Savanna stopped and straightened her immaculate hair. 'Do I look OK?'

'I'm trying not to think about it,' said Aron, with a grim smile. The enchanted evening before was still in the forefront of memory. Both had held back from what both had wanted because they needed the magic of anticipation to last longer. But they were on their way, and this meeting would cement their relationship. Neither had any real doubt that 'Roots and Wings' would sweep all before it. Pete Cook was no novice. He owned ten per cent of a Polymark subsidiary and effectively controlled the shots at it. He was Nashville's equivalent of a Hollywood green-light man.

'Come on in,' yelled Pete as they knocked, and he bounded round the big desk with its cargo of photographs of stars, family, and now the brand-new fishing boat.

'How did the sailfish run?' said Aron cunningly. Nashville needed its banter.

'Oh boy. Oh boy,' said Pete. 'I never looked forward to retirement until this minute. Well, wait a minute here, so this is Savanna.'

'Savanna Carson Stone. Tomorrow's Shania. Meet Pete Cook. Pete is in the artist discovery business. Knows more about country music than Hank Williams did.'

'Even though he died before I was born,' said Pete with a wink. But his bonhomie hardly hid the sizing-up process. Appearance counted for so much more nowadays than it ever had. And personality. He was waiting for the spark. He was watching Savanna closely. 'Aron tells me your family are from around here,' he said pleasantly.

'Yeah, but I hope that won't count against me.' She smiled a big open relaxed smile. It was the right kind of answer.

'We sure don't have nothing against Tennessee music or against Tennesseans here in Nashville, do we, Aron?' He laughed jovially, signalling that he already liked her. 'You want some water, a Coke, some coffee? This demo listening business is thirsty work.'

Savanna felt the squirt of adrenaline. Aron tried to hold on to his cool.

'You hear about all that trouble with Dwight?' he said.

'That tabloid stuff and Cassie's suicide?'

'Yeah. Not a pretty business.'

'That was so sad,' said Savanna.

She somehow wished sadness hadn't emerged as a topic right at this moment. But Cassie Stewart's death had made an impression. It was the unacceptable face of fame. It was the other side of the coin that was as ugly and defaced as the front side was bright and burnished. For every country legend beside his guitar-shaped pool, there were a score of drunks, derelicts and walking disasters of human beings who had been destroyed by the destruction of their dreams.

Pete Cook and Aron exchanged glances. Cassie Stewart's suicide might be 'sad', but the 'not a pretty business' referred to the tabloid attack on Deacon, the Polymark star.

'All I can say is Deacon's got balls of brass. Climbed right back into the saddle. Has a break on his tour, and he comes right back here and lays down half a dozen tracks on his new CD. I was over there this morning at the studio. One of those songs has single written all over it.'

'What's he calling that thing?' said Aron.

'The CD? "Homefires" is the working title. Based on the one they think will be the first single, thing called "You've Got to Go Away to Come Back Home". Real soulful. Slow ballad. Reaches deep. Deacon's about ready for another of those. The boys next door are *real* excited. "Ace of Hearts" will be a hard act to follow. But I wouldn't mind that problem . . . following a quadruple platinum.'

'It's sold four?' Aron was astonished.

'Will have done any time now. There's the Good Lord upstairs, and there's Dwight Deacon down here. Made me nervous just saying "good morning" to him and having those eyes of his look into me like he can X-ray my brain.' He turned to Savanna. 'So, little lady, Aron here says you can sing prettier than a nightingale, and he made me put my hand into my pocket and stake your demo. I never tried that one before!' He laughed in a not very reassuring way.

'Shall we get it on?' said Aron.

He reached into the pocket of his jacket and handed Pete the tape. 'This equipment isn't the greatest, but it'll do the job.'

The sound system in Pete's office might not have cut it in a recording studio. However, there were not many sound aficionados throughout the land who wouldn't cheerfully have traded their rigs for his.

Pete jabbed at the play button. He walked back behind his desk, and stuck his feet up on it, in relaxed listening mode. 'Roots and Wings', the volume cranked up nice and loud, filled the room.

'Real pretty voice,' he said, closing his eyes and swaying his head to the music. Still with his eyes closed, he then said, 'Real pretty tune.'

Aron's hand crept out for Savanna's below the desk, out of sight of Pete. She grabbed it gratefully in her nervousness, and he squeezed it tightly and gave her a little nod. Pete's closed eyes, complimentary remarks and head swaying motions were, apparently, good omens. Aron began to relax. He had seen executives switch off demo tapes after the first few bars, hovering by the machine before deciding whether or not they had the stomach to sit through the whole thing. But this was going smooth as honey. The sound was real neat, and the JBL speakers were doing justice to the demo's quality.

And then Pete opened his eyes, quite suddenly, as if he had been startled by something. It was as if he had forgotten a vitally important meeting, or remembered he had left the stove on at home. He sat bolt upright in his chair, and his eyes widened. 'Wait a minute,' he said. And then, 'What is this?'

Savanna stared at Aron. Aron stared at Pete. What on earth was going on? Pete now looked as if he had been stung by a wasp.

'What's what?' said Aron, as 'Roots and Wings' continued to fill the room.

Pete Cook's face was undergoing a series of contortions. Puzzlement merged into frank shock, which slowly became surprise. Bewilderment gave way to a mini-smile, the sort of weak one you just about managed when somebody had made a joke in poor taste. None of these expressions had anything to do with his original ones when the song had begun to play. They were about as appropriate and as welcome as ants in pants.

'It's a joke, right?' said Pete, his eyes glinting strangely.

'What is a joke?' said Aron. For one milli-second, he wondered if this was Pete's idiosyncratic way of saying he didn't like the song. But that was impossible. Pete was a gentleman, and the song was great.

'This is Dwight Deacon's song, with a few of the words changed. Right? It's a cover. She covered "You've Got to Go Away to Come Back Home".'

He said the last sentence as if a supreme blasphemy had been per-petrated. And he looked at Aron askance, as if to say, 'How could you, with all your experience of the way things are done in this town, possibly be a party to sacrilegious nonsense like this?'

'It's my song,' said Savanna. 'I wrote it with my mother, years ago. I've sung it a thousand times. More.'

Now Pete's face was a mask of confusion and disbelief. He leaned forward in his chair.

'Listen, Aron, I don't know what this shit is, and maybe I am having some sort of a mental crisis here, but I've just been over at Soundsplash at Deacon's recording session, and this here damned song is going to be his single "You've Got to Go Away to Come Back Home". I don't know . . . there's maybe a C minor for a C, and G7 for a G here and there, but that song is this song. And Deacon wrote it, words and lyrics. He told me with his own lips. Said he thought it up when he was alone one night on tour. Told me how he remembered his mommy giving him some bullshit about having a firm base to build on . . . I don't know. It came with a whole story attached.'

'He stole it,' said Savanna. 'If it's the same, he stole it,' she repeated. Her hand flew to her mouth. She had put it in his tape deck. Oh, God, he had heard it after all, and he had simply stolen it. She turned to Aron. His eyes were open wide; he was thinking exactly the same thing. But Aron was several steps further on into the game. Dwight Deacon was claiming the song as his. He was recording it on an album, whose title seemed to reflect that this song would be its lead single. That meant one thing. Nobody on God's earth, or in Nashville, which was basically the same thing, was going to stand up and call him a liar.

'Deacon doesn't steal songs,' said Pete harshly. 'You can't say things like that in this office.' He made as if to stand up.

Aron put up his hand. He knew this was a minefield. Pete already had the look of a hunted man. 'Look, Pete, listen to me. Trust me. We've known each other a long time. Nothing goes outside this room, OK?'

'But if he stole my song . . .' said Savanna.

'Savanna, *please*!' snapped Aron. 'Let me handle this. Please! Look, Pete. Here it is. A few weeks ago, Savanna went out to Deacon's place. She had a raw tape of her song, and she wanted him to hear it. She didn't know a thing about the way things get done in this town. She stuck the tape in the deck in his car. She never heard a thing from him. That was it. But she told me about. That's how this thing must have happened. Maybe Deacon forgot he had heard the song, but it stuck in his memory, you know, the subliminal thing. Nothing is totally original. He probably didn't even realise he had heard the song before.'

Pete Cook started to calm. Only one thing was impossible. It was simply not possible that Dwight Deacon should be accused by him, or by someone with the remotest connection to him, of stealing songs. That would have one certain consequence. He would be fired. He would be obliterated by a thunderbolt from the skies. All hopes of fishing in the Gulf Stream during a happy retirement, all hopes *period*, would be terminated. Deacon was Polymark's profits. Deacon was not a reasonable man. He was a career murderer, and well known to be. All round Music Row there were people who had bought trampolines so that when Deacon shouted 'jump' they could put on a decent show.

Aron had offered an 'out'. Deacon had not consciously copied the song. But it would be far cleaner, far safer, if the party line could be that this no-hope hustler of a girl had somehow heard Deacon's song and tried to rip it off. Yes, that would be a far safer line of approach. Pete would get these two out of his office, and ring Deacon's people then and there. 'I thought you should be the first to know. Thank God it was me and nobody else she came to. Thank God, I was there at your session and remembered that brilliant tune. No. No problem, Dwight. What are friends for? Yeah, the lawyers, that's the way to do it. Put the Polymark boys on to her. Jeez! The things kids try to get away with nowadays.'

But even as he dreamed up the conversation, Pete recognised its impossibility. Dwight Deacon had been unusually talkative this morning in the studio, and he'd talked up a storm about the song. 'Never played it before, Pete. Never even to myself. Can you believe that? All up here,' and he had touched his head, where the bald patch was usually covered by the black hat. 'Never wrote it down, not on the chord system, nowhere. Came to me from Heaven, and the Good God produced it today. Ain't that something? Makes one a believer all over again. Praise the Lord.' If Deacon was telling the truth there was no way this kid could have heard it and stolen it.

He sat back in his chair. Aron and he knew the implications of what had happened. The girl did not. Could not. He ran his hand through his thick grey hair in desperation. He supposed he must have known worse moments. He couldn't recall them.

'No proof she owns the copyright,' he said.

'None,' Aron confirmed. 'But it's hers. Believe me.' He paused. 'Coincidence,' he tried.

Pete Cook shook his head. 'Identical. Same song,' he said. And then, 'Oh, shit, we got one helluva problem here.'

CHAPTER

TWENTY-FOUR

Savanna curled up on the bed and wrapped the blanket around her. Jeez, it was cold! Cold as poverty. She propped her mother's diary on her knee, getting ready to open it. She rationed herself, like a child with candy. There was so much wisdom, and so much love between its pages. She felt like a miser counting out the pennies that were her mother's words.

Life is so strange, my darling Savanna. You never know what is going to happen, but you always think you do. I thought I would be a doctor at Vanderbilt, and I ended up working in the admissions office to help pay Luke's medical bills. So then I thought I would be a secretary, or a clerk, while I worked on being a singer, and then along came Dad, and I was rich and married into a grand old Tennessee family. Nothing planned. Just the Good Lord dealing cards. Probably there were Carsons in the same boat from England as the Stones, but in steerage, not first class, and luckily it wasn't the *Titanic*! You know what brought that home to me . . . Grandma Stone. I was terrified the first time I met her, but I ended up adoring her. More commonsense in her little finger than the rest of the family put together. Remember that, darling. When you are in a fix, ask her advice. You will be. Everyone is sooner or later, and it's the problems that make you strong and worthwhile. That first time

Jason picked us up at the airport, he called me 'Mrs LeAnne'. I sat in the back of this big old Cadillac that seemed like it was a hundred years old, and I was in this off-the-peg frock and I was dreading eating with all those knives and forks I didn't know how to use properly, or when, or for what. The young master had married the girl from the wrong side of the tracks, and I expected Harbour Court to be like a vast, velvet-lined torture chamber. And there in this huge marble hallway, big as a railway station, was little old Granny. She said, 'Welcome to the family, LeAnne. Welcome to your home.' And she gave a hug, a tight one, a real one, although she was frail even then. And she said, 'I never thought Henry would marry a girl as pretty as you. Always had him down for a mealy-mouthed mouse with peanut butter for brains.' And Dad got cross and Grandma just laughed at him, and took me in and gave me a Bourbon that took the top of my head off. I've never been so relieved in all my life. When you meet a man, Savanna, take him to see Grandma, and watch out if she says he's no good!

Savanna had to laugh, although as always there was mist in her eyes when she read the diaries. Well, she was in a fix right now. And she had a man in her life. It was weird how everything in the diaries seemed to apply to her here and now. That morning, a terrible thing had happened. Not only had the demo been turned down, her song had been stolen. By someone who, in this town, was as powerful as the President in Washington. Aron had tried to explain to her the implications of what had happened. She could see the situation only in black and white, right and wrong terms, but he had been trying to persuade her that there were all sorts of shades of grey. Deacon had acted like a thief, but the theory seemed to be that he was allowed to steal, because he was so special. If she stood up for her rights, the consequences would apparently be appalling for everyone, chiefly Savanna.

So much for American justice and the American way. But although he had tried to explain the realities, she had seen the fury inside Aron

Wallis. He, too, was appalled by what had happened. However, he was trying to keep the lid on her steam. He didn't want her to do anything that she would regret later as a result of her failing to understand the odd way things happened in Nashville. He had asked her to give him a few hours. He would talk to some people, and see what could be done. In other words, a deal of some kind. But in Savanna's world, copyright theft was not something about which you 'dealt'. She could feel Aron being pulled in two directions . . . by his natural sense of honour and his feelings for her, and by the music world in which he lived and earned his living.

She so desperately needed to get some perspective on her life, on Aron and her non-existent career. Might this be the time to eat humble pie and call her grandma? Ask her if she could come and see her in Belle Meade, perhaps bring Aron and Stephanie?

She picked up the telephone. The butler answered. Mrs Stone was out in the garden doing something to the roses to prepare them for winter. At eighty-six, with the wind-chill pushing the temperature down towards zero!

'Would you tell her I'm in town and ask her if I could bring my cousin and a male friend for dinner. Pot luck. Nothing grand.'

'Certainly, Miss Savanna.'

She left the telephone number She knew the big old house was stiff with under-occupied servants. Dinner for Steph, Aron, Savanna and Grandma would present no problems at all. The three of them had planned to meet anyway. There was no reason at all why it shouldn't be in Belle Meade.

Next, she called Aron. He sounded harassed in his office at Polymark. 'I'm not making much headway,' he said. 'I never knew there was so much fear in this town.' He sounded relieved when she didn't push him for more information, and more relieved still when she wanted to firm up dinner. 'You're asking me to meet your family?' he said, just a trace of humour in his voice.

'Yup, best behaviour time. Clean time.' Savanna laughed, glad that she was able to after such a depressing day. She simply couldn't get her mind around the fact that Deacon was going to pretend her and her mother's song was his. It was the sort of thing that she had thought couldn't happen, but then she reminded herself it wasn't unusual for people to sue famous singers for plagiarism.

'Shall I pick you up at your cousin's house?'

She gave him the address and explained where he could find it. The tumble-down termite-infested wooden house would be an enormous contrast to Harbour Court in Belle Meade. Aron Wallis would be getting the full bird's-eye view of the way her family straddled the great divide between the 'haves' and the 'have-nots'.

The telephone rang almost immediately she had put it down.

'Savanna, it's Grandma. How come you're in Nashville and not staying with me? You had a row with your father?' She spoke loudly as deaf people often do. As always she cut right to the point.

'Hi, Grandma. How are you?'

'Still alive. I think that's supposed to be good. So you're coming to dinner. With a cousin, and a man! Wonderful. We can all get drunk. Haven't had any young people in here for an age. I long to hear about all the horrible things that are happening amongst today's youth. Make me feel smug. You all right, Savanna?'

She added the last bit sharply. God, she was shrewd. She was asking if trouble was brewing and if that was the reason for the visit.

'Fine, Grandma. Nothing that I can't handle.'

'That son of mine who doubles as your father was bleating on about you dropping out of university. Wanting to be a singer. Sick as a dog about it, he is. 'Spect he told you.'

'Uh-oh!' said Savanna.

'Good for you, I said. Far too much education about nowadays. Expensive rubbish, that's all you pick up at those Ivy League schools. Other ones, too, I imagine. Only useful thing you learn is to hold your liquor. Look at your father, poking around in people's chests all day. Interferin' with the Lord's timetable, I say. When it's time, you go, and no nonsense. What's the man's name?'

Savanna was laughing with relief. It was so good to have Grandma on her side. Her father, who was not taking Savanna's calls right now, was terrified of Grandma.

'The man who's coming to dinner? Aron Wallis. He's a record producer. A very good one.'

'That's a Southern name,' said Grandma.

'I think he's in the Social Register, Grandma,' Savanna said with a laugh.

'Got it propping up the top of my bed to stop the acid coming up into my gullet at night. Doc Smedley told me it helps if you sleep on a slope. Works about as well as brandy and milk. So what time are you coming? Better get here early so we can all get to know each other before the food. Don't like to eat in front of strangers. Bad for the indigestion. Most things are.'

'We'll come in plenty of time. Longing to see you, Grandma.'

'The only thing about the singing business,' said Grandma, 'is that it's full of crooks,' and she put down the telephone.

CHAPTER

TWENTY-FIVE

Aron knew Steph's song, and the two were singing 'Patiently Waiting' in the front seats of the BMW, Savanna happy to be scrunched up in the back. She wanted her cousin, and the guy she was on the edges of thinking about as 'her man', to get along . . . and they were. She had thought they would. Already there was real warmth in the car. The evening at Grandma's looked set fair.

'Left here. Here. There!' shouted Savanna as they overshot the turning. Aron backed up, and soon they were travelling down the broad streets of Belle Meade, lined with dogwood trees. Great mansions stretched off on either side, separated from each other by maybe a quarter mile of gardens. Then there was the familiar driveway, with its black iron gates drawn back against discreet stone columns. Gravel crunched beneath the wheels and silence descended in the car as expectations rose.

'I haven't been here for so many years,' said Steph. 'As a child I remember it as a castle.'

'Wind down the windows, Aron,' said Savanna excitedly. She wanted him to see the house in which she had been born. It was like sharing an intimacy. The scent of the dying gardenias, brown now, no longer milky white, wafted in to merge with the luxurious leather of the car. It was the sweet fragrance of old Dixie, once driven down, but now rising again. On either side of them, banks of rhododendrons, their leaves falling and rotting, flourished in the rich soil, a faded quilt of once-bright colours. Then, around a bend in the drive-way, was the old house itself, Harbour Court. If buildings could be self-satisfied this one was, its Palladian ante-bellum splendour made more gracious, far from withered, by time. Aron, whose own house predated the war, speculated how many times it would fit inside this one. As a Southerner, he wondered what deal with the Yankees had saved it after Shiloh and the fall of Nashville to the Union. The South was littered with architectural gems that had survived William Tecumseh Sherman's destructive march through burning Atlanta to the sea because sweet-talking ancestors had found the right connec-tions with the hated, but victorious enemy. Savannah, Aron's home town, Sherman had saved on a whim, 'giving it' to President Lincoln as a 'gift'.

He parked the car a reasonable distance from the steps that led up to the front door, and then set about getting the ladies out. They had all dressed for the occasion, Savanna in a wickedly short black dress that turned her emergence from the cramped confines of the back seat into a deeply erotic performance. Steph had a similar, but longer, dark blue dress, whose shininess said it had seen heavy duty. Aron was safe as the house itself in a Savile Row suit he had treated him-self to while at Cambridge. He knew Southern grandmas. However much personality they possessed, the snobbery of the old South was impossible totally to eliminate.

Forrest, the butler, in dark coat, black tie and pinstriped pants, opened the door as if by magic as they reached it. Aron stood back to let the girls in.

'Good evening, Miss Savanna,' said the butler. 'How very nice to see you, miss, and looking so well, if I may say so. And is this Miss Stephanie? You won't remember me, but I remember you when you were a little girl.'

Forrest led the way and they clicked and clacked across the faded marble, past the gracious curved stairway, dominated by its old Flemish tapestry and topped by a domed ceiling, with chandelier and intricate Georgian cornices. Aron took in the ancestors that stared down at him accusingly. Much like his own, they sat in chairs next to tables with books, globes and eye-glasses upon them. In future generations these would probably be replaced by mobile phones, computer attachments, maybe bottles of 'feel good' pills. The men wore mostly brown suits. The women's uniform seemed to be fur coats, indicating that sitting for portraits was a cold experience, and the frosty temperature seemed to have transferred its effect to their eyes, which watched Aron carefully as he walked past them. Were they judging his genes? Wondering whether one day he would become one of them? If so, they didn't seem reassured by the prospect. Savanna sashayed in front of him, her bottom accentuated by the tight black dress she wore, its swaying motion encouraged by her fashionably high and thick platform shoes. Aron thought he wouldn't mind spending eternity on the walls of Harbour Court. It seemed a small price to pay for Savanna.

The library opened up before them, rich Eastern carpets, old cherry-wood panelling, chandeliers and yet more ancestors dotted around the walls. The books looked as if they had been bought long, long ago by length rather than individual selection.

Grandma Stone, looking a bit like Whistler's mother, was sitting in a comfortable wing-back chair by a crackling fire as they entered the room.

Savanna rushed over to kiss and hug her.

'And this is . . .' said Grandma.

'Oh, this is Mr Aron Wallis. My grandmother, Mrs Stone.'

'Mary Stone,' said Grandma, extending a wrinkled hand. 'Is that Wallis with an "ace" or an "is"?'

Aron was acutely aware that there was a right and wrong answer to this seemingly artless question.

'Is,' he said. 'My family is from Savannah.'

Grandma nodded. Nothing the matter with Savannah.

'I don't believe I know your people,' she said. 'But then most of the people I know are dead.'

'And this is my cousin Steph who has been here before as a child.'

'Hello, Stephanie, dear. I won't say I remember you, because all children look alike to me, but welcome anyway. Your aunt was a great favourite of mine, God rest her soul. Best thing that ever happened to this family in the last hundred years. Gave me my sweet Savanna.' She squeezed her granddaughter's hand, and eyed Aron speculatively, a bit like one might a stud bull. He could dress all right. That looked like an English suit with its box cut and square shoulders, the pants longer than Americans would wear them.

'What may we get you to drink, sir?'

'Bourbon, please, ma'am.' He felt like he was going to need one.

'And Stephanie?'

Stephanie chose Coke, aware that it was not the right answer, despite the fact that Coca-Cola had been invented in Atlanta the year after Lee surrendered to Grant at Appomattox.

'I'll join Mr Wallis in a Bourbon,' the old lady said firmly. 'And don't drown it, Forrest. It's nice to share a glass of Tennessee sour with a gentleman for a change. Not enough men in this house for too long. That's the trouble with us women being the stronger sex. The men drop dead and leave us.' She laughed, quite happy around the subject of death, perhaps quite looking forward to the peace that her own would bring.

Aron was warming to her. She might not know his people, but she didn't come across as a snob. She looked near to ninety, and yet she was telling the butler not to water down her Bourbon. Her ancestors would have fought like lions at Chattanooga. She smelled strongly of Chanel Number 5, and the stone of her diamond engagement ring looked as if it weighed more than her scrawny forearm. Her dress was of ancient lace, and her grey hair was piled high by somebody who would have visited the house for that single purpose. She looked incredibly rich and classy, but she also looked as if she would know a hard time if she saw one.

'What are you drinking, Savanna?'

'Mint Julep, please. One of your specials, Forrest,' she added to the butler.

At Harbour Court, they were made the traditional way – twelve sprigs of mint covered with powdered sugar and crushed in a bowl with a pestle. Half the crushed mint and liquid were then placed in the bottom of a sterling-silver tankard which was then filled with finely crushed ice. The rest of the crushed mint was added and whiskey poured over it until the glass was brimming. The tankard was then placed in the icebox for a minimum of two hours, and when ready to serve, it was decorated with powdered sugar and fresh mint sprigs.

Forrest had been anticipating the order and Mint Juleps were ready as they always were when there were guests. If there was no call for them, he drank them himself, like a priest dealing with the left-over communion wine.

'Now you come and sit here by the fire with me, Mr Wallis, and tell me anything you like. It's downright quiet round here nowadays. Heck, I feel like a darn good conversation with somebody who doesn't work for me.'

Aron sat down in the other chair by the fire. It would have been old Mr Stone's chair. Savanna's grandfather stared down at them both from above the mantel, his expression registering mild disapproval, his hand resting on the head of a favourite bird dog.

'Your home is magnificent,' tried Aron.

'Why, thank you, sir. It's been home to us for quite a time now. After the second fight, when Nashville was taken by the Union, we were lucky enough to have a distant cousin who was a major-general in command of the blue-belly First Corps. He commandeered the house and prevented it being wrecked. He and his family never did get invited back since, though. There's about three branches of the family tree buried out there at Shiloh.'

Aron felt the surreality of it. It was history to Savanna and him, but to people like Grandma these were not so distant personal memories. Her grandparents would have lived through it, or died in it, with bitter tales to tell the grandchildren round this very fire. His family had moved South more recently, but to the Stones a grudge dating back to the Civil War would still rankle like a Balkan feud.

The Bourbons, the Mint Julep and Steph's Coke arrived on a silver salver in record time. Aron took the crystal goblet, heavy cut glass that might have been Waterford, and raised it to his host. 'It's a real pleasure to be here, Mrs Stone.'

'There you are, I knew Savanna would end up with somebody with good manners.'

She raised her glass to him and then drank surprisingly deep on it. Grandma was going to have a high old time tonight. Aron, too, was beginning to enjoy himself. He had been in private houses as grand as this, but not many. The country music megastars that he knew had the money to buy taste like this from some 'Southern Living' designer. But none of them had the nerve to try it . . . and it would have looked somehow wrong. One platinum record, one copy of *Billboard*, one guitar would have ruined the timeless effect of the house.

'Grandma, I'm going to show Steph my old nursery, OK? Will you two be all right for a few minutes?'

Grandma waved her away with the Bourbon. 'Don't hurry back, dear. Mr Wallis and I are going to sit here and have a couple of glasses of whiskey and shoot the breeze.'

'So,' she said, the moment they were gone, leaning forward conspiratorially in her chair. 'Is she any good?' And she winked.

For one dreadful second, Aron was not sure what the question meant.

'At the singing,' prompted Grandma.

'Oh, oh, yes, indeed she is, Mrs Stone. She is very, very good. I think she has what it takes to be a big success.'

'Are you a success? Savanna says you are.'

He laughed at her directness. 'Yes, I think I would have to say I am. I've worked with the top people.'

'In other words, you know what you are talking about. Are you in love with her? That can affect a man's judgement, you know. That's the only reason I ask,' said Grandma with a slow smile.

'Savanna is a very pretty girl with a wonderful personality, but that doesn't influence my opinion of her singing voice, her talent, and her whole persona as a potential songwriter and singer.'

Grandma nodded, seemingly satisfied with the answer. 'Well, her mother sure could sing, and Savanna as a child, so I'm not surprised. Of course, my son wants her to be a doctor. He's gotten himself into a terrible state about the whole business. Won't speak to her. I never could understand the attraction to medicine. Too many doctors. Too many people pretending to be ill. Somewhere between the frontier and the New Deal, we turned into a nation of hypochondriacs. Everyone wants to live for ever, have sex for ever, rush about making money for ever. Way I see it, the trick in life is to make people happy, not just healthy. Singers do that, don't they? What's the matter with being a singer? Savanna's never going to starve unless the Treasury stops paying interest. Sing is what I say, if that's what she wants.'

'I can see how it must be a disappointment to your son. My family were not over the moon when I wanted to be a record producer.'

'Nope. Not what a nice boy goes and does,' said Grandma with a laugh. 'But it's not the end of the world. When I was young, half the old men were missing legs, arms and eyes and other bits and pieces. And there's my Henry like a chicken with his head cut off on account Savanna doesn't want to spend the rest of her life getting sued and filling forms for insurance companies. Two decent wars I've lived through, not counting those sideshows in Korea and Vietnam, and a son of mine won't talk to his daughter because she wants to be a country singer. And he thinks *I've* lost my mind.'

Aron laughed. It was true. The material world had lost its perspective. Although, to give his parents their due, they hadn't bothered much about *his* career move.

Grandma's Bourbon had gone. Aron's was hardly half finished. 'Drink up, young man,' said Grandma briskly. 'Or is that Bourbon not to your liking? It's Rebel Yell whiskey. You ever had that brand before? I get it through the United Daughters of the Confederacy.'

As if on cue, the butler reappeared, clearly used to the speed of Mrs Stone's drinking. Aron's own half-finished glass was swept from his hand to be freshened up in case the ice had melted and diluted the spirit. Aron took a grip on himself. *This* was the Deep South. Music Row and Downtown Nashville, where they drank as much Perrier as anything else, was hardly a part of it. Good ol' boys had to be able to drink.

'Never tried Rebel Yell,' said Aron. 'But it's smooth. Very good.'

'It's stirring, that's what it is. You know they invented that yell at First Bull Run. Apparently, Lee used to say it was worth ten thousand men. Don't know when they invented the whiskey.'

'What was Savanna's mom like?'

'Fresh air,' said Grandma, her face lighting up. 'Beautiful. Clever. Kind. Pure country from Pigeon Forge. Hill folk. Carson, they were called. My son was lucky to get her. He was a good-looking boy, and clever, but frankly I always found him a little dull. But LeAnne was bright as a daisy in a cornfield. Had a place at Vanderbilt Medical School, but gave it up to earn money for her sick brother's medical treatment. Helluva girl. And Savanna is just like her. She might not have been from a grand family, but it was a big old one, and the Stones needed some new blood with a bit of a kick to it. Beginning to run a bit sluggish, it was, like a stream drying up in summer. Henry was an intern at Vandy. LeAnne worked in one of the offices, and he set his cap at her. Later he got her little brother transferred up to Sloan-Kettering in New York, and they gave him everything medical that anyone had ever dreamed up. 'Course, he died anyway. People do. But she'd married him . . . out of gratitude as much as anything else, I imagine. And she bore him Savanna and put up with him all these years. Then she went and died, when she was the sort of person that should have lived for ever.'

Suddenly Grandma was quiet, staring away into the fireplace.

'You know,' she said, 'I think I loved her more than my own son, Henry.'

At which point, Savanna and Steph, laughing loudly, returned. The butler followed on their heels.

'Dinner is served,' said Forrest.

CHAPTER

TWENTY-SIX

Aron's heart was in overdrive. He had the AC on maximum, but he was sweating like a pig. Why were the things in life that were good for you designed to be so unpleasant? Exercise was the prime example, and he cursed inwardly as he tried to hold the split time on the rowing machine steady at 146. He looked out at the Cumberland River, meandering so slowly underneath the bridge. The contrast was painful. Five thousand metres and he had 1,000 left to do. Oh, Jesus. But he got there. He always did. It was the final straight that was the hardest part. Then he was finished, the race with himself over. And he hadn't moved a single inch. A bit like life, really. He stood up, feeling a little sick and a little faint. Both were good on the no-pain, no-gain principle. He wiped his face down with the towel, and thought briefly of vanity. He had had a regular exercise programme before Savanna, but was it with a Savanna figure in mind? And had he increased his distance to 5,000 from 4,000 on account of her? Probably!

He thought back to the night before. The dining room at Harbour Court certainly had not been its least grand reception room, and the first fast ball had been Grandma asking him to say grace. All he had been able to think of at first was 'Good grub, good meat, Good God, let's eat', but he had finally managed the one they said at Trinity, Cambridge: 'For what we are about to receive may the Lord make us truly thankful.' To which Grandma had responded, 'So you're an Anglican?' as the butler had poured pink champagne into Baccarat glasses and the formal dinner had begun. A huge silver bowl of seafood gumbo with fire powder and Zatarain's had been passed round the faded mahogany table from which leaves had been removed to make for greater intimacy. The gumbo was hotter than hellfire and Grandma had watched him carefully to see just how Southern his digestive system was. Savanna, noticing her interest, had chimed in, 'Don't worry, Grandma, Aron's family have been here long enough to know to put Tabasco on vanilla ice-cream.'

Aron had smiled wanly through the firestorm in his throat, managing to put some of it out with the champagne. Then Savanna had raised the ante by saying in a conversational manner, 'Oh, Grandma, there was something we wanted to ask your advice about. There's a famous singer in Nashville called Dwight Deacon, and he's stolen one of my songs. One that Mother and I wrote. The man is saying he wrote it himself.'

'Told you the music business was full of crooks,' said Grandma. 'Present company excluded,' she added without quite enough conviction.

They had explained the situation, but old Mrs Stone had simply not been able to understand why and how a man like Deacon could not, and would not, be punished for doing a dishonourable thing, and the situation rectified. Her whole life had been about honour and the interpretation of it. Her family's men had died for honour. Their bones filled the fields of Tennessee. The vast majority of the Confederate Army had never owned a slave. They had fought not to overthrow the United States Government, but for the right to secede from it, and run their own affairs like the Bosnians, the Kosovans, the Chechnyans. So how come this Yankee carpetbagger who called himself a cowboy, whatever that was, could steal a song that belonged to her granddaughter and not be made to give it back? In vain, Savanna and Aron had tried to explain that it was to do with record sales . . .

'But that's about money,' Grandma had insisted. 'What's money got to do with a man stealing what isn't his?'

It had been an all but unanswerable question. Because of the culture we live in? Because honour doesn't matter any more? Because only winning matters and money is the method of keeping the score and determining who emerges the victor?

'What if this Deacon was a no-hope drifter with a voice like a toad and face like a wart-hog? Is he allowed to steal Savanna's song then?'

Grandma asked the good ones. No, of course not. He gets drummed out of town, his card marked, and if anyone bothers to remember him they call him a crook, Aron had thought. But they had all been looking at him then. He was management of sorts. A producer. He was an employee of a company that would commit little short of murder to keep their megastar sweet.

'Aron's on my side,' Savanna had said, 'but if I get an attorney and file a breach of copyright on Deacon, I apparently become an outlaw in Nashville . . . and not an outlaw like Willie and Waylon and the boys. I am out of the music business for good. I couldn't record a hip-hop song. Couldn't invent an African-American ancestor and float a rap thing. I am history. Aron is going to try to talk to Deacon, but he's taking his career in his hands even if he does that.'

But Grandma's eyes had said that was hardly enough. 'Pistols at dawn' would have been her solution, as the Trout Amandine with the Alexander Valley Chardonnay Jordan replaced the champagne and the shrimp gumbo. Failing that, a halfway honourable man would have resigned from the company rather than work for people who condoned theft amongst their high and mighty. So what he'd be out of a job? At least he would have his self-respect intact.

The telephone cut into Aron's far from comfortable memories. He hoped it was Savanna, but it wasn't. It was a call from on high. What's more, Mike Gramm who ran Polymark Records was calling Aron directly. It was Mike himself on the line, not his assistant or his secretary.

'Aron. Mike Gramm. How are you?'

'Mike. I'm well. I'm well.'

'You busy?'

'Right now?'

'Yeah.'

'Not really.'

'Any chance you getting over to my office right away?'

'Sure.'

The foreboding was strong. It was hardly unheard of for Gramm to summon him to a meeting, but not in person . . . and there was usually an explanation . . . to discuss a contract, the handling of an artist, the marketing of a CD. Costs-in-general was a regular topic.

'How long will it take you to get over here. Twenty?'

'I'm on my way, Mike.'

Aron sat down and wondered what was going on. Had Pete Cook talked? It was possible, but unlikely.

He called him anyway.

'Pete? Aron. Listen, I've got a mystery meeting with Gramm in ten minutes. Any idea what it's about?'

'Not your girl and the Deacon song, if that's on your mind. Not from me, anyways. Jesus, that one is dynamite. Anybody plays with that one's going to be lucky to lose only fingers.'

'Yeah,' said Aron with feeling. 'Just checking.'

He put the telephone down. There were other possible sources. Every session player on the demo, the engineer, knew people who knew people. The Deacon musicians were a league above the people he and Savanna had used, but Nashville was a small town. Someone might easily have their hands on a tape of the new Deacon CD. It would give them street cred. Family and friends would be impressed. It was way within the realms of possibility that someone, somewhere had recognised that the same song was being passed off as their own by two different composers. And when one of those writers was Dwight Deacon, and the other a beautiful, unknown girl, it was hot news of the juiciest kind.

Aron ran a cold shower and washed quickly. It didn't sound like the sort of meeting to which it would be advisable to be late.

A few minutes later, as he drove across the big suspension bridge across the Cumberland, the one that seemed to have been built by an engineer with no artistic pretensions at all, he looked back at his redbrick loft, picking out the plate-glass window he had been staring through minutes before. Mid-river, this would have been the view from the ships carrying their cargoes of cattle and pig-iron, cotton and corn up to the railhead that had been the start of Nashville, the place that was within half a day's drive of seven states. Soon, he was on Music Row and the sense of foreboding was heavy within him. He had the strong sense that something was going to have to go . . . his principles, his integrity – hell, his job and his future in this town he had come to love.

TWENTY-SEVEN

The atmosphere in the busy reception area of Polymark was giving nothing away. Nobody looked at him strangely. But there was, to a peculiarly sensitive and paranoid antenna, perhaps just a little extra excitement in the air. He walked up to the receptionist, a pretty girl he hardly knew. She had the look – although you could never tell in Nashville – of someone who had men rather than music on her mind. Perhaps marriage to serious money was her objective rather than making it the hard way through records and the road. In short, she seemed to Aron to be one of the few people in town who were not hooked on either God or fame.

'Yup, Aron, Mr Gramm is expecting you. Oh, and you got lucky. Mr Dwight Deacon is sitting in on your meeting.' She smiled brightly, unaware that she had not brought good news. Aron's brow furrowed. Many producers would have been thrilled to bask in the reflected glory of the biggest name in music, period. 'I was just saying to Dwight the other day . . . he told me this great joke about . . . you know, he said he has a lot of problems with his sinuses. Not a lot of people around town know that . . .' They would all be worth points in the conversations that lubricated business in Music City.

He went up the stairs with a heavy heart. It was difficult, if not impossible, now not to expect the worst. He felt like a spectator at an unavoidable, but as yet to happen, traffic accident. How would Aron react in his moment of crisis? They must have felt something like this on the Western Front in the First World War as they waited for the whistle that would send them over the top. Would they be brave? Would they survive? Would it hurt? How would they do in the ultimate test? He wondered if Gramm himself was sharing his misgivings. When it came to Deacon even the hardest could fall.

He gave what he hoped was a cheery knock – the rat-a-tat-tat of someone who is at ease and who expects to receive a friendly welcome.

'Come in.'

Gramm was behind his desk, which seemed to be unusually tidy. He looked his usual small, neat, slightly aggressive self in an openneck blue shirt which matched the colour of his eyes. Gramm, however, was hardly the point. The room was controlled, as Hitler's study in the Reichstag would have been, by somebody else. By, in fact, Dwight Deacon. He sat, or rather sprawled, across the big leather chair in the corner. His buckskin boots were all over the coffee table, scattering magazines, ashtrays and photographs of the famous *tête-à-tête* with Gramm as if they were the detritus on some college freshman's desk and he the senior and quarterback of the football team who had deigned to call.

'Hello, Aron,' said Gramm with what seemed like a forced exuberance.

Gramm half stood, half sat as he gestured to the chair opposite his desk. He shot a quick glance of the 'how-am-I-doing' variety at the superstar in the corner of his office.

'Of course, you know Dwight?' he said in magnificent afterthought.

'Dwight!' said Aron, standing there, and waiting for his cue. Was this a standing up and hand-shaking moment? A lot would depend upon that. Apparently it wasn't. Dwight Deacon leaned his head back to one side. He looked at Aron Wallis as one might at a rare, but slightly disgusting reptile you had been introduced to by the natural history teacher at the zoo. He had a baseball magazine in his lap. This he now cast aside, much as if it had been Aron Wallis's entire career, reputation, and place in the pecking order of Nashville. The magazine skidded across the table. It knocked over a photograph . . . no damage . . . before colliding with another couple of periodicals and sweeping them before it on to the floor of the office of Mike Gramm, one of the most powerful label heads in Music City. Deacon made absolutely no attempt to retrieve what he had spilled.

'Yeah, I know Aron,' said Deacon. He smiled. It wasn't one of his nicer smiles, but the truth was that Deacon was not much of a smiler. The fans preferred it that way. You didn't want to crack jokes on Judgement Day with the Almighty. 'We cut one a few years ago,' he added. His words sounded dangerously past tense.

Aron forced a smile on to his face. He sat down on the chair he had been offered. There was a slight problem in that his back was now to Dwight Deacon, who did not do backs. Aron manipulated the chair, repositioning it so that it included an attenuated view of both Deacon and Gramm. He was the pig in the middle, if not the pig in the poke.

'The truth is,' said Gramm tentatively, 'Dwight asked that we all meet up to discuss a little something that has come up which has the potential to embarrass us all.' He looked down and gave a nervous cough. He did not seem convinced that 'corporate speak' was going to cut cookies in this particular situation.

'Truth is,' said Deacon, mimicking the words of the man whose signature appeared on his mammoth pay cheque, '*I* have been embarrassed by this "little something" that has come up.' He spoke ponderously in a Southern accent on which he had worked hard and long and with a certain amount of surface success. Grandma Stone would not have believed it for a second. She would have stuck him slap bang in the middle of the blue-belly state of Pennsylvania from where, rumour had it, he had originally hailed. His mighty PR machine, however, was working hard on somewhere that included the borders of North Carolina, West Virginia, Kentucky and Tennessee.

'And what might that be?' tried Aron. He was surprised that he managed to sound very vaguely threatening.

'Well,' said Gramm nervously, 'it seems like . . .'

'It seems like . . .' boomed Deacon. He was taking over again. His face coloured up to order, and his wide eyes widened. 'Seems like you recorded a song the other day, for some hillbilly looker you found somewhere down the back alleys, that was a cover of one of the songs off my album. And I for one would like to hear what you have to say on that subject.'

Gramm looked up. It was speaking time.

There were several ways to go. There was no point in trying to discover where Deacon had obtained his information. It was not usual in such situations for the truth to be the best plan, but Aron decided to give it a try.

'I heard a girl on the Broadway singing. One of the songs she sang was a thing called "Roots and Wings". She told me she wrote it with her mother, years ago. She also told me that a few weeks back, she went out to your place and stuck it in the tape player of your car. Said she never heard anything more about it. I thought it had a hell of a lot of potential. I got Vantage to stake a demo.' He looked quickly at Gramm. 'I took it there, because I knew Polymark was all filled up with new faces, and anyway it was all in-house, in-family.'

'You are right about one thing, Mr Wallis,' said Deacon from the corner. He was now coloured a very unpleasant shade of ripe tomato, whose brown cracked bits looked like they could explode at any minute. He paused.

It seemed pointless for Aron to ask about which part he had been correct. He was going to be told.

'You are right about that song having great potential . . . *my* song having great potential . . . because it is going to be the title song and the very first single of the CD that I am cutting this week right here in Nashville. And come Christmas, the CD is going to provide maybe thirty per cent of Polymark's North American profits. It will be paying thirty per cent of Mr Michael Gramm's salary, here, and possibly, just possibly, thirty per cent of your own, Mr Aron Wallis. Are you getting the drift of what I am saying?'

Gramm nodded quickly. Aron less so. Sooner or later, he was going to have to answer back to this sonofabitch. Sooner or later, the last trump was going to sound. It seemed wiser not to hurry the process. He pictured Savanna singing 'Roots and Wings', and the memory strengthened him. You could only die once, and it was better to do so in a good cause. He had no doubt what had happened. Deacon had played the song by mistake. He had liked it like hell. And he had stolen it. His car. His land. His CD player. His song. He hadn't made the effort to contact Savanna at the address and telephone number she had written in black marker on the tape. 'It had come off,' he might argue. He hadn't stolen it because he wanted to save himself paying Savanna a writer's royalty; that was chickenfeed. He simply wanted to have written that song. He wanted his fans to think he had written it. He wanted his fans to believe he had the sensitivity to know all about 'Roots and Wings'. When he had stumbled upon 'Roots', he had wanted to hijack it for his own legend. He had simply used it as icon polish. Life was not supposed to be fair, but there were limits, and Aron Wallis was creeping close to the edge of this.

'So how', said Aron slowly, 'did this girl get to hear your original song? And how do we know that the demo is a copy of it?'

Attorneys always say that the cardinal rule in a courtroom is not to ask a question to which you don't already know the answer.

'Pete Cook played the demo for us. And he told me he played an out-take of Dwight's song to you. So I think we can all quit playing games here.' Gramm spoke quickly, almost sadly. Pete Cook had done a Judas. If it came to it, so would Gramm. It was just a question of when, and if, Aron would. Cards were now on the table. But there was still one card missing.

'I still don't understand how my girl got to hear Dwight's song. Pete Cook told me that Dwight hadn't written it down, not even in the numbers. Had it "in his head". Said that was the first time he'd ever sung it, when he laid it down the other day. That true, Dwight?'

Aron swivelled around in his chair to look at the legend. Out of the corner of his eye, he saw Gramm's face sink into his hands.

'Well, goddamn it to hell, I don't know how your piece of white trash ass heard my song, an' I sure as hell do not care. Seein' as how she was hanging round my place like a groupie on heat, maybe she walked right into my shithouse and heard me singin' it on the john. That's for you to find out if it interests you any. What I *do* know is that I'm getting all bent out of shape sitting here listenin' to this crap. You got a lot of gall sittin' there and near as nothin' callin' me a liar to my face. This is Nashville, boy. An' this is Polymark, and don't you forget whose songs pay the overheads around here. An' it sure as hell ain't some underage hooker hayseed who takes your fancy in some down and dirty beer joint in the tourist part of town. You want to get your pecker goin', boy, you be my guest. But you got one fuck of a lot of gall insinuatin' my word ain't my goddamn bond round here. This is Dwight Deacon you are talkin' to, son, and don't you forget it, boy. An' next time you cut a record with trailer trash . . . *if* you ever cut another record, that is . . . you make sure as God is in His Heaven that it ain't one of my songs she's stolen.'

He was halfway standing, pulsating with rage. The vein on his forehead throbbed like a beacon. His eyes bulged like tennis balls. It was as genuine an act of genuine anger as Aron had ever seen, and he wondered at its strange and terrifying magnificence. He also knew that it was faked. Somehow that made it all the more impressive. If Deacon could fake like this for an audience of two, what could he do for a stadium full of hundred per cent believers? This was the politics of power on a massive scale. Behind the CEO's desk, Gramm was an inch away from tears, and Gramm was a man on whom people would place bets not to cry at his wife's funeral.

Aron tried to take stock of the situation. Disaster of stupendous proportions had struck. He was effectively fired. The second that happened he would be a pariah in Nashville, in New York and in LA, too. Nobody would go up against Deacon while he was astride the charts like the Colossus he was. Nobody sane, wise, or sadistic – which was ninety-nine per cent of the record industry. He would have to find a card-carrying masochist to employ him, or somebody who wanted one good last joke before his suicide attempt.

And what would he be fighting for? Savanna had done a silly thing. She had trespassed. She had possibly broken the law by entering Deacon's car in the dead of night. The tape was probably, in the circumstances, legally a gift. With her name and address wiped off it, if indeed it still survived, a battery of $1,000-an-hour lawyers would make mincemeat of her in a copyright case. It would be a Nashville jury, and every one of them would have Deacon's CDs at home. The guy even had a reputation in town for looking after songwriters. Even the Stone money and social rank would count against their case. Poor little rich-kid college dropout has dreams of making it on the wrong side of the tracks. Her family indulges her fantasy that the great Dwight Deacon, who has no need to steal anything, has pinched one of the nobody's songs. It would be a classic case of the old Nashville continuing to turn up its decadent nose at the new, vibrant Nashville that was paying the bills and providing the jobs. It would be no contest. Savanna hadn't a prayer. It might be as ugly as home-made sin, but Deacon was going to come out of this thing smelling like prize-winning gardenias.

Gramm's eyes tried to tell him. But the phrases the star had used about Savanna kept on stacking up . . . Still, Aron tried to hang on to it. For Savanna's sake. If he went down, she went down, too. She would never work in this town again. Might not even *walk* in this town again.

He had two choices. Maybe less. He could let it go, and begin the very serious business of consuming gigantic proportions of humble pie. Deacon was a bully. A full and abject apology and capitulation might mollify him. He would have exercised his power and found it as potent as ever. Who knew, perhaps he would even turn the whole thing round and be magnanimous in victory. One thing was certain. Unless Aron recanted now, this instant, both he and Savanna would be dead in the world of country music. Dead as if they had never been. Gramm's silence said it all. So did Aron's knowledge of the industry. They would all be done, done . . . as they said around here. On the one side there was musical hope, other songs, other chances. On the other side there was musical and career oblivion. The price for the former, of course, was pride, self-respect, a mighty chunk of one's soul. The reward for the latter was loyalty, self-esteem, and one's essence intact and enhanced as one trolled the job market with increasing desperation. Savanna would survive either way, but her dreams would not. What was the far, far better thing to do? On the sharp horns of his ethical dilemma, Aron genuinely didn't know. He only knew that time was running out.

He stood up. Deacon stood too. So, for some reason, did Gramm. The consensus seemed to be that whatever happened now, standing up would be required for it. Aron was slim, but tall; Gramm thickset, but very short. Deacon was large, but the jury was out as to whether he was mainly muscle or mainly flab. For the very first time, Aron saw what might be fear in the star's eyes. He had pushed the envelope way out. If Aron and the songstress were an item, the barroom brawls Deacon had spent the early part of his career mostly avoiding might just be put into the shade by one right here in the office of the Chief Executive of Polymark Records.

But Aron dropped his hands. His face sagged. He looked down. When he looked up again, there was moisture in his eyes.

'Look, man, I'm sorry,' he said and there was a break in his voice. 'I didn't mean to doubt you. I admire you so much. We all look up to you in Nashville, sir. You've turned this town around and I for one am proud, genuinely proud, to be in your company. I am sorry, real, real sorry, that we got into this discussion. I can see now that I have been naive, and taken in, and I should know better even though I am young. But you are right, Mr Deacon, sir. That this is your song and your finest, too, if my word counts for anything round here. And I wish you well with it, sir. And I wish the company well with it. And I don't know that I have the right to stay on here, after behaving like this through my inexperience. That's for you gentlemen to decide. I just want to say that I am truly, truly sorry. And if you would, sir, I would like to shake your hand and wish you well and thank you from the bottom of my heart for everything you have done for all of us.'

Dwight Deacon, for one of the first times in his life, looked genuinely surprised. Shocked even, but relief was not far behind. He reacted in an astonishing way. The disbelief, as it happened, registered most clearly on Mike Gramm's face as he hovered on the brink of crisis behind his desk.

Deacon took one step forward, and his own eyes filled rapidly with tears. He opened both his arms wide, and he surrounded Aron with them as if lassoing a calf at a rodeo. Then and there, he hugged him.

'Took a big, big man to say that,' he said.

He stepped back, and then reached out and slapped Aron across the shoulder and his big eyes shone once again with deep sincerity.

'That was a mighty fine apology,' he said. 'And I accept it in the spirit in which it was intended. No hard feelings, man. And I'm sorry if I said some things back there in the heat of the moment.'

And then he smiled. His whole face broke into a beatific smile as if the spirit of God Himself were suddenly pouring down through separating clouds.

'That's what I love about cowboys,' he said simply.

It was impossible to have the faintest idea what he meant.

CHAPTER

TWENTY-EIGHT

This wasn't telephone information. Aron leaned on the doorbell of the old house, and somehow hoped it would be Steph who answered the door. Outside the cold wind blew, and he shivered from its blast and from the thought of the reception he might get. He had caved in to Deacon, and he had done it for Savanna. It was the wise thing to do. Discretion the better part of valour and all that. Living to fight again another day. What was the purpose of sacrificing everything to make a point and paying for it with your future? Savanna was too young for martyrdom. But then, so was he. His stomach rumbled in protest. That was the crux. How much of what he had done had been for Savanna, and how much for himself? He remembered the poem about Horatius on the bridge . . .

> And how can man die better,
> Than facing fearful odds,
> For the ashes of his fathers,
> And the temples of his Gods.

Steph opened the door.

'Aron! Wow! Early. Are we expecting you?'

'I had something to discuss with Savanna. Face to face,' he added. 'Is she in?'

'Sure. Come in out of the cold.'

Aron sat down in the tiny room where the family lived. So much of Nashville lived like this. He remembered the old rooming house he had lived in when he had first arrived in town. He had heard the other tenants, mostly elderly, coughing at night and moving stiffly over creaking boards. But like roaches he had seldom seen them. Society thought of them as people of the twilight who had passed their 'sell-by' date.

'Aron. Hi. Why didn't you call? I'd have put on a face for you.'

Savanna's natural face looked better than perfect to him. He cherished the smile of pleasure and welcome. He sensed that it would not survive his news, even though he had done the only thing he could in the circumstances. At moments like these freedom did not exist. Aron felt the pang of guilt. In life you could understand those who had given in to the ultimate pressure, but did you admire them? He was going to find out where Savanna stood. He didn't want to do it here, with an audience.

'You look wonderful,' he said, his voice distant, distracted.

'Is everything OK?' she said. Her smile tightened a little.

'Yeah, great, in fact. Some pretty good news, in a way . . .' It sounded like a tragedy of cosmic proportions, the way it came out.

'Oh, great,' said Savanna, far from convinced.

'Look, I missed breakfast this morning and there's a diner down the street. You wouldn't have some coffee while I eat something, would you?'

'I can rustle up some eggs over easy and bacon,' said Steph.

'No,' he said, too fast, 'I wouldn't want to put you through the trouble.'

They all got the message. He had something important to say, the 'pretty good news' that was only good 'in a way'.

'I'll get my coat,' said Savanna. 'Looks cold out there.' It didn't take her long. 'Breakfast, here we come,' she said bravely, without knowing why she needed to feel brave.

They walked down the street, bent against the wind.

'So what's up?' shouted Savanna, but her words were lost in the gale. The conversation would have to wait. He mouthed back a 'Can't hear.'

They cascaded into the diner, an old 'Happy Days' place, or one that had been got up to look like it was from the fifties. Waitresses in nurse-like whites roamed with pots of coffee. There was a bar at which noisy cooks grilled fatty things. There were booths along one wall with windows to the street.

'Sit wherever,' said the waitress. 'I'll be right with ya.'

They sat in one of the booths and began to peel off clothes in the greasy heat. The plastic menu, long and thick, was lying on the table.

'You have some news,' said Savanna. It was a statement not a question.

'Yeah, sure do,' said Aron. And he told her. Just like that. All about the meeting in Gramm's office. What he had said. What Deacon had said. How it had been resolved. He told it straight, without comment and explanation. Just the facts. Justification, explanation would come later. Or would they?

Savanna had just stared at him blankly throughout. She had remained totally silent. It was difficult to read any expression at all on her face, although Aron tried as the words spilled out. Then he stopped, simply because he had finished.

Savanna's smile was not a nice one. She stared at him as if she had never seen him before in her life. Instead of Aron Wallis, human being, it appeared as if some ludicrous creature from the swamp had crawled out to join her breakfast table.

'You sold me out,' she said simply. Then she said it again. Louder.

'Coffee?' said the waitress, pouring it anyway.

'You spineless, pathetic, cowardly bastard,' she spat out at him.

'Uh-oh,' said the waitress. 'I'll give you folks a little more time.'

Aron shook his head from side to side in a doomed attempt to deny everything that was going on in Savanna's mind. He thought she had got a handle on this, but she couldn't really understand the brutal truths of the politics of Nashville. She hadn't been here long enough, hadn't cared for a lifetime. He had seen terrible, unjust things happen. He had watched careers burn on the whim of far less powerful people than Dwight Deacon. It probably happened in the offices of corporations, too; and in the banks on Main Street.

'You . . . *you* . . . of all people . . . caved in to that ass-hole?' She was all but shouting now. People were looking at them, and unlike the famous movie scene of Meg Ryan's diner orgasm, nobody was asking what they were eating and ordering up the same. 'Who *are* you, Aron Wallis? How do you stand up straight when you haven't got a spine? I thought, I thought . . . oh, my God . . .' Sorrow had not replaced anger yet, but it might.

'Could you keep your voice down if you are goin' to cuss,' said a Bible-Belter at the next banquette.

'Oh, shut up,' said Savanna, turning to the woman and silencing her with a look of withering scorn.

Aron could not help thinking, even in the midst of what was a terminal crisis in their fledgling relationship, that he had seldom seen Savanna more beautiful. Rage suited her. It would be nice to see her cross more often. Preferably with someone other than him. However, he was acutely aware that this might be the last time he and Savanna saw each other.

'Look,' he said, his voice low and urgent in the neon diner. 'Don't you get it? I did this for you. For both of us. Because of what I did, we are still alive in this town. We can still win. Bigger than before. Better than before. The ass-hole might even help us. I ate crow, and he actually *liked* me for it. OK, you've lost something incredibly special to you. Your song. And that is wrong, and mean and wicked, and Deacon is the Devil, or would be if he wasn't close to being insane. But you know you wrote it. I know. It's not gone, it's just got Deacon's name on it, and it's going to be a number one hit. And in this industry there are few secrets. Everybody knows where the bodies are buried. That song is going to work for you. I guarantee it. We'll get you dates at the Bluebird. The Gibson. The Station Café. OK, so you haven't got a contract, but everybody knows what happened. Gramm knows. Pete Cook knows. I know. Hell, Deacon knows. And *you* know. That hit will be your hit. That talent is your talent. Can't you see that?'

'You know what I see?' said Savanna, her voice as cold as Arctic ice. 'I see a guy who sold a friend to save his own hide. You did what they all did, Aron. You dumped on me, and did the wrong thing, because it suited you. And now you are trying to talk your way out of it with all that English college BS. I bought you "Roots and Wings". It was a part of me, in here, this part,' and she tapped her heart. 'I trusted you with it because I liked you, and you were a professional. And what did you do? You gave it to Dwight Deacon, your biggest star, on a plate like Herod got the head of John the Baptist. You all just treated me like the little people. You took your opportunity, and now you're going to ride off into the sunset with your new fake cowboy superstar friend, and pretend that I don't exist any more.'

'That is really, really unfair,' said Aron. His face began to redden. His voice, too, began to rise. 'Just remember the facts here, Miss Savanna. You took that song and put it in Deacon's car. You. Nobody else. And why? Because you wanted the great big star to hear it, like it, and use it, and then turn *you* into a great big star. You went out to that thing he calls his ranch and you broke in like some groupie backstage at a Stones concert. You put yourself in this shit, because you are too stupid and too naive to know how this town, and every other town in this country, works. Stars don't make stars, or help stars. They are too busy *remaining* stars. That, believe me, is the fullest-time occupation in the entire wide world. If Dwight Deacon hears a song worth stealing, and he thinks he can get away with it without denting his image, then it's gone, baby, it's stolen. Deacon walks around all day, I'm telling you, and every minute, every second, of that day, he is thinking, Is this the moment where it's all going to start going wrong? Is it now? Is this the top of the hill? Is that the abyss I see before me? So don't give me rubbish about helping to steal your song. I made a business decision in there. I kept you alive, but you can't appreciate that. Grow up, Savanna. Join the real world. If I'd stood up to Deacon, it would have been the ultimate empty gesture. You would have been history in Nashville. That's it. That's God's honest truth.'

But was it? Aron had asked himself the question a hundred times. He had done, perhaps, the 'sensible thing', but he had stood by and allowed a great wrong to be done. OK, so nothing *would* have put it

right, but where was the heroic gesture, the sacrifice of the brave soldier? Martyrs had died in agony because they refused to deny a truth
they believed in. Would they have been considered more noble if they
had crossed their fingers and denied their God, so that they could hang
on to life and spend the rest of it working secretly on His behalf? Was
sacrifice always pointless? No, was the answer. There was a time when
futile gestures were right because any other course of action would be
appeasing wickedness . . . because any other way of behaving would be
letting others down, and, most of all, letting yourself down.

'You know what, Aron Wallis? You are not a man. I thought you
were. But you aren't. You sit here in front of me and tell me about
empty gestures and "still being alive in this town"? Listen, I *am* alive
in this town, even though Dwight fucking Deacon says that I am
dead. You're the one that's dead, Aron. And you know what they say,
a body begins to stink from the head down.'

Aron opened his mouth to say something, but there was nothing to
say. Was righteous indignation a luxury that only the rich and sheltered, like Savanna, could afford? Part of him said 'yes', part of him
said 'no' – an age-old dilemma. Savanna had looked inside him, and
had seen something she despised. Aron might not be hypocrisy-free,
but there was a part of Savanna Stone that wasn't as righteous as she
had just made out. Could it be argued that she was a spoilt little rich
kid who didn't like it when things went wrong?

The waitress tried again, recommending the omelette and the grits
and the orange juice squeezed fresh five minutes ago. But it was too
late for breakfast. Savanna stood up, and picked up her coat. There
wasn't much more to say.

So he simply watched her go, past the fat Midwesterners who
made up most of Nashville's tourists; past the shiny counter with its
hungover metal-workers in their baseball caps; past the waitresses
who looked like nurses who would take your temperature, or serve
your corn flakes. He watched her go from the back, and he remembered that that was how he had seen her first at the C. It seemed a
lifetime ago. He would see her again. That he knew.

But would she ever see him?

CHAPTER

TWENTY-NINE

The telephone rang. Aron opened his eyes. It was early. Way early for business hours. Savanna? More abuse? An apology? While there was sleep there was hope. He reached out for the receiver, and flapped his tongue around inside his mouth to loosen it up, as he tried to get his mind straight. Last night he had been in the upstairs room at Tootsies for a private performance for a guy that Mercury had just signed . . . an Elvis Presley country meets R 'n' B singer by the name of Eric Heatherly. Aron had taken the opportunity to tuck into the Scotch. Now, he had the hangover to show for it.

The voice on the telephone sounded as if it had been up and making calls for hours. In fact, it sounded permanently 'up', as if being 'up' were a moral imperative without which the world might quite easily stop spinning, with the result that everyone would fall off.

'Hi, man, what you doin' still in bed? I can just hear that sleep in your voice.'

It was Dwight Deacon.

'Dwight?' said Aron unnecessarily. This was not the telephone call he had been expecting. One thing was clear, Deacon was not in aggressive mode. He was in friendly fashion. Aron wondered which was worse.

'Fact is, man, I've been doin' a lot of thinking about you since that meeting yesterday. You know, and I say this sincerely, there's not a lot of people stand up to me in this here town of ours. Used to be in the early days. But not now. Not now.' He paused. He seemed to be contemplating the downfall of all those who had once 'stood up' to him, in the days before his monstrous fame had made that a non-viable option. 'Yup, you got spunk, boy. An' I like that in a man. You had your say and I had mine, and then you had the courage to admit that there was another way to see this thing. A man who can stand up to someone, and then admit when he's wrong, is a man, an' that was what I was ringing up to say. You may be a lazy sonofabitch, asleep at the best part of God's day, but you're my sort of a sonofabitch.' He laughed heartily at his own joviality, and it *was* infectious. Aron could actually feel himself warming to the man. Good old Deacon. A fella's fella. A cowboy at the end of the day, after all.

'It's nice of you to say that, Dwight,' said Aron. He felt guilty as he spoke. Savanna's furious face, pretty as summer flowers in a summer storm, filled his mind.

Aron knew there was more. Deacon was a dealer. This call had a purpose that was not simply cowboy to cowboy. Aron ran through the possibilities, trying to stay a step ahead of the Deacon game, which was a bit like taking out a Russian grandmaster at chess. It could be that he was making sure this whole business had a lid on it. Nashville was gossip. Gramm and Pete Cook would have been silenced. Now, Deacon had to know if Aron was on his team, or not. Deacon could not know the relationship, if any, between Aron and the girl singer who had cut the demo. But Aron had reacted visibly and strongly to Deacon's rude remarks about her. That was an indication that his interest in her might be a little more than merely professional.

'Listen, man. A lot of people forget that I wasn't always Dwight Deacon, you know. That I paid my dues. That I was poor and looking for work and wanting all the things that the others want. It's pretty easy to forget that nowadays, but I want you to know that I never forget it. Not for one minute of each day. People find that hard to believe about success. But you don't forget. You don't forget.'

Aron couldn't find it in his heart to produce the compliment that was now expected. He heard the short silence at the end of the telephone which registered the fact.

'The point is this. That girl of yours. I don't know a thing about her, but she sure has a voice and she sure did some justice to that song of mine. Now, I don't know where she came by that thing. Who knows? I've heard some songs in this business that have never met, but have sounded exactly like each other, almost twins even. People can look like each other. Songs can sound like one another. Don't mean they have to be related. So I am not saying anything derogatory about that girl you found. I want you to know that, man. I do realise that my words have a certain amount of authority in this great land of ours. Sometimes people just knowing what I'm thinking will go ahead and do something as a result. Give someone's career a leg-up, for instance. Give someone else a little push in the other direction, if you get my drift . . .'

He paused. This time Aron had to say something.

'I surely do understand that, Dwight.'

'So I suppose what I'm trying to say here is, if that girl of yours wants some showcasing around town, I think a couple of words I might be able to say can do her a bit of good. Like she could maybe do the Bluebird. Hell, that was where I started out. You think she might appreciate that?'

Aron knew that Savanna would go to hell and back before she did the Bluebird on Dwight Deacon's say-so . . . or his, for that matter. But the Bluebird was *the* place. Tucked away out in a split mall ten miles outside Nashville, it was where the best music was. The tourists hadn't found it, and every night it was stuffed with record people, talent scouts, and people who specialised in being 'in the know' before anyone else. It was true Deacon had gotten his start at the Bluebird. So had Faith Hill. So had Patty Loveless. Trisha Yearwood had played it a lot. Every singer/songwriter in town with big dreams and talent prayed for a slot on their showcase nights.

'I know she would,' said Aron. It was a reflex action. You could not say 'no' to the Bluebird. It was the equivalent of a Catholic turning down the communion wafer at St Peter's in Rome.

'Well, look, man. I'll make a telephone call. I know they will . . . ah . . . look kindly at my humble request. You leave her telephone number with my people, an' she'll be hearin' from that ol' club. Boy, that takes me back. Way back. People say these are the good old days, but, you know, those were. It was a simpler place in time, man. Simpler place in time. Hey, that sounds like a real good idea for a song. I'll say goodbye.'

He put the telephone down real quick. Aron could see him grabbing his guitar and trying out a few riffs based on that simpler place in time, or whatever fantasy surrounded and obscured the reality of it. Aron replaced the receiver and looked at his watch. It was 6.45 in the morning. You could say a lot of things about Deacon, but you could not say he was a man who had not worked for his success. Maybe that made him not so bad after all.

Later that morning, as he left for work, he called Dwight's people, of whom there were a decently large number. He rose through the ranks of three of them, and all had been expecting his call. He finally left Savanna's telephone number with somebody who rejoiced in the title of 'special relations assistant'. 'Tell her to expect a call from the Bluebird within twenty-four hours,' the clipped voice said.

CHAPTER

THIRTY

The Bluebird was filling up. Technically there were no table reservations, but rules in Nashville as elsewhere were made to provide the exceptions that proved them. Two of the best tables were empty. Everyone knew they would not be when the show started. The Bluebird was always full. It was not large, in fact it was very small for the importance it had in what was now a multi-billion-dollar industry. At the back was the small bar with stools. Immediately to its left, as you looked at it, was the mixing board where the sound engineer controlled the relative volumes of the voice and acoustic guitar mikes that each of the four singers had. To the left of his station were about six rows of church pews. These were for members of the audience who had missed out on the tables and the bar stools. The tables were dressed with blue chequered cloths, and the décor was signed black and white photograph traditional. Replicas of the great mingled with the nearly famous, the megastars and the ones who had disappeared without trace into the bottomless pit that consumed country singers when they had passed on . . . often way before they had passed on.

Savanna sat at the stage far left and adjusted her microphone. The '29 Gibson was in her lap, and she could see some of the *cognoscenti* in the audience commenting on it enviously. She felt the strength it gave her, and she smiled across the room at Steph who had arrived early to take the bar-stool with the most central view of the room. She raised her hand in a half wave, and Steph returned it, again surreptitiously. Here in the Mecca of cool country, everyone was on their best behaviour. There was no smoking in the Bluebird café. And no drunks. Nor was there conversation in the place once the singers had started singing, nor during the introduction of their acts. This was serious business. Careers could be launched. Although the performers were singing for free, each and every one would have paid what little money they had to be there.

The atmosphere was low-key excited. The waitresses glided silently between the tables, taking orders that were muttered to them in low voices. It was left to the singer/songwriter whose showcase it was – in that she had been asked to bring along three of her friends – to warm up the audience, during the sound checks. Tonight it was a pretty girl with big eyes and a sensitive mouth who was well known in Nashville as being an up-and-coming talent. Her name was Lori Lawton and she headed up a band called Shyne, whose only member here tonight was her husband, Brett McGuire. Their CD 'Sooner or Later' had made medium waves. The title said it all. Sooner or later Lori Lawton was going to get her shot at the starshine. That the crowd recognised this was one of the reasons her showcase was so well attended and with such important people. Curb, Tim McGraw's label, had a table, and there was another at which sat a couple of members of the hot new group Blackhawk, and a pair from Nashville's oldest 'new discovery', the BR5-49's. Lori, who knew most people in Nashville, had whispered to Savanna where the movers and shakers were sitting, but Savanna, not good with names, had forgotten most of them already.

What she could not understand was why she was here. The call had come from Lori personally. 'Would you like to be in my showcase this weekend at the Bluebird?' Answer: 'Yes.' Question: 'Why?' She had not actually asked that, realising it would be uncool, and Lori had simply said, 'A couple of people around town have said you are really good.' Again Savanna had not asked their names. Aron, of course, was a possibility, actually a probability, and the 'couple of names' could easily be just him. But she was trying hard not to think about Aron and how he had behaved towards her. He had hurt her deeply, and she didn't understand how she could have got him so wrong. He certainly wasn't in the audience tonight, and he would have been if he had been responsible for her invitation. Or perhaps again, guilt had been his motive . . . a belated attempt to make amends . . . but he could no longer face her in the flesh. It had to have been Aron. Who else would have known her telephone number?

Lori had questioned her briefly about her repertoire. 'We usually take the songs in turn and it maybe works out at six each. There'll be a mix of ballads and up-tempo, but it's unstructured. Sometimes we all sing along on a cover, or help out on the harmonies, if it feels right. That sound about all right to you? No cash, I'm afraid, but the drinks are free. If you want to join us, we usually go across the road and eat Italian afterwards, and moan about the music industry.'

Savanna liked her on the telephone, and more in the flesh. Lori wore braces over a very white, very clean shirt, and she played the trumpet, as well as the acoustic guitar, because, she cheerfully admitted, it had helped her get boys when she was younger. 'Everyone else in Nashville played the guitar.'

The 'feel' at the Bluebird was that everyone was amongst friends whom they knew slightly. However, they were all there for a purpose that transcended mere networking and social intercourse. To that extent, it was not unlike a church service. You nodded at people, made perfunctory small talk, but ultimately concentration was on the music. Was this the night that you would witness the birth of a star, and have the licence for the rest of your life to bore everyone to death about it? 'I was there when Garth played the Bluebird for the very first time. You could tell right there and then, he had the magic.'

The performers were both separate from the crowd, and a part of it. This was because the crowd was not the usual sort in Nashville – fans, paying members of the public who needed to be entertained, or beer drinkers wanting background noise to their booze. This audience was a cross-section of the music industry itself. Tomorrow, they would be talking about what they had heard tonight. Important people would be listening to the reports at morning conferences, at coffee breaks, in the corridors of Music Row power. So, as they did

their sound check, Lori and the others waved at an agent here, a producer there, mouthing soundless 'hi's' from the stage. It was an all-girl
evening, and the other singers were introduced to Savanna more or
less as they bumped into each other amidst the snakework of cables
and islands of loudspeakers that were a feature of the cramped stage.
Camille Harrison was a beautiful, shy girl who had been around
Nashville for a long time and written songs for more or less everyone.
Shy, that is, until she was performing. Then her back-chat with the
audience and other performers showed a sharp wit and a whiff of
steel behind the guileless, big blue eyes. Cindy Kalmenson, tall, thin,
and interesting-looking, had learned her 'country' in Sherman Oaks
in the San Fernando Valley, but her style was no less authentic for
that. They both greeted Savanna warmly. There was no bitchiness
here. This was the tough, cutting edge of Nashville breakthrough
dreams, and God was with these people, in their songs, in their
hearts. They were fellow travellers on the road and the failure of any
diminished all of them, while the success of one gave hope and inspi-
ration.

'You gonna go first, Camille?'

'OK, I'll go with "Too Much Memphis". It's sort of slow, but
insistent, if that helps whoever's next.'

Savanna would follow. Then Cindy. Lori would play last, having
introduced each singer individually.

Savanna was all set up, and there were still a few minutes until
starting time. She noticed a few eyes on the door, where a pretty
maître d' guarded a lectern and portioned out the much-sought-after
seats. The two big tables were still empty, and there was only just
time for them to be filled. Whoever had engineered reservations at the
Bluebird was pretty certain of their welcome, didn't mind being
unpunctual, or enjoyed making an entrance – possibly all three.
Savanna was more interested in having a few words with Steph before
the act. Shared nerves were somehow better than lonely ones.

Steph sat bolt upright in the middle of the bar. The entertainment
industry type who was next to her came with a date so she was in no
danger of being irritated by barflies, not that the Bluebird was that

kind of place. She nursed a beer, and had tried to eat some of a bowl of hot chili, but had mostly failed.

'Jeez, I'm terrified. What do you feel like?'

'Kinda not as bad as I thought,' said Savanna. 'Everyone's real friendly, and non-competitive. You know, like a family jam at sunset feel. Even the crowd feels kinda warm, you know, rooting for you.'

'Well, good for you, honey. I just keep looking at all these photographs!' Steph waved a hand at the walls. 'Like, do you get to have yours up there now you've played here? It's a pretty big deal, isn't it?'

'Yeah,' said Savanna, 'I guess it is. Not like 300 spotty would-be doctors getting lectured by the Dean of the Med School about not playing games with the body parts from the dissection rooms.' She laughed, but she knew what she meant. Doctors were just doctors. And there were an awful lot of them, mostly quite dull, and often not very clever, although all reasonably well heeled. They would work their guts out, have high suicide and alcoholism rates and they were well below the national average for life expectancy. Everybody they saw would be either ill or potentially ill. How much of a life was it? Compared to this, for instance. The excitement in the room was palpable as a mass in a gut. These people were looking forward to a good time and Savanna was going to help provide it. There was being and becoming in this room, and on these walls. It looked like the staging post for a journey out West on a wagon train of hope to a distant red horizon and a gold-dust future.

'There's Aron,' said Steph suddenly.

Savanna turned, almost too quickly, her heart quickening as she remembered the taste of his lips, but the expression of distaste arriving on her face just a tad later. Aron arrived with seven others to make up one of the empty tables of eight. Savanna saw him before he saw her, and she noticed him look first to the stage, and then begin to scan the room. He was quite obviously looking for her. She did not want to be seen by him, and moved a little to the side of and behind her cousin. It was now clear why the table had been reserved. The Vantage record head, Pete Cook, was there with someone who had to be his wife, petite and pretty, around fifty. Gramm, the chairman of

Polymark, came with a girl who was not his wife, but looked like she hoped to be. She was a toucher and her hands never left some part of the label boss's body, which Gramm didn't seem to mind at all. Aron, too, was not alone. In fact, he had pulled something of a rabbit from a hat. He was escorting Faith Hill, easily the most beautiful, and talented, female singer in Nashville and now a superstar of diva status. Her husband Tim McGraw, also very much the man of the moment, was away on business. This would be a strictly platonic date, but to have taken Faith Hill away from her two adored baby daughters was a recognisable achievement in Nashville. There was a scattered round of muted applause as she entered. She smiled and waved back, and then pointed out where her picture was to Aron. She, too, had made her start at the Bluebird – of all things, as a back-up singer.

'So he brought Faith Hill to make you jealous, but not too jealous because everyone knows she's besotted by her husband,' said Steph, with a knowing smile.

'Screw him,' said Savanna. But at the same time she was glad he was there. The presence of the Polymark and Vantage top brass meant that she was very much more than *persona grata* in the town. The other two at the table, she didn't know. However, they seemed to know everyone, and vice versa. There was a brief flurry of table-hopping. Then Savanna caught sight of Lori signalling her from the stage. It was time to take up positions. The show was all but on the road. Savanna avoided Aron's eyes as she squeezed past an outer table and took refuge on her stool behind the ambivalent anonymity of the stage lights. Savanna smiled pleasantly at the audience, catching the eyes of two or three men who were already singling her out for special attention.

'Welcome to the Bluebird everyone,' said Lori. 'No strangers here tonight. Lots of friends. So I don't have to explain to you how these nights work. I do just want to say a special hello and thank you for coming to Faith Hill . . .' She paused for the polite round of applause. 'Faith has her picture on the wall here, an' so do I. And if, one day, I go a tenth as far as she has gone, then thank you, Lord,' she said with a good-natured laugh, in which everyone joined.

Savanna saw Aron trying to establish eye contact. She smiled past him at Faith Hill, who did catch her eye, surveying her with some interest. Camille, Cindy and Lori were old Nashville hands, but the Bluebird was humming tonight in a very special way. Did that mean that Savanna whoever was the main attraction? Curb, Polymark, Vantage, a brace of Blackhawks were all here, and a lot of agents and A & R people. Faith herself had been more or less bullied into paying back a couple of IOUs to Aron Wallis by putting in a showing when she would rather be relaxing with the kids at home, eating her favourite tomato sandwiches.

'Well, hi, Camille!' Lori continued. 'Camille Harrison is an old friend, which does not mean she isn't young and pretty and as talented a writer and singer as we have in Nashville. She has a new CD which you can buy after the show, and she will be playing Thursday nights at Central Station. So, welcome, Camille, and thank you for agreeing to be part of my showcase tonight.'

Camille Harrison had been born in Memphis and was therefore allowed to launch into a catchy mid-tempo number about having to shed her blues roots to find her country ones. It was not a million miles from the Deacon mega-hit in terms of sentiment, but way different in terms of tune. Savanna was thinking that, when the next event threw the whole laid-back atmosphere of the Bluebird into a crisis of major proportions. There was a commotion at the door. Something very significant was happening. It was not clear what. Camille Harrison's Memphis problems faded into immateriality as all heads turned to see what was unfolding.

There by the lectern, far larger than life, in a jet-black stetson, stood Dwight Deacon. Behind him were serried ranks of hierarchical hangers-on. There were about eight of these, maybe ten. Too many for the size of the empty table that clearly awaited them. If Faith Hill and the power panjandrums of Music Row had created an impression, this latest coming was registering seven or eight on the seismic Richter scale. The words 'Dwight Deacon' flashed around the room in insistent whispers. The net effect was to make the utterance of his name very loud indeed. This drew a smile to the face of the legend which he managed to mix with an expression of sanctimonious apology for his obvious disruption of proceedings. For a second or two, Camille attempted to hold on to them with 'Too Much Memphis'. Then she simply ceased to try.

The bubbly song and the whispers ceased on cue, leaving an eerie silence in their place. At the bar, Steph took a deep breath and held it. Then she reached for her beer. Savanna's eyes opened in horror. Aron Wallis was one thing at her Bluebird opening. Dwight Deacon was quite another.

'OK, OK,' said Lori Lawton, holding up both hands to stop what had already stopped. 'We don't usually break in mid-song here at the Bluebird, but special events deserve special treatment. I had no idea . . . nobody told me . . . that we were going to have Mr Dwight Deacon here tonight. But it seems we do, or I need new contact lenses . . . I wondered about that empty table . . . I guess my wondering time is over.'

She began to clap. This lead was taken up around the room as the Deacon party, led by the great man himself, threaded themselves through the tables to the position of honour, where waitresses were already finding extra chairs to accommodate the additional members of his entourage. Throughout the room, as he passed, the Nashville movers and shakers attempted to reach out and touch him, by hand or voice. But he fended them off with a series of hand gestures. He managed to imply he meant no disrespect to them personally, but as a performer himself he did not want to interfere with the act in progress. That he had totally and completely disrupted it, seemingly on purpose, was effectively disclaimed by this charade.

Nobody held it against him. Deacon was at a point in his career where nothing except possibly a brutal murder would be held against him. Later, on the ebb-tide that came to everyone who had hit the high-water mark, there would be time for the sharpening of gutting knives. It was not now.

Like everyone else at the Bluebird, Steph had been thrown completely by Dwight Deacon's unexpected entrance. Her mind moved fast. Why was he here? She knew instinctively that he had come to see Savanna. Why? He had stolen her song, and not given her credit for it. Did he feel guilty about that? Was he attempting to make amends for his poor behaviour? Had he, in the mysterious way that Nashville worked, been responsible for arranging for the gig in the first place? Was he one of the 'couple of people' who Lori Lawton said had talked up Savanna's talent? You played the Bluebird for free, but pints of blood would change hands amongst desperate songwriters for the honour. Could a Deacon word have been spoken in a receptive ear, and Savanna magically invited as a result? If so, then he clearly was under the impression that Savanna realised that she was there under his auspices . . . that tonight she was a Dwight Deacon production. Otherwise he would never have risked being in Savanna's audience, at the wrong end of a mike. Steph knew her cousin pretty well by now. Savanna was about to be confronted by a man she had reason to despise. Savanna lived by her morals. Savanna had a violent temper. And Savanna was afraid of no one, having been brought up to believe that whatever happened in her life, there would be a family safety-net beneath her. Fireworks were definitely on the menu, along with the indigestible chili and the dull sandwiches. 'O God,' prayed Steph quietly, 'let this not be a disaster.'

In answer the good Lord sent two bright specks of red to the upper reaches of her cousin's cheeks, as she adjusted the mike for her song. She shot a look at Dwight Deacon that was full of daggers. Blissfully insensitive, in the manner of supreme egotists, he beamed back at her encouragingly.

Dwight Deacon seldom ever made anything that was not a career move and, invariably, a canny one. However, he was not 100 per cent certain why he was here. Already, however, he was happy so to be. His welcome at this trendy shrine of country music had been as ecstatic as he could have wished for. In the limo, he had wondered about it. The *cognoscenti* could be hard on the super-successful. They were always awaiting failure, trying to pick the peak of a career like cagey investors in an over-the-top bull market. But he had passed the test with flying colours. If they weren't worried about his crossover success here at the heart of Nashville, about his 'authenticity', his business savvy, then it was hardly an issue anywhere. He leaned back on his chair, tipping the front legs upwards and draping a casual hand over its back. His bass player, a man who had perfected the art of saying 'yes' in a million subtle ways, whispered in his ear. 'The one that's about to sing is a babe.'

The Deacon eyes rounded out as he studied her. She was very sweet. Neat and clean, and prettier than a field of poppies in summer. And she could write. Boy, could she write. The song he had lifted from her was the foundation of his album. Was she a one-shot girl? They often were. One hit, and then a mountain of misses until the Greyhound out of Nashville for the humbling return to the folks back home, and the 'I told you so' eyes of 'friends' and neighbours. That was the fear of Nashville. Dwight himself lived in it, and the thought of it made his blood run momentarily cold in the warm room. But there was the girl again, coming back into focus. She was looking right at him, and smiling, pretty like a sweet song, like her sweet song. He smiled back knowingly. Oh, yes, they had a secret, and she would keep it. In return for her song he had given her this chance at the Bluebird, and he would give her more, through Aron whatever he was called. Tomorrow he was lunching at Arista. The Capitol people were coming for brunch on Sunday. Warners wanted him for their charity thing. To each and all he would mention the name of the Savanna girl and how good she had been at the Bluebird, and they should get her ink dry on a contract before some scumbag scooped them . . . and out they all would troop to the 'bathroom' to get their mobiles going and their A & R people mobilised, and to blast minions for not knowing about Savanna someone whose name dropped from the lips of none other than Dwight friggin' Deacon . . .

Yup, that was how it worked in this wonderful world of the new Nashville that he had largely created single-handed. She could have had a few hundred grand, and a credit on the disc. This way she had his goodwill; goodwill that could become worth billions. He settled back, serious now. Because he cared about music. And because he was an expert in it. He hadn't been more interested in hearing a singer sing in a very long while, maybe never. That was good. That made life good. That was how a cowboy felt.

A low buzz of conversation had started again, reverential, excited.

'I'll tell y'all what,' said Lori. 'Why don't we give Camille time to catch her breath and make a fresh start after Savanna Carson has sung her song. That sound like a good idea?'

In the mood of the place, everything sounded like a good idea. Savanna held up her hand, and said 'Hi' into the microphone as the buzz of conversation faded to silence.

Deacon waited. She would have to acknowledge him in her introduction. Faith, too. It was a hell of a debut, and he had put it together. It was worth a song. Tomorrow the town would be talking about nothing but the surprise crowd at the Bluebird the night before. If the girl could hold a tune, she might even be on her way without him.

'I'm Savanna Carson,' said Savanna in a quiet voice. 'And I want to thank Lori for inviting me here tonight. The Bluebird! What can I say? What can I sing?' There was muted laughter. 'Obviously, this is my first time here, but my family are from the Smokies and my mother taught me to sing. Thanks for everything, Mom. I know you are upstairs listening tonight and you and your family gave me whatever it is I have in the music department. And thank you, Faith Hill, for coming. I'm a big fan . . . me and the rest of the country.'

There was sporadic clapping. Faith Hill gave a gracious smile. Aron shifted uncomfortably in his seat next to her. He was not going to be mentioned. That wasn't the problem. Deacon was. What would Savanna say about him, to him? He knew her well enough to know that she set a hell of a lot of store by principles. Rich kids could often afford those, where poor kids couldn't. It was the arrogance of *noblesse oblige*. When an empty stomach and cold wet streets were options out there in the future, morals could be more easily compromised. He held his breath, but the butterflies in his stomach were not an encouraging feeling.

'Anyway,' said Savanna, 'thank you all for coming, and this first song I'm going to sing for you is about a boy whose name I have almost forgotten, and who has surely forgotten mine. It's called "It Was a Lucky Day When You Broke My Heart".'

She launched into it fast.

Do you remember the sunset on the day we parted,
You held me close, I was broken-hearted,
But I realise now in this brand-new start,
That it was a lucky day when you broke my heart.

The song was catchy, with an easy rhythm. It was deeply country, and Savanna's voice with its Loretta and Patsy twang was instantly distinctive. The knowledgeable ears of the audience picked up. The title caught their attention. The lyrics were simple. As they should be. There were no prizes for guessing what the song was about. Everyone could identify. Luck and love. The first love hurt like hell, but it was usually a mistake. What did kids know? Kids weren't wise like grown-ups. For example, kids would not be wondering what everybody else was wondering. Why had the good-looking nobody from nowhere with the catchy tune and snatchy voice just made a strategic error of monstrous proportions? Why had she made a mistake, the gigantic size of which relegated the broken heart of her first love affair to the banal level of over-scrambled eggs? Why hadn't she acknowledged the presence of the most powerful man in Music City? She'd known to say 'hello' to Faith Hill. Why had she ignored Deacon? It was an oversight from which a career might not recover, however plaintive the voice and wide and open the eyes and mouth.

Everyone turned to Deacon to see how he was taking it. He was not taking it at all well. His eyes narrowed, and his expansive, self-confident body language evaporated. Now, he leaned forward on to the table, his arms clenched across his chest, his big black hat sending dark shadows down across his face. He knew everything. Protocol had been ravaged. He had in effect been insulted by being ignored. The girl with the mike had just said 'hello' to the Secretary of State but passed on the President. All was not well in the world of the Bluebird café, nor in the heart of Dwight Deacon's own personal universe. He could feel them waiting for his reaction. He had to act one out. So he smiled a smile he didn't feel. He simply switched it on like an electric light in the way that he could. Nearly everyone but the most shrewd thought that he had graciously overlooked the oversight and was enjoying the song.

Savanna had them now. This was her opener. It would not be her best. She would warm up to that, but already the audience was waiting for her next one, anticipating it, a little sorry they had to wait three more songs for it. The girl had talent everywhere it mattered, except in the tact department. There she was clearly a natural disaster on a cosmic scale.

The song came to an end, and the applause was a little restrained. The power panjandrums were biding their time. How were the others taking it – the label heads, Faith Hill, hell, Deacon himself? If he didn't clap, then those who clapped loudest wouldn't want him to see them doing it.

Deacon did clap. He clapped loudly, and beamed around the table at his entourage, giving them permission to do the same. However, his smile had a frostiness around its edges. His big round eyes caught Savanna's and she did not smile back at him. He recognised that fact and drew his conclusions from it. The failure to mention his presence at the Bluebird had not been the innocent mistake of a nervous novice. It had been premeditated *lèse-majesté*. The girl had not forgiven him for the song. He shot a look across the room, but Aron was busy whispering to Faith Hill. Was it possible the producer had not told the girl that he, Dwight, had organised the Bluebird? The bastard had stolen the credit for it for himself?

Deacon stood up, as Cindy Kalmenson made up for the first girl's lack of respect. 'It's an honour to play here in front of Dwight Deacon and Faith Hill, but it hasn't done anything for my nerves,' she said charmingly. 'This one's called "Rock 'n' Roll Hero". Remember those teenage crushes on rock stars? In answer to your question, "Neil Young".'

'Got to take a leak,' said Deacon. This time he did not hurry through the room. He worked it. Despite the fact that poor Cindy was trying to explain what it was like to love Neil Young when you were merely a face in a crowd. At every table there was someone who knew him, and several who wanted to with the desperation of the damned. He kept his voice down to a loud whisper, with the paradoxical effect that most people could hear what he was saying. The Bluebird rule about silence while singers were singing was not made for the Dwight Deacons to follow. It was a power-play pure and simple, and recognised as such. The mighty stood to clasp his hand. He saved Faith Hill for last, star-to-star protocol. 'Hear Tim's standing room only in the North West. Folk givin' fingers for tickets. You triple platinum on that album yet? Heck, I'd have liked to have had that one about the sunset of the heart. Helluva song. Mike Walker knows how to turn out tears. Yes, ma'am, how are the kids?' To Aron, he simply nodded curtly. On it went, until he made it to the bathroom. When he got there, he simply dabbed some water on his face, and made it back through the still eager crowd. Lori Lawton was halfway through a sweet song called 'Daddy's Here'. The girl he had come to see would be up again next. She had a chance to rectify her mistake, if that's what it had been. The power show had been to remind her of her oversight.

At the bar, Steph's knuckles were white. Across the room she watched her cousin, and now she feared the very worst. There was that look in Savanna's eye. The 'I will not brush my teeth' look; the 'I will not go to the party' look. It was terribly, dreadfully calm. Her expression was almost serene in its certainty. The very worst was going to happen, and somehow several people in the room sensed that without having a clue just what it would be.

The silence when she came to speak was total. Savanna's face was flushed with excitement. This was something that had to be done. It wasn't wise; it wasn't clever, cunning, or businesslike. But it was the inescapably right thing to do. She struck a chord, a G, and it lingered in the quiet.

'It's quite a coincidence,' she said, 'that Mr Dwight Deacon is here with us tonight . . .' She paused. It was a strange attempt to rectify an impoliteness. The silence deepened. 'Because, a few weeks ago, I gave him a tape of a song I had written many years ago with my mother. It was called "Roots and Wings".'

She peered out into the darkness of the audience. A hundred eyes were fixed upon her. The girl had sent Deacon a song. Obviously, he had just thrown it away. No 'name' singer took unsolicited tapes in Nashville. It wasn't done . . . although the fans passed them on all the time, and traffic cops, busboys, and the guy who came to clean the pool. The girl was new to the industry and was miffed at the lack of response. Now, she was going to throw some sarcasm Dwight Deacon's way. Everybody waited. It was the equivalent of knowing that someone was going to shout an obscenity in church.

'Well, the other day I recorded a demo of that song with Aron Wallis. Vantage financed it. Hi there, Aron, thanks for coming along tonight. Hi there, Mr Cook.'

The eyes shifted to Aron and Cook, the Vantage boss. Most people in the room knew them. Aron lifted his eyes to the ceiling in a gesture that said he could not believe what was about to happen.

'Anyways, I just thought you'd all like to know that Mr Dwight Deacon recorded my song. He changed a word or two and the title. Called it "You've Got to Go Away to Come Back Home". It's gonna be his next single. On his new album. I didn't get any credit for that song. No money, and no thanks. In fact it makes me downright nervous sitting up here in front of Dwight Deacon 'cos I surely am not certain which of my tunes he'll be stealing next. Anyway, right now I'm going to go right ahead and play "Roots and Wings" for you all because he can't steal something twice. And, Mr Deacon, I'm sorry for any embarrassment this might cause you. But where I was raised people who steal things from people who don't have very much can expect to suffer a little embarrassment in life from time to time. Way I see it, a song you write contains a little, bitty piece of your soul. I don't like to lose bits of my soul, although there are a few people in this room tonight who seem pretty happy about parting with bits of theirs. So I guess it takes all sorts to make a world, and here is "Roots and Wings" . . . the original version, the one that *won't* be a hit. And I dedicate it to my mom who helped me write it, and who was one of the finest singers and writers ever to come out of this great state of Tennessee. Thank you, Mom . . .' and she looked up at the ceiling to where the sky would be.

She struck the chords . . . G. C. G. Savanna's roots had wings.

The rest of the room, however, was on its own agenda. Shock, horror, excitement, vicarious thrills collided in the air like sub-atomic particles in a university physics experiment. Unseen, unheard, the emotions were nonetheless palpable. Everyone looked at everyone else as if each were in a competition to see who would win the best expression of disbelief. The slower minds were simply dumbfounded. It was simply unthinkable that somebody who was a singer, a song-writer, in *Nashville*, would say to Dwight Deacon what had just been said. He had been called a thief. In public. In the town he owned. The girl had already sung a pretty song. She wasn't drunk or drugged, although she was clearly unhinged.

The sharper minds however had already moved on. They were analysing the charges. Were they true? And if so, what then? A scandal of epic proportions was in the making. What would Deacon do? He had a reputation for a quick temper, but he was also a cool customer. Still, he had been thrown a public curveball that looked all but unhittable. To deny the accusation would be to dignify it. To ignore it would be simply impossible. To admit it would be suicidal. What would the star do? The eyes that had been consulting each other in astonishment now sought out Deacon in amazed curiosity.

'Roots and Wings' warbled on from the stage despite a sudden hum of conversation. The few serious players in the audience who had heard the as yet unpublished Deacon version made the mental note that it *was* the same song. This was not one of those borderline disputes when two people had a similar idea at different times. Either Deacon had stolen the girl's song, or she had stolen his. Whatever, Music City telephone companies were going to have one helluva day tomorrow.

Dwight Deacon was busy turning beetroot-red, as the initial surprise in the audience was expressed as a collective intake of breath that seemed to suck the oxygen from the atmosphere. He sat quite straight in his chair, and he wore an expression of the purest bewilderment. Here in Nashville, in public, in what many regarded as the centre of the beating heart of Music City, he had been called a thief by a girl with a spotlight on her. That gave her credibility. It was way past obscene; it was surreal. Could this conceivably be a dream from which he would shortly awake? He stared around him wildly, and saw the shocked faces of the audience. Reality was biting hard. Details were filtering in from the edges of his consciousness. Stealing songs was not new in Nashville. Nor had stealing horses been uncommon way out west on the Old Frontier which he had so often sung about. But both were hanging offences. Everyone agreed on that. Song-stealers were the lowest of the low, because they hit at the heart of the industry. Song-rustlers stole from the poor, the hopeful and the hopeless, and there was no health in them. Country was about honour or it was about nothing. Train songs, jail songs, whiskey and broken hearts songs celebrated the toughness of life and its troubles. They were hymns to suffering. But their underlying message was always clear. No matter how deep you were mired in the mud and the muck, a cowboy kept the faith. If you could be true to yourself, even the lowest loser was a winner. If you sold yourself out, the highest and the mightiest was a nobody.

A nobody! Deacon braced himself at the horrible, hideous thought. All his life had been dedicated to being the opposite of a nobody. Every breath he took was for that purpose. Every movement he made was in the service of that ambition. He had long since ceased to ask the question why. 'Why' questions didn't sell a single CD. They were therefore superficial and irrelevant. They were better left to pointy-headed intellectuals with more sense than money, whose names had never seen neon, and whose eyes had never seen grown female strangers cry in lust.

Dwight remembered the tape, of course. He had played it by mistake, but listened right on through it, before taking it out and seeing some girl's name and telephone number on it in black marker. He had worked out what had happened. A more than usually determined hustler had snuck out to his ranch, trespassed and stuck the tape in his car. The song he had been listening to was sitting neatly on the passenger seat. His quick mind had worked fast. The tape was unsolicited. It was on his property. It had been left by someone who had at the very least trespassed to get there and had possibly committed some felony if she had broken to enter. That made the tape his. Legally, if not morally, he owned it. He had played it again, and then two more times, and each time he had heard it, he had heard a hit. It didn't happen often in Nashville. A nobody's demo was nearly always worth nothing. Hell, the *good* songwriters mostly turned out shit. But this was different. This had the sincerity even he couldn't fake. This was genuinely authentic country, full of blue mountain mist and the warmth of crackling pine fires. It came deep from some young girl's heart, and was sung by a voice that could talk the heart's language. He had sat there, transfixed, in his car, as the world had gone away and he had heard over and over again the flagship song for his next CD, the single that would do what 'Memphis' had done, and 'Hurry up to Heartache', and 'There's Two of Us in this One-Horse Town'.

He hadn't thought about it for long. He had wiped off the name and the telephone number with the bottom part of his shirt and a bit of spit and he'd taken it right out to the small studio he had in the barn. He had subtracted a line here and added a note there, and changed the title. That was about it. He hadn't felt any guilt because he had known that the law was on his side, not just because he was Dwight Deacon and the law was kindly *disposed* to be on his side, but because legally he was entitled to do what he was doing. Did you own the crowbar that the burglar had left behind? Of course you did. In a country where attorneys had replaced consciences, what was the *point* of guilt any more? Law had made morals redundant. If it was legal . . . and profitable . . . then it was right.

But now the chickens were home to roost. Rather than doing it in the henhouse, as was traditional, they had decided instead to congregate on the fan that was, metaphorically, whirring around his head. The rights and wrongs of the thing were not the issue. He was being accused of one of the most terrible crimes in Nashville, in a place that meant more to country music than any of the 700 churches that surrounded it. Tomorrow Suzie would have it on WKRM, and that guy at the *Tennessean*, and the day after the tabloids would be on to his PR hacks. The whole mighty organisation he had built with his bare hands would be under siege again.

The girl was actually singing it now, her own big blue eyes boring into his own famously blue ones. She was singing her song at him, for him, and to everyone else, including a co-writing 'mom' who it seemed had died.

> Slamming doors, breaking hearts,
> Running free with our emotions
> You took a home and made it hurt,
> You made us cry . . .

She was willing him to sit there. He felt the panic and the anger rise within him. He turned around and they were all looking at him. They were waiting to see how he would react. He was in the audience, but he had never been more prominently centre-stage than he was right now. Fury had the better of panic. He lifted both of his big hands up into the air and slammed them down on the table so that all the glasses jumped and a couple of them spilled. 'Bullshit!' he thundered into the sweet melody of Savanna's 'Roots and Wings'.

But it didn't stop her. She sang right on, and as the phrases piled up, and the lines became verses, her eyes never wavered. They were honest eyes, unblinking in righteous indignation, and the master of deception could recognise the magnificence of her truth. This wasn't a cover. This wasn't a borrowed tune. This belonged to her like her cute little nose, and perfect blue-jeaned butt. It was hers, along with the cold, accusing fury that wafted on her words across the few feet that separated them. Indignation did not get much more righteous than this.

Deacon computed the odds. He could read the minds around him. They were thinking that the pretty girl with the honest eyes, only two steps from the low end of the Nashville ladder, had either stolen Deacon's song, or the megastar had pinched hers. Somehow the middle way was ruled out. Coincidence was simply not an option. The feelings in the room were wrapped right around the black and white atmosphere of the confrontation. It was evening, but the sun was 'metaphorically' as high as noon. Deacon had shouted 'Bullshit'. She had accused him of theft. One of them was lying. Which?

> Better by far than losing you,
> Was finally finding me . . .

Aron Wallis watched, mesmerised by the magnificence of it. This was raw, red courage. No foot-soldier in Pickett's famous charge at the Union's impregnable centre at Gettysburg had shown bravery like this. Deacon sat there, pulsating with anger, and he would never forgive Savanna for what she had done to him. For Savanna, the girl Aron wanted, Nashville was over. Despite her talent. Despite her wonderful song. Despite everything. From now on she would be the sound in the forest unheard. It was an enormously courageous but deeply sad ending to a career that might have been. Nobody would touch her now. She was an outlaw in town, and she would be forced to leave it. Beside him Faith Hill touched his arm. 'What *is* this?' She spoke urgently. The great and the glorious liked to stick together. She would have to react, and some people would copy her reaction. The situation hung in the balance. It could go either way. What people did in the next few seconds mattered dreadfully. Aron leaned towards Faith, the star from Star, Mississippi, who more than anything else symbolised Nashville family values, the girl who put career after motherhood, and whose career had exploded to the skies as a reward.

'Deacon stole the song,' said Aron quickly. 'I know the whole story.'

'Oh, God,' said Faith. 'This is not going to be a good moment.'

At the bar, Steph was frozen like Lot's wife. The bottle of Bud which, country style, she was sipping from the bottle, remained half an inch away from her lips where it had been for the best part of a minute. It was all going on in her mind. There simply wasn't enough mental space to organise bodily movement. Savanna had behaved just like Savanna. The words of the Frenchman who had witnessed the Light Brigade's suicidal ride to the Russian guns in the valley of death at Balaclava had it right: '*C'est magnifique, mais ce n'est pas la guerre*' – 'It's magnificent, but it isn't war.' Savanna had just committed country suicide in the Bluebird café. Her trust fund might well have to peel off a million or two to fight the libel litigation into the bargain.

Dwight Deacon had to do something. The question was what. He could not just sit there and leave it at 'Bullshit'. He could storm out with his entourage, and take most of the room with him. The heavy hitters like Gramm and Cook would leave with him on cue. He was certain of that. They couldn't afford to be on his enemies list. They were practical men, who would not side with a nobody against the biggest somebody in Nashville. But there was a wild card in the pack. There was Aron Wallis who had brought the mighty Faith Hill along to the Bluebird. Faith was getting bigger every day, bigger than Shania, a female rival for the Deacon crown. She was turning into a country queen with her film-star looks and sweet little girls. In the meantime, her husband, McGraw, was on the edge of taking over Garth Brooks's position as country's greatest star after the incomparable Dwight Deacon. Yes, Faith was the wild card, and Dwight hardly knew her. If she didn't walk, others would stay . . . perhaps too many others. And Faith might easily depend on Wallis. Did Dwight own Wallis? That was the big question. His gut said only the loosest 'maybe'. The man had apologised, but his heart had not been in it. And he had liked the girl who had caused all the trouble. The analytical part of Deacon's very far from unsophisticated mind could see why. She had beauty and talent, both as a singer and a composer. Far and away above that, she had balls. She was awash with testosterone. Nobody in Nashville would have pulled the stunt she had just pulled. To stick it to Dwight Deacon like this defined devil-may-care courage. It was so cowboy, it was almost untrue. The OK Corral had nothing on this. Five hundred years from now, they might well be singing ballads about it.

So he turned around in his chair, and fixed his eyes on Aron Wallis, at the moment Wallis's head came up from his *tête-à-tête* with Faith Hill.

'Aron,' he shouted out in a voice that carried right across the room. 'You gonna sit there and let this songbird get away with this *bullshit* when you know the story of what went down?' He turned right round in his chair, giving Aron the full frontal view of his immense fury. He literally vibrated with anger. Anything that had been said or threatened in the Polymark offices on their last meeting was gentle netball in comparison to this. The threat oozed with the sweat from his pores. It blew off him like an aura. It radiated from him in rays of dreadful promise. Aron had to put this right. Now. In a way that left no doubt. Or Aron was dead as if he had never, ever been.

Aron had never been here before. And at the moment of truth, he discovered a truth. That you never knew yourself. He would not have predicted his reaction. Some fudged half truth would have been his most hopeful prediction of his own response. Worse, he wondered if it was possible that he might deliver up total capitulation to the megastar who was so clearly and so publicly demanding it. After all, Peter had not covered himself in glory after the arrest of Jesus. But he did not react in either way. He didn't even think about it. It was his voice when it came out, but it sounded like the voice of another person, a bigger, deeper voice, louder, more expressive than his usual style of speech. It carried right across the Bluebird, distinct and clear like a bird in flight.

'You stole the song, Deacon,' he said. 'You know it. I know it. And now everybody else knows it.'

> Better by far than losing you
> Was finally finding me.

Savanna finished 'Roots and Wings' milliseconds before Aron Wallis spoke. The effect was to make his words sound like an explosion in the middle of a dark, quiet night because they had been uttered originally with background music in mind. Silences are never deafening, but they do have a quality of their own. One silence is not like another. This one was unique. Savanna's head flicked back as she caught Aron's words. Steph, once again, felt the numbness creep over her. Everyone else in the room was on hold. Some, the outsiders, were just thrilled to be there at this spectacular moment in Nashville history. Others, the players, were acutely aware that they had major career decisions thrust upon them at a moment when none was even remotely prepared for such an eventuality. Some looked at Deacon for a lead. Some at Faith Hill. The subordinates of the label bosses looked to their superiors for guidance. Everyone looked at everyone else. And nobody had a clue exactly what to do.

Dwight Deacon was on his feet. The silence surrounded him. It was as if a fearsome teacher had been stood up to by the new kid in the class. Mortgages, marriages, mistresses hung in the balance. A wrong step now, and carefully constructed careers could end. Few were thinking about morality, about right and wrong. Those issues could always be fudged, argued and re-argued. The question was simply how to play a game which had suddenly revealed a peculiarly nasty and un-anticipated twist.

Aron turned to face the place where the music had come from, the disputed music. He turned to face Savanna. She was looking back at him, a bewildered expression on her face.

But Deacon had not finished.

'You redneck bitch,' he screamed. 'You dare to call me a thief here in Nashville, in this place where I started. I'm walking out of here now, and if anybody can find you tomorrow I'll bury you in writs. Do you hear me? Bury you! Bury you! You two-bit hustler. You are dead meat, baby. Do you hear? Dead meat. I promise you. I personally promise you.'

His entourage jumped up with him. Deacon turned around to Aron Wallis.

'And that goes for you, too, you lying sonofabitch. If I hear of anybody who *speaks* to you in this town again . . . *speaks* to you . . . offers you a place to piss in . . . they'll never talk to me again. You hear that, ass-hole? Does everybody hear that?'

Everybody heard that. It was delivered at maximum decibel level, and it was preceded by a purposeful march of the megastar towards the door of the Bluebird café. About half the audience went with him. Everybody major left. Except Faith Hill, who kept the faith. She was the only one in the room who was big enough as a performer, as a woman and as a human being to do the right thing.

The sound of banging doors and shifted chairs, mumbled outrage, and whispered wonderment took a little while to subside. And then it was over. Deacon and his acolytes, big and small, had gone. The

Bluebird was stripped of half of its customers, but the show, as always, had to go on.

Savanna spoke again. 'Lori, I wonder if you'd do me a really big favour. My cousin is in the audience this evening, and I don't think she walked out with Mr Deacon and his friends . . .' There was a tiny ripple of laughter, and someone clapped. 'She is the best song-writer I know, and I wondered if you'd mind if she joined me in one of her songs . . . now that the excitement seems to have died down and the real country music people are still here. This may be the last shot I get at a stage in Dixie . . . so perhaps you wouldn't mind bending the rules this one crazy time.'

Lori Lawton, sweet and dazed as an angel who had just been hit by a brick, simply nodded 'yes'.

And so it was that Steph's dream came true as, heart hammering, mouth dry, she threaded her way through the partially empty room to join her cousin on the stage. Faith Hill turned around to clap her, and so did Aron and a handful of people who just happened to be there and had nothing to lose. Somebody pulled out a stool for Steph and she sat down, smiling in the unaccustomed light and wishing she had had her hair done.

There were people who remembered the night in the Bluebird café as the time Dwight Deacon was called a crook by a nobody singer from the stage. There were others who remembered it as the first Nashville appearance of the two cousins singing duet. Over the years the first group tended to revise their memories. They had not left to show solidarity with a superstar. They had stayed on because they had sensed that special something in the air that canny Nashville noses could. Then they had wined and dined and told stories directly from 'memory' that they had come themselves in their later years to believe . . . memory being funny like that.

So in the end, the stories of the two groups had merged, as legends and myths do over time. The story had homogenised into one with several features on which everyone agreed, some true, some half true, and some not true at all.

It started, as these things do, unpractised and unrehearsed, with promise alone. Together they sang a verse and a chorus of 'Roots and Wings', and they sang it tight and sweet and deep in a way that proved beyond the word of God that this was their family's sound, their music, their words. No judge hearing them would have hesitated in finding in their favour. But soon, those thoughts had moved on, like the urgent memories of childhood, important once then meaningless as even moments passed. Lori had conceded them extra time because of all the 'interruptions', and Savanna and Steph conversed for a second before agreeing on 'Mountain Memories'.

And that was when magic had arrived for the second time at the Bluebird café.

Country music was honest or it was nothing. When it was sad, it said it was sad. When it was glad, it said it was glad. And sometimes, deliciously like now, it could be both at the same time. Here were two girls from the Appalachian Mountains, a few hours' drive from where they all sat, whose family had moved on from those days of poverty in the hills, to relative prosperity, and the trappings of the American dream. But memories remained in the genes, and they sang of them now, and they lived on in the music as real as the day they had first imprinted themselves on the mind of a musician.

> It isn't hard to live if you've got love,
> It isn't hard to hope when you believe in God above,
> In the dark cold of winter, there is the warmth that
>   we dreamed of,
> Yes, it isn't hard to live if you've got love.

It was not in the words. Dreams, God, hardship, cold, the healing power of love. These were country themes of the old school, and the ballad was slow, but steady . . . but the voices and the plucking of the strings of that ancient Gibson guitar were not usual, not for Nashville, not for the Bluebird. Nor were the harmonies. They came tight, as if bound together by an umbilical cord that had never quite separated. They coiled in and around each other, like snakes dancing to a charmer's music, writhing, slipping, sliding in perfect rhythm.

The two merged to become one, and then, tantalisingly, they flew apart again so far that you feared they would not return. When they did, the relief was so great it squeezed moisture to the eyes. Steph was deeper, the anchor, the bed-rock; Savanna tended to soar above her, like a bird experimenting with distance from its nest, but always coming back to the safety and warmth, refreshed by her break for freedom. It was a personification of the roots that enabled a person to fly, and in these mountain memories whole lives were being lived, an entire family raised, locked together by love and by the music that they were sharing tonight.

Aron sat as still as a rock. In all his life, he had never heard anything as good. Savanna had the voice and the personality, but Steph had written the wonderful song, and was the perfect complement to her cousin's brilliance. The sound they made had taken his breath away. 'Breathe,' he said to himself, and when he did he realised how still he had been before.

His heart went out to Savanna. At this moment he fell in love with her a second time. He had known she had great talent and loved music, but this was on a different level of goodness. He turned to Faith Hill by his side. She had her head cocked, and the expression on her face was of puzzlement busily turning into amazement. It was there, too, on the faces of the others that knew . . . the singers and songwriters who shared the stage and the back-up guitarist who sat behind them. Lori Lawton was transfixed, a half smile of heaven on her face, swaying gently to the rhythm of 'Mountain Memories'. Camille, too, was distant, transported by the sound. And Cindy, all the way from the Valley in California, wore an expression of awe that singers who had spent a year or two in Nashville did not give away for free.

Aron tried to make sense of it, but he didn't want to miss a syllable of the song. This might never get as good again. Could the rest be rubbish? No! It was impossible. To be half as good as this would be to fill a stadium. To be a quarter as good would be to send a CD spinning into the top ten. Something deeply wonderful was happening before his eyes. He smiled at the ridiculousness of life, at the weird impossibility of dreams. Anything could happen. Nothing had to. Yet none of us lived if that was true. We lived by maps. Yet there was no life to map, only the unknown future, a wild west of possibility and mystery where the landscape was uncharted. That future life was rich in rivers and trees, wide-open spaces, tall mountains, a paradise of expectancy where things could be made up as you went along, and the only thing that you could not afford to lose was your courage.

When they had finished, the room went wild with applause, the half-filled tables making more noise than a full house. Aron applauded. So did Faith. The clapping rolled on and on, the other performers joining in.

'We didn't forget those mountain memories,' said Savanna, holding out her hand to her cousin and raising it up to acknowledge the applause.

'I can't believe tonight,' said Steph, a faraway look on her flushed face.

'Aron didn't leave,' said Savanna. 'You hear what he said to Deacon?'

She, too, was flushed with their success, but she hadn't thought it through. She was thinking of Aron again. He had made an enemy of Dwight Deacon in public . . . for her. He had placed his career on the railway track, and the Midnight Special was right on time. He had done it all for her, and she felt the love for him well up inside.

'Deacon won't forgive him,' said Steph, practically.

'Screw Deacon,' said Savanna.

'Yeah, right!!'

But Savanna had already forgotten Deacon, who had not forgotten her. As the round went on, she peered past the spotlight to find Aron, and when she caught his eyes her lips were a little bit apart, and her breath was coming faster.

CHAPTER

THIRTY-ONE

Dwight Deacon had made a career out of being a good guy. His formidable politeness was legendary. 'Yes, ma'am', 'No, ma'am', 'Yes, sir', 'No, sir'. Even the most humble interviewers got the DD treatment. The only thing Deacon could be accused of was wanting too badly to be a success. In America, that was not a crime, it was a virtue. So, he might not be quite as 'genuine' as some country purists would have it. So, he was a little ruthless with former friends and business partners. So, there was a little question about the depth of his 'sincerity', whatever that was. But nobody had stuck any real, good, old-fashioned dirt on Dwight Deacon . . . so here was a first.

The conference room at Polymark was full of lesser mortals. A cold, rather heartless room, it was in the genre of such places . . . a long mahogany table, neutral carpet, expensive drapes. A few badly dressed, irritable-looking former executives stared down from the walls, poorly painted, and prematurely dead of stress-related illnesses. The record company lower orders who now milled about it were on some form of red alert. The atmosphere was heavily caffeinated, and people talked intensely into each other's faces, and pored over copies of the newspapers. As always, several huddled in corners making seemingly important cellular telephone calls.

Bit by horrendous bit, the story was coming together. Nobody had gotten to the girl yet, but already they knew who she was. Old Nashville versus new might be the angle . . . a genuine class struggle in the famously 'classless' society. The power freak had been accused of stealing a little person's song. Dwight Deacon had a reputation for going to bat for impoverished songwriters, and put out a lot of PR about how important it was to recognise your sources, and ensure that they got paid. So you had hypocrisy; a little person against a big person; major league insincerity. It was fact that there had been an unseemly row in the revered Bluebird café, where Deacon himself had sung as an unknown. It was magical stuff for the tabloid world whose job it was to reassure Mr and Mrs Average at the check-out desk that there was pain and heartache at the top, too.

At precisely twelve noon, the door to an adjacent office opened. Dwight Deacon strode through it. He came first. The chairpeople and nominal leaders of the various companies that employed him came second. For a couple of uncomfortable hours, Mike Gramm, Pete Cook and the others had been listening to their major profit-earner, and none of them was feeling any better than lousy. There had been a discussion of sorts. Several of the more senior people had suggested that the whole situation be handled in the Nashville way, with the exchange of telephone calls, discreet meetings, the passing of favours and IOUs. Finally, of course, there would be the customary greenback silence with everything laid to rest underneath the thick blanket of untraceable banknotes. But Deacon had not been in dealing mode.

Deacon stood at the end of the boardroom table and banged it with his fist to get the attention he already had.

'Here's like it is,' he said without any preamble at all. 'Last night, I was wronged in public. I was called a thief, and a liar and a cheat in front of a roomful of witnesses. My character was defamed and degraded, and my career has been seriously damaged. That girl lied when she said I had stolen her song. She will be sued for every penny she hasn't got, and she will be driven out of this town. Nobody that has any dealings with me will have any dealings with her, or with anybody who sides with her in this unhappy situation. Now, before I say another word, I want to know this. Is there anybody in this room who does not believe 100 per cent what I have just said? I want them to say so now. Not later. Not ever. Now, or never. Do I make myself very clear?'

Very, very clear.

A very junior and inexperienced attorney tried it.

'Could I just ask, Mr Deacon, if it is true that the Stone girl ever did leave a tape in your car, and if so did you ever hear that tape . . . just for the record?'

Deacon turned to him slowly, as if to a condemned man. 'I do not recall,' he said. 'There's more tapes in my car than bullshit paper in your briefcase, sir. But if there was a tape, and she put it there, she did so without my permission. That is trespass. The tape is technically a gift. That is maybe breaking to enter. It's a felony; at least a misdemeanour; an invasion of privacy; harassment; there may be things missing from my car when I check through . . . and that will make it theft. As far as I know, I never heard that tape. I do not recall it. I do not recall. And now, sir, I would like you to leave this room, and not come back into it again. And I want whoever you work for to take you off my case and out of my interests now and for all time. I would also consider it a personal courtesy to me from Polymark and its subsidiaries if they could arrange to dispense with your services permanently, now and for ever, amen. You have sought to question my integrity at a time when my friends should be supporting me with every ounce of their hearts and minds. I hope you find other business in Nashville, sir, but I am not betting the farm on it and that is not a threat . . . it is a sincere prediction.'

The lawyer whitened. He looked around for support; he did not find it. A couple of his senior partners simply nodded their heads. He gathered up his papers and he left. He did not even protest. He was dead anyway. It set the tone for the meeting as it was intended to. A man had been executed to 'encourage' the others.

'What I need to know from you good people,' Deacon nodded at the remaining lawyers and he nodded at the publicists, 'is what we are gonna do about this little piece of misfortune that has befallen us all.'

He held out his hands to encompass everyone. He was Polymark's

profits. Polymark was their income. Indirectly he was paying everyone in the room. His disasters were their disasters.

The lead attorney spoke quickly. 'The early signs are that she is
of legal age, but has no assets except a large trust fund we can't
touch. Her father is no longer legally responsible for her, but he
does have funds. Very substantial funds. We could use our influence
with the police to get them to issue an exploratory arrest warrant.
They could infer probable cause, if she admits she was in your car,
and if there is anything missing. There usually is something missing
from one's car, in my experience,' he said with a poker-straight
face.

'I surely have not recently seen my solid-gold spectacle case,' said
Deacon. 'Never thought to look for it before all this happened. You
know how it is. Something in your car. Safe on your property. Why
would a man look?'

'What might its value be, sir?'

'Five thousand dollars. Maybe more on account of it being mine,'
said Deacon slowly, allowing himself the beginnings of a smile.

'If she was arrested,' said the lawyer, 'this thing would lose its
sting. Even if there is no proof she took it, she had no right to be
there. An arrest would definitely cool this thing down.'

Deacon looked at the head publicist. 'How could it play?' he
snapped.

'It might be OK if you magnanimously refused to press charges.
You know, a young, stupid girl, got carried away in the excitement of
it all. A kid who's spent her whole life up North. A de facto Yankee
who doesn't know how to behave down here in Tennessee. Kid with
crazy Nashville dreams. Needs to see a shrink.'

'But you don't like it? You don't like we get her locked up?'
Deacon was thinking hard now. This was what he was good at.
Image was everything.

'I think that people might get the wrong idea there . . . you know,
a big man and a little girl . . . that kind of thing.'

'That hussy called me a thief in public. If she had a husband, I'd
have shot him.' DD's fantasies were occasionally so bizarre that most

people had learned how not to smile when he expressed them. Extra effort was needed now in that respect.

'And there were others there . . .'

'Aron Wallis will not be working with us any more,' said Mike Gramm from behind left. 'He's terminated. The lawyers are working on it now.'

'Terminated he certainly is,' said Deacon. He began to tour the room, creeping up inside people's private spaces before moving on again to someone else, as if sniffing them for fear, disloyalty, or some other unacceptable emotion.

'So there are no problems about the copyright of my record,' he said at last.

'None, sir. They can't be stopped from trying, but they couldn't win. She left the tape in your car unsolicited of her own free volition, if indeed she left it there at all. That would make it a gift. Nobody can prove you heard the song, anyway.'

'But there's going to be this . . . this shadow . . . hanging over it.'

The lawyer looked nervous. There was always the deal. But it was dangerous to talk to megastars who thought they were cowboys about doing deals. John Wayne never did deals. The attorney chose his words with great care.

'Of course, someone could talk to the girl. Get her to retract. Point out the downside of not doing so. Word is she has a place at Columbia. Her family are respected in these parts, and in New York. Father is a professor of surgery at the Columbia College of Physicians and Surgeons. The investigators suggest he was unhappy about her dropping out. I'm sure it could be arranged for her to go back there. It would be sensible for her to do so. Make lots of sense to her. Of course, you might not want her to have that escape route after the way she has treated you, sir, and in public like that. But if she retracted, then those tabloids would be running scared on any story they wrote, what with them being so close to malicious intent with regard to your private life, sir, and that lady who came to that unfortunate end. Comes to the carrot or the stick in this life, sir, then a young girl is going to be advised to reach out and grab that carrot, what with her future ahead of her an' all.'

It was pure old Southern-style Tennessee sweet-talk, shrewd and polite. And of course it made sweet Southern sense, smooth as sippin' whiskey.

And then something very odd happened. Dwight Deacon laughed. Whether it was because he could see the light at the end of the tunnel, or for some other reason nobody quite knew, including himself.

'So just who do you think is going to be the person who sits down with little Miss Spitfire and her great big mouth an' her cute little butt and gets her to "retract" – as you so delicately put it, sir?'

There was silence. Nobody appeared to want the dangerous mission. But somebody did.

'You know what? I think it should be me!' said Dwight, and he laughed again. 'Because she might be a lyin' no-good loony-tune hayseed with Yankee money and no sense, but she has for sure got a lot of balls to do what she did to someone like me.'

He looked around the room imperiously. The implication was clear. There was little or no testosterone here.

'So I think I shall seek her out, and have a few quiet words and see if I can explain to this little señorita the error of her ways. Yessir, that is what this man is going to do. When you have a little mess in your backyard, it's always quicker and easier to clean it up yourself. My momma taught me that. And weren't nothin' she was ever wrong about.'

CHAPTER

THIRTY-TWO

Savanna walked up the stairs, remembering the last time she had done so. It hadn't seemed so far up before, but then she wasn't so sure of her reception now. She didn't know what sort of greeting she would get, but she knew the one she wanted. Since she had told Aron she never wanted to see him again, he had stood up to Deacon in the Bluebird in front of a jury of Nashville players, and told him to his face he was a thief. It was one thing for her to do that. It was quite another for him to do it. He worked for Polymark, or had worked for them. He had had a career. A life to lose. A life he loved. It was easy to work a big mouth, and be brave behind the silly optimism of youth. What would Aron's alternatives be now? Uncertain, for sure. Would this apartment be up for sale soon? Was it up for sale now? She hadn't thought to look. Savanna was beginning to realise that thinking things out ahead was not her speciality. Maybe, selfishness and self-righteousness were.

She tried to imagine what she would say to him, but feelings kept getting in the way. She had done him a wrong. She knew now that it was wisdom, not cowardice, that had caused him to back down in his office confrontation with Deacon. He had realised the consequences of doing what his gut had told him to do, and he had had the self-control to know when to walk away and fight another day. He had proved his courage in the Bluebird. The big picture windows were on the stairs too, and Savanna could all but see the big sacks of grain swinging through them. Corn from the heartland would have passed through them on joists from the ships moored on the banks of the Cumberland below.

Nashville. What a place it was. It seemed that she had never left. It seemed that all those years up North had been but a dream, and that she had woken up at home after being away on her travels like Gulliver. Her telephone had been busy this morning. It was amazing just how much determined people could discover in the shortest time. The earliest had been from the Bluebird, saying that she would never be welcome there again, either as a guest or a singer. Next, there had been a series of reporters digging for facts. They had all agreed cheerfully on one thing. Her singing career in Nashville would be strictly a street corner business from now on. ''Course, you could wait till he dies, hon. You sure got time on your side, if not much else,' one of the more cheerful had predicted. 'Pity, 'cos I heard you and your cousin were good, but "good" don't matter in Nashville unless you're good *and* have friends in the business.' In desperation she had actually rung the Crazy C, but the word had reached there, too, a place that was only one step up from a street corner. 'Wouldn't have you as a waitress, sweetheart!' the barman had said with brutal honesty.

Savanna reached the door and checked her watch. She hadn't liked to call first. Was she too early or too late? Whatever. Her timing seemed to be way off right now. Aron opened the door in his dressing gown. It was 9 a.m. More than likely his early morning meetings had been cancelled for some time to come. He smiled when he saw her, wryly, ruefully, but she could tell he was pleased to see her.

'I'm sorry,' she said.

'Come in. Do you want to come in?' She had hesitated without meaning to.

'Oh yes, please. That's if you want me in.'

'Well, you can't stand out there. It's cold.'

'Oh, yeah,' said Savanna slipping past him into the big warm studio.

'I've got some coffee on. Want some?'

'Yeah, please.'

'Toast?'

'No. Just coffee would be fine.'

She wandered into the kitchen. He didn't seem to be wearing anything beneath the dressing gown. No slippers. Yet he wasn't embarrassed. If anything, he seemed to have gained in composure. He poured the coffee into a big mug.

'Milk? Cream?'

'Oh, cream. Just a dash.'

It was funny how conversation had a way of formalising itself. This could have been a Geisha tea ceremony, American style . . . with most of the more intricate bits sacrificed to the saving of precious time.

The pine table in the kitchen seemed to be where he was having breakfast. The *Tennessean* lay on it.

'The good news is you were too late for the morning editions,' he said with a little laugh that was a tad short on humour.

He looked tousled, unshaven, sort of woolly, and cosy. Savanna hadn't seen him like this before.

'I bet you wish you never went into the Crazy C that time,' she said. It was a fishing trip.

'Actually, I haven't gotten around to wishing that yet.' He smiled and sat down, and indicated for her to do the same. She did. 'But then it's early days, isn't it? Right now Deacon will be marshalling the big battalions. My secretary didn't make it into work this morning. I wonder what that means?'

'Look, Aron, I am truly sorry for dragging you into all this. I was just thinking of myself and what is right and wrong, and I guess I wasn't thinking about anyone else at all. That means I'm selfish, and self-centred and I am real, real sorry if this has done you damage.'

He laughed. 'Honey, if you only knew . . .'

'But Polymark can't fire you . . .'

He held up both his hands. 'Spare me, Savanna. I don't think I can take a lecture right now on how this town works or ought to work. It's too early. Or too late. I'm not quite sure which.'

'Yes, I know. I did not intend to come round with that sort of a speech.'

'What sort had you got prepared?'

He kept the sarcasm out of it. There was friendliness in his brown eyes, and the spark of something else, that something else that had been there all along.

'An apology speech. An "Anything I can do" one. Later on perhaps, a "Can you ever forgive me" speech. Humble pie. You get the picture.'

'Yes, but I'd like it painted up a bit, you know, the numbers all filled in with colours. Then I can stick it up on the wall of my memory for those long cold nights up ahead delivering mail or sweeping streets.'

'Oh, don't, Aron! It isn't as bad as that, is it?'

'Not quite.'

'You mean you have a plan?' Savanna smiled her excitement.

'Sort of.'

'We prove he stole my song, and then everybody . . .'

'Forget it, Savanna. Dear God, let that one go . . .'

She looked crestfallen, then apparently decided not to be.

'OK. OK. I'm not going down that road again . . . unless you tell me I can.' She smiled a little bit at the end. The insinuation, flirtatious, was that she might put some of her energies to trying that direction.

'No, my plan is to go sort of independent in the manager/producer category. Maybe out of New York. Maybe out of LA. I don't know. Hell, maybe even out of Nashville, if I can find someone who'll give me a shoe-shine round here.'

'That's great, Aron. And some of your people will go with you.'

'No, they won't. None of them. *I* wouldn't go with me. They won't. They can't afford to. Nobody that I have is that big. Faith could, and Tim, Garth, Shania. But I don't work with those people. I'd even advise Newt Fulsome to find another producer.'

'So who will you work with, or for?'

'You . . . and Steph. That row with Deacon wasn't the only thing that happened at the Bluebird last night. "Mountain Memories" happened. That may turn out to be the event that gets remembered.'

'You liked it.'

'No.'

'You *didn't* like it?' Savanna's face fell away.

'That song is a platinum single on a platinum album. It's not "like" or "dislike". It's just a hit. A great big monster hit. I know them when I hear them. And yes, of course, I *loved* it.'

'Wow,' said Savanna, relieved and pleased. 'You liked it that much. Like "Roots and Wings".'

'*Hold* "Roots and Wings"!' said Aron laughing, and amazed that he still could.

He watched her over the top of his coffee cup. Her eyes were wide at the idea he was opening up to her. She had never looked lovelier to him. So he sent his hand out across the table to where hers lingered, and he touched her fingers, and she did not withdraw her hand from his.

'You know, you make me feel so good about myself. So confident,' said Savanna suddenly. 'You're kinda like Kryptonite! Make me feel like I can fly.'

'You can fly, Savanna. Musically, you can walk on water. Maybe in other ways, too.'

She smiled gently. They were touching still, but their fingers were not moving. Then, almost absent-mindedly, her fingers moved against his, playing with his hand. But she seemed hardly aware of it, because she was concentrating on what she was saying.

'My mom never had a man to make her feel like that. Maybe it was all she needed. She'd sing sometimes after a dinner party, and people would be so condescending. "Oh, that is so cute, LeAnne. Where did you learn to sing like that?" They didn't mean to be cruel, they were just the sort of people who didn't know country from catfish. They were the type that found Mozart a little "obvious" and Brahms a bad joke . . . you know, in this patronising way, and I'd be sitting there thinking that song is a shit-load better than the latest Crystal Gayle or EmmyLou Harris and that Mom's voice was twice as interesting. But those snobbish friends of my father's, who thought they were so clever, were just pig-ignorant. They were the kind of people who thought vegetables grew in supermarkets, and that cheating songs were for those who didn't know the name of a good divorce attorney, or couldn't afford one.'

Aron laughed, pleased by the compliment. What was there better in life than to empower people? What worse than to belittle them, and pour cold water on their talent and dreams? You didn't have to kill to commit murder.

He concentrated on the finger thing. It was still going on. Savanna was playing with them as if they were cutlery, or something. It was strangely nice, and he didn't want Savanna to stop and realise what she was doing. She was at once miles away, and yet more 'here' than she had ever been before.

'But you understand, don't you?' said Savanna. 'That's the thing I like about you best so far. You understand me. You know about the longing and how strong it is, and how secret. You keep it secret because you can't help feeling it's ridiculous, and yet it's the strongest thing about you.'

'Yes, I know,' he said gently. 'Not personally. No producer knows personally what you're talking about. But I've heard many artists trying to articulate it. They all say the same thing. The fire on stage. The world lighting up. Everything coming alive. The rest of life being like some sort of a sideshow. Not really real. The enormous knowledge that the talent is there, coupled with doubt because nobody else sees it. Then, one day, apparently for no reason, they suddenly see it. And it happens, and you haven't changed. You haven't done anything different. You've just gone on being you, but suddenly you are visible, and before you weren't.'

'That is so right, Aron. That is *it*. You came by that dirty old honky-tonk and you heard me sing. All the other drunks did, too. All three of them, and the barman who must have heard a singer or two in his time. But you *heard* heard. That was the difference. I wasn't trying extra hard to please. I was just doing my thing. Wow! Is that how it happens?'

She squeezed his hand really hard now.

'Yeah, that's how it happens. And then you insult the biggest star in the American recording industry, and then we all get thrown out of work and then we all catch the Greyhound out of Nashville, and that's the end of the story.'

He laughed. So did Savanna.

'I can't believe we're laughing about this,' she said.

'I can't believe you're holding my hand,' he said.

'Oh. Jeez. Am I?'

She looked down and she was, and he was smiling at her across the table. The moment happened very fast. Like him discovering her. Like her being discovered. Savanna worked emotionally at electricity speed, in anger, in love, in longing, maybe in everything. It was part of why she would be a great artist, but Aron wasn't thinking of her artistry. He was thinking of his longing. And he was wondering about hers.

'Did you just get out of bed?' she said.

It was not really a question at all.

CHAPTER

THIRTY-THREE

Savanna woke slowly in that way you did when you knew something very good had happened in the night. It might have been a dream, or even a particularly relaxing sleep, but this morning, of course, it was neither of those things . . . it was Aron. He lay there still asleep, his arm thrown out casually to lie across her tummy. It was an act of ownership, of claim, and Savanna, who had never been owned or claimed, was uncertain about the brand-new feeling. So she slid out from underneath his arm, trying not to wake him in the process, and failing. He moaned gently in the no-man's-land between sleep and wakefulness.

'Where you going?' he said, trying to open his eyes. He reached out and put her hand back where it had been, effectively stalling any escape.

'Nowhere,' said Savanna. She hooked herself up on her elbow and looked down at him dreamily. He had no way of knowing it was her first time, because she hadn't told him. It had felt right. And that was enough for her.

'Not ever,' he said. He closed his eyes and snuggled in more closely to her, adding his leg to his arm as an inducement against leaving.

His action raised the desire in her again. She didn't want to get up today. She just wanted to lie there in the great big room, and make love until she broke, or cracked, or whatever people did when they had made too much love. Was it always like this the first time? Did you just want it to go on and on, and the world to go away and leave you forever loving? Could that little clock go spinning around for a week, and this go on getting better and better? She could ask him. Oh, God, he might know. He would know. The thought came as a shock. There would have been others. The wife for a start. He was twenty-five. Several? A score? More? But how many more? And how had the enthusiastic novice rated amongst the serried ranks of past lovers? Savanna smiled at the wonderful ridiculousness of early-morning jealousy after a night of passion. Somehow, it underlined the mystery of life. How little one knew. Of oneself. Of anybody else. She had given her virginity, freely and with what seemed like the purest love, to this man who was fundamentally a stranger to her. OK, he was a stranger who had sacrificed his career because he believed in her. He was a stranger who thought he loved her, maybe. Surely that must count for a lot on top of all the other somehow less reputable things . . . like lust, and passion, and animal desire. Would this be it? Would he be the one? The first and the last? The odds said 'no', but the feelings said 'yes'. And feelings ruled, OK?

'Do we get to stay here all day?' she asked, subtly acknowledging that he was the expert here.

'We could,' he said, opening his eyes wide. He reached forward and touched her breast, tracing its line with his finger.

'Look, I can do this. And I couldn't do this yesterday,' he said.

'How do you know you can do it now? You didn't ask my permission,' she laughed.

'Because I *am* doing it, and you are not complaining. And because, in fact, your nipple is beginning to tighten when I touch it. There. See? Mmm! I think that is permission. That looks like permission to me.'

'OK. OK. You have permission for that. I do give you permission.' Savanna could feel the blood rushing to her breast, and to the other one, the one he also had permission to touch.

'In fact,' he said, 'I think I also have permission to do this.' He leaned forward, looking into her eyes as he did so. Very gently, he opened his mouth and put out his tongue, and laid it on the hot and hardening nipple, running round the tip of it, filling it up with blood, feeling it pulsate against his tongue. 'But I might be wrong,' he said, taking his tongue away, and smiling, teasing her.

'Not wrong,' she said. Her lips were suddenly dry. Her whole mouth was dry. He could hardly enunciate the words. His tongue had to get back there quickly. Immediately. 'Not wrong' was too long a speech in the urgency of the circumstances. He didn't wait. His whole mouth surrounded her nipple and she felt it swell inside the wetness, felt it taut and tight, throbbing shamelessly against his tongue. He moved his hand up to touch the other one. But his neglect had not held it back. Savanna was very far from expert in this, but apparently the body had its own wisdom, and breasts had a way of acting in concert. She was glad they were so beautiful. It had been nice to look at them in the mirror and know they were good, and to see people react to them, that hypnotised male stare, at once reassuring and ridiculous. There were two sorts of breasts, she and her friends had decided. Those that had button nipples, and those that didn't. The latter were rare, although Nubian tribeswomen had them, and quite a lot of Italian women, if the glossy magazines swimsuit sections could be believed. Hers were conical, pre-pregnancy, pure pink, and they made a straight line with the white skin of her perfect young breasts. The only difference between nipple and breast was colour, and the gentle upcurve at their end, a tiny ski-jump that could send a slippery tongue sliding off into the thinnest air . . .

Savanna's low moan submerged her thoughts. His mouth sucked gently on her, and she felt the wetness explode once again between her legs. There was a rhythm about this. No ecstasy could stay still. Everything led to something else, and all was urgent. A second before Savanna had thought that her life would be full if his tongue could touch the sharpening point of her nipple. If it could but throb there hotly, wetly, indenting his tongue with its tension, that would be enough, for an hour, maybe more. But now, there was already more. Another part of her was screaming for his touch, and it could not wait another second. Permission, indeed. She reached down below the covers for his leg, and she shifted, lying back and opening herself to whatever he would give her. But it must be soon. It must be now.

His hand found the heat of her, and he laid its palm against the place of longing, but still he held her breast in his mouth and Savanna began to understand the game of love. It must be slowed, but not for too long. It must hurry, but not too quickly. For every tide there was time. Each part of her body had its moment, which it was forced to surrender in turn to one with more urgent claims. It had been like that constantly through the long night of lovemaking. The pinnacle of release followed by the gentle and tender rebuilding before the crashing descent into the abyss of desire from the highest point of the mountain of lust.

'Aron, please, please,' she moaned, unable to wait as he could.

He moved on top of her, and then he was inside her. The dance began again with all the hopeless and wonderful promise of the tiny death that would only be the end of a wonderful new beginning.

Savanna's thoughts went away as she lost her young body to its blissful senses. As she slipped into the timeless joy, there was one thought that merged into her ecstasy.

'Welcome to life,' it said.

CHAPTER

THIRTY-FOUR

In the library at Harbour Court the atmosphere was an extraordinary mixture of fear, joy, despair and excitement. Savanna and Aron sat on the vast sofa, needlessly close. Grandma, watching them across the room, knew immediately that they were lovers. The natural cynicism of old age had not left her untouched, but she was warmed by the sight of young love in all its passion and crazed inconsistency as much as her old bones were warmed by the hot fire.

They had told her everything, but events were still unfolding. Sometimes they were defiant, and confident, but then, as the facts mounted up against them and their dreams, pessimism would drown optimism.

'Whatever happens, I'm not going back to New York. If Aron has to leave Nashville, I'm going where he goes. That's the bottom line.'

Grandma watched her. How much of this was about love? When love came in the door, sense had a way of flying out of the window. But then Aron, a man who apparently knew his job, had bet heavily on Savanna way before Cupid had appeared on the scene.

'Explain to me again,' she said, shaking her head from side to side, 'why young Aron here is being drummed out of town. Because somebody else stole something? That's the reason?'

'I don't want to leave, Mrs Stone. But I just have to face reality. I've made some telephone calls. Business. Friends. People I thought really liked me haven't called back. People I would have trusted with my life are not *speaking* to me. I can't find a Nashville attorney to advise me on the employment contract that Polymark are trying to cancel. The people that have talked to me say I should go to Europe. One even said the Far East. Somehow, I don't see Savanna singing in Tiananmen Square!'

It was barely a joke.

Grandma nodded, but she shifted in her chair and plucked at her earlobe. It was a subtle sign that she was getting angry. But Grandma didn't get angry in a vacuum. When she was angry, she acted.

'I'd sing in China. Anywhere,' said Savanna. 'With you' was the unspoken sentiment. Suddenly, she felt very bad. She knew about Aron's situation, but hearing him describe it to Grandma brought it home hard. Out of fury and a rich kid's pride, she had rained not only on her own parade, but on Aron's too. She hadn't bothered to learn the rules of the town's games, because she had felt that rules didn't apply to her. She had wrecked Aron's career and then, to add insult to injury, persuaded him to fall in love with her. Scott Fitzgerald had been right when he said the rich were different, and Hemingway had been wrong when he had answered that they were merely richer. Pride, gall, and insensitivity came with old money, but it had no right to wreck the lives of those who had had to work their guts out in this world for the things they'd got.

Then suddenly, Savanna, too, started to get angry. Aron could not be treated that way. It was wrong. It was wicked. It was simply not fair.

'You know,' she said, and her voice was cold, 'I think I might just go out to that ranch . . . I know where it is . . . and shoot that son-ofabitch. With good behaviour I'd be out of jail in a year or two these days. Yeah, shoot the bastard right between the eyes.'

'And I for one will drink to that,' said Grandma. She pulled on a sash and somewhere in the depths of the house a bell sounded. 'I'll tell you, that is fighting talk of the kind I like to hear down in Dixie now and again. It sounds to me we got some genuine un-American activities taking place in this city of ours, or fixing to take place, and I say head 'em off at the pass. That's what I say.'

The butler arrived to answer the bell.

'We'll have a bottle of the Dom Perignon '52,' she said. 'I know we are not supposed to drink champagne so old, but to me that '52 has the sweetest taste of any wine that came out of France. There's only a few cases left, and I'm planning to finish them before I die.'

She turned around in her chair, and her eyes were full of fight.

'Now here's what it seems to this foolish old woman. It seems about time that I had a little word with old Senator Forbush. I've lost count of the amount of dreary fundraisers I've had for him in this here house. I've listened to enough of his boring stories. He can sure as hell listen to one of mine. And that goes for that young governor, too, with the pretty wife. He was real polite when he came here last. And all those congressmen we've been writing those cheques to for years. Send them out like Christmas cards. Probably most of those representatives are dead now, but I could ring up old Arthur who heads up the law firm still, and ask him if any of those weasels been cashing those cheques. That law firm of Arthur's represents that new bank I'm told that the city are using for the downtown redevelopment programme. I haven't talked to the mayor in six months. I bet he'd like to come out to luncheon on Sunday. He was a family values man last time I heard. Don't seem as if this Deacon fella is too sound on the kind of family values we have down here in Tennessee.'

'Go, Grandma!' said Savanna.

Aron hadn't seen that side of things in Nashville. He'd seen the other, and in a way it wasn't so different. This was good ol' boy power. It was like the Mafia, which had perhaps been modelled upon it. IOUs were accumulated for years, uncollected, uncalled, like cash in a bank for a rainy day. They might never be needed. Often weren't. Then, when a rare crisis hit, the old wheels would be set in motion. In the corporate world it was much more immediate. A favour would be repaid within a day, a week or a month. That was because the power of businessmen could wax and wane. You had to collect what you were owed before the debtor lost his ability to pay. But ancient Stone lawyers would pay long-term Southern congressmen for years on end without a favour asked. Grandma was right. Some of them might even be dead. But some would not be and they would have long memories and records of contributions that had been badly needed in the days before political and pecuniary plenty had struck. A good ol' boy ball could be gotten rolling well and good. And it could gather a lot of moss as old friends who hadn't talked in years found time for a game of golf or bridge or a spine-stiffening Mint Julep on the porch of an ante-bellum home. It wouldn't take much to stimulate the irritation of the old guard, especially when the subject of the collective ire was some jumped-up singing man from the 'entertainment' business. That darned thing seemed to have taken over the country like some communist revival, turning everything upside down and frightening the damned horses.

'It might be worth a try,' said Aron.

'Tell you what's worth a try, my boy,' said Grandma, 'and that's this champagne,' as the butler poured the amber liquid, still sparkling, but mellow now with age, its acidity deliciously tempered, its rich thickness somehow symbolic of the subtle power that permeated the ancient library of Harbour Court.

CHAPTER

THIRTY-FIVE

For the second morning running, Savanna awoke in Aron's arms. It didn't feel any less good. She peered at the clock. It was six-thirty, which was a little early for the telephone. It was on his side of the bed, and she was perversely glad of the call, because it would wake him, and then . . . and then . . .

He woke with a start, and then a scowl. 'Six-thirty,' he mouthed silently.

'Well, if it isn't ol' sleepy-head. Aron, boy, I told you about the early mornings. Those late nights are for rock 'n' rollers. We country folk like to watch that good ol' sun come up.'

It was Dwight Deacon.

Aron mouthed the word across at Savanna. 'Deacon.'

She opened her eyes wide.

'You know what you are thinking, Aron? You are thinking: Now why on God's good earth is Dwight Deacon calling me up at six-thirty in the morning when I didn't think he was kindly disposed towards me on account of what a lot of guys I telephoned yesterday intimated to me? The ones that called back, that is . . . Well, boy, I'll tell you what I want. Now, I had a few calls of my own yesterday. The governor for one. Big fan of mine, the governor. I raised a lot of money for that governor. Boy, I sure did. And Forbush, the senator, he called round sundown. He'd had a few whiskeys, I'd bet. And then you know what, I had calls from a few congressmen . . . some I never even heard of . . . and a couple I done never campaigned for 'cos they were not my sort of people. Anyways, to make a long story short, I'd sure as hell like to have a quick word with that little girl of yours. My spending money is saying she is lyin' right next to you in that warm bed of yours at six-thirty on this bright mornin' when God's day is startin' right on out there without you both.'

Aron tried to clear his brain. How the hell did Deacon know where Savanna was sleeping? Had he got the place staked out? No. He didn't need to. He was shrewd. Deacon was the shrewdest man Aron had ever met. He didn't know who Homer was, and he'd hardly heard of Shakespeare. He prided himself on not reading books. But he knew things. Things like who was sleeping beside whom. Things like how to set up the scaffolding of a deal. He had managed to intimate that the Stones had struck back. That there might be some point in negotiation. That it wasn't just his brute strength any more. But should Aron give Savanna to him? Savanna was all sorts of things, but she couldn't handle Deacon. Or could she? She'd as good as thrown him out of the Bluebird. She'd been the one left sitting prettier than a rainbow at the microphone.

'He wants to talk to you,' said Aron, holding his hand over the mouthpiece.

'What does he want?'

'Don't know. Sounds like Grandma got the politicians on his back.'

Savanna beckoned for the phone. She sat up in bed, naked to the waist, and tried to compose herself. Aron stared unashamedly at her. Her breasts defied gravity. Her hair, unkempt, fell over half her face.

'Yes,' she said.

'Savanna Carson Stone, I am presumin'.'

'Yes.'

'This here is Dwight Deacon.'

'Yes.'

'Is that all you say, "yes"?'

'No.'

'Ah well, I suppose it is early in the morning . . .'

'What do you want?'

'Direct, I see. I like that in a woman. Well, I'd like to talk to you. Face to face. One to one. Just you an' me. It seems we have a situation that has blown up here, and it is not doing any of us, nor this town of ours, any good. An' I thought that the intelligent thing would be for us to sit down and talk things through. Get a few things off our chests, so to speak. Of course, ain't no big deal to me either way. My life goes on, and life is good. But a couple of friends whose advice I value have had a word with me, and the view we took was that talking, like rain, helps to clear the air on a foggy day. I was thinking you might be thinking that, too. Now you, bein' young and proud and pretty, you didn't like to call first. It's us guys supposed to do the callin' in this life, is it not, Ms Savanna?'

'I'll talk to you. Where? When?'

'*Very* direct. Well, I'm glad you take that view. I'll tell you something you may not believe but I am sitting in my car – that will be a Range Rover you may well recognise – parked right here beside the Cumberland River. Right now, I am looking up at a big window that I believe to be the window of the room that just a few minutes ago you were sleepin' in. How's about that for a nice surprise to wake up to?'

Savanna was yards from the window, but she instinctively drew the sheets around her to cover her nakedness . . .

'He's right outside. In a cellphone, on his car. In, on. On, in,' she whispered as she tried to correct herself in her confusion.

'Bastard!' said Aron. He wasn't quite sure why that was his first reaction. There was something voyeuristic about it, something not quite nice.

'And you are suggesting?' said Savanna to Deacon.

'I am suggesting that I sit here and eat my breakfast, which I just picked up at McDonald's. And in the fullness of time, when you have done all the things you need to do, eaten your own breakfast perhaps, you might care to come down to my car, and we could go for a little drive. How does that sound to you?'

'OK. Wonderful,' said Savanna coldly, her voice thick with sarcasm.

'I will just wait on you, then, ma'am. Please do not hurry yourself. I am just drinkin' coffee in the early mornin' here, and composin' me a song. If you don't mind me joking about our little situation here, I won't tell you what my song is about.' He laughed quite pleasantly, and switched off his phone.

'Are you going to go?' said Aron. His head had been close to the telephone. He tiptoed out of bed, buck-naked, and approached the window indirectly, peering out of it from the edge.

'Shit, he's there, all right. Range Rover. Was that the one you left the tape in?'

'I guess,' said Savanna. 'Cute butt.'

'Thanks.' He smiled ruefully, hurrying back to bed.

'What harm can I do?'

'Nothing, I guess. He can't kill you.'

'Or rape me?'

'Jeez, Savanna. Don't even talk about . . .'

'I've never had anybody else, you know.'

'You haven't?'

'Well, I'm glad you didn't say you guessed.' She giggled.

'Listen, Savanna, this is serious. This maniac is sitting outside there in his car, and you are talking about sex!'

'It's what's on my mind.'

'It's on my mind, too, but I'm trying to work out what this freak is up to. He'll probably have the conversation recorded. Think what you're saying.'

'Not evidence in this State unless both parties agree.'

'Oh, thank you, Ms Attorney. Jesus, Savanna, can you put those breasts away. They are making my mind go numb.'

'Well . . . if my breasts are making your mind go numb, what do you think my butt might do to it?' She flipped over and threw back the sheets.

'Oh, God.'

Aron put his hand to his head. Life in Nashville was not supposed to be like this. Wasn't country about being laid-back? What was happening here?

'Savanna, I know what we all think of the bastard, but that is Dwight Deacon down there. He is waiting in his car. I've just seen him. I don't think anybody in Nashville has seen him wait for anything for the last five years. We could sell tickets for it. Twenty bucks a pop!'

Savanna rolled over and stretched like a sleepy cat.

'Oh, Dwight Deacon. Dwight Deacon. He's only a singer!'

She looked completely irresistible. Aron hesitated.

'Savanna!'

'OK, but I've got to take a shower. Got to get all cleaned up for the dream thief. You know that's what he is, isn't he? A dream thief. Can you get any lower than that?'

She got up and walked across the room, totally unselfconscious of her body. It was as if she had known him all her life. He prayed that she would. Aron had never been much of an early-morning man. Things were going to change in that department. He grabbed a terry-cloth robe as Savanna disappeared inside the bathroom, and double-checked the superstar. He was tapping on the wheel of his car. It would be in time to one of his own CDs. At the Deacon level of fame you only ever listened to your own music.

She took an age in the bathroom. Aron walked the line. He had to admire her guts. But he was also thinking of the future. Deacon might get pissed off waiting and pull right out of there, sick of being jerked around by somebody he basically considered a nobody. Then where would they all be? Back to square one. There was a window of opportunity here, and Savanna was in the bathroom taking a leisurely shower. It was the rich again, wasn't it, and their damned safety-net of cash and confidence. Still, Aron was a dealer, too. If you had the balls to play it cool when you were the one without the cards, sometimes you walked away from the table with the whole pile of chips. You could never know when to hold 'em, fold 'em, walk away or run. The song had been wrong about that. Savanna's delaying tactics might just be exactly what the doctor ordered.

Eventually she emerged, looking newer than brand.

'He still there?' she asked, buttoning her blouse.

'God knows why, but he is.'

'Must want to see the girl,' she said, throwing back her head and her hair and laughing. 'Maybe he has this old man's thing for me. You know how guys do.'

'Jeez, Savanna, you are not trying to make me jealous now, are you? Look, baby, I am clean out of emotions here. I am sizzled like an overdone steak in a greasy pan. I need a Librium and a quart of Jack Daniels.'

'Or a nice clean woman.'

She walked over to him and threw her arms round his neck, plastering her body against his, feeling his instant excitement.

'Savanna, no!'

'OK. OK. I'm going. I'm going. If I'm not back in a couple of hours, call the cops and start looking for newly dug graves by the side of the road.'

'Just don't agree to anything. Don't sign anything. Don't be taken in by his BS. Don't . . .'

'Oh, Aron. Really. Anybody would think this dick-head is important or something . . .' Again, she laughed, and she was gone.

He breathed in deeply and checked the window once again. Deacon was still there. He saw Savanna walk out across the sidewalk and tap on the window, saw Deacon let it down. Then she walked around and got into the passenger seat through a door that Deacon leaned across to open for her. He caught the ghost of a smile on the star's face before it disappeared from view.

And then Aron Wallis felt the pang of regret that he had allowed this meeting to happen. He had the feeling that he had made a mistake, and that he would be the one who would suffer most as a result of it.

CHAPTER

THIRTY-SIX

'You sure know how to keep a fellow waiting,' said Deacon. He made it sound rueful rather than aggressive, and he upped his black Stetson to her as he spoke.

'Didn't know you were coming,' said Savanna, quite coldly, but not quite as coldly as she had hoped.

'Well, you sure look pretty as a picture and cool as a cucumber. I guess country singers are just two a penny to a rich kid like you.' He laughed, impressed by the fact that she was not impressed by him.

'I'm through the autograph-for-my-kid-sister routine,' declared Savanna, allowing herself a faint smile.

'Apparently you and your family got friends in high places. Not just a hayseed singer after all, Ms Stone. Ol' Senator Forbush said he used to dandle you on his knee. Bet he'd like to try that now, the old lecher.'

'So that's why I'm sitting here in your car and you are trying your best to be nice to me. Because my family have done a lot of dying for this State and managed to hold on to their money and influence while they were doing it.'

'Nice way to put it. But yes, well OK, you like to be straight up . . . so do I. I listen to my friends.'

'The ones in high places.'

He just laughed at the semi-insult. 'Like that Garth song, it's the friends in low places you need to worry about.' It didn't come out like a threat.

'Are we doing our meeting here?'

'No, ma'am. If it is acceptable to you, I would like to take you on a short drive. Out to my spread, if that would be all right. Show you where I live. *Invite* you on to the property as it were.'

'OK,' said Savanna, getting his point. 'Was this the car I stuck the tape into?'

In answer, he jerked his thumb over his shoulder to a back seat. A cardboard box sat on it. It was stuffed to the brim with tapes, apparently blank. 'That's about three months' worth of the tapes I get handed every day. Can you believe that? If I listen to them all, I wouldn't have time to wash.' He had borrowed the box from the receptionist at Polymark the night before. She kept it under her desk, and deposited the dreams of the hopeless hopefuls in it.

'Seems like you listen to the stuff that makes it into your player,' said Savanna. 'Or do you check it first to see which particular one of your songs you want to start the morning with?'

He started up the car, and went silent for a moment or two.

Above them, Aron watched him pull out suddenly from the parking space. Deacon narrowly missed a car that was overtaking them, which honked its horn angrily. It was the action of an irritated driver. Shit, what had Savanna just said to him?

'Listen, missy. I had hoped this little chat would be a pleasant one. I am still hopin' for that. But you called me a thief in front of people who count for a lot in this town. Now, here I am driving you out to my ranch. I don't want you to feel you got the right to insult me, because I am behavin' like a gentleman here. Now here is the way I see it. We are in Tennessee. In Nashville. We are not in Detroit or New York City. Why do we not just have a few words about the world in general, and get ourselves down to specifics later? I believe your family would know about small talk . . . a lot better than mine.'

'Just where do your family come from, Mr Deacon?' asked Savanna in her best drawing-room voice. 'As my grandfather would have said, I don't believe I know your people.'

He laughed. 'You don't give up, do you? An' I like that in a woman. You don't take no shit, if you excuse my French, but you sure as hell are not afraid to dish it out. Reminds me of myself when I was young.'

'Or of you now, perhaps.' Savanna laughed openly. It was a good sound and she felt like it. There was something strangely likeable about Deacon, and she had never expected there to be. He was so awful, he was somehow nice. It was as if he had turned the full circle on himself.

'You're not afraid of nothin' or nobody, are you?' There was a kind of awe in his voice. 'Is that just grand old genes?'

'No. Just tight new blue ones, and being young, I guess. I think you have to learn how to be afraid . . .'

'Darn right, you do. Habit like anything else. Nothing to fear except fear itself. Who said that?'

'Roosevelt.'

'Well, you cottoned on to something important there, missy. Being afraid is a bad habit that others like you to have. They like you to be weak and generous, too. Then when they got a bead on you, they can smell your fear and take advantage of it. Before too long you're just a mouse like all the rest, just hangin' round waitin' to be spat out by the cat.'

'Listen, you can just call me Savanna.'

'That's a right pretty name.'

She looked at him sideways. Was he flirting with her? He seemed to like her naturally, almost unconsciously, because he for sure had no reason to. The stupid thing was that she felt the same way. That was downright crazy, almost obscene. It wasn't a sexual thing. Oh no, for sure it was not that.

They were through the outer strips of Nashville now, passing brown Vanderbilt, and the funky shops that seemed to attach themselves to rich universities – bars and eateries, clothes stores and bookshops, coffee joints that catered to a young crowd. He would turn right soon, to Hendersonville, where his 'ranch' was, or what passed for one in the suburbia where most Nashville stars lived.

'You mind me askin' what you are doing slumming it round beer joints, when you could be going to a place like this?' He jerked a finger at Vanderbilt.

'Had a place in an Ivy League school up North. But I wanted to do this. My mother's family were mountain people.'

'Were they now? So you are a creature of contradictions, Savanna. Class and money and brains versus poverty, music and talent. Sounds like America to me. Dreams or safety. Excitement or security. Not too many get that choice to make. Don't know if it's easier to have the choice, or harder. Too much freedom can tangle you up, you know. That's why shrinks are not poor. Yup, in the old days it was simpler. Just getting ahead was the only game in town. Only one way up. Ten thousand ways down.'

She looked at him with renewed interest. He was quite a thinker. She sensed the loneliness like a lead weight at the centre of his gravity, pulling him lower. He carried cares, this one. There was sadness at his core, and not just career sadness.

'How do you write a song?' he said suddenly.

It was a serious question. He was a songwriter, possibly the most famous one in the world at this very moment. So was she, but an unknown. He was talking shop to her.

'At night. In a diner. Too much coffee. Legal pad, felt-tip pen. Words first, melody a few seconds later, but the melody just stays in my head.'

'Me, it's the morning. I wake up, don't open my eyes, lie still as a dead dog, and start composin'. The tunes have been going round all night in my dreams. Then they come together, and I jump out of bed and start scribblin', but it's exactly the same time I need to take a leak. Boy, do my days sometimes start badly!'

She laughed out loud, and he turned to her with those hypnotic, big, round eyes. He seemed startled that he had actually been funny. It was as if nobody had ever accused him of being that before. Then he started to laugh.

'Oh, that is so original. I never read that about you, in interviews I mean,' said Savanna.

'Those ain't the kind of things a man tells *journalists*!' They are the sort of things he tells songwriters that he respects, was the unspoken subtext.

Savanna was charmed. Was she meant to be? Was this the Deacon magic working on her, being aimed at her, to prepare her for some cunning pitch? Aron had warned her, but her attitude towards this man was changing. She reminded herself he had still stolen her song. She hung on to that, surprised that she needed to reinforce the memory.

'You know 'em when they are good, don't you?' he said.

'Oh, you do know that.'

'Because they excite *you*,' hc said.

'That's it.'

'Your song excited me,' said Deacon suddenly.

'What!'

He had just thrown it out, like a bone to a dog. She wondered if she had heard him right.

'You wrote "Roots and Wings" in a diner. Too much coffee. No, that was an old one, wasn't it. Way back. That was why you got so pissed.'

'Are you saying you heard "Roots and Wings" and you used it?'

'Wasn't that why you left it in there?' He pointed at the tape deck.

'For credit, and for royalties. Not to be stolen.'

'You got 'em.'

'I have not got them.'

'You have now, Savanna.'

'What do you mean?' Her eyes were wide open. They had reached the gates of a long drive. Deacon pressed a button. The gates opened.

'But I heard that disc went to press,' said Savanna.

'Not them covers didn't. Nor the press handouts.'

'Why are you doing this?'

'Don't know.'

'You don't know?'

He stopped the car in the driveway, and turned to her. 'As God is my witness, I do not know why I have said what I have just said. To be frank, I made this meeting to bullshit you this way and that. Buy you off. Frighten you. Charm you. Jeez, brainwash you. I don't know, but I knew I could fix something. That damned song was the best thing I heard in ten years, and I wanted to be the one who wrote it. Those early mornings haven't been turning out too well lately, truth be told. So I took advantage of a sweet girl who was innocent enough to make me a legal gift of a tape. I did not do the decent thing. I did not do the decent thing because I thought I had the power to get away with it. And you know what is weird? I did have that power, and I do have that power. But I am not going to use it. You get writer's credit on your song, and you can cover it too, if you like. You can have that, too. Why? Beats me. Something about you, Savanna. Something strange. You opened that pretty mouth of yours and you called me a crook in front of Polymark and Curb and Faith Hill, and a whole bunch of guys who *fawn* on me. That makes you special. And that goddamned song is worth a million bucks in songwriters' royalties, or I never sold a CD. So there. Next time you open that big mouth of yours, I'm gonna kiss it shut.'

Savanna had had no very great surprises in her life this far. This was one of them. Like all great surprises, it came with subsidiary surprises of its own. All she could think about at this moment of the deliverance of her dreams was the extraordinary, unpredictable, and totally obsessing personality of Dwight Deacon. She looked at him. Her mouth was wide open. The look of frank astonishment on her face mirrored the sense of absolute bewilderment in her heart. Expecting one thing, she had got another. That was the essence of shock in life. A million dollars. OK. Dwight Deacon's hit of the decade written by her. Her own cover of the song that alone would launch her career. OK. OK. But the interesting thing was why? And what was that about kissing?

'Why?' she said again.

'I don't know,' he repeated. He turned to look at her and she had the overwhelming impression that he was as bemused as she. The popular wisdom was that you knew what you were doing in this life. In the case of Dwight Deacon, it had just been proved spectacularly wrong.

'There's cattle,' he said suddenly in the silence that had developed amidst the whirring thoughts.

There indeed were cattle. A cowboy's 'ranch' should have them. Savanna dutifully looked at them. They were corralled into a paddock that looked as if it had been designed for horses. These were the 'show' cattle, kept near the entrance of the estate to show that it was a 'working' place, not just some dude affair owned by a Roy Rogers cowboy whose swimming pool might well resemble some musical instrument. In fact, the cattle looked as if they had been groomed like racehorses. They were sleek and shiny, giving the impression that they would come when called. They would require nothing as drastic as a lasso, but had perhaps been trained to put up with one on days when they were on 'show'. Savanna kept thinking of the herd of sheep that some artist had up north in a field. Cardboard cutouts. Probably very valuable. Surreality was everywhere. Why was she staring at nearly fake cattle, when one of the most mysterious men in the world had decided on a whim to make her a star? The rollercoaster that was becoming her life was making her dizzy. She had experienced the bottom . . . you didn't get much lower than the C, then Aron had 'discovered' her. Next she had become an outcast, a pariah, a non-person. Now, here she was again on the brink of stardom. Was this a dream, a nightmare, or reality? Was there any difference between the three?

'You'll be an overnight star,' he said suddenly, as if he were right inside her mind. He looked at her again, as if at a Martian who had landed by mistake in his car. He shook his head, as if to clear it. Was this the flu? Was this the onset of a mental illness that had been lurking in the undergrowth for years, and had finally manifested itself . . . brought on by the cattle? Some osmotic mad cow disease?

'Yes,' she said.

He could have cut a deal. A five per cent royalty, $100,000 cash. No cover. 'Written in conjunction with . . .', 'By Dwight Deacon and Savanna Stone', 'Words by Savanna Stone'. The kid would have leaped at any of these offers. What had happened to the deal? The blessed deal? It wasn't too late, of course. The slap on the leg, the hearty laugh. 'Just joking, Savanna. Now, let's talk turkey.' But no, there would be none of that.

Savanna closed her mouth. For some reason she could not get the remark out of her mind about him kissing it shut. That lingered strangely, weirdly, like an indecent, but oddly perverse delight. He shot a look at her, that seemed to say he was thinking the same thing. Then he shot the stick into first and the Range Rover lurched away from the acting cattle. For a few hundred yards they drove in silence, past manicured paddocks in which high-stepping, small-gaited walking-horses roamed. The house, large and square on the Tennessee flatlands, held no mystery. Soon they were beneath its imposing late 1920s' size.

The car crunched to a stop on gravel that looked like quicksand. As if to stop Savanna drowning in it, Dwight jumped out quickly. He opened the door for her like a Southern gentleman might have done a generation or two before.

He took her hand as she stepped from the car. Scarlett and Ashley. Rhett wouldn't have bothered. Savanna blushed. He looked away.

'Thank you,' she said. There was no trace of the irreverent mockery she might usually have injected into such a situation.

'Welcome to my home,' he said as he led her up stone steps to a large hall that had come with stags' heads from the previous owner. The hallway was vast, and he seemed uncomfortable in it. He hurried her off to the side, where a warren of rooms merged into each other, each bearing the unmistakeable stamp of the house's owner. Grammys littered the walls. Signed photographs of the famous dripped from Steinway pianos and long tables, fighting for space with Remington bronzes of Indians and frontiersmen. The Wild West was the subject matter of the pictures, too. Many were of museum quality, others firmly the wrong side of kitsch, garish and bright against the dark panelling on which they hung.

There were plaques commemorating awards won, trees planted, hospitals opened. The covers of magazines like *Time* and *Life*, *Newsweek* and *People* hovered grandly above lesser publications, and already, although Savanna had not seen him touch a thing, the tones of Dwight Deacon's music emanated mysteriously from cupboards, drapes, cornices and lamps. There did not seem to be anything resembling a loudspeaker anywhere.

He flopped down on a sofa, and stuck his boots on a coffee table which bore books about the artists whose work hung on the walls. His body language hinted at an attempt to reassert some form of control.

'Would you like a Coke, ma'am?'

'No, thanks. Some coffee would be nice.'

'Oh, yeah.'

The house seemed empty. It was as if Deacon didn't trust himself with people. Yet, it was spotless. Armies of ghostly cleaners must do their thing at some time or another. Did he cook for himself? Surely not. It was all but impossible to imagine him giving a dinner party, or even having folk round to watch football. The thought bordered on the grotesque. He stood up again. 'Let's go find some,' he said, as if a coffee-seeking mission were quite an adventure.

A vast, impersonal dining room gradually gave way via a series of sculleries, pantries and other rooms to a huge, slightly old-fashioned kitchen. Its main features were an outsize wooden table surrounded by chairs and the largest Aga that Savanna had ever seen. A coffee machine was plugged in on a grey marble counter. He bypassed that for a plain water heater, and reached into a cupboard for a mug, and some Taster's Instant. Milk came from a Sub-Zero that looked like an outsize jukebox. So did a box of Coco Pops. He poured these into a bowl, and drowned them with milk. This would be the second Deacon breakfast.

'You want I make you some ham and eggs,' he said. He was strangely diffident, as if embarrassed to be revealing so much of his private life.

'No really, coffee's fine,' said Savanna, holding up her hand.

'Don't mind instant?'

'No, it's what I have at home,' she lied.

'It's not,' he said.

'What?'

275

'Not what you have at home. You would have fancy percolated coffee.'

To continue to lie, or not to lie was the question.

'OK, actually Kenya. From the Rift Valley. Obviously, I'm not a very good liar.'

'Takes one to know one.' They both laughed. An awkward silence descended. He heated the water and poured her coffee. Then he sat at the table and got down to the munching of Coco Pops. Savanna knew somehow this would be his staple diet. Whenever he was hungry . . . in the middle of the night, or the middle of the morning, he would come in here and do the Coco Pops. He leaned low as he ate, his head right down by the dish, like a Chinaman scooping rice into his mouth from a bowl with chopsticks. Deacon used a spoon that looked too small for the task.

'You mean that . . . what you said back in the car?' said Savanna carefully.

It seemed like the time for some cementing of the verbal agreement. Here they were eating a fifty-cent breakfast in a $3,000,000-dollar house as if nothing but small talk had taken place in the car. Strangely, the deal itself didn't seem so important. It was getting to know Dwight Deacon that was oddly beguiling. Savanna simply didn't understand it. He was so different. The self-confident BS that surrounded him like an aura in public had evaporated. Where had it gone to? Where was it hiding? When would it reappear? These seemed more interesting questions than the one she had just asked. But then people were much more fascinating than things.

'Yes, I did, and after breakfast we will go into my study and I will write you what is known as a statement of intent, or sometimes a deal memorandum. We will both sign and have the signatures witnessed by one of my staff – if I can find any – and that will be that.'

'Oh, your word is good enough for me.'

'You don't look like a fool, Savanna. Best not to talk like one.' He laughed to soften the lesson. 'Getting to the top in singing is just like getting to the top in General Motors. Rule number one: get it in writing.'

'Oh? What's rule number two?'

'Don't call the most powerful man in country music a crook in his own backyard. But you seem to have gotten away with that one. You and precisely nobody else. I promise you that.' He laughed out loud, and spilt a bit of the Coco Pops on his chin.

Savanna had an urge to wipe it off for him, but there wasn't a napkin. He did it with the back of his hand. She felt maternal towards him, and yes, attracted to him. It was pointless to deny it. The two emotions might have conflicted, but they didn't.

'So you never got married, Dwight Deacon,' she said. Her remark seemed to flow from the two thoughts she had just had.

'Nope. Married to my career.'

Married to my fans, was the standard reply in magazine articles. 'Career' rang truer, but didn't play quite so well.

'Never tempted?'

'What about you? You tempted by that Aron Wallis? He's a good producer. And a brave man. Bit like you.'

There was no law against answering a question with another question. But somehow with famous people you felt a little cheated by not getting a straight answer. Surely they should be in the question-answering business as a price, a penalty perhaps, for their fame.

'No,' she said, just a little too quickly. 'I mean, I hardly know him. What I mean by that is that I know him well, but we've only just met. Like a few weeks ago . . .'

He knew she had slept with Aron. That was why she had revised her reply. She didn't want to give the impression that she routinely slept with people she hardly knew. Yet she also wanted to avoid giving the impression that Aron and she were anywhere near talking about marriage. The fact that they weren't raised the question, why was it so important to establish that?

Savanna felt a touch of guilt. She remembered her last words to Aron: 'If I am not back in a couple of hours, call the cops.' Something like that. Well, she had been gone that long, and the very last people of all that she wanted to see were the cops.

'So I still have a chance,' he laughed. 'If I can lose twenty pounds and ten years.'

'I think you might be a bit of a handful for a girl like me,' laughed Savanna, joining in the joke and not finding it distasteful at all.

'In fact, there was a girl. First love. Only love. All that BS. Remember that song of mine . . . "Our Times Didn't Meet" . . . that was about her.'

'"But they will in another world,"' Savanna quoted from the Deacon mega-hit.

'Yup, that's the one.' He liked that she knew his lyrics.

'We all used to argue whether the other world was Heaven or another part of this one, another place, another occasion, another time.'

'That's a nice idea,' he said, fixing the big blues on to her, 'you and your friends speculatin' 'bout my song. What did you decide?'

'Is there a "right" answer?'

'Yes.'

'They said Heaven. I went for this world.'

'You went right.'

'I knew it.' Savanna clapped her hands in excitement. She could remember the high-school heart-to-heart discussion as if it were yesterday . . . she the minority of one.

'What went wrong with the timing?'

'Another man. The things she needed. I wasn't Dwight Deacon then. I mean, I wasn't the man in the black hat. I wasn't . . .' He shrugged his shoulders to express the impossibility of even beginning to describe the change in his circumstances, the 'now' to his 'then'. 'Guess I wasn't the man on the radio in those days.'

'I don't think we really change, whatever happens,' said Savanna. 'And I think that lady made the wrong choice,' she said in a softer voice. 'And I thought that in ninth grade, too,' she added.

'But you didn't think it back in the Bluebird café?'

Why had he said that? Why had he injected just a little bit of poison into a promising moment, a nice moment. Did he not like to get close to people? Was that what he found dangerous? Was it easier to sing about relationships and make millions from them rather than live, love and enjoy them? Was that what the mysterious 'only love' of his life had decided? Was mistaken timing really just about a character flaw, after all, a difficult personality that in the end couldn't be dealt with?

'No. OK, I didn't think it back in the Bluebird, but I just said I think it now. Is "now" less believable, or just less comfortable to believe?' She was probing in a little deep, but she couldn't help it.

'You have to be fucked up to be famous,' he said. The words sort of exploded from him, like an oath. 'Sorry 'bout the language.'

'Do you? Why do you?'

He stared away into space, and took a deep breath, as if trying to decide whether or not to go for it. He wasn't good with explanations. The whole 'word' thing never came out quite right and made you sound like some crazed ass-hole.

'OK, why would you want to be? I'm asking why would you want to be *famous*, not why would you want to be President, or quarterback for the Cowboys, or sell a hundred million CDs. Those things *bring* fame. But to want to be famous, like in a void, that means you are like lost, man. You feel like a fucking nobody, and everybody else looks to you like a somebody. So you daydream. You dream of everyone knowing your name, it don't matter what for, just that they *know* you, and talk about you, and think about you. That you are *there*, man. That you are not invisible. You can't be ignored, then. You have to be listened to. You have their *attention*. So you kill someone. Like Lennon. Or shoot Reagan. Or you blow away your classmates at Columbine. Or you fight and claw your way to the top of the music business, over the dead bodies. You do your personal deal with the Devil so that Savanna Stone will be squealin' in the school yard about whether "another world" meant Heaven or Tulsa. What's the difference? What's the difference between a fame-junkie and a sick, wacko psycho? A few hundred million in the bank, and the front page of *People*, and that is about *it*.'

'Wow,' said Savanna. 'I had no idea . . . I mean . . .'

'But you asked, little girl. You asked. Only difference, I told you the truth. This whole country is based on a great big lie and you know what that lie is . . . it's called the American Dream, and it's supposed to be the big OK. And you know what the American Dream is built on? Freedom, equality and the chance for everyone to have a shot at happiness. You know what that means, Savanna, in real language, in real time, in goddamned reality? It means getting rich, that's what it means. It means getting rich, and richer, and then richer than everyone else until money is just the method of keeping the score of how *superior* you are. In the fifties it meant a washing machine, a car, a college education for the kids. Now it's how many times did you triple your money on your dot-com stocks, and it's going to the shrink because the neighbours are doing better than you. I tell you we are up against the limits of materialism here. Our noses are pressed right up against those walls, baby, and we are going to be squashed flat by the pressure any goddamn moment now. Fame is money. Fame is exposing yourself or getting exposed. Or fame is doing something so horrible that people can't ignore you any more. I got it, babe. I got it bad. It's like an illness. And it's why famous people screw up . . . Betty Ford, divorces, kids a mess because everything has to go to get it and keep it . . . *everything* . . . everything has to be focused on that fame. And if that is not the definition of being fucked up, then you tell me what is.'

His eyes were filmed over with tears. This was straight from the heart. Savanna had never seen somebody so famous and so miserable. And so honest about it. She wanted to hold him, to hug him, because it sounded so horrible, and so sad because there was probably not a red-blooded male in America who did not want to *be* Dwight Deacon. This speech of his would not have deterred them. They would have accepted the misery, and the madness, the loneliness and the despair. They would all to a man have done their deal with the Devil for the fame and the cash that came with him. Dr Faustus was alive and well and living on Main Street, USA. He had been renamed Mr Everyman, and there was nothingness at the centre of his being.

'So if the timing had been right, and you had married that woman, way back then, would it have been a mess? Is that part of what you are saying?'

'Yes, I guess so. Part of the thing I have that's good is that I recognise just an inch or two,' and he held up his pinkie, 'what a disaster I am as a human being. I would destroy a woman. I would destroy kids. I would take a marriage and turn it into a hell on earth. So I never did those things. I did my deal with the Devil alone, and we left the others out of it.'

'I do not think you are a disaster as a human being. I think you are quite fine,' said Savanna, and she knew that there were tears in her eyes as she spoke. 'Whom have you hurt? It's your life and you have led it and chosen it. I bet there have been great big pay-offs. Like setting all those concert halls on fire, and making fans happy, and, and . . .'

'But I killed a woman.'

'You did what?'

'Cassie Stewart. You may recall her. She committed suicide. I used her and her band to get where I wanted. I didn't leave her with a safety-net. I owed her, and I never paid her, not money, not chances, not favours. I knew she had been important to me, and that she had helped me, and I didn't like that. I didn't like the feeling that I had not done it all by myself.'

'We all do things we are not proud of. I cheated in a biology exam and I snuck on Anne Miller when she brought a mouse into school . . .'

He smiled through what were almost tears, and he reached out a hand to her across the table. And she took it. It was the first time they had touched.

'You know,' he said, 'I guess it would feel like this to have a daughter.'

But Savanna was not sure that it felt like that at all.

CHAPTER

THIRTY-SEVEN

It was late when he drove her back to Steph's place. The sun had long gone down, and the hours had flown away, although it had been difficult to say just how they had spent their day together. Mostly they had talked, wandering the rooms of his vast house; played a game of billiards on his pristine table; made sandwiches at sunset and watched the fire fade as the evening drew in. Savanna didn't know there were so many words in her. She particularly did not know why she was spilling them out to this perfect stranger. Dwight Deacon had to be the least likely candidate for confessor in this whole wide world.

His face, so famous, had seemed as semi-permanently perplexed as Savanna's, at the great mutual outpouring of feelings. Usually, Deacon did not talk much. He listened. That was how the powerful got more powerful. They received information, used it, withheld their own. But today, he had talked about his childhood to a girl who was only just finished with her own. He had talked of what it felt like to have your father leave, just walk away without a goodbye, or a reason, or even an angry word. They had not been close, but neither had they been distant. He had 'loved' the man as hard as a ten-year-old could love and as wisely. And then one day, his dad had walked away, to some preplanned new life that had revealed itself over the years in bits and pieces. His mother had fallen apart, because she was never very 'together' in the first place. Dwight had raised his younger brother and sister, and had never forgiven either of them for it, nor they him. So all were guilty in Dwight Deacon's world . . . men, women, children, families. You had to rely on yourself. You, you could trust. You and you alone were what mattered, because you and you alone would always be there. There was no long walk away from the world that you could take, although he had thought about it sometimes, and discarded it for reasons that were mostly to do with revenge. What he had had to become was the Duke, alone as always in a strange town; at the end of the bar, with the shot of whiskey. The guitar had been his gun. The love of strangers had become his objective, because when they loved you, you had power over them. When they loved you, they stayed and did not leave. But they could stop loving you at any time. That was their nature. Fickle as fate. A turn-down in album sales was the sight of a father's back walking away down a lonely road. A decision to reduce the PR budget for a tour was a mother's madness in the back room. A concert that was not sold out was the needy cries of children who were not his in the front room. Career setbacks were a threat, but they were a threat about which something could be done and was done. Dwight Deacon relied on himself because he had learned the hardest way that he was the only one in the world who was reliable.

Sometimes she had wept gently, when he told her the little stories. The Christmas card that his father had sent from Hawaii after years of silence. 'Having a wonderful time. Wish you were here!' That exclamation mark had been the cruellest thing that Dwight Deacon had seen in all his time on this earth. But he had written a hit about it. That was how he reacted to tragedy, by making it work for him. 'The Mark of Exclamation is Branded on my Soul'. He tried to explain the hurt that fired him, the rage and frustration that fuelled him, and all his failures as a man and a human being made perfect sense in the context of it all.

Only about the woman had he remained silent, and Savanna had wondered why. Because that was too hot to handle? Because that was the only other time Deacon had risked his fragile heart only to have it broken once again? Or was it because he did not want to talk of a great love before her, another woman, a woman he was opening up to in a way that Savanna felt sure he had never opened up to anyone before.

Savanna had had so few sad tales to tell, few tears, and such silly heartaches, apart from the tragedy of her mom's death. He had been formed by disaster and had risen, burned but a survivor, from the flames of a childhood that would have sent other men snivelling to shrinks for the rest of their natural days. But Elizabeth the Great's father had chopped off her mother's head. She had lived in mortal terror until she ascended, through luck alone, to the throne of England, amid a blizzard of unsigned death warrants, and the permanent threat of her head on a stick. She had pleaded with her half-sister for her own life, and by God had she made something of it thereafter. Choices. It all came down to choices. Which way did you go when tragedy struck . . . to the wall or to the top? Whichever direction you took, the damage walked beside you like a black shadow for the rest of your days.

Late in the evening, he had driven her home, but first he had wanted to see the house in Belle Meade where her family had come from. He hadn't wanted to go in, just to see it from the outside. So they had parked in the driveway surrounded by its old trees and velvet lawns, so big and wide. The rhododendrons were as big as hillocks, and the ivy climbed the walls behind the ante-bellum columns growing from roots that were almost as old as the house itself.

'You know, Savanna, it must have been harder for you,' he said as he stared at her home. He seemed to be unwilling to reach the time he must leave her. He wanted to talk some more. Seemingly for ever. 'What did you ever have to fight against? Where could your motives have come from? I *had* to do it. You didn't have to do a damned thing, yet you did. That is something. Sometimes I thank God that my father left, and I raised my brother and sister, and Mom was all burned out . . . I thank God for hardship and hell because it made me so strong. But you, I mean you . . .'

He swept his arms out to encompass the riches and security that the old house represented.

'I had you to fight against,' said Savanna with a laugh, patting his knee. 'I slew Goliath. You were my first and only battle.'

He held her hand with his, and turned to look at her. The famous eyes were round with tears.

'You beat me, Savanna. The world, I can handle. You, I couldn't. You called me a low-down thief, yet you won't be able to play that radio for the next six months without hearin' your song, either your version or mine. And if my version don't bury yours, then I will personally have the guts of every executive at Polymark and every station programme in America, and I will wear them round my neck as a scarf.' He smiled through the tears.

There was no threat in his words, nor would they ever again be anything to Savanna but bluster. She had seen through the window into the soul of the man, and she knew him. When you knew, you could forgive, because you had the answer to the question 'why'.

Later he stopped the car outside Steph's house. As before, he got out to open the door for her as John Wayne would have opened the stagecoach door to the pretty lady he had travelled with across the range.

'Will you come in and meet my mom's family?'

She knew he would not.

'Another time, it would be a pleasure,' he said. He was already planning his retreat back into his private world, that less dangerous place that he could control.

'Goodbye, then. And thanks, Dwight. I mean for everything, not just the piece of paper . . .'

'I know,' he said simply.

On a whim, she hugged him, and kissed him on the side of his cheek. He stood there quite still, not knowing how to react, although he hugged a thousand strangers a week with all the unbridled enthusiasm of the star that he was. So she turned and left him in his confusion, and she tried to deal with the confusion in her own heart.

'Thank you, Savanna,' he called out after her.

For listening. For hearing the secrets. He had never told them before.

She smiled and waved back at him in the twilight of a silver moon, its beams surrounding her.

'Catch you,' he murmured, his voice a whisper.

THIRTY-EIGHT

Savanna closed the door at Steph's house quietly behind her. She looked at her watch, something she had not done all day. It was 10.30 p.m. She felt the shock. Time had simply disappeared. There was no other way to describe it. But the world would have been going on, the world she left this morning, outside Aron's place. He would be wondering where she was. Possibly even wondering frantically. He would have called this house. The 'Savanna-has-disappeared-with-Dwight-Deacon' story would be up and running in at least two homes in Nashville, and if Savanna knew Nashville, possibly in a whole lot more. Steph's parents, she remembered, were out for the evening, and Steph had been thinking of joining them. Savanna hoped she would have the house to herself, which was odd because she had so much good news to share.

'So Savanna Stone disappears with a Mr Dwight Deacon and hugs him outside the door of her home, and all the time her close friend Aron Wallis is having to be persuaded that this is not the moment to call the police.'

Steph didn't exactly emerge from the shadows, but her voice arrived before she did. 'Ha! So much for the discreet entrance and the noiseless journey upstairs for the "early night"!'

'Oh, hi, Steph. God, what a day! You will never guess what happened.'

Steph's whole expression said she was going to die in the act of trying.

'He sweet-talked you into saying that you didn't write "Roots and Wings", by saying that he would "make you a star",' said Steph.

The peck on the cheek and the hug had said 'good vibrations'. Deacon only vibrated well when he had got what he wanted.

'Oh, right, Ms Pessimism! Thanks for your faith in me, cousin. In fact,' she said, walking over to the sofa and flopping down on it, 'I think this is a Miller moment.'

'Oh yeah,' said Steph, still deeply suspicious. Savanna was a sheep ripe for shearing by an old pro like Deacon. Whatever the deal, the small print would turn everything upside down. But she went over to the refrigerator which stood in the corner of the small living room because there wasn't space for it in the smaller kitchen. She took out a couple of Miller Lites, and handed one to Savanna, flicking her own open expertly with a thumbnail.

Savanna took her own and opened it slowly. She had wanted time to digest all this, quiet time when the secret was hers and hers alone. She hardly knew what she thought, because things had only just stopped happening. She could still feel Dwight's arms around her. The touch of the skin on his neck was only just a memory. Somehow, these were more real than the 'deal' that so interested Steph.

Steph dropped down into her father's armchair. 'I should say there are telephone messages for you,' she said. 'Aron has called so many times, I have lost count. He seems to think Deacon might have murdered you. It certainly didn't look like murder from behind the hall drapes, although the moonlight might have been a little more revealing. Looked to this girl like a Southern gentleman escortin' his belle back from the ball. That's what it looked like to your cousin, sneakin' a look on the sly.'

Savanna laughed. 'I guess I should call Aron,' she said. 'I thought the whole thing would take an hour at the outside.'

'Yeah,' said Steph with a knowing smile, 'but time just flies by when you are havin' fun, don't it?'

She reached out and pushed the redial combination.

'Aron? Steph. She is back. Not murdered. Not mutilated.'

Quite suddenly, Savanna felt she couldn't face him. Not right this minute. He was obviously in a state of some kind, and she was still trying to work out exactly what state *she* was in. She waved her hands frantically at Steph, mouthing 'no'.

'She's in the bathroom, freshenin' up,' said Steph. 'I'll get her to call you when she's through.'

It was clear that this was not what Aron had in mind, but a woman could not be extracted from a bathroom.

'OK. OK,' said Steph, and put the telephone down. 'My change money says he is fixin' to come right on over unannounced,' said Steph shrewdly.

'Aron wouldn't do that. I'll call him later. OK, do you want to hear it, or do you want to hear it?'

'Shoot.'

Savanna started to talk from the hip, her words tumbling out like bullets.

'He gave me the record. I get full writer's credit . . . plus, wait for it . . . *plus* he gives me permission to cover it and to compete with his version head-to-head. He withdraws all objections. He calls off his attack dogs. His friends are now our friends. He was *so* charming, I cannot tell you how charming he was. And he told me things, things about himself that made me cry. And he is just not at all like everyone thinks he is. I mean, if you knew what I knew about his family, you would understand how brave he has been, and how admirable to do what he has done. I am just so pole-axed by this. I mean, I have never met anybody like him. It was like I had known him as well as I know you. And I told him all my bad stuff, not that I've got so much except for Mom, and he listened to that like it was the most important stuff in the world. And we played billiards, and fooled around in his recording studio, and he has these funny cattle, like for show, but it's kinda sweet because he has this whole cowboy thing. I mean it's a defence mechanism, of course. He is just protecting himself from all that pain, but he's made it work for him. So many people go whimpering off with their tails between their legs and moan on to anybody that will listen about how godawful their lives are . . . and he just puts the emotional BS on the back burner and gets his revenge on everyone by becoming Dwight Deacon . . .'

'Oh, my God,' said Steph, her hand to her mouth. 'Oh, my God! A Deacon single. Getting to *cover* it? In real time?' Of course, it could not be. There would be a catch. But just the *idea* of it was a mind-bending moment.

'Look,' said Savanna. She fished around in the back pocket of her jeans. 'I got it in writing.'

Steph took the piece of paper, her hand trembling. 'This is wonderful, Savanna, unbelievable.'

She tried to read what it said, but she was too excited.

'But what did you give up for it? What did he get? What was the deal? There doesn't seem to be anything that *he* gets.'

'That's it. There isn't. It's an absolute and unqualified act of total generosity.'

'I guess he did try to steal the song in the first place . . .' said Steph half-heartedly. She couldn't really see that that was relevant any more.

'Of course he did. I left it in his car. I *wanted* him to buy it. And, legally, it was probably a gift. He was probably within his rights to steal it. But this guy who has only ever cared about winning, and staying on top and getting bigger and bigger to get rid of all his pain, just turns around and gives me this thing . . . and so much more . . . so much more . . .' There seemed to be a mist forming in Savanna's eyes. Quite suddenly, she burst into tears.

'Savanna?' Steph jumped up and hurried over to her cousin. Already the penny was beginning to drop. Girls knew these things. The day had lasted all day for reasons that were not only to do with business negotiations, perhaps hardly to do with business relations at all. It was possible that Savanna hadn't a clue, but from where Steph was standing, which was close enough, it looked suspiciously like that old thing called love.

'What is it, darling? What is it? Isn't this good news? Are we crying for joy here?'

'For him. For him,' sobbed Savanna. 'I have just spent an entire day with someone who is just so misunderstood, and *alone*, and who everybody gets wrong, because he messes up his signals all the time. It is so unfair, and that makes me want to cry that it's so unfair . . .'

'Are we the only two people in the world in the sorry-for-Dwight-Deacon club?' tried Steph, trying to inject a little humorous reality into the situation.

'Oh, that's just the obvious thing, isn't it? He's rich. He's famous. So he must be lucky. QED. But it isn't like that, Steph. We have so much love, and warmth, and support . . . and he never had that. Everyone left him, or depended on him, or let him down. There was no one for *him*. What does that do to a man? He's only human like the rest of us. And he is so unhappy inside his heart. It's wounded. It's bleeding. It is so sad. It is *so* sad.'

'Don't, Savanna,' said Steph, stroking her cousin's hair, 'don't, hon.'

But it was catching. There were tears in Steph's eyes, too.

CHAPTER

THIRTY-NINE

Aron arrived in the space of time it took him to drive there. The short length of that time suggested he had driven like a maniac on the way. He burst into the house to find Steph and Savanna halfway through their Miller celebration.

Within a few minutes Aron had managed to extinguish the atmosphere of joy that had replaced the initial sadness. With an air of general *angst* and agitation he listened to the news, speed-read the contract, and failed to be mightily moved by it. What was on his mind was that Savanna had apparently spent an entire day with Dwight Deacon, until 10.30 at night, and had left his warm bed that very morning in order to do so.

His displeasure was bursting out of his seams, and now as the row came up like a twister over a Kansas horizon, visible from miles away, Steph diplomatically remembered something important she wanted to watch on TV upstairs.

Left alone, the lovers of last night circled each other warily like prize fighters at the start of a championship match.

'Just tell me one thing. One thing,' said Savanna, raising her voice. 'Why are you not pleased about this? Why are you not over-the-moon happy for me, for you, for everyone, that the whole thing turned from a great big nightmare into a wonderful dream? Just tell me that. I need to know.'

Aron continued to walk the quarterdeck of Steph's parents' tiny living room with the intensity of a man about to be hanged from the yardarm.

'I *am* pleased. I am *thrilled*. I am ecstatic. It is just that I don't see why I should be the last to know, at ten-thirty at *night* by the way, ten-thirty at night, why this ass-hole changed his great big egocentric mind, and why the hell he won't change it back again.'

'Because, idiot, he signed this paper, and we had it witnessed by a Filipino sushi chef and a Filipino something else, and those two guys, baby, are going *nowhere*. They are sitting in Paradise, USA. You said yourself it was legal. You see, silly little airhead Savanna Stone actually got it in writing. Just like a man would. Let's go ahead and make her an honorary man for a minute or two, and stop talking bullshit at her.'

Aron ran his fingers through his hair. His was not the best debating position. He wasn't fighting the fight he wanted to fight, because the *real* fight was all about jealousy, and he did not have serious grounds for jealousy.

'Well, OK. OK. I admit it was wise of you to get this in writing. That was clever of you . . . you see, I am admitting something here . . .'

'Big deal, Aron. Clever little Savanna. Who else would have gotten Dwight Deacon to sign this piece of paper? The Devil? The Spanish Inquisition? The Gestapo? This is a deal memorandum, or something like that, worth a million bucks and a career, and gets everybody what they wanted at his expense . . . what I am missing here is some sort of recognition of that fact.'

'Why did he sign it? Why, that's what I'd like to know.'

'Why? Who knows? Who cares?' Savanna set off on her own walkabout. 'And they say men are the logical ones. Maybe he felt like it. Maybe it was a whim. Maybe I made him feel guilty. I haven't a clue. But he did, Aron. He did. Isn't that what matters? Isn't this a fucking champagne moment?'

It for sure didn't feel like one.

Of course, they were getting close to the crux. It wouldn't be long now. Points, however, would be lost by the person who brought it up first, and every argument in life was designed to be won . . . no matter how petty, or stupid, or irrelevant it was. Aron was jealous. He had waited all day not knowing where Savanna was. He had worried about her. But he didn't want to admit that. She wanted him to. End of story. Life was simple, really. She had climbed out of his bed that morning and spent the day with possibly the most eligible bachelor in the world, and dared to say that she had found him charming and touching. And he had given her something for nothing, which in recorded history Dwight Deacon had never been accused of doing. Then there was 10.30 at night. In a reasonable world, that of Henry VIII for example, that would have been treason. Savanna would be in danger of having her head cut off. Only Aron's personal intercession would save it. Where had the world gone wrong?

He had to go for it.

'I mean, what did you do for it . . . until ten-thirty at night?'

Savanna stopped in mid-patrol. So did he. Her face registered a cynical smile of pure triumph.

'Oh, I *see*. *I* get it. Why didn't you say so? Why did you not spell it out? *Now* we get to the nitty-gritty. I slept with you all night, then got right up and slept with Dwight Deacon all day, *until ten-thirty p.m.*, just so I could do a deal with him. Excuse me while I vomit, Aron Wallis. Is that the only way a woman gets something in this world, by screwing for it? Well, *sorry*. I had not got you down as Chauvinist-in-chief in my working woman's little black book. And anyway, remember, when we did it last night you hadn't even got a *job* at the time. I got that back today while I was giving Deacon his ride to the moon on my own personal Starship *Enterprise*.'

'That is not what I said . . . Savanna . . . I didn't say that.'

'You did. You did!' She actually stamped her foot. 'What did you do for it? . . . Until ten-thirty at night. That's what you said. What does that mean, Aron? Tell me what it means.'

He waved away what it could have meant. 'I mean, he obviously used his famous charm on you. You were obviously taken in by that.'

Savanna's eyes narrowed. She had had enough of this. Way enough. 'Yes, I was. Absolutely. Taken in by it. Bowled over by it. I was charmed by him. I found him deeply charming, and totally mis-understood. I can see now why he is not close to the minnows who swim around this town, and why he does not need to be, because he is so much bigger than them . . .'

'Oh, so I am a minnow now, am I . . .'

'You are what you feel you are, Aron. I don't know, and frankly I no longer care what you are. If minnow describes you, be a minnow. All I am saying is that Dwight Deacon is not one. He is a big man who has overcome more misery than most of us ever know, and I admire him for that. And, yes, I find it attractive. And, yes, I find him attractive, although I *know* you never suggested anything of the sort. But, no, we did not make love today, and I think you are a worm for even suggesting that we did. He is a much older man, but then you are older, too. The difference is that he has matured. You, apparently, have not. So if you want to give me a call one day, when you have done a bit of growing up, then be my guest. I shall not be waiting around holding my breath.'

She turned and made for the stairs.

'Hold your breath and you will suffocate,' Aron shouted after her.

'And the man can't even muster a decent last line,' she said over her shoulder as she disappeared from his sight.

CHAPTER

FORTY

'Congratulations,' said the nurse, as Henry Stone walked on to the ward, trailing medical students and a couple of visiting professors from Zimbabwe.

He looked at her sharply. 'On what?' he said. He couldn't think of a single thing on which he was to be congratulated. First, he had lost his wife. Now, it seemed he had lost his daughter, too. He had failed to return two of her calls, and being a Stone, she had not tried again. Being also a Stone, he had not found himself able to break the impasse of pride that father and daughter had managed to set up.

'On the news from Nashville. Your daughter's recording contract. With Polymark. It's on page six of the *Daily News*.'

She had a copy of the paper there on the desk of the nurse's station. Henry Stone was not a dramatic man. He looked at the nurse; at the students; at the two beaming visiting professors who were about to enjoy the grand man's grand round.

'Yes,' he said. And then he said 'Yes' again.

It wasn't clear, in the context, what 'Yes' meant. What he had felt like saying was 'Shit'. The other possibility had been 'No!' 'Yes' seemed better. 'Yes, I know.' 'Yes, how nice.' 'Yes, congratulations are in order.' Just 'Yes'.

He smiled at everyone, aware that his smile was rather fatuous. He reached out and tried to touch the newspaper, withdrawing his hand at the last minute, as if he could not bring himself to lay it on the tabloid. 'Where, exactly?'

The nurse was very helpful. She found the page and pointed out the segment with some pride, as if finding it made her a contributor to the triumph.

Old Nashville surely met new today, when Savanna Stone, daughter of the Belle Meade Stones of Harbour Court, signed a contract with Polymark Records to produce two albums for the vast Music City label. Savanna was discovered by none other than singing super-legend Dwight Deacon, who generates fully sixty per cent of Polymark's North American profits. Deacon's office said that his own personal producer, Brad Van Zandt, would work on both her albums. A couple of days in Nashville is a long time. Only the other night, at an 'in-the-round' session at the Bluebird café, Savanna Stone accused superstar Deacon of 'stealing' one of her songs. Spokespeople for Deacon and Polymark describe this as 'a giant misunderstanding based on a series of extraordinary coincidences'. Savanna's father, Henry Stone, MD, presently Professor of Cardio-Thoracic Surgery at Columbia College of Physicians and Surgeons in New York, will find his heart beating a little faster today.

Henry Stone's smile had turned from fatuous to frankly sickly. If the article was correct about nothing else, it had made the right prediction on his heart rate.

He tried to remember if there was a spare bed in intensive care.

CHAPTER

FORTY-ONE

Aron Wallis sat at the bar of the Crazy C, and felt like all the country songs that had ever been written. Hurting. Lying. Cheating. Broken hearts. Lost love. The consolations of whiskey and beer. A freight train caught to someplace else to escape the pain. Wrong done. The ways of a woman. Eternal triangles. The only thing missing was little children, and it looked now as if they would be missing permanently. He had come back here on a maudlin mission of memory. It was pathetic. Savanna had sung here, where the big brassy blonde now sang. She had been as spirited and as magnificent as the performer *du jour* was flat and stale. There were three or four afternoon drunks, those saddest of men who didn't have the balls to start at breakfast, or the self-control to wait until sundown. Maybe they were even the same ones who had been here when Savanna had sung. They all wore pointless, seemingly 'knowing' smiles that said that their addled minds were on the fast track to somewhere which was not the Crazy C.

Aron sipped at his beer.

'Wanna 'nother?' said the barman.

'I haven't finished this one,' he snapped back.

'Doesn't stop most of 'em,' said the barman, without a smile and without taking offence.

'Oh,' said Aron, trying to make amends for his tone.

'Where you from?' said the guy a couple of seats down. He was a tourist, not yet drunk, just on the clean side of dirty.

'Here,' said Aron, cursing inwardly. He had not come out to find the company that misery was supposed to love.

'I'm from Florida,' said the guy. 'Randy.'

Aron smiled. 'Randy.' Was it a name, a statement, or a question?

'Went there when I was a kid,' said Aron. 'Don't remember any of it.' That should be enough to stop the conversation in its tracks.

'Yeah, not much to remember, I guess. Flat, heat, rain, skeeters, blue-plate specials, old folk. Otherwise, much like anywhere else.'

There was a depression about the guy that Aron was rather drawn to in his present mood.

'Ain't that America,' said Aron. John Mellencamp when he had still had the 'Cougar'. Today was obviously going to be conversation by song.

The blonde completed a dismal and downbeat rendition of Tammy Wynette's 'Apartment Number Nine'. Nobody clapped. Everybody looked all clapped-out. The song was depressing, about an apartment in which the sun had ceased to shine and in which there was nothing much else but loneliness.

Aron thought of his own bright apartment into which the sun shone permanently. Would it stop doing so now that Savanna had blown him away? Had it been his fault? Hers? OK, he had over-reacted, but she hadn't helped him any. It was as if she had been waiting for the first excuse to walk. Was that the way it really was? Or did it just seem like that? Would the dreary bore from Florida know or care? Would the busty singer with the dyed roots and gravel voice who seemed to specialise in heartache? She was working the room for tips, and now she hovered at Aron's shoulder. She might.

'Liked my set, hon?' she said. Aron fished in his jeans for a five. He could only find a twenty and he gave it to her anyway. What the heck! Her broad ass had sat on the same stool that Savanna had sat on. That was worth twenty bucks.

'Hey, thanks, cowboy. Looks like you did – like my set,' she added by way of clarification.

'We gotta big spender here,' said Aron's new best friend, excusing the single dollar he was planning to donate.

'Where you from?' said the blonde.

Aron did not usually talk to strangers. That made him a little un-American. 'Where you from?' was what you were supposed to say to each other. Names came second. Mary-Lou, Aron, and Randy, sitting at the bar in the Crazy C, drinking Bud from bottles at a quarter past three. That would make a very bad song, but then 'Bobby McGee' hadn't sounded much on paper.

'Nashville,' said Aron.

'And Florida,' reminded Randy.

'You with each other?' said Mary-Lou in a tone which said she believed they were not.

'No, we just got to talking,' said Aron.

'This is a real friendly place,' said Mary-Lou.

'Yeah, it is. Met me a girl in here. Fell in love with her. Then she dumped me. Real friendly place,' said Aron with a bitter laugh.

'It happens,' said Randy.

'Sure does,' said Mary-Lou. Both looked as if they had some experience of the situation. Perhaps a lot.

'I guess so,' said Aron. Was this humans reaching out to one another? Probably, in a way, it was. He felt a tiny bit better for the fact that Randy and Mary-Lou could confirm that he was not the only man on earth to fall for a woman who had dumped him.

'I'll have that Bud now,' he called out. 'And one for the lady, and one for Randy from Florida.'

That made them his audience, technically. It was a role they seemed happy to settle into.

'Another man?' tried Mary-Lou. You didn't dump people until you had a spare.

'You could say so.' But could you? Would you? Was it correct? Had Savanna dumped him for another man? No, not at all, in fact. She had walked out because he had insinuated that Deacon fitted the 'other man' hat. But that was an overreaction. Why? Wasn't that what the guilty did? Or maybe she just had PMS. Maybe this. Maybe that. He took the second Bud without hanging around. The barman plonked a third in front of him without even asking.

'You were in here before,' he said as he did so.

'Yes, I was,' said Aron, startled. 'I'm surprised you remember.'

'You sat with that singer. The one who could sing,' said the barman. His face was blank.

'Yes, I did.'

'Name of Savanna. Savanna Carson Stone.'

'Jeez, you got a memory on you.'

'What the booze left me,' said the barman without smiling.

'That the one that dumped you? Never trust a singer,' said Mary-Lou with a laugh. 'You spin her a twenty, too?'

He ignored her.

'Singers are in love with singing,' said Randy, not without wisdom.

'Yeah, Savanna Stone. Not surprised you ran into some trouble with her now she signed with Polymark. Two-album deal. Brad Van Zandt producin'. Dwight Deacon's blue-eyed boy. I guess the Crazy C ain't on her stump no more. You'd best go hang around the Bluebird café,' said the barman with a sarcastic laugh, and he moved away.

Aron sat back in his chair. 'Where did you hear that stuff?' he shouted after the retreating figure.

'Morning papers. Not like it's no secret, or nothing.'

Aron felt the faintness well up inside him. He hadn't seen the *Tennessean* this morning, and he hadn't been into the office. But this must have happened fast for him not to know about it. Fast, as in faster than anything that had ever been done in Nashville before. Fast, in fact, as a deal masterminded by none other than Deacon himself, who was accustomed to hearing 'how high?' when he said the word 'jump'. The blow seemed to come at Aron from all sides. He was out of the loop, although technically back in the fold, his job returned, apologies made, a small pay rise agreed. But he was not producing Savanna's albums. Van Zandt was and Van Zandt not only outranked him, Van Zandt was better than he. He freely admitted it. The guy was a wizard in the studio . . . Aron's hero in fact, the man he one day aspired to be. And Van Zandt worked exclusively for Deacon. So this was Deacon's baby all the way.

Now, the row he had had with Savanna had to be seen in this new context. Had she known about the recording deal at the time of the argument? It seemed possible . . . and it made the whole thing more explicable. Made it worse. Made it better. Made it harder. Made it easier. Had she purposely picked a fight to free her to walk away from him? Had he become baggage already? Or, horror of horrors, had his own jealously precipitated the sequence of events that the barman had so casually described? The timing of it all was suddenly vital. As always, in love and war, and everything else, it was a question of who knew what and when.

'There's always more fish in the sea . . .' started Randy from Florida.

'Sounds like a scheming bitch to me . . .' said Mary-Lou, thinking about the twenty and wondering how much more there might be when this guy had loaded up on a few more Buds.

But Aron just dropped a twenty on the bar, said 'Keep the change' to no one in particular and walked straight out of the Crazy C to see what he could salvage of his life.

CHAPTER

FORTY-TWO

'Please, silence everybody. Quiet, please, ladies and gentlemen.' Mike Gramm shrugged his shoulders and smiled broadly as the party crowd ignored him. They were having too much fun, and that was the best news of all at Nashville parties. Unlike New York and LA, where the only thing that mattered was who put in an appearance, in Music City the columnists still reported on whether or not the event had gone with a swing. Country liked to hang on to just a little of its naivety, although that was going fast.

He tried again, but this time he played a trump card . . . 'Dwight Deacon, Dwight Deacon has, has . . .'

The curious quieted their chatter – the eager questions, 'How did your record do?' and the ready answers, 'I've sold more in the past, but this one was from the heart, ya know' – all faded away. The 'DD' name could silence a Nashville crowd as the chairman of Polymark, who was throwing the event, well knew. He waved a tape, like a talisman. Words from the great man? A song?

'Thank you all. I'm so pleased to see y'all havin' so much fun. Well, friends, as you know, Dwight Deacon is back on tour and if this is Thursday it must be Seattle . . . you know the drill. But as you also all know, Dwight is very, very sad to miss this party because he has a special interest in the lady we are honourin' here tonight, Miss Savanna Carson. This tape here in my hand is a decoy. We have the real one plugged in and ready to go, so without more ado we are going to play it for you all tonight. Here is Dwight from somewhere on the road.' (In the cabin of his 707 he sounded a little over the top for Nashville.)

'Hi, Savanna, so beautiful and so talented. Well, this is your night. You have a great contract, and a huge career ahead of you. I have listened to your tapes, and they are some of the best music I have heard in my life. I tell you all this from the bottom of my heart, and I never lie, but I especially do not lie about music . . .' The tape paused to anticipate the general laughter. 'I want you all to know that I hope to be working together writing with Savanna. So as long as Dwight Deacon is around, she will be too . . . and I ain't never goin' nowhere. You have my word on that . . .' Another pause. People started to clap. There were endorsements, puff endorsements, and then there was this. And 'DD' didn't ever do endorsements. He had never been heard to mention the name of a country singer in his entire career. For music heritage, it was always Elvis, Muddy Waters, Dylan, Bob Seger . . . not even Hank Williams had made his cut.

'And I'd just like to end up with the last phrases of a song I'm busy writing, and it's about meeting you, Savanna, that day at the ranch, and what we talked about and what it meant to me. It is a song of thank-you, and it's about friendship, and how it is never too late to find a soulmate. Here you are, Savanna. It's called "I Found a Friend in You".

> As I get older than
> The man I started as,
> The worst part always is
> My inner loneliness.
>
> Friends are hard to find,
> As habits set in time,
> Then you came along,
> And showed me I was wrong.

Now, I know it's true,
I found a friend in you,
I was searching for another,
Maybe looking for a lover,
But I found a friend in you.

There was silence, a haunting silence. The sound system sent the song straight from Dwight Deacon's heart. It was marked with his blood. And there were those in the audience who reckoned that he didn't have a heart.

Savanna, looking adorable in a plain white dress, tasselled at the bottom with white leather cowboy boots to match, and no jewellery, was crying. The tears streamed down her face, and she was unable to stop the quiet noise she made in the almost silence. Nashville watched and waited and listened. They were all there. Every would-be and wannabe and a sprinkling of stars not too grand or too mean of spirit to lend their power to a sometime rival at the request of their record company. Agents, PRs, the press, the grey men from Music Row who pulled the strings behind the scenes, the invisible men from the mighty banks, and from Gaylord who owned so much of Nashville, clustered around, savouring the moment.

The Polymark president leaned in to the microphone. 'If that is Savanna's tears I'm hearin', let me sweeten them by saying that those words that Dwight has just sung about you sound like pure platinum to me . . .'

They clapped again, and some cheered. Platinum was everywhere, and it felt *good*. Savanna felt her world peak. It had all started with her mother from the Smoky Mountains, where the morning mist formed from the ground wetness and the mineral oils of the trees' leaves, and where the grass was tinged with blue in May. Now the circle was complete. The Carson in her had survived and triumphed. Savanna had never felt closer to her mother than at this moment, or as grateful. Everything she had came from her mother: her character, her upbringing, her talent, voice and soul. She felt her closeness, as she felt her father's absence. He was not here for this party, and in a deeper way he was not here for Savanna's success. He had not wanted this.

'I wish Daddy was here,' said Savanna to Steph, who was standing by her side, her arm around Savanna's waist. Mike Gramm came up behind and bear-hugged them both as a battery of flashbulbs went off on cue.

'Congratulations. Congratulations. Oh, by heck, this is the start of something big. I just know it. I know these things.'

He was bubbling over with enthusiasm, as if by willing it he could make it happen. But he was not alone in the room in thinking these thoughts. In the savvy eyes of the insiders, you could see the cash registers ringing up the word 'success'. PRs clustered hopefully, as did the agents and top-end bookers. It wasn't too late for them. The smell of rich pickings was everywhere as business managers straightened their ties, as well as their smiles, and personal managers surreptitiously smelled their breath in their hands. Only the male singers looked truly relaxed. Vince Gill – Mr Nashville Nice Guy – and Alan Jackson, cool and gentlemanly with his shy smile, came over to congratulate, while lesser mortals lined up behind to take their turn. And all the time the Veuve Clicquot went round and round with the trays of canapés . . . polenta cakes, marinated duck egg rolls and pieces of salmon and tuna sushi.

Savanna tried to hold the moment. Here it was. The first sweet touch of success. Here was fame without responsibility. Soon, the work would have to be produced, agonising decisions made, as the whole business on which the fame was ultimately based took over. Dwight Deacon had talked of it . . . the joy tarnished by the responsibility. And she knew he was right. How many operations did her father enjoy nowadays, compared to that first magic time he had been allowed to suture a long saphenous vein to a damaged coronary artery? Habit made drudgery of excitement. The trick was to keep up momentum, to keep on going, until the inevitable moment when the younger, hungrier and more energetic passed you, heading up as you headed down. 'Not to fade away' became the problem, almost as soon as the problem had ceased to be 'making it'. So God, with his paradoxes, had the very last laugh, and the Devil took those who could not learn to see the point of the joke.

'Hi,' said Aron.

Savanna spun around, and the colour shot to her face. She had confronted this in her mind. Aron was a producer at Polymark once again, after the briefest hiatus. She had imagined he would be at the party. How would he react? More important, how would she react?

'Hi,' was what she said.

'So?' said Aron, trying a small smile.

'So!' said Savanna, trying an even smaller one.

'I'm glad it all worked out for you, Savanna. I hear Van Zandt is producing. He's great. I'm not as good as he is.'

'Oh, I'm sure you will be,' said Savanna. What did she feel? Still angry, but only just. She hadn't totally forgiven him, but her heart raced at the sight of him. So many warm memories came flooding back, but it was too soon to say if there was any going back.

'A two-album deal. Brad Van Zandt. A personal tape from DD about friendship at a big-label launch party. You sure didn't let the grass grow under your feet after you left my apartment that morning.'

Aron kicked himself inside. That had sounded like a criticism, and he had wanted it to be a kind of congratulation. But had he? Things usually came out the way you deep down intended them. That was what a Freudian slip was all about.

'Yup,' said Savanna, her colour deepening, and her quick temper boiling over. 'You were just the bottom rung of the ladder, baby. Hope you manage to get my footprint off it.'

That was nasty. Savanna knew it the moment she had let it fly.

He didn't move, but his eyes took a step back.

'I'll get the smell of you off my pillow first,' he said.

Savanna began to feel she was in a small Balkan conflict that had the possibility of turning into a third world war any minute.

'Maybe it won't be so easy to get the memory of me out of your mind,' said Savanna. She held her head back, high and proud. The pillow remark had really gotten to her. She felt quite suddenly on the verge of tears. It was as if, subtly and politely, she had been called a whore . . . a woman who had used a man for financial gain, and then dumped him the moment someone better had shown up. That was as far from her personality as it was possible to get. Or was it? After all, you are what you do, she thought.

'Maybe that will be the easiest part,' he said with a gentle smile. 'The girl I met on that bar stool that day seems to have just blown away with the wind.'

'That's not true,' she said. That signalled defeat, of course. But she couldn't allow him to walk away with that line lingering in the air and in her memory.

'What's not true?'

'What you said . . . that I am a different girl. I'm the same girl.'

'Oh?'

Once again there were tears in Savanna's eyes, on the night of her triumph. Aron had never been so relieved to see tears before.

'What happened,' she said, taking a deep breath, 'was that you insulted me out of jealousy. And you insinuated I was cheap.'

'Yes,' he said. 'I did all those things, and I am deeply, deeply sorry for them. And I apologise for them, and for anything else I said. I *was* jealous, and I had no right to be. And jealous is what you are when you like someone very much, and when you spend the whole night with your head buried in the pillow they used, just trying not to lose the scent of them.'

'Oh,' said Savanna. 'Well, that was a very handsome apology . . . I . . . I . . .'

'Apologise? Apologise? What has my smart young producer been doing to apologise for? Say the word, Savanna, and I will chop off his head. Although he was the one who found you. Maybe just a year or two in the Tower!' Mike Gramm had arrived at a critical moment, which could not be reclaimed. He had a whole load of people for Savanna to meet, and she was swept away from Aron at the moment she most wanted to talk to him, and he to her.

Gramm steered her away through the waitresses with their trays of canapés and champagne, and the awed crowd parted at the approach of the best sort of star, the newest one. But from several feet away, over her shoulder, she said, 'Don't leave without speaking to me, please.' And she was gone.

Aron felt the loneliness close around him in the crowded room. He had lost her. She still had feelings for him, but now she was caught up in the surging sea of success, and nothing would be the same again except the void in his already aching heart. He had seen what fame could do to good intentions, and the steadiest soul. To fall in love was a full-time job. So was making it in Nashville. So he shook his head sadly from side to side, and he reached out for a passing glass of champagne.

As he took it, it was knocked flying from his hand. The man who had spilled it was clearly in a hurry. Now, confused by his clumsiness, he stopped and made ineffectual efforts to clean up the mess he had made. The waitress, as waitresses do, had managed to avoid 'seeing' the spillage. 'I'm surely sorry,' said the man, in a gruff tone that was formally polite without being emotionally so. The implication lingered that Aron had been waving his champagne about, and that innocent passers-by were quite likely to bump into it. Most of the wine had landed on Aron's Armani suit. Now the stranger pulled a large handkerchief from his pocket, and mopped inefficiently at the stain. Aron had more important things to be sorry about. 'No, it's fine. It was an accident. And you don't look as if you have had much practice at cleaning up messes.'

'Nonsense,' said the man. 'I do it for a living. I'm a surgeon.' He said this without the trace of a smile. Clearly, he was either in a very bad mood, or lacked a sense of humour and did not realise he had made a passably good joke . . . perhaps both.

'A surgeon?' said Aron. Two and two clicked together. This was Savanna's party. The father could have relented, and turned up after all.

'You're not by any chance Doctor Stone?' said Aron.

'Yes. Who are you?'

'Aron Wallis.'

'How do you know me?'

'I know your daughter.'

'So do I. And I'm looking for her. Have you see her? I have just arrived.'

Aron checked him out. He was formidably well dressed in a charcoal-grey suit, double breasted, with a splendid Hermès tie, Cole-Haan loafers, highly polished. His hair looked like a sculpture. He smelled of Eau Sauvage cologne. In fact, he looked very much the sort of man you would trust with your beating heart, if less so with your naked emotions. Those might be best kept out of Dr Stone's way. In short, he was rather frightening. Aron could see where Savanna's temper and pride came from.

Aron had a strong desire to hang on to Dr Stone for a little bit longer, to investigate him properly. However, Stone clearly wanted to escape from this irritating nobody as soon as he possibly could and move on to what looked like his main mission . . . wrecking his daughter's party. Aron couldn't help wondering if his own objective were not much the same as Dr Stone's. He grabbed another glass of champagne.

'I think she is in the middle of a photo-op in the next room,' said Aron quickly. 'That usually takes ten minutes or so.'

Stone scowled. 'Are you in this dreadful business? Sounds like it.' He looked at the cut of Aron's trendy Armani suit. 'Looks like it,' his expression added.

'The music business, or the general business of nobody doing quite what they are supposed to be doing?'

'What do you mean?' said Stone. This man was a gentleman of sorts, but he couldn't decide on what sort. Was that a Savannah accent, with a trace of English, tinge of California?

'Well, Savanna giving up med school to be a country singer. You having to come all the way down from New York to try and straighten out the whole mess, when you are busy and have patients . . .'

'Who on earth *are* you?' said Dr Stone. He seemed enormously put out that a stranger should know his business so thoroughly.

'I'm afraid that I am the man who started this whole ball rolling. Then it just sort of rolled away from me, and now it's gathering moss all over the place, totally out of control . . . that happens in Nashville.'

'I've no idea what you are talking about, but Nashville used to be a very quiet and reasonable place. It's all this silly music for stupid people. It's all pure fantasy. Very dangerous. Done America a lot of harm. Glorifies a lack of education, and education is our only hope of getting the population to grow up.'

'Fighting words in Music City.'

'Music City! Rubbish! Banking. Insurance. Religion. Publishing. That's what the real Nashville is about. Before that: railheads, pig-iron, cattle, cotton. My family have lived here for generations. All nonsense, this music stuff, all nonsense.'

'I've been to your home, Harbour Court. I met your mother. A very fine woman.'

'Good Lord,' said Stone, quite taken aback. 'Did she like you?' He peered at Aron closely as if he were a specimen beneath a microscope, possibly contagious, possibly benign, more than likely malignant. His mother's seal of approval obviously meant a great deal to him. Mary Stone did not break bread with rubbish. 'You had a meal there?'

'Dinner.'

'Good Lord,' he said again.

'You sound surprised,' said Aron, gently pointing out the doctor's rudeness in assuming him an unlikely candidate for a dinner date at a Belle Meade home, particularly his mother's.

'Do I? Oh. Well, frankly this whole thing is a big surprise. Actually, a nightmare, from beginning to end. I've simply got to sort it out.' He grabbed a waitress. 'Do you have anything except champagne? Some Bourbon, for example?' She hurried away to find some. 'Gives me gas,' he said. 'Champagne,' he added.

'Your mother is fond of it.'

'Never had gas in her life. Cast-iron stomach. I didn't inherit it, that's for sure.' He sniffed at the unfairness of the world. Aron, despite himself, was beginning to like Dr Stone. You would know where you stood with Henry Stone. It might not be at all where you would like to be standing, but you would have the GPS reading on your position at all times.

Stone now, quite clearly, had an idea. This Wallis person obviously knew the ins and outs of the situation far better than he did. He was quite talkative. It might be a good plan to interrogate him. You always got the real lowdown on a patient's condition from the people who were living with them. Patients hardly ever told the truth about anything.

Aron saw Stone's thoughts written clearly across his face as if in neon.

'I'm sorry if I was a bit abrupt, earlier. Rather out of my depth here. Bit of a fish out of water, or is that to mix metaphors?'

The Bourbon arrived. He took a decent gulp at it. He seemed to talk a bit like an Englishman in a black and white movie about the Royal Navy in the Second World War, although his accent was Southern. Maybe when Southerners transplanted to New York, they learned to economise with words. Or perhaps this was the way he dealt habitually with strangers, treating them as if they were patients in a particularly busy schedule. Now, it seemed he was going to make an attempt to be more polite. The party roared around them.

'So what do you do, Mr Wallis? I'm sorry to ask. It's a Northern habit, isn't it?'

'I'm a record producer . . . like a film producer only with records. Country music.'

'Yes, this isn't exactly rap around here, or hip-hop, come to that.'

Both laughed rather nervously in the way that you do when making vaguely politically incorrect jokes in front of people you don't know well.

'I am the man who in your eyes would probably be called "guilty" of discovering Savanna.'

Henry Stone looked at him closely. Just what exactly did 'discovering' involve these days? 'Look, do you think you could do me a big favour and just fill me in on the details of events down here. I suspect that I am the only person in this room who hasn't much of a clue what is going on.'

And so Aron told him, leaving out the bits that a father would not want to know.

Henry Stone listened carefully. He wore an expression throughout the monologue that he might well have assumed in the midst of prolonged root-canal work.

'God, what a way to run a business!' he said at last. Then he went quiet. His mind, obviously a formidable object, would be working on the finer points of the plot.

'You don't seem to have come out of this as much of a winner,' he said at last, implying that there was honour in that. 'In fact, the only person who has done worse than yourself would appear to be me. Unless . . .' He paused. 'Unless one takes the wholly defensible position that all and sundry have made complete and utter fools of themselves.' He seemed happiest with that conclusion. For the first time, he smiled. 'It will all end in disaster,' he said in summary, and with the greatest confidence.

There was a part of Aron that agreed with him. From now on this was Dwight Deacon's party. Disaster as an outcome was therefore far from impossible.

The photo-op in the next room, which had been more or less spontaneous in its onset, was now coming to a close. A backflow of onlookers, and guests who liked to be near the action wherever it was, now began to drift into the sparsely populated room where Aron and Dr Stone stood.

Henry Stone straightened himself up. There was about to be a family reunion. It would be an unexpected one. He had only decided at the last minute to attend the party, and had had to use his considerable powers of persuasion to be allowed past the guardians at the gate, always a feature of Nashville 'A'-list events.

Savanna saw him almost immediately. Her face ran through a list of emotions which embraced pleasure, fear, regret, excitement, and confusion in equal measure. Henry Stone's more or less mirrored them in a different sequence. Savanna looked very sexy, showing lots of cleavage in her white tasselled dress. Aron's dream. Presumably, Henry Stone's worst nightmare. She looked as far from a ward round as it was possible to get. She walked towards him, her expression registering a jolt of displeasure that he should be so obviously joined together with Aron Wallis.

'Daddy! Daddy! You came. I am so glad. I am so, so glad!'

She took off into arms that made a slightly less than enthusiastic effort to receive her. They kissed, and she stood back to look at her father, determined that at least this meeting should start well. It was what she had dreaded since she had arrived in Nashville. It was one thing to be playing the Crazy C versus Columbia. It was another to have the city's biggest label throwing your two-album-deal contract party. She had already earned on paper what a doctor without much bedside manner might expect to earn in thirty years. Not that that mattered to her father. But at least the rest of the country would understand . . . useful for the arguments that would surely follow.

Gramm, congenitally drawn towards scenes of tension, material-ised once again at Savanna's side.

'Look, here's Mike Gramm, he's the head of Polymark Records, and this is Laurie Standish who runs the PR department. This is my father, Dr Henry Stone, who decided to come at the very last minute, all the way from New York . . .'

Stone shook hands with them as one might with one's executioner to show there was no personal ill will. Whatever had happened was hardly their fault, although he couldn't help feeling there was enough blame to go round to include everybody.

Gramm slipped into effusive mode: '. . . great talent . . . must be so proud . . . your beautiful daughter . . . keeping her hidden for so long, ha, ha . . .'

The PR gushed like a geyser by his side with similar platitudes.

Savanna and Aron exchanged glances. 'What did you tell him?' she hissed.

'Just the story,' he said with a quiet smile.

'Thanks a lot.' There was sarcasm in Savanna's voice, but she was grateful that she hadn't had to do it.

Somehow the bubble of conversation burst, leaving a damp silence.

'I had always thought that Savanna would be a doctor,' said Henry Stone in the middle of it.

Everyone stared at him as if he had gone quite mad. And quite sud-denly he began to get the drift, as the party rolled around him like surf on a beach.

Who the hell wanted to be a doctor when you could be a star?

CHAPTER

FORTY-THREE

Dwight Deacon sat on the sofa of the suite in the Seattle hotel, and he said, 'I have had one hell of an idea.'

Several people leaned forward to agree with it, whatever it was. It seemed decent to wait until the idea was expressed before saying how great it was, but whoever was first scored points. One eager young publicist, new on the Deacon tour trail, tried, 'Well, if you think it's a hell of an idea, it will be, Dwight.'

Even Deacon joined in the general laughter at the levels to which sycophancy could fall . . . or rise.

'I think it would be a real neat idea to have that girl who just signed with the company come right on out here and join me for part of the tour. She can sing the wheels off a wagon. Wouldn't want her to open and spoil the special effects, but she could come on in the second half . . . give the men in the audience something to see . . . do a couple of songs, maybe three. How about it?' He sat back and beamed around the room encouragingly.

There was silence. Nobody could bring themselves to say it was a good idea, because it was a disastrous one. It was also weird to the point of craziness.

Deacon was suggesting that someone else appear on his stage! Deacon giving away a single photon of his limelight? What had they got for shrinks here in Seattle? Somebody had better find out who the top guy was.

'Hey!' said Deacon. 'My idea, boys. Savanna Carson Stone.' For a ringmaster, this would have been the crack of a whip.

The road manager won the red badge of courage. 'Well, I don't know, Dwight. Way I see it is people pay money to see you and nobody else at your concerts.'

Several of the braver nodded their heads in agreement.

The business manager actually ventured a 'yes'.

'Course they do. But you don't know what you are getting till you get it. Can't like oysters till you try 'em. Can't learn to dance sittin' on your ass.'

There was nothing to disagree with there. Or to agree with. An uneasy silence reigned again.

'It might work, just a couple of songs,' said the weasel who picked the girls out of the audience when the band was feeling sociable after the show. He got a few dirty looks for his trouble.

'Sure it will work. There you are, Harry. Right again. Takes Harry to know the value of a pretty face. What do you boys do for testosterone round here? Seems y'all better get down to the health food store and stock up on vitamins or somethin'. I mean, this girl is good. Not just good, she is great. When she is playing Yankee Stadium, people gonna remember she started here with good ol' Dwight Deacon. Put her on the map. And boy is she genuine country. You can hear the gurgling of those Smoky Mountain streams in her music, feel that sunrise dew in her voice. I'm telling you, boys, if we got crossover problems, authenticity problems, this girl solves 'em overnight. I am not just a guy who sells a shitload of records, you know. There is method in my madness.'

There was nodding and a general level of agreement on this. It was true. Still, the idea stank.

'Maybe she's tied up with the album back in town,' said the bass player hopefully.

'Not if I offer her a slot on my tour, she's not. Tell you what. I'll give a hundred bucks to a five that if I pick up that phone and call Gramm, that girl will be on the next plane out of Nashville. Any takers?'

There were no takers.

'Jeez, hanging round with you guys is like swimming through a pool of molasses. You wouldn't know a good idea if it sat on your faces. So that's settled then. Matt, you work out the details with the girl and Gramm and her agent. She got an agent yet? Give her decent money. And let's get some beers up here. Jesus, I am as dry as a Belle Meade Martini.'

CHAPTER

FORTY-FOUR

Savanna's telephone had been busy all morning, but Aron got through at last.

'I heard the news,' said Aron. 'You're going on the Deacon tour.'

'I guess it's all round Polymark.'

'All around the nation,' said Aron.

'How have you been?' said Savanna.

'Better.'

'On account of me?'

'Yup.'

'That's nice.'

'Is it?' His voice took off on an up beat.

But she wouldn't go any further. She couldn't. She had a plane to catch to Seattle. The limo was outside.

'When you come back, you are already a star. You know that.'

'But you knew it first, Aron. I'll never forget that. It's the first one who knows it that counts.'

'It's the first one who knows it who can do anything *about* it that counts.'

'Well, that was you, too.'

'I'm just sorry we didn't have more time, or time in the right place, or something like that.'

'We did have some time in the right place.'

His heart quickened. That was flirtatious. That definitely was.

'Listen, can I drive you to the airport?'

'What do I tell the guy in the hundred-foot limo outside?'

'You could try "goodbye".'

'OK. Is that how music people carry on? That's a 500-buck limo.'

'Baby, you ain't seen nuthin' yet. I'll be there in ten.'

And he jammed down the telephone before she could change her mind.

The limo was still there when he arrived at Steph's house. Savanna was on the doorstep, waiting. The neighbours had their heads out of the window.

'You didn't trust me?' He smiled. Savanna would trust no one with her career. Perhaps especially a man with a vague vested interest in her missing her plane.

'You tell him,' she said, laughing.

So it was Aron's job to send the limo home, mission unaccomplished.

'Are you ready?'

'Yup.'

'Bags?'

'Yup.' She hurried towards his car. It seemed from her demeanour that he had been well and truly forgiven for crimes committed in the name of his passion for her.

'So Dwight Deacon just snapped his fingers and here you are off to Seattle on the very next plane.' He just couldn't resist saying it as he swept away from the kerb.

'Aron!'

'OK, OK. I know it is a career move, and nothing more nor less.'

'Remember that.'

'I will try to.'

'Succeed!'

'I will succeed.'

'Good.'

'If I were to succeed, and if I were, at some stage, to fly out to one of your concerts, would you be pleased to see me?'

'I might be.' She looked at him and smiled a big smile.

'Like pleased enough to, well, to let me tickle your neck behind your ears the way you like . . . liked.'

'You never know your luck. You might even get to be allowed to do that little thing with your tongue you said you liked. You know, where you . . .'

'Savanna, stop it. I've got to drive this thing.' He turned to look at her. His voice was deadly serious. 'So it's not over . . . between us.'

'Whoever suggested it was?'

'You did.'

'Did not.'

He jammed on the brakes and pulled the car over to the side of the road.

'OK, prove it.'

'And how would a lady do that?'

'Kiss me.'

And so she did.

CHAPTER

FORTY-FIVE

He met her at the airport, and gave her the big hug that she had been hoping would be there to greet her. In his arms Savanna felt so safe and right, and the warmth of that feeling overshadowed the extraordinary career opportunity he had given her. Now, she knew that had been true from the moment she had heard the news. Dwight Deacon had become her mentor, but, tight in his welcoming embrace, he seemed, once again, to be far more than that.

'*Jesus*, have I done my fans a good turn today? Look at you. Will you just look at you. Pretty as an angel of God, and with a way better voice.'

'This is *so* exciting,' said Savanna. Her tone was breathless, partly because it was exciting to see him, and partly because he had squeezed most of the air from her lungs. A small crowd was already gathering. A flash bulb went off. 'Hi, Dwight,' said some stranger as if he had known him all his life. 'How'd you like Seattle?'

'Just love rain, man,' he replied, signing an autograph and reaching out to grab the stranger's shoulder.

'Meet country's newest star,' he shouted out to the crowd of onlookers that was swelling by the second. A babble of voices all murmuring his name was accompanied by a feverish rustling through handbags and briefcases, pockets and hand luggage for pens and pieces of paper. Some simply offered the magazines or newspapers they carried for him to autograph.

'Wait a second, honey. Got to do some work here,' he whispered to her. He was especially quiet when he said the word 'work'. She stood back and watched him operate. He was one vital bundle of charm, and the fact that she had seen his other side didn't seem to matter. He had words for folk for whom no one had words any more . . . losers whose wives had stopped talking to them, the vast mysterious mass of faceless humanity who became people at last in the presence of his fame. They were grateful for it. Many would go straight to the airport record store and buy all his CDs as a result of this one magic meeting.

And then he was back to her. Men appeared from nowhere, and suddenly they were a posse or a gang, Dwight Deacon's boys. Some were employees, relieving Savanna of bags, of her guitar case, and even the magazine she was carrying. Others seemed to be from the airport management. There was a policeman; reporters and a cameraman who were making a documentary of Deacon's life on the road; and there were others, including the stray fans who were not content to stand and stare, but were going along for the ride until a stern bodyguard finally parted them from the superstar.

He reached out and held her hand, and she almost had to run to keep up with him. 'Welcome to my world,' was what he meant, with its mad craziness, and its fishbowl obviousness. Ordinary life had been suspended. Savanna could feel it. She wanted to pee. But peeing was simply not an option, somehow. It was normal. Too slow. Too 'beside the point' of the whole issue, which was what . . . to get somewhere, do something important, and then hurry on. Savanna suddenly felt larger than a life that had fitted quite nicely before, but perhaps never would again.

There were three limos, each guarded by a policeman, and there was a motorcycle escort of four dark-glassed robocops on big Harleys. Would there be sirens? Savanna could all but hear them.

He opened the door for her and she was sucked into a velvet world of softness and silence, of cool and low lights. For a second, she thought she would have to swim on the back seat. It felt so liquid. As she disappeared amongst the cushions, she wondered whether a seven or a five would be needed to hit a golf ball that would reach the driver's partition.

He jumped in beside her and simply said 'Go', which they simply did. They roared away from the sidewalk with a screech of tyre rubber while passers-by gawped and craned to look, and cops held back the traffic for the motorcade.

'How does all this work?' said Savanna simply, lost in cushions and wonderment.

'Well,' laughed Deacon. 'But it took some shit-kicking to get it this way . . . over the years.'

'But the cops, and the motorcycle escort. Do you find those in the Yellow Pages?'

'Governor's mansion, babe. Those guys give blood for celebrity endorsements. Some of your best friends from now on are going to be politicians, I promise you. Democrats, Republicans, don't matter which. They will be on to you like fleas on a dog when they sniff out the fact that you can deliver a vote or two. Restores your faith in democracy.' He laughed and turned the big mesmeric eyes on her.

'You know my dad came to the Polymark party?'

'I'm glad,' he said. 'I know that whole thing worried you. You only have one father in this life.'

Savanna felt the dreaded postcard's wicked exclamation mark hovering like a ghost in the conditioned air of the limo.

'So, is it true we go on tonight, unrehearsed, and just blaze away in front of . . . just how many people?'

'Eighty thousand official. More unofficial.'

'Oh, God, I don't think I can handle that.' Savanna felt the sudden panic.

'Oh yes, you can, missy. You can handle that just fine. You just stand there and you sing a song. And by the time you come on that audience will be well oiled, man. Running like a freight train on greased wheels.'

'But they'll just want more of you.'

If the Deacon entourage had been present, they would all have chorused 'Amen', but they weren't.

'I'll tell 'em what to want. Then you'll show 'em what they wanted. Simple as that.'

'Two songs, and a duet with you, for "Roots and Wings".'

'That is it. Simple as that. And I have a little speech all planned, that will get 'em going good. People like to be there at the beginning of things. Most people never realise they are until afterwards. This lot are going to *know* that they were there the night it happened for you.' He paused. Then in a more reflective tone, he said, 'Wonderful thing, that power. Frightening, too. You understand what dictators must feel. For those minutes, an hour, you own eighty thousand people. They are all looking at you, thinking about you, dreaming about you. You. You. You. Me. Me. Me. Adoration. Escape from all the worries of their lives. The mortgage, the rows with the neighbours, the dead dog. All gone. All vanished into the moment. And you released them from all that. That is an awesome thing. An awesome thing.'

He seemed lost suddenly in the contemplation of it. Savanna could understand his words, but they had no meaning divorced from the experience. And yet there had been inklings of it. Whenever she had performed, she had felt a tiny bit of what he was talking about. Mostly it was the focus, the contact. You and the audience, bound together. But what she was about to experience was the *scale* of the thing.

'It's the gratitude that turns you on,' he said. 'The sheer weight of all that gratitude, sort of like diluted love, just beaming across at you. Old women screaming. Grown men yelling. Kids crying. You can touch it. It is that real.'

And he crunched up his hand into a tight fist and brandished it in the air, as if it contained the essence he was talking about. 'It's like an addiction to feel that, Savanna. People write books, make movies, become President, but only a live entertainer gets the instant feedback from their moment. You are out there in The Place, and it's like no place on earth although it may be what Heaven feels like. Time passes, and yet it stands still. It is you, but you are someone else. You can do anything in The Place. You are a god. You are God. Sounds like blasphemy, but I am only trying to tell you what is real, and not real, all at the same time.'

Savanna could feel the intensity of the man. His words were somehow unimportant beside that. He glowed. He vibrated. He pulsated with a form of raw energy she had never been close to before. That day at his place, she had been touched by his sadness, his sorrow, his seeming lostness in a world he had ceased to understand. But this was another side of him. The flipside. The naked power. He was sad and sorry most of the time, because he could only get to feel like this sometimes. Grey was gone from his life. Only black and white remained. He was flashes of brilliant whiteness against a canvas of ghostly dark. That was the deal the mighty made with the Devil. There was no normality in it, but it was part illusion and part real. And fame was a fact. Fame facts were everywhere. In the record sales; in the roar of the Seattle stadium tonight; in this crazy motorcade which existed solely to transport a couple of country singers from an airport to a Hilton when they could just as well have gone in a yellow cab like everyone else.

'I thought we might stop by the stadium, maybe try a sound check, play a few chords.'

'Really!'

Savanna took a deep breath. Things never happened this quickly in life. It was one of the clichés about fame. Overnight success took twenty years to achieve. Somehow, the idea that she would be on stage with Deacon in perhaps less than twenty minutes, singing with a legend, hammered home what was happening to her.

He called out to the driver. 'Tell the others we're stopping at the stadium. Tell 'em to bring out Ms Savanna's guitar. And my Fender. We're goin' to pick a little to loosen our fingers. Goin' to see just how good we are.' He laughed and banged his knee.

For the first time, Savanna felt his competitiveness. He would try and swamp her on the stage, she knew that. He wouldn't know how not to. But she wouldn't be swamped. She knew that, just as he knew it. Swamped was simply not what she would be . . . if they rolled Hank Williams from the crypt to play against her.

She also knew he would play fair. He would line the mike output up so that she had his volume. He would not feel the need to cheat. His ego wouldn't let him. But if the left side of the stadium played better than the right, he would take the left side. But then so would she. She knew him so damned well. It was uncanny. He wanted to make her a little nervous for the show. There was a graph – too much adrenaline and you were off; too little and you were short of your peak. He sensed her confidence. She would need just a little taken off the top.

'You're going to try to intimidate me a bit, aren't you,' she said suddenly with a smile.

'Now why would you think that? Why would I want to do a thing like that?'

'Because you think I am just a little bit over-confident.'

'Ah,' he said. 'So you do that telepathy thing. Actually, I was not thinking that.'

'Liar.'

'That is the second time you have called me that. Least this time it's in private.'

He smiled to show he didn't mind at all. Then his smile widened to show that he didn't mind anything she did. Pretty much liked it all. From the turned-up nose, to the dimple in her chin, to her classy accent, and her patrician confidence. He liked the way she sang, and wrote. She was not afraid of him, and almost everyone he ever saw was.

They arrived at the stadium to some confusion, the visit being unexpected. People ran around, and there was a lot of shouting and talking into mobile telephones and shortwave radios. The set was already constructed, as this was the first night of a five-night sell-out Seattle date. Savanna looked up at it in awe.

'You got those guitars, man?' Dwight yelled out. 'Set us up a four-mike stand, couple of chairs. We gonna play around for a while. If Willie is here he can fiddle with the sound. Somebody said there was flatness in the back east. If there's a black hole we'd better be on top of it.'

Savanna made a note. East was left stage. She wanted to be singing on Dwight's right.

They wandered together through the vast auditorium, dwarfed by the mighty Deacon set. There were knots of people doing things everywhere; riggers manipulating lights; sound engineers tracing miles of black cable; people cleaning. The sense of anticipation was electric.

Savanna felt the first thrill of nervousness. She swallowed hard. This was a long way from the Bluebird stage. He was watching her out of the corner of his eye as she walked beside him. Was he a rival now? Was competition about to unfold?

From the stage, everything looked bigger still. Savanna moved fast. She took the chair to Dwight's right. In reflex mode, his eyes shot out to the dark spot in the back east. He couldn't help it. But he didn't think she had noticed him steal the glance. She was far too inexperienced to have worked out that one. For a second, he wondered whether or not to ask her to change seats. A winner was a winner first and foremost. Then he discarded the idea.

Not! 'Savanna, would you mind if I took the right position . . . it's a force of habit thing.'

'And me with my little voice sing right out into that black hole,' laughed Savanna. 'Forget it.'

'Oh, boy,' said Dwight, his eyes widening. 'And this is only the beginning!'

She undid her Gibson.

'That is a real nice guitar,' he said.

'Yeah,' said Savanna warily.

He pulled out his Fender and reeled off a finger part that Clapton or Rivers would have been proud of. 'There!' he seemed to say. 'Now you are batting in the majors, babe.'

The stadium quieted. The groups of workers took a break. It would not do to disturb Deacon in action. Nor would it be something they wanted to miss. Who was the little looker? Nobody had a clue. What the hell was she doing sharing a stage with Deacon? He didn't like to share the stage with his shadow.

He pulled off another ambitious guitar solo.

'Finger-lickin' good,' said Savanna. There was the mildest cutdown in there somewhere. 'Do you feel the need to impress this little girl?' was the underlying message. Apparently the answer was 'yes', which were points to her. She could not play an eight as well as he could, but then he couldn't play as well as Vince Gill or Ricky Skaggs.

'Wo! Wo!' He tested in the mike, adjusting it for height. He called out to the back. 'That about right, kids?'

Someone from the sound crew shouted back. 'Great, nice and rich and plenty of bass.'

Deacon was well known to know near a thousand songs from the long days on the road to his 'instant' stardom. So Savanna didn't even bother to mess with asking him what he wanted to sing.

'Ladies first,' she said simply. It was not a question.

> So what, I'm sad and lonely,
> It ain't what cowboys do,
> I know, it ain't convincin',
> But I am allowed to be blue.

She hit it hard, singing low and gruff, with a heavy right hand, and the feeling burbled up from her guts. It was a man's song. I can sing men's songs. I'm better than a man. I can do anything. Those were Savanna's messages.

'Right,' said Deacon with a big smile. 'Nice one, honey. Big girl's song.'

He took the guitar solo, letting it rip in descant. Her voice reached out into the world, filling it with ease. It was surprisingly powerful. Deacon watched her in wonder. He had expected the sweetness, the accuracy of the notes, the certain chords, but he hadn't foreseen the power. He would sing the last verse with her, go over the top of her and force her lower by dropping to E minor. That would throw her. The bass was rich out there, apparently. It would sound empty as hell if it wasn't filled. It was a low trick, but all was fair in love and country music. She shouldn't have been so damned good.

Now words they don't come easy,
And feelings harder still,
Somehow I gotta make you love me,
The way that I love you.

He went up high, forcing her low, and it didn't faze her at all. She crept around the low notes like a well-known house in the dark, bumping into nothing, finding her way effortlessly. And, if anything, she made him sound a trifle shrill up there hanging above her. The people who knew, out there in the auditorium, had seen all the moves. They had all reached the same conclusion. This girl could more than hold her own with Deacon, and she was riding a horse that was trying to unseat her. He came back down from the attic for the last chorus, and she came up from the basement. They met in perfect harmony in the living room of the song.

'The way that I love you.'

She cut off her vocals just before him, but had the last chord with her guitar, holding it up high and closing with a fast five-chord riff.

'Shit, Savanna,' said Deacon. There was sweat on his brow beneath the black hat.

'Yeah,' said Savanna, smiling back at him. 'Think I felt the outer edges of The Place there.'

But he was looking at her strangely. His head was cocked to one side. 'Never heard no girl sing that song before.' He tried to make the remark inconsequential. However, that effort was undermined by the sporadic clapping that broke out from the pockets of people around the stadium. These were people who paid their bills with music, lived by it, died by it, got screwed by it . . . and, as a result, knew it from back to front.

Savanna waved to acknowledge the applause. It had been her song, although technically a duet. So she was entitled to thank for both of them.

Deacon wiped his brow. This was where he should be angry, would be angry. But he wasn't angry. He was proud. This was deeply strange. He had tried to murder this girl in a song she had no business being able to sing anyways, and he had failed dismally to do so. He had failed. In a musical objective. Dwight Deacon. That usually equalled terror, anger, and the burning desire for revenge. Not this time, it didn't. Something was going on. What was it? He was not an introspective man. Introspection was not for the famous in the entertainment industry, maybe not for the famous anywhere. Most of his 'feelings', such as they were, coruscated into the final common pathway of anger. But here he was with this funny feeling of warmth in his chest, and something that just might be, just could be, the beginnings of a thing called love in his heart. He laughed. That was his usual response to anything ridiculous.

'About what are we laughing?' said Savanna, laughing, too. But she knew. She knew. She had heard him go high, to force her low. She had followed his sneaky trip into E minor, and she had rattled her ribs with the 'feelings harder still'. He was older than her, but she was a woman and he a man. It was not impossible, but it was uncannily unsettling, that both might be in the business of making the other love them. She felt herself blush, and saw him notice it.

'How do I follow that?' he said into the microphone. He knew, of course. It was so right for the moment, the context, for everything. Shania's 'From This Moment On'. If she could sing a man's song, he could sing Twain.

And so the time-honoured battle began, a competition between competitors with a sub-plot of the heart. Or was the competition already the sub-plot? People were sitting down now in the auditorium, all pretence at casual interest abandoned. Roadies, tattooed stagehands, caterers, anybody who was near, and some who had heard the unmistakeable voice and walked a quarter mile to linger and listen. They played together as if they had been made together. And when Dwight stopped competing with Savanna, and tried to complement her voice, then magic happened. All agreed on it. This late-afternoon sound check would be talked about for years to come. I was there, man. I was in the rigging when they started. Darnedest thing I ever heard, before or since. Man, that was a moment. It had to end soon. Both knew Deacon mustn't sing himself out before the evening concert.

'Shall we wrap it with "Roots and Wings"?' said Savanna.

'I guess so.' He didn't want it to end. Nobody did. But good things had to, so that they could get better.

Then, quite suddenly, he stood up, and when she looked up he was standing in front of her, the strangest expression on his face. She knew instantly what it meant. There were tears in his eyes.

'You have made me so happy this day,' he said. 'I thought I'd forgotten how.'

'Oh, Dwight.' There was a lump in Savanna's throat.

A tear broke loose on his cheek. She, too, stood up, the guitar dangling by her side, and she wiped away the tear with her thumb.

'Oh!' she said again, her heart full of wonderful tenderness. 'That felt so right,' she said.

And so he kissed her. He leaned down and he took her in his arms and he laid his lips against hers as gently as the touch of a breeze on a field of ripened corn.

CHAPTER

FORTY-SIX

Dwight Deacon's voice boomed around the stadium, into the air already shaken by the quivering A minor chord that was his trademark. 'Memphis' had gotten them going, but this time there would be a difference. The ghostly voice issued the time-honoured incantation:

'May the spirit of his music, and the love in his heart, warm you all tonight with the help of God.'

There was the man in black, symbolically crucified, rising from the platform on the stage. Now, a shower of brilliant fireworks rose crackling and screaming above the stadium, the grand finale of some super state occasion, some monstrous celebration. Nobody had seen anything like it on the 4th of July. The millennium firework displays had hardly surpassed it. Dwight had ordered it up specially . . . a quarter of a million bucks worth to explode in precisely one minute. The heavens were on fire, and so was his heart.

'God bless you, my friends,' he started as the roar of awe at the mighty display of heavenly light subsided at last. 'And good evening, Seattle.' He paused, increasing the tension. They were hung, drawn and quartered by his words. 'Believe me when I say that tonight will be different. I have had an experience this day that has brought joy to my soul, and later it will bring happiness to yours. I will be joined later in this show by a young lady who is destined to become a legend in country music. Friends . . . friends . . . DO YOU TRUST ME?'

The 'YES' roared back at a deafening decibel level.

'You are here tonight at the first live concert performance of a person that your great-grandchildren will be talking about way after the Good Lord has taken you to his heart.' He paused. 'Her name is Savanna, and she is . . . and she is . . .'

He paused. With a thrill of shock, the audience realised he was choking up. He wiped a tear from his eye. Nobody could believe it. DD was all but weeping. The tension was in overdrive, the fireworks, the birth of a legend, Dwight Deacon crying real tears on stage. Oh boy, was this special or what!

'So anyways, come with me on the most important night of my life so far . . .'

He struck a chord, lifted the guitar high and kicked into 'Beyond Glory'.

Henry Stone sat back on the swivel chair in his office at home in Connecticut, and looked over his shoulder at the small TV. It nestled secretly amidst its surround of leather-bound books. Stone didn't watch TV often, except occasionally for the stock quotes. This was an activity of which he was a little ashamed and liked, as a result, to conduct in private. So the television was small and old, and it hardly did justice to the TV 'spectacular' that CBS was mounting with such pride this evening. Dwight Deacon was 'live' from Seattle, and the word was that his only daughter was going to be, too. It was all somewhere between a joke, an event, and an embarrassment . . . Stone couldn't decide which . . . and Deacon's verbal melodramatics at the start of the thing seemed to set the tone at a tastelessly low level. That was why Henry Stone was watching it over his shoulder. It was the way you watched something that someone has insisted you watch when your heart isn't in it. Savanna? A legend in country music? An 'experience' that had brought joy to his soul? What was the dreadful man talking about? It was perfectly clear from his bovine, glistening, child-like face that the imbecile hadn't got a soul. He was about as deep, and transparent, as a sheet of tracing paper.

*

Mary Stone sat in the servants' quarters with the servants, watching their TV . . . a large RCA . . . and the ice-cold atmosphere of embarrassment would have been the pride of any meat storage facility. Of course, Grandma Stone didn't recognise it. She sat in the butler's chair, while he hovered behind her. The cooks and housemaids and other 'help' perched on the corners of sofas and chairs and prayed for the ordeal to be over.

'Quite impressive, the fireworks,' said Mary Stone to the sort of mumbled assent given to a preacher's admonition in church. She had not seen such good fireworks at the Rockefeller wedding, or anywhere else for that matter, and she liked them. The stage props, while in poor taste and well over the top, were clever for a 'mass' audience. Grandma had even been quite moved by the general sense of ecstatic anticipation that Deacon had been able to conjure up. Clearly Deacon had acquired his millions the hard way, by earning them, rather than the old-fashioned way, by inheriting them. That was creditable in Grandma's book, but she was relieved that they didn't need tricks like this at Carnegie Hall. Yes, she was impressed – or had been until the speech. That was her granddaughter that Deacon was getting all emotional about, and that was very bad manners indeed, especially in front of the servants. She didn't at all like the sound of the 'experience' that had brought joy to Deacon's soul. One should keep quiet about experiences that brought one 'joy'. And what was all this nonsense about a 'legend'? Surely that was just hyperbole from a man who clearly had never heard of understatement. But was it? Deacon was something of an expert in such things, presumably. People who made billions out of something usually knew their subject. She had never dared contradict J. P. Morgan Jr. when he was talking finance, and she didn't like it when people laid down the law to her about the growing of roses. Now, the singer was on the verge of tears, or so it seemed. He looked tired and emotional. Had he been drinking? Why was he talking about Savanna in this way? Good Lord, surely he couldn't be in love with her!

'Forrest,' she said in the clear voice she reserved for crises, 'can you fetch me another Bourbon, and don't drown it this time, please.'

In his apartment overlooking the river, Aron watched on a Mitsubishi TV, larger by far than any Japanese who might have made it, up to and including a retired sumo wrestler. Around him burbled the 'surround' sound. The TV had a flat high-definition 100 megahertz screen, and he had a better view by far than anyone in the vast Seattle stadium. He could have told Deacon to have a crack at his nose hairs with the little electronic clipper device from Sharper Image. Or he could have ordered him to disappear into the vast abyss he wished with every fibre of his being would emerge from somewhere to swallow up the superstar and take him out of circulation for ever.

Deacon was all but in tears, and the reason for those tears was Savanna, the girl Aron hoped was his. It was not good karma. You did not cry about friends and acquaintances. You cried about people you loved. You cried, in fact, about people with whom you had enjoyed 'experiences' that brought you 'joy'. What had happened that very day to bring Deacon 'joy'? The only thing the zombie was supposed to care about was his career. Aron felt the worm of jealousy turn within him. He shifted uncomfortably in the leather massage chair that had fifty different programmes to calm you down. He had never felt so 'uptight'.

He took a deep breath. He could hear the star clearing his throat, all but hear his stomach rumble, all but feel his pumping heart. There was not much escaping it. It was clear to Aron as philosophy's law of excluded middle that Deacon had 'fallen' for Savanna. Bullies sometimes reacted like that to women who stood up to them. There was only one question of paramount interest. Did Savanna return his affection, and if so, where did that leave Aron? The answer was inescapable . . . stuck like a leaf between the pages of an old leather book authored by Pushkin. It was not at all where he wanted to be.

Steph and her family, never accused of resembling a James Bond Martini, were both shaken *and* stirred. They sat in the cramped living room with its dung-coloured carpet and creaky old GE television, and watched transfixed as the extravaganza from Seattle exploded into their world. Steph, curled up in the scuffed leather chair, was biting the nails of her chord fingers. She had imagined, from the whole business of Savanna being invited to appear on the spectacular, that Deacon had developed some sort of feelings for her; but nothing like the ones he seemed to be referring to. She hadn't been able to get hold of Savanna, who had, almost overnight, become surrounded by an anti-ballistic missile shield of Polymark people who filtered every telephone call. Overnight success. Yet Savanna had been on the verge of throwing it all away. A year of banging against a brick wall, and then, suddenly the wall was gone, and Savanna was charging forward, way off balance, into some crazy future. A 'legend'! Jeez! In the mouth of anyone but Deacon that would have sounded like PR popcorn rubbish. But what about Aron? Shit, would Savanna's *dad* be watching?

Her mom said what was on all their minds, as she sipped at a can of Bud on a sofa whose guts were hanging out.

'Heck, I think he's gonna pop the question. Tom, listen up! Steph! That oddling's gonna ask Savanna to marry him . . . right there on the stage!'

Dwight Deacon had become DD as he always did on stage, and he was slap-bang in the middle of his Place. He was also aware that something was different. Usually, he shed his old persona like a lizard an old skin in this situation. Tonight, however, Dwight Deacon was up there with DD, and the two, like strangers without much in common, were having problems relating to each other. DD was lost in the act, deep in 'Beyond Glory', one of his first biggest hits. But Dwight Deacon had other things on his mind, or rather one. He was thinking of Savanna.

> I'm a-riding on that glory train
> And headin' back to you
> And baby when I get there,
> You'll know just what to do . . .

Dwight knew he was an obsessive. Focus. Single-mindedness. Laser-like purpose. These were the qualities that had made him a winner. The poor losers out there in the crowd thought it was all to do with his voice, the songs he wrote, and the energy with which he delivered them. In his life of struggle towards the Nirvana he now lived in, there had been room for nothing but the next hurdle in the race to fame.

Now there was something else. Someone else. And the time was right for them. He hadn't agonised about Savanna. He didn't think long about decisions. He just made them. When he had kissed her on the stage after their extraordinary duet that afternoon, he had fallen in love with her. That meant all sorts of things. That she would love him, too. That she was his first and last love. That they would get married, have children, and she, too, would become famous. She would be the Queen to his King and he would write a number one song about it. Everything else . . . Aron Wallis, her family's antagonism, even Savanna's own feelings in the matter, were just part of the detail, the small print, that had to be worked out by the minions after the basic deal was done.

Dwight wanted. Dwight got. If you wanted hard enough, and with sufficient energy and power, the goods got delivered. Was that romantic? Who cared? Love was like anything else. It was a business. It had rules and penalties, procedures and rituals, ups and downs. You simply had to learn the game and get better at it than the others. Right now, nearly a hundred thousand strangers were going through the motions of loving him. What chance had Savanna got? She had been chosen, and her life . . . their life . . . would be blessed from now on. Everything was coming together. DD and Dwight Deacon. Sense was emerging. Savanna would share his future as tonight she would share his stage.

The vibrating chords of the final line of the song crashed to a close, but the audience could still see that the star's eyes were wet with his tears, and they loved it. They adored the public display of private and inexplicable, yet, deliciously perhaps, soon-to-be-revealed emotion. What nobody could know, because Dwight Deacon had only just decided it himself, was that tonight, on stage, live on CBS, he was going to ask Savanna to marry him.

In the dressing room, Savanna paced up and down. She was dressed in virgin-white with white leather boots and a white headband, looking like some Druidic virgin sacrifice of extreme beauty. The thunder of the crowd invaded the dressing room. God, she mustn't let them all down! A wave of insecurity broke over her. Would they boo her off the stage for taking time away from the man they had all come to see? 'No,' she thought. 'Dwight won't let them.' She felt very sure of that. Sure about him.

Her life was turning into a kaleidoscope, but the colours were dazzling. In the panic of the moment she hardly dared to think about the kiss, but it had been a dramatic turning-point. She had thought before that he had an idle crush on her, the whim of a famous man for a little person. He would turn her into a star as a demonstration of his power, and allow himself the luxury of a brief flirtation in the process. But it hadn't been that sort of kiss. She had seen love in his eyes, real love, love of the frightening intensity that Deacon brought to anything he did. It had moved her, and she had already been on the move. From that day at his ranch, he had captivated her. It had not been his power that she had been drawn to but his touching vulnerability, his loneliness at the peak of fame where the air was too thin to be breathed by mere mortals. But then there was his godlike authority, too. The mixture of the two was explosive. A woman would be so protected by him. There was security in his arms, and safety in his future, and children and everything you could want. And the price? To be owned by him. To give up freedom. Like her mother had? To be Dwight Deacon's woman would not be the sort of relationship in which you kept your own second name! Savanna smiled at the thought. What would happen? What about Aron, her 'other' lover? Oh, God, it was all too much to think about at this frantic moment. She looked at her watch, and listened to the howl of the crowd.

She had been told to be ready for anything, and she was.

CHAPTER

FORTY-SEVEN

Dwight had decided to abandon his usual practice of strict control, and go for spontaneity. Rather than give Savanna a specific time slot, he would use his legendary 'feel' for the audience to judge when they were primed for an interruption to the usual flow. Savanna was therefore on permanent stand-by. A knock on the door would precede a ninety-second dash to the floodlit glare of the stage, and the eyes of 80,000 strangers. Adrenaline gurgled in Savanna's veins. This was what she had waited for. Any moment now, it would be time for answered prayers.

On stage, Dwight had decided to slow the pace.

'This next song means a lot to me,' he said, 'especially this evening. It's called "First and Last Love".'

He felt the song in his gut. It was full of the *angst* of that first-time romance, and he knew that he could milk it for the performance of a lifetime. Then, after it, he would bring on Savanna. It made a nonsense of the pace of the show, but sometimes in art, and in life, nonsense made the best sense of all. The audience would be teary-eyed, dreaming of their own first loves, trying to remember over the years what they had looked like; the magic touch of hands; the first anguished brush of lips, a time so amazing and new that it would last a lifetime. And then he would show them his. He wouldn't spell it out, though he might. But the inference would be there. In the centre of The Place, God was at work. That was its beauty.

He wrenched the song from his heart and soul. He squeezed it from the essence of him. Tears rolled freely down his cheeks unashamedly as he sang.

> Your first love will be your last love,
> And there will be nothing but good lovin' in between.

And then it was over. He bowed his head, and 80,000 people went wild with the joy of his sadness. There might be some dry eyes in the house, but all Dwight could see was a sea of Kleenex. He knew it was his finest performance ever of that song, and so did they. They simply did not know why.

It was time to show them. And it was time to tell them.

'Ladies and gentlemen, friends . . . all of you good people who share my life . . . boy, do I love that song . . .'

The cheers rocked the stadium. 'So do we, Dwight.' 'You are my first love, Dwight.' 'Sing it again.'

He waved them into quietness, wiping the tracks of his tears from his cheek with the back of his hand, in case anyone had not noticed that he had wept.

'I love that song about my first love, and I have a secret.' He paused. The silence was so real it had acquired a life of its own. Not a throat cleared. Not a person moved. He had a secret love. And as sure as the Tennessee moon was silver in the sky, he was going to share his secret with them.

'And tonight, my friends, I want to introduce you personally to a girl . . . a girl . . . and you will see she is a beautiful, beautiful lady.'

The stage manager punched the intercom. 'Get her out here. He's introducin' her. In the wings, five minutes ago.'

The knock on the door of Savanna's dressing room was all but instantaneous with the command.

'You are on, miss,' said the stagehand.

'God help me,' said Savanna.

She hurried through the backstage area. In seconds, she was within sight of him while Dwight Deacon, pinpointed in the spotlight's glare, talked on into the eerie silence. What had he said to make it this quiet? It was like church without babies crying.

The audience were digesting his words. He had said in a round-about way that the girl they were about to meet was his. And he was famously unmarried. Could this be the big one? A proposal, on stage, in front of *them*?

Aron leaned forward in his chair. He was beginning to sweat. Hell! He had thought of flying to Seattle. Then he had done what everyone else did nowadays. Watched it on TV. Get the big picture. The bird's-eye view. Every nuance, every expression, every gesture. The surround sound had picked up on the silence of the arena. To Aron's confused mind, it sounded like the loudest silence he had ever heard.

The madman on the stage had basically declared his undying love for Savanna. Oh, it was all filtered through the cunning magic of the Deacon stage performance, and it still might be some kind of wind-up, some hideous trick of the master showman. That was all there was left to hope for. The jealousy he had felt seconds earlier was already ancient history. It had faded away, to be replaced by an awful pregnant nothingness that was already beginning to emerge into something very much like panic. Here it was on big-screen TV, where everything should, and one day would, be. On CBS, America was hearing about Dwight Deacon's secret love, the secret, secret love that so soon would be a secret love no more. Did Savanna know? Could she have any idea what was going on here? Surely not. You couldn't walk straight from one man's arms into another's . . . just like that. Could you? Fate didn't deal in tricks that dirty. Did it? Somebody had to do something. But who? What? Aron was in Nashville. But the place to be was in Seattle.

Kirstie was in Seattle. Crammed up against the stage she was within six feet of the man she loved more than anyone, or rather anything, on this earth. Like the rest of the audience she was in the silence of shock. There were hundreds of girls who felt almost as badly as she did, but there was not one who felt the betrayal so deeply. Her world hovered at the brink. Dwight Deacon belonged to her. He was her. He had become her reason for living, breathing, eating. There was nothing that she did not do that was not for him, and nothing that she was that would be anything without him. She knew that every moment of every day. But you don't really know what you have lost until you lose it.

Kirstie's face was a mask of horror. Her mouth was wide open, and her eyes stared blankly at the object of her obsession. He hadn't said the words, but he had done everything else. He was telling the world, or rather he was telling Kirstie, up close and very personally, that he did not love her. He loved someone else. Never, ever now could her fantasy become reality, and yet fantasy had *been* her reality for as long as she could remember. It was ending, but it had not ended. There was time.

She pulled the bag from her shoulder, and laid her hand on the rubber butt of the Dan Wesson .357 Magnum.

'Come on out here, Savanna Carson Stone,' said Dwight Deacon, and he signalled to the wings.

Savanna took a deep breath and walked on to the stage, to a roar of stupendous proportions from the crowd. Deacon's introduction had sparked that most potent form of emotion . . . curiosity. Savanna was buoyed up on the carpet of sound. It seemed her feet hardly touched the ground on their way to the limelight.

Deacon greeted her with a bear-hug, as the crowd continued to howl its approval. Dwight Deacon's first and last love was one hell of a looker. Could she sing?

Savanna took up her position, and adjusted the microphones. 'Thank you. Thank you,' she said. But the sea of noise did not abate. If anything, it intensified at the sound of her voice. The crowd had been thoroughly primed, and here was a beauty in virginal white, and there was their hero about to claim her. She could stand there and say 'thank you' all evening as far as the fans were concerned. It took Dwight to quiet them. 'Please, please, everyone. Now you seen her, you gotta hear her. Trust me. You're gonna thank me.'

And then some sort of quiet descended.

'I am just overwhelmed,' said Savanna. 'Thank you, Dwight, for giving me this chance . . .'

The crowd roared its excitement, and again Dwight held up his hands for silence, a big smile on his face. 'Let her sing first,' was the message he conveyed to the crowd he could handle so well.

'This one is called "Roots and Wings", and I wrote it with my mother. Dwight has it on his CD, and I will be bringing it out on mine, too.'

And Savanna began to play. It was easy, but far more than that it was magnificent. She felt the wings beneath her, her voice strong and true and straight, lifted by the power of the amplification system to a sublime level where it had never ventured before. When dreams come true, then magic rules. There was no disappointment. It was better by far than she had dared to imagine. Her own music, and a crowd so big it was as if the entire world was watching, listening to the music she made. Nothing in her life so far had come close. No single thing. She had arrived and she could not leave. Her old life was over. Into this brand-new world, she had been born.

She came to the last verse, and Dwight joined her in duet. It was not hard to summon up the feelings that make the best duets. Savanna owed this to him, and he looked down at her with the love light shining in his eyes.

And so the two of them, to the adoration of the multitude, sang the song that would be remembered for ever. Then it was over, and, as the applause at last began to wane, Deacon simply followed his heart. Wasn't it what a cowboy was supposed to do?

He dropped to his knees, his black guitar across his heart, and he looked up at Savanna, who looked down in amazement at him.

'Savanna,' he said. 'Marry me.'

Kirstie actually heard the words, as she read his lips. They were the ones she had dreamed about on so many fevered and magic nights. There was nothing wrong with the words. They were word-perfect. It was just that they were being delivered to the wrong girl. So she pulled out the gun, quite quickly, and laid its butt on the stage against which she was leaning, and then, at last, she had Dwight Deacon's attention. For some reason, his gaze shifted from the girl he had just asked to marry him and, with the sixth sense of the supreme show-man, he focused in on the one trouble spot in his audience. From six feet away the barrel of the big hand-gun was not large. But to Dwight Deacon it looked like the black hole of Eternity. He opened his mouth wide, as Kirstie fired twice.

The bullets raced after each other like a pair of dark angels, and splintered the black guitar two inches apart directly over the heart that had so recently been promised to another.

Aron saw it best of all. For the next three days, in slow action replay, this scene would be repeated for a breathless America with the relentless overkill of the Kennedy assassination, and the Oswald murder. But Aron's mind slowed it down as it happened, breaking it up into its constituent parts of horror.

He saw the song end; heard the applause surrounding him fade at last; saw Deacon drop to his knees. The CBS camera crew, and the control room director, were up to every moment of it. In they went on the closest of close-ups. 'Marry me,' said Dwight Deacon's lips with the certainty of the prodigy in the elocution class. Aron heard it softly in 'real time' as they called it now, and he saw it in high-definition visuals, better by far than Savanna did. Then they shot to her face, again in closest close-up. There, by Mitsubishi, was the wonder of her beauty. There in Japanese super-reality was the expression of dumb-founded amazement on her face. OK. She had not been expecting it. Question answered. Aron was aware that he had never been so still. Time had stopped, but it would start again. What came after amaze-ment? Tenderness, warmth . . . hell, assent? But none of the above came afterwards, because the camera was once again on Deacon. He had apparently been distracted by something in the crowd at a moment when his focus should surely have been on his intended bride. His mouth opened in a big round 'O', and his eyes widened to two large and similar circles. Simultaneously, shots rang out – two, close together – and the black guitar seemed to explode over his chest. The wood splintered, and Dwight Deacon, on his knees still, simply toppled over, very slowly, backwards. As he did so, his hat fell off, and somehow that was the most significant fact of all. The guitar slipped back over his head, and hit the stage, partially hiding his face. In superb televisiual colour, a dark red stain began to spread over his shirt. Aron simply watched. Nobody had got as far as recognising what had happened. A stunt! An appalling, misconceived, ratings-peaking, bad-taste . . . no, not. Not at all. The quickest reactions were those of the trained professional in the control booth. The camera shot cut to Savanna's face in close-up, and all the horror in the world was there in her expression for the world to see.

'Oh, God,' said Aron. Dwight Deacon had been shot. He had been shot dead, on the stage, seconds after he had proposed to the girl that Aron loved.

The camera panned back as Savanna dropped to her knees and held him, cradling his head, trying to pick him up to the sitting position. As she did so, his blood covered her, red on white, stars and stripes, and she held him tight. Aron saw her say Deacon's name again and again . . . as if to summon his spirit from the vast deep into which it had vanished. Now, there was the mighty wail from the crowd, and people running, and the chaos that America did so well at moments of peak emotion.

A voice came over the TV sound system. 'Oh, my God, he's been shot. Dwight Deacon has been shot. Oh, my God.'

There was some sort of scrimmage in the crowd by the stage, and then the cameras were back in a feeding frenzy to the live carnage, to the quick and to the dead. Tears ran down Savanna's cheeks, as she squeezed the lifeless superstar to her, willing him back, denying the truth. 'Oh, no! Oh, no! Dwight. Dwight,' she was saying. And then she turned fully towards the camera and looked right into it. It zoomed in on her until her whole face was jammed up against the corners of the vast screen, her face bigger by far than it would ever be in her life again. And she screamed. Aron, 2,000 miles away, had never been closer to her. And it was his name that she screamed.

'Aron! Aron! Help me. Help me.'

CHAPTER

FORTY-EIGHT

'Mom used to say that her family used to call Nashville the City of Rocks,' said Savanna. 'It was an old ridge-runner expression.'

Her voice was distant, like the cold mountain on which they stood. The mist that looked like smoke billowed around them as they looked down to the Tennessee flatlands far beneath.

Aron took her hand in his, hearing the deep melancholy in her voice, the hillbilly secret harmonies that he had learned to love. It had been her idea to come on up here, stay the night at the Cataloochee ranch, and commune with the ghosts of her mother and her family. The Smokies stretched away from them, like wave after wave on a mountain sea. Last night, they had made bittersweet love in their cabin, and afterwards her face had been wet with tears melded from both passion and sorrow. He had won her by chance and by commitment, but who was she now, this Savanna Carson Stone? Well, she was a living legend, as well as the woman he loved. Dwight Deacon had not gone quietly into the night with his fame. His death and its pomp and terrible circumstance had given him the one dimension his mighty celebrity had never had . . . heart. He had been gunned down, at the moment he had asked a beautiful young girl to be his wife, and America had seen it, and America could not and would not forget it.

Nashville and Polymark had not let the moment pass. So now the Dwight Deacon memorial tour rolled across America and every singer with a name and a conscience and a following bled real blood to get a chance to play on it. On and on it went, gathering the extraordinary moss of momentum, because one thing it guaranteed. At the end, at the last was the best . . . the lady that Dwight Deacon had loved, singing her heart out in his memory, and creeping as she did so into the hearts that were primed to receive her. That had been his legacy. He had passed on to her his legend.

She looked up at Aron, and she squeezed his hand. One day, they would marry. She knew that. But not now, not yet. The glory days, painted with the delicate sorrow of tragedy, were beginning for her. Her mother was with her in the mists, and Dwight, who had never much cared for mists, was there, too. She could feel their presence, as she could feel her lover's hand. Dwight Deacon had touched her heart, and she had touched his. In America, land of dreamers, his life had been the stuff that dreams were made of. He had died like a soldier for ideals that maybe were long dead before he was born . . . and he had loved her. At the going down of the Nashville sun, and in the Tennessee morning, she would remember him.